Seducing the Widow

"I wouldn't mind a houseful as long as they take after their mother," he said, nuzzling her neck.

"I would like the boys to look like their Papa." Breathing deeply, Elizabeth leaned her head back, baring herself more openly. He caressed the curve of her throat, sending tingles down to her core. "Curly blond hair, blue eyes, and ears that turn pink, so we'll know when they are fibbing." Lord, he made her want to abandon herself right here in the hall.

"We will see if that can be arranged." Continuing to kiss his way across her neck, he turned and went up behind her ear.

Shivers wracked her, then she flushed with desire.

He walked her backward until her bottom hit the wall, and he pushed himself against her, settling into the V of her legs as though he was a missing part of her. "I would say we could start now, but we already have."

Seizing her lips, he thrust his tongue into her, and the heat exploded all over her.

She relaxed into his arms, drinking him in as their tongues tangled. With an effort, she slid heavy arms around him, pulling him closer, urging him to give her more . . .

Books by Jenna Jaxon

The Widows' Club
TO WOO A WICKED WIDOW
WEDDING THE WIDOW

The House of Pleasure Series
ONLY SEDUCTION WILL DO
ONLY A MISTRESS WILL DO
ONLY MARRIAGE WILL DO
ONLY SCANDAL WILL DO

Published by Kensington Publishing Corporation

Wedding the Widow

Jenna Jaxon

LYRICAL PRESS
Kensington Publishing Corp.
www.kensingtonbooks.com

LYRICAL PRESS BOOKS are published by

Kensington Publishing Corp.
119 West 40th Street
New York, NY 10018

All Kensington titles, imprints, and distributed lines are available at special quantity discounts for bulk purchases for sales promotion, premiums, fund-raising, educational, or institutional use.

Special book excerpts or customized printings can also be created to fit specific needs. For details, write or phone the office of the Kensington Sales Manager: Attn.: Sales Department. Kensington Publishing Corp., 119 West 40th Street, New York, NY 10018. Phone: 1-800-221-2647.

Lyrical and the Lyrical logo Reg. U.S. Pat. & TM Off.

First Kensington Printing: August 2018
ISBN-13: 978-1-5161-0327-0
ISBN-10: 1-5161-0327-0

First Electronic Edition: August 2018
eISBN-13: 978-1-5161-0326-3
eISBN-10: 1-5161-0326-2

10 9 8 7 6 5 4 3 2 1

Printed in the United States of America

For my Aunt Joyce and cousin Valerie, two of my biggest fans and supporters. Love you to the moon and back!

Acknowledgments

This book would not have been possible without the help of a great many people.

To my dedicated beta team, Ella Quinn, Alexandra Christle, and Mairi Norris: Thank you for helping me smooth out all the many bumps in Elizabeth and Jemmy's story.

To my editor, John Scognamiglio, and agent, Kathy Green: Thank you so very much for your help and patience in steering me through this amazing process.

And the biggest thank you to my wonderful family, because your love for me allows me to neglect you while I write.

Chapter 1

Village of Wrotham, Kent, England
October 1816

"Here you go, Mrs. Easton." James, Lord Brack, handed her a pint glass of Wrotham ale.

"Thank you, my lord." Shivers of delight coursed through Elizabeth Easton as she accepted the dripping libation and took a long sip, cool and nutty with a pleasant bite. She'd initially encountered the brew this past summer during her friend Charlotte's first house party, at the insistence of her neighbor, Lord Wrotham. Even though ladies weren't supposed to drink it, she'd enjoyed it, and Lord Brack had remembered.

This weekend party had held more pleasurable sensation for her than she'd known since she'd lost her husband over a year before. Much of it because of the Harvest Festival, here in the village of Wrotham. Some of it was sparked by her best friend's announcement an hour ago that she and Lord Wrotham were to marry before the New Year.

The bulk of it, she suspected, however, came from the handsome young man dancing attendance on her, whose arm she now clasped. Lord Brack, or Jemmy, as his sister Georgina called him, had escorted her about the county festival all day, seemingly to their mutual satisfaction. They had enjoyed shopping among stalls—he'd insisted on buying her one of the sweet little dolls made of stalks of wheat—had a delicious tea, and laughed themselves giddy at the antics of the participants during the various games. With their sizable party, he could easily have changed partners several times during the festivities. Lord Brack, however, had remained at Elizabeth's side all day long. Quite flattering for a widow of six and twenty.

Now they were enjoying a quick pint of ale before the final and, as some had said, most important activity of the day: the crowning of the Corn Maiden.

She wrinkled her nose at the sharp smell of hops. "I wonder why ladies are not supposed to drink ale. Gentlemen should not be allowed to have all the fun."

"We cannot give up all of our best secret pleasures, Mrs. Easton." Lord Brack's sky-blue eyes crinkled as he grinned. He was certainly one of the best-natured gentlemen of her acquaintance.

They strolled away from Mr. Micklefield's temporary stall toward the center of the field where the games had been played earlier. Even though she'd been sensible and worn her sturdy half boots, the newly mown stubble made her wobble. She clutched Lord Brack's strong arm tighter, the startling warmth of him seeping through his green superfine coat.

"Careful there, Mrs. Easton. We don't want you to come to grief."

Lord, don't let her spill the ale on either one of them.

Lord Brack led them to the edge of the circle that had formed around the hulking Michael Thorne, the Harvest Lord, and four young women—local girls vying for the honor of being crowned Wrotham's Corn Maiden.

"They do look pretty," Elizabeth said, motioning to the figures obviously decked out in their finest, most colorful garb, their hair unbound, flowing around their shoulders and spilling over their breasts.

"Yes, they are a bevy of country beauties, aren't they? Mr. Thorne's going to have a difficult time choosing his Corn Maiden." Lord Brack's eyes sparkled as he sipped more ale. "The three not chosen will be quite disappointed, I fear. Michael Thorne's a very handsome lad."

"Does he choose a girl to marry him?" How scandalous that would be, to be chosen—or not chosen—before all the assembled tenants and members of the village.

"Oh, no. Nothing quite so permanent." Brack's smile flashed again. "He claims a kiss only, said to keep the fields fertile through the winter and into the spring."

"That must be some kiss." The four girls preened and giggled as Mr. Thorne walked around them, looking them over with a keen eye.

Lord Brack took another pull at his ale, the torchlight throwing his features into sharp relief. "According to Lord Wrotham, it used to be quite a bit more than just a kiss." He gazed into her face, the gleam in his eyes transforming suddenly into hunger.

"More?" she squeaked. Heat blasted her face, as though she stood too close to the flickering torches. The chilly night became hot as midday.

"Long ago, the Harvest Lord chose his Corn Maiden as his Bride of the Fields. After the toasts and celebration ended, the Lord took his Bride into the fields, and the two spent the night together in a makeshift bridal tent. The next spring, if the Corn Maiden was increasing, it was considered an auspicious sign for a good crop, and the two married."

"And if there was no child?"

"Then no wedding."

"Oh, dear." Elizabeth clutched her glass of ale, her heart

beating furiously. "How . . . pagan." Aware now of her arm through his, she slipped it out and transferred her glass to that hand. "How could the girl's parents allow such a thing?"

Brack shrugged. "It was the custom, Wrotham said. Pagan perhaps," his voice deepened, "but it was considered a great honor for the girl to be chosen." He nodded toward the Harvest Lord, busy inspecting a harvest bouquet of stalks of wheat and field flowers offered by a very pretty dark-haired maiden on the end. The offering was supposed to be the measure by which the girl was judged, and this one certainly showed hers off to best advantage by holding it in front of her ample bosom. Michael Thorne was getting an eyeful of more than flowers.

Infectious excitement blazed across the girls' faces. Elizabeth's pulse beat faster as Mr. Thorne bent his tall frame to sniff the bouquet. From the tented look of the man's breeches, he was interested in much more than a kiss. A sheer animal heat seemed to leap from him to the girl, their gazes now locked. The power that emanated from them wafted over Elizabeth, making her want to loosen her spencer to cool her body. Lord, she should never drink Wrotham ale again if it made her this fanciful and uncomfortable.

Had the display affected Lord Brack? She sneaked a look at her escort. His cheeks had taken on a reddish hue. He stared at the couple, as enthralled as she.

Too scandalous for their modern time, this pagan performance should be stopped. Yet even in her censure, her gaze inexorably strayed back to the scene unfolding before them inside the ring of torches.

"Has the Harvest Lord chosen his Corn Maiden?" Mr. Smith, the unofficial master of the festival, called from the edge of the circle.

"He has." Michael Thorne spoke, his deep bass voice echoing down Elizabeth's spine.

The power in that voice had her grabbing Lord Brack's

arm once more. She needed an anchor if she was to hear this pronouncement.

Lord Brack seemed just as affected as she. Scarcely taking his eyes off the couple, he tossed back the last of his ale, then dropped the thick glass to the ground. His big hand came down and covered hers, heat streaming through her gloves.

She wanted to grasp his hand as well but couldn't think what to do with her own glass. It still contained some ale, which she could not drink, though she loathed to spill it on the ground. It somehow seemed sacrilegious. Still, she wanted more contact with the strong male protection next to her. So she stepped closer toward him, almost leaning against him.

He plucked the glass from her hands, swallowed almost half in one gulp, then deliberately poured what remained on the ground around their feet.

Protection against the pagan gods or sacrifice to them? Where had these fanciful notions sprung from all of a sudden?

Again, the raw animal power of the moment washed over her, and she grasped his hand, pressing it to his arm. If she got much hotter, she'd likely steam in the cold air.

"As the seed goes to the fertile ground, so goes the Harvest Lord to his Maiden . . . Nora Burns." Michael Thorne intoned the ages-old chant, then seized the dark-haired Nora, her face alight with joy and triumph, by the hand and pulled her to him.

A jubilant cry went up from the crowd, a wail of lament from the three would-be Corn Maidens. They scurried out of the circle, arms around each other.

Elizabeth's heart thumped so hard she gasped for breath. Could Lord Brack feel her pulse pounding in the hand he held so tightly?

The Harvest Lord led his Maiden into the center of the circle, grabbed her around the waist, and lifted her above his head, spinning them around. After making a complete circle, he lowered her inch by inch to the ground. As soon as her feet touched the field stubble, he grasped her face—her cheeks red, her eyes snapping with excitement—and lowered his mouth to hers.

A stab of desire jolted Elizabeth, tearing through her like a lightning bolt straight to the apex of her thighs. Her breasts tingled as the Harvest Lord claimed his Corn Maiden.

As Thorne deepened the kiss, Nora threw her arms around his neck, pressing herself against the powerful body before her.

Panting, Elizabeth strained forward as well, her hands clasped, viselike, around Lord Brack's arm. A moan of need began in her throat, but she bit it back. What was happening to her?

She'd not been this aroused in over a year, not since her husband Richard—or Dickon, as she'd called him—had gone away to war. She'd felt his death so sharply she'd not even thought about love or desire for another man. Not until Charlotte had dragged her to the house party in August. There she'd met Lord Brack, who she'd found very amiable but hadn't thought of as desirable. Well, not exactly. Nor had she paid much attention to his obvious interest in her. Until now.

His arm tensed as he watched the crowning of the Corn Maiden. From the corner of her eye, she marked his Grecian profile as it stood stark against the flickering torchlight, his gaze fixed on the couple before them. His jaw clenched so tightly she could almost hear it creak. He turned his head to peer down at her, his eyes dark with a desire of his own.

Slipping his arm around her shoulders, he turned them away from the sight of Michael and Nora as applause from the surrounding crowd crashed around them. He led her from the lighted circle, toward a stand of trees at the edge of the field.

Elizabeth had expected her senses would return once she

no longer bore witness to the incredible raw sexual power of that kiss. Her body, however, continued to throb, then to ache with the need to feel a man's touch once more.

Lord Brack stopped just at the tree line, well out of the light. He loosed her hands from their grip on his arm, then cupped her face, just as Michael Thorne had done to Nora, and sank his mouth onto hers.

A bolt of fire shot through her, down her arms and legs, through her fingers and toes. Her core heated as though a sun burned at the center, and the ache deep inside her, begun while they had watched the Harvest couple, became a demand she could not ignore.

Brack deepened the kiss, his tongue stealing warm and welcome into her mouth. She arched her neck back, opening herself fully. Let him take her here and now.

As if reading her mind, he wrapped his arms around her, pulling her so tightly to him that every muscle in his chest pressed into her, hard as granite, yet comforting as a safe harbor against her hurts and fears. Ah, but she had missed that sense of safety so very much.

Still his tongue explored, now her mouth, now her ear, where his rough, panting breath sent new shivers down her spine. His lips traveled lower, down her neck. She couldn't repress the moan this time. Her whole body trembled, ached for Dickon to lay her down here on the ground and take her, as he had so many times before.

This wasn't Dickon.

Like a spray of cold water shaken from a rowan tree onto her naked body, Elizabeth jumped back from Lord Brack, suddenly very aware of who he was and where they were.

He too stepped back, blinking as if roused from a dream. "Elizabeth?"

Covering her face with one hand, she held the other out as if to fend him off. What had come over her?

He didn't move toward her but looked away, toward the still-lighted circle where Michael and Nora danced wildly with several other couples. "Please forgive me, Mrs. Easton. I'm not sure what just came over me."

"No, my lord, I must beg your pardon." Elizabeth didn't quite know where to look. Not at him, not at the dancing couples. She settled for the ground at her feet. It was probably best he didn't see her fiery cheeks.

"I am afraid the spectacle of the Harvest Lord claiming the Corn Maiden quite carried me away." He sighed deeply. "I think you may have been affected by it as well?"

Elizabeth risked raising her head. "It was . . . most powerful. I believe many pagan rituals are."

"Yes, well, I am sorry I took advantage of you in the moment." He shook his head. "Most unforgivable."

"I forgive you, my lord." She leaned forward, putting a hand on his arm to reassure him. "I was as much to blame." Heat stole through her palm where she touched his arm, and she snatched it back. "One wonders if it is the ritual or the very place itself that channels these feelings."

"You felt it as well?" His eager voice touched that ache deep inside her.

"I must confess I did." She almost whispered the admission. Could she actually be standing here in a field, in the middle of the night, saying these indelicate things to a man? A particularly nice gentleman too. What *must* he think of her?

He seized her hands, startling her afresh. "Do not be ashamed, Mrs. Easton, I beg of you. I hope you have noticed these last few days of the house party—no, even before that, when first we met—that I have come to have the greatest respect and admiration for you. Gratitude as well for your friendship with Georgina."

"Lady Georgina is a dear, dear friend. I would do anything within my power for her." The pleasurable tingles where he held her hands had begun anew.

"You are one of the kindest spirits I have ever known."

He pulled her a step closer. "I have been waiting for the right moment to tell you just how much I admire you."

His gaze warmed her as much as his words. She could fall into those big blue eyes and be lost forever. Willingly. Oh, dear, was she doing it again?

"Lord Brack." She leaned back, pulling her hands from his and winding them firmly around her reticule. "I fear a headache has come upon me suddenly. Likely brought on by that potent Wrotham ale."

"Mrs. Easton—"

She started toward the area where the horses and carriages waited. "Perhaps that is why ladies are seldom supposed to indulge in it." She must get away from this place, before she was truly lost. "Will you please see me to the carriage? I believe it is time I returned to Lyttlefield Park."

"Allow me to escort you back." He fell in step beside her but didn't offer his arm.

Perceptive man. If she touched him again she would completely lose control and quite likely abandon herself to him here and now. And while that prospect had a wild appeal to her at the moment and in this place, in the light of day it simply would not do. "Thank you, my lord, for the offer, but I cannot allow you to leave the festivities on my account." The short drive back to Wrotham Park alone would give her time to cool this unusual desire for him. If she remained here, in the wild sensuality of the night, she might ravish Lord Brack on the spot.

"I believe it has concluded." He swept his hand toward the now-ragged circle where the locals were milling about.

Indeed, the festival seemed at an end.

"It would be my greatest pleasure to see you home safely." He chuckled. "Even though the robbers in the area have been apprehended, a lady at night alone is never a wise choice."

Although this might be the one exception to that rule.

"Very well then." Elizabeth resisted a sigh. He'd got what she called a "stubborn man face" on—Dickon had shown it to her enough times that she recognized it on other gentlemen. She would simply have to keep a vigilant distance from this most attractive man. "I thank you for your kind offer."

His joyful smile did nothing to buoy her confidence.

She steeled herself for the touch of his hand. "Should we wait for the others, perhaps? They will be needing the carriage as well." If others accompanied them, surely she'd be less inclined to think heated thoughts about the gentleman seated across from her.

"The distance is less than half a mile. We will send it back directly we arrive." He tapped on the roof, and the coachman started the team. "If you are in distress, we must get you home so you can have some tea as quickly as possible."

"You are truly kind, my lord." Elizabeth relaxed against the soft leather seat and smiled at the personable young man. He would make any woman an excellent husband in due time. It might even be her, if only she were ready to give up her love for Dickon.

She firmed her lips into a pleasant smile. Even though Charlotte and Georgie had been actively advocating a match between her and Lord Brack, that didn't mean she was ready for it. Such a major change in her life must take more sober consideration than a few days' acquaintance, delightful though the gentleman might be. She had Dickon's children, Colin and Kate, to think of, after all. There was no need to rush into marriage.

Not even to satisfy the hollow ache deep in her core that suddenly yearned to be filled by the man in the carriage.

Chapter 2

Jemmy leaned back in the carriage, wishing for more light. He'd give anything to know what Mrs. Easton—Elizabeth, as he already called her to himself—was thinking right now. But the shadows fell across her lovely face, masking any inner thoughts that might help him to gauge her reactions.

The leather seat creaked as he eased his position. Perhaps the darkness was a blessing. While it shielded Elizabeth's face, it also very effectively hid the lingering effects their passionate encounter had caused in his groin. His breeches had tented as soon as that indecent pagan kiss had taken place in the circle. Not from desire for Nora Burns—God, no—but from his fantasy that he was the Harvest Lord and Elizabeth his Corn Maiden.

Best not think along those lines at the moment. At least not until he was safely away from Elizabeth. Mrs. Easton. Damn it. He thought of her as Elizabeth. His Elizabeth, although after rushing his fences like that tonight he'd surely set himself back in his campaign to make her his wife. Perhaps some simple solicitude would help offset his blunder.

"Are you cold, Mrs. Easton? There's a carriage blanket here." She looked pale whenever the moonlight flashed in through the window, illuminating the sweet, heart-shaped face that so often wore a worried frown.

"No, thank you, my lord. I am fine. And we are almost at Lyttlefield Park." She smiled, and his member leaped afresh.

Earlier in the year, Jemmy'd had no notion of wanting a wife. At just twenty-nine, he'd returned from a grand tour, not only of the normal places in France, Italy, and Germany; he'd also taken excursions to Egypt and Greece as well. He'd waited years for the war to be over, and he'd insisted on a complete tour before coming back home. Just arrived in London in May, he'd come to Town this Season to sow his final wild oats. Of course, he'd managed his share of that in various places across Europe and now throughout London as well, with several delectable birds-of-paradise.

Lady Cavendish's house party had been one more stop in a summer dedicated to passion and frolic, a way to see his sister again with his father none the wiser—until he had met Elizabeth Easton. When Georgie had introduced her as a widow, he'd immediately assumed the woman desired a casual romp. To say he'd been grossly mistaken was to put it lightly.

"Here we are, Mrs. Easton."

The carriage rolled up to the manor house door, and Jemmy jumped down, waving away the groom and handing Elizabeth down as gently as if she were a porcelain doll.

"Thank you so much, my lord." She smiled, a dimple appearing in her right cheek.

Oh, to have that dimple to kiss at will.

Jemmy offered his arm, not at all certain she'd take it. Although their kiss earlier had steamed with passion, she'd broken from it and him rather abruptly.

Elizabeth placed her hand lightly through the crook of his arm, and he thrilled to the delicate touch. Heat curled around his cock as though she'd gripped it instead.

From the moment he'd been introduced to her, the woman had entranced him. Her beautiful face, lush figure, and pleasing voice had attractions of their own. Her sweet nature, however, had enchanted him. A very womanly lady who had been someone's perfect wife.

She'd mentioned both her husband and children that first evening in August, dispelling any idea she'd come to the party with a mere dalliance in mind. Despite the initial disappointment, he'd discovered he didn't care. He'd been drawn to her as a cold man is drawn to a roaring fire. Even when she'd hinted she still grieved for her late husband, a war hero, Jemmy had found hope. A woman who had once loved so deeply would likely need that physical love once more.

Tonight, he'd been sure of it. Her passionate response to him had given him even greater hope that she was at last ready to forget the past and think about a future with him. Unfortunately, he had to admit, accepting his arm didn't necessarily indicate she would accept further advances. His body simmered with the memory of her mouth, craving more.

As they entered Lyttlefield Hall, the butler claimed their wraps.

"Can you fetch tea for us, Fisk? Mrs. Easton and I are chilled to the bone." Jemmy steered Elizabeth into the drawing room, where earlier so much excitement had occurred. Perhaps a quiet cup of tea would put them both back into a more affable mood.

"I am afraid I am too tired even for tea, Lord Brack." She still gripped her reticule tightly, her gaze darting repeatedly toward the door. Seeking escape. "I will give you good night and thank you for a lovely day."

"I am sorry your headache is no better, my dear." He might as well sneak that endearment in while he could. "Don't you think hot tea would make a world of difference?" Desperation made him grasp any straw that presented itself to keep her here.

To his dismay, she shook her head and smiled sadly. "I

think the only thing that will rid me of this pain is an early night."

"Then let me come with you."

Eyes widening, she stumbled back a step. "What do you mean?"

Putting every ounce of charm into his smile, Jemmy offered his arm once more. "Only that I beg to be allowed to escort you to your chamber. I would have this day and your company last as long as possible."

The tension in her shoulders melted away as she relaxed toward him. "You are very kind. Thank you so much for your excellent company all day." She cast her gaze down, then back up at him through long, golden lashes. "It would be lovely to extend it a little more."

Grinning at his victory, Jenny enjoyed the thrill of her small hand as it perched, light as a hummingbird, in the crook of his arm. Oh, that they were bound for the same chamber.

"Do you stay long here at Lyttlefield? I believe the party is scheduled to last through Monday." He'd accepted an invitation to Braeton's Hunt Ball next week but might stay on here if Elizabeth elected to remain. "Have you other engagements, or do you return to your parents in London?"

"I will leave for London on Tuesday. I suspect Charlotte will have much more to do now to accomplish another move and plan her wedding by December. Such a pity she will have to repack nearly everything to move only a mile or so down the road." Elizabeth shook her head at the daunting task. They mounted the steps, and she tightened her grip on his arm.

The slight pressure filled him with desire once more. Desire to seize her lips, devour that red, luscious mouth, and more. If only they'd had more time out at the festival. "I will be truly sorry to see you leave." He laid his hand over hers as they neared the landing. "I fear I can never have enough of your company."

A nearby sconce threw light on her cheek, revealing a blush. "Lord Brack—"

"Why did you break our kiss?" He stopped her, needing to know. "I have waited for months for that kiss, and then it was over before I even knew it had begun." He stroked her cheek, soft as a flower petal, with the back of his hand. "Did you not enjoy it?"

A quick gasp, and she released his arm. "Of course, I enjoyed it." One stricken look at him, and she turned away, striding quickly toward her room with short, jerky steps.

"Then why did you end it?"

He caught her at her chamber door, the last one at the end of the corridor.

"I . . . I was thinking about my husband." Her voice had lowered to a whisper. "That wasn't fair to you."

A pang of jealousy shot through his breast, but he dismissed it. It had likely been her first kiss since the man's death, therefore a normal reaction. "Let me see if I can make you forget him this time." He grasped her face, ignored her startled blue eyes, and brought their lips together again.

Elizabeth didn't protest, couldn't protest when Lord Brack's gentle but firm hands took control of her for the second time that night. Secretly, she'd wanted another kiss and had been appalled by that desire. She still loved Dickon, didn't she? How could she want another man's lips on her? Want to feel his hands all over her body? It was a betrayal of Dickon, of the memory of his love.

At the touch of Lord Brack's lips, however, her struggle melted like snow in the sunlight. Passion ignited earlier out in the dark field flamed anew throughout her being, licking into all the little recesses of her body, starved for attention these long months. Every inch of her quivered, longing for his touch. Her breasts swelled, her core ached with new intensity. What was it about this man that drove her into such a frenzy of need? Had the pagan god of the festival followed them back to work his powers of lust on them once more?

She moaned into his mouth, searching greedily for his tongue. In her urgency, she leaned into him, rubbing her breasts against his rock-hard chest with even more insistence than before. Madness descended, as her hips thrust wildly, seeking a different hardness.

Sliding his hands down her back, he cupped her bottom with firm fingers, and pulled her right into him before slamming them both into the door. The stiffness in his trousers prodded her mound in perfect placement, drawing a groan from deep within his throat. He thrust his tongue in and out of her mouth, the invitation clear as a summer's day. He wanted her.

And heaven help her, she wanted him as well. Desperately. She felt for the handle, pushing it down with such force the door popped inward and they staggered into the room. Still locked in their frantic embrace, she fought to stay upright.

He tried to put her from him, but she clung closer, sending her hands into his curly hair, closing her fingers around the short strands. Disengaging their mouths for a moment, he rasped, "Let me shut the door."

She nodded but wouldn't let go, forcing him to walk them both back to the door to give it a shove. It crashed into the frame with a force that made the painting on the wall jump and the lone candle in the room waver. Then he was back, his lips on her mouth, her throat, the swell of her heaving breast as it spilled over the neckline of her dress. Lord, she wanted more of him. Her nipples drew into points, aching to be freed from their confinement. She guided his hands to them.

He needed no further urging. With a flick of his wrists, her breasts popped free, his hot mouth engulfing first one nipple, then the other. Moaning her delight, she pressed his head to her, reveling in the exquisite sensations so long denied. And still she craved more of him. Her raw panting sounded loudly in the semidarkness. If only she could feel his hands on her skin, all over her body. Lord, it had been so long. "Undress me now."

His sharp intake of breath swelled her desire to new heights. He spun her around, his fingers fumbling first at the buttons of her dress, then the laces of her stays. Soon her clothes puddled at her feet, and she stood only in shift, stockings, and shoes. Delicious chills coursed through her as she stooped to remove her half-boots. At last she turned to find him almost as divested of his clothes as she. All that remained to cover his taut form were his breeches and boots.

Drawn to his sleek, broad chest, she skimmed her hands lightly over his nipples, then down the firm, beautifully made muscles of his abdomen to the top of his tight, buff trousers.

"One more moment, love." His husky voice sent another frisson of heat streaking to her core. He bent, and she chaffed with impatience until his boots hit the floor with dull thuds. There was a soft plop, plop of buttons being ripped through their holes, and he towered over her again. With one swift motion, his hands grasped her shoulders and peeled the shift from her, exposing her to his hot gaze. He ran his thumb from her neck down to the tip of one nipple, her skin pebbling at his touch, her breast swelling tight, its tip furled into a tiny, eager point. Continuing downward, he stroked over her stomach, making it tremble, and onward to the thicket that covered her mons.

Staring at her with a hunger she'd not seen in years, he pressed through her curls until he found her nub, dipped lower to gather the moisture that drenched her sex, then massaged it gently over the sensitive spot.

Knees weak, she quivered as he circled and rubbed, staring into his eyes, though intensely aware of his fingers at play. A squeeze of her nub drew a gasp, then a moan that seemed to well up from her core. Desperate to touch him, she grabbed his face, captured his mouth, and thrust her tongue into him. Their tongues battled as he stroked faster. Little mews of pleasure escaped her as he drove her to the long-denied brink and pushed her over.

Waves of passion crashed over her as her body gave itself up to the pleasure once more. She clutched him to her, crying and panting as the waves receded.

He scooped her up in his arms and carried her to the bed. With one hand, he raked the covers down and laid her on the crisp white sheet, then climbed up and spread his body over hers. His cock searched eagerly for access between her thighs.

Immediately, she opened them, inviting him in, wanting—no, craving—more of the pleasure he had generously given her. It had been too long since she'd felt these wonderful sensations that had left her all but breathless. "Don't stop."

"As if I could, my love," he chuckled, then licked her nipples, first one, then the other.

The cool air on her wet flesh made it pebble again, and the tips teased back into their hard, aching points. They had always enjoyed such attention. But she wanted more. She surged against him, her hips bumping his, seeking his heat.

"Hmm, not yet, love." He left her breasts and trailed his tongue down her stomach. Lower still, he brushed her mons with a kiss that set her afire.

"Ah. Ahh." Had anything ever felt so wonderful? She hadn't realized how much she'd missed these feelings, how good they felt. Arching her back, she pressed herself into his mouth.

His questing tongue drew deeper and deeper moans from her until he found her nub again and pressed it.

"Ohhh, yess." Once more like that, and she would complete again.

Instead, he replaced his mouth with something hard and

hot that stroked through her moisture, seeking entrance at last.

"Ready?" The deep, husky growl brought every nerve in her body alive.

"Yes, oh, yes," she breathed, straining toward his heat.

With one smooth thrust, thick and hard, he flowed into her, filling her emptiness with life once more. She wanted to savor that fullness, that connection to another she had missed so much, but as a starving man cannot settle for a mere taste, she couldn't stay her need to push quickly for the glorious end.

Maddeningly, he began long, slow thrusts that should have satisfied but didn't.

Impatient, she raised her hips to meet each thrust, urging him to quicken his pace.

"Slow and steady, love. Let us enjoy this together."

Yes, enjoy. Enjoy the pleasure as long as they could. She relaxed back on the mattress, and he buried his face in her neck. His hot breath sounded ragged in her ear as he moaned with each lunge.

The slow, deliberate strokes kindled a beginning blaze, like a single flame licking deep within her. Heat sizzled down her arms and legs, radiating from her core, where he stoked her fire to a white-hot intensity she'd never experienced before. The spark must have leaped to him, for he abruptly abandoned his leisured pace, thrusting harder, with a frenzied power that left her breathless. Harder, deeper, faster he plunged into her as if trying to touch her very soul, until with a great cry he exploded within her, hot seed scorching her womb.

She clasped him deep within, shuddering around him, shattering into a thousand pieces as she cried out, "Dickon, Dickon! Oh, yes, yes, my love."

Chapter 3

In the deathly silence following her outcry, Elizabeth held her breath, hoping against hope she'd awakened from an incredibly intense dream of Dickon. It had happened before, though never quite so vividly.

The man breathing heavily above her, however, was no dream. A sticky sheen of sweat covered them both, and her body ached in places long unused.

Oh, God, what had she done?

With a grunt, Lord Brack withdrew from her and flopped onto the bed next to her, flinging his arm over his face.

"I'm so sorry." What else could she say? If she could die this minute, she would do so and be thankful. Unfortunately, that option seemed unavailable at the moment. At least in the semidarkness he couldn't see her face, burning hotter than a blacksmith's forge.

"It's all right, Elizabeth." He sighed and turned on his side to face her. "Please don't fret about it. You'd said earlier you'd been missing your husband."

The kind understanding in his voice, hushed in the darkness, filled her with even more humiliation. "I don't . . . I can't . . ." Words failed as tears choked her throat.

"Shhh." He kissed her bare shoulder, a fiery brand that seared her soul. "Please don't distress yourself, my dear." Taking her cold hand, he laced their fingers together. "One often loses oneself in the throes of passion." His warm lips brushed their entwined hands. "You are a very passionate woman, Elizabeth." His husky voice sent shivers down her body.

"My lord—"

"Please, call me Jemmy." A chuckle underlay the words. "After this evening, I don't believe we need stand on ceremony any longer, do you?" He rose up on his elbow to peer into her face. A boyish grin showed in the faint firelight.

Beyond words, Elizabeth shook her head slowly. How would she ever be able to face him in the light without this feeling of mortification surging through her? Much less calling him by his Christian name. The idea of meeting him out in society made her chest tighten, as though a hand squeezed it. Not only had she taken a strange man into her bed, but at the most intimate moment possible, she'd called him by her dead husband's name. By Dickon's name.

"Lord Br—"

The glint in his eyes stopped her cold.

"Jemmy." She forced the name out. So odd to say it aloud, though she'd heard Georgie call him that since the summer. "I think it might be best if you go before you are discovered here." Perhaps if he left, she could think what to do about this ghastly mess. His warm presence in her bed was too disconcerting, too distracting. Any thought she might have had flew right out again with his slightest movement.

"Ah, but it's scarcely midnight. We have the whole night before us." He kissed her nipple.

She gasped, a bolt of desire streaking down to her core. What was wrong with her? She'd never been so insatiable, not even with—No! She couldn't think of Dickon. Not when another man was fondling her breasts, making her want to moan with pleasure she'd not felt in over a year. Tears spilled down her cheeks. It was wrong to feel this way.

"Elizabeth? Did I hurt you?" The concern in his low, in-sistent voice sent the tears streaming faster.

Yes! she wanted to scream. He had hurt her grievously. For he had made her betray not only him, but her love for Dickon. She'd clung to that with every morsel of strength she possessed for the past year and a half. But she couldn't confess that to him. So she shook her head and whispered, "I'm just terribly embarrassed."

"Don't be, love." With a long finger, he followed the track of a tear as it hurried down her cheek, catching it on his thumb. "I'm certain when we enjoy one another again, everything will be forgotten." He kissed her lips, then swung a leg over her body, straddling her legs once more. His shaft, magically hard again, lay snug on her stomach.

His readiness surprised her. Dickon had never been able again so quickly. And she just . . . couldn't. What if she called him Dickon again? Her stomach clenched at the thought. "Jemmy, please. I don't think I can . . . I don't think this is right." She turned her face from him. "I truly think you should go."

A frown immediately shadowed his face. "You wish me to leave?"

The hurt in his voice sent a pang of guilt through her, but she ignored it and nodded. "I simply can't." Tears flooded her eyes. "We shouldn't have done this at all. I'm not done . . ." She took a ragged breath, angry at its pathetic mewling sound. "I still love my husband, so I'm sorry, but I can't have you in my bed."

He tensed, then vanished from above her, leaving her ex-posed and cold. "I understand, Elizabeth."

She raised up on her elbow, pulling up the covers and peering into the dim room.

He pulled on his breeches, fastening his fall with lightning speed, his short jerky movements punctuating his anger.

Sorry as she might be, she couldn't help that. He needed to leave, so she could cry alone. A sudden chill made her shiver and draw the covers more tightly around her neck.

After pulling on his boots, he stomped his feet, too loud in the accusing silence. When he turned toward her again, his shirt was tucked, his cravat in place around his neck, but not tied. A stray shaft of light lit his face—it reminded her of the statuary in her father's garden at home, frozen in harsh, stony lines.

Guilt flooded her again. He looked angry and miserable, like an eager puppy that had been shoved aside. "Jemmy—"

"No, my dear. I am simply very sorry for misunderstanding you."

"Please, Jemmy, I am truly sorry." She couldn't bear the hurt on his face. He had been a boon companion this past summer as well as this weekend. Kind, friendly, attentive, and so handsome. He should be the perfect man to help lead her out of her grief for her husband. If only it were the proper time. If only she hadn't ruined everything. He could never really forgive her calling him by another man's name. And having done so once, she would not risk lying with him a second time, even to try and dispel the lapse.

He watched her, his eyes still hungry. "I take my leave of you, Mrs. Easton."

The formality cut like a knife to her heart.

Before she could say a word, he swept her a bow and strode to the door. Opening it a crack, he first listened to the corridor, then eased it open enough to look up and down the hall. He slipped out without a backward glance. The door clicked shut, leaving her alone at last.

Hand flung over her eyes, Elizabeth lay completely still, unable to keep from seeing images of her and Jemmy entwined in her bed. She rolled over, staring into the dying embers of the fire, willing herself to sleep. The tick tick of the clock on the mantle told her time continued to pass, still she felt frozen, reliving in her mind that one horrifying moment when she'd called Jemmy "Dickon." She curled up as her stomach threatened to cast up its contents. She could never look Jemmy—no, Lord Brack, much better to think of him as that once more—in the face again, knowing that.

Flopping onto her back, Elizabeth stared at the frilly white canopy overhead, still unable to sleep, despite her exhaustion. Marital relations with Dickon had always left them both panting and sated, ready to talk quietly as they lay in each other's arms, drowsing off to sleep.

The very same activity with Jemmy—no, Lord Brack—seemed to have the opposite effect. She was wide awake and might be until the sun came up. She should have slept like the dead after such a strenuous—

Her whole face flushed with heat at the image of him over top of her, thrusting vigorously into her over and over.

By God, but she had enjoyed it.

"I did not." Speaking the words aloud, she sat up in the darkened room, ready to deny it to anyone except herself. "I did not enjoy it like I did with Dickon." But she had enjoyed it nonetheless.

It was different, of course. Jemmy was quite a bit younger than her late husband, more her own age. That youth had shown in his vigor and stamina, and the forceful way he'd swept her off her feet, literally, and into the bed.

Her husband had been slow and steady. Nothing wrong with that during their almost seven years together. But—

How could she lie here and compare them? She sat up and punched her pillow. It was indecent. No nice woman would dream of doing such a thing. Of course, most women didn't have the experience to make a comparison between two men. Two very different men, yet each called to her.

Dickon had been a gallant soldier, yet tender and kind when they closed off the rest of the world in the bedchamber they always shared.

Tonight had been all wild passion, as if another Elizabeth had taken over her body and allowed a secret part of her to be free. It must have been that dreadful scene at the festival. So pagan it had stirred her blood to a fever pitch. Lord Brack's as well.

"Jemmy."

The name on her tongue set her body to throbbing, especially her core at the apex of her thighs. What was wrong with her? Was she truly so wanton a woman she already thought of bedroom pleasures a second time in one night? After almost a year and a half without such urges, to now crave such intimacies said little for her delicacy or her loyalty. She should still be mourning her husband, not taking a new lover between her sheets.

Still, the memory of Jemmy's hard body over her, in her, driving her to the heights of ecstasy would not be denied. Even now, her body tingled with the anticipation of his touch. She wanted to experience it again and again. She strained upward with longing for him, but it could never be. Not with Jemmy.

Despite his words, he could scarcely overlook such a breach of propriety as she had committed, much less forgive it. If she'd rather die than look him in the face again, how was she to be intimate with him? Blow out the candles? As if he'd expose himself to the possibility of such a thing happening again.

Not that she'd make a habit of falling into bed with a man to whom she wasn't married. If she married Jemmy, oh my, but the nights would never be cold or lonely. Hot, passionate, tender. Yes, that would be a life to live to the fullest. Jemmy would be the perfect man to warm her bed.

Impossible. She flopped over on her other side. Not that he'd likely make an offer after tonight's wretched performance. No. Better to remain true to the memory of her dead husband. A cold bed was a small price to pay for the appearance of loyalty.

The final ember in the fireplace broke apart, and the darkness closed around her. As she began to sink into sleep at last, another disconcerting question raised itself. Was she more disturbed that she had shown disloyalty to Dickon, or that she had so easily abandoned herself to passion in Jemmy's arms?

Jemmy snicked the door closed, alert for any sound that might indicate someone else lurked in the corridor. He moved away from Elizabeth's door with a brisk step that quickly took him toward the landing. He crossed it, noting no activity downstairs. Good. He'd have time to make himself presentable before appearing later.

He hurried to his chamber before someone saw him so disheveled and started asking questions—he'd thrown on his clothes so quickly he'd slipped his shirt on backward and he'd missed a few buttonholes in his breeches. This dishabille could indicate a dalliance on his part, though he was close enough to his own room now that no one would necessarily suspect a particular person. Clawing at his neck, he stopped at his door. He'd simply wound his cravat around his throat, where it currently threatened to choke him. At the moment, death was far less alarming than his anger at Elizabeth Easton.

"Fellowes," he bellowed as soon as he'd shut his chamber door. His valet would put him to rights in good time with no questions asked.

"My lord?" The short, thin man with graying hair bounded out of his dressing room.

"I require some attention."

Fellowes took in his master's rumpled appearance and, with a long-suffering sigh, replied, "Of course, my lord." The valet began to strip him methodically, if somewhat distastefully. Fellowes took inordinate pride in turning Jemmy out impeccably every time he set foot outside his room. Jemmy's current state would have set a blot on his valet's internal copybook had he been seen by anyone.

Relaxing in Fellowes capable hands, Jemmy gave himself over to calm, cool inner reflection.

What the deuce had happened tonight between him and Elizabeth? He forced himself to relax and groaned with the effort as the valet continued his adjustments. The sheer power of the Harvest Festival's ritual crowning had affected them both more than he'd ever expected. The claiming of the Corn Maiden, Wrotham had called it. Fertility rite indeed. The utter sexual frenzy that had come upon him as he watched the Harvest Lord kiss the Corn Maiden had shaken him to his soul. Truth to tell, he'd had to restrain himself from laying Elizabeth down on the newly spaded earth and taking her within yards of the festival revelers.

Fellowes began his efficient removal of Jemmy's linen shirt.

Elizabeth had felt the power as well. Her passionate response to his kiss had told him that. His cock had ached all the way back to Lyttlefield, much as he tried to hide it. And he would swear on a Bible, as he stood on his mother's grave, that Elizabeth had wanted him as deeply as he had wanted her.

If he'd had doubts about the appetite that burned beneath the cool, dignified veneer that was the world's view of Elizabeth Easton, they'd been put forever to rest in the last hour. Actually, Jemmy'd had few doubts about Mrs. Easton's true nature even before the festival. From the moment he'd met her, he'd sensed that although she might appear prim and proper, deep within her burned an impassioned soul. That, as much as her comely face, had drawn him to her last summer. How satisfying to have been proved right.

He groaned quietly, trying to hold still as Fellowes straightened his trousers. His unruly flesh strained embarrassingly as the memory of his recent satisfaction in Elizabeth's bed fanned the flames of hunger and lust yet again. Not even the sound of her rich, husky voice crying out her husband's name had been able to stifle his desire for her. He'd been shocked by that slip of course, but understood it better than Elizabeth likely gave him credit for.

Georgie had told him early on of the deep love and regard Elizabeth had had for her husband, and of her terrible grief over his death at the Battle of Waterloo. His sister had professed a similar love and grief for her own husband, Isaac Kirkpatrick. So he understood that such a profound and abiding attachment could not be overcome even after a year of mourning. He could not fault Elizabeth for being carried away during the moment of completion, calling out the name of the only man who had excited such pleasure in her before. What he did regret was that her inability to move past her natural embarrassment had prevented him from making love to her once more, from the chance to bring his own name to her lips at that sweet ultimate surrender of herself.

Handing Jemmy a fresh shirt, Fellowes assisted him in dropping it over his head, the correct way this time.

Would she ever allow him to become close to her again? He feared she'd allow that one lapse to keep them from another intimate encounter. She said she still grieved for her husband, which he suspected was true. However, he'd wager she now intended to keep him at arm's length because of her embarrassment, not her grief.

Finally, the valet draped a new cravat around his neck almost lovingly.

As a matter of habit, Jemmy raised his hands to begin tying the knot, then paused, shooting a frantic look at the little man still fussing with his clothing. "Was it in a Napoleon tie earlier, or a Ball Room, Fellowes?"

"I believe a Napoleon, my lord; however—"

"Be certain, for God's sake. If it was in a Napoleon, then it must be tied in a Napoleon once again. I must not look as though I have changed clothes." Jemmy began adjusting the length of the long silk cloth, trying to remember which way he had tied it earlier.

"But gentlemen are not looked down upon for changing such things, my lord." Fellowes brushed at the shoulder and back of his jacket. The valet's pride in his master's looks was usually an endearing quality, but this was not the time.

"Tonight, Fellowes, I wish to give the impression that I have not changed since the company dined and returned to the festival. Let us say it is a point of honor—a lady's honor, mind you—that I appear so." Adjusting the dents in the cravat, Jemmy finished tying it and looked at his appearance critically in the mirror.

"Ah, I see, my lord." Fellowes nodded so quickly his head bobbed. "Indeed, I do. May I suggest you adjust the cloth slightly? If you loosen it somewhat, it will suggest that it has been worn for some hours, and assist with your deception."

"Thank you, Fellowes." Jemmy's fingers flew as he retied the snowy white cravat more loosely until he could swallow with relative freedom. "What would I ever do without you?"

"I am pleased to ever be at your lordship's service."

Jemmy gazed at his reflection, taking in point after point of his dress, remembering how he'd looked before he'd escorted Elizabeth to the festival. Before the madness had descended upon him.

Fellowes had worked another miracle. His suit approached the crisp look of earlier, only slightly relaxed. The cravat, however, was the masterpiece. Draped with exactly the correct degree of looseness, it suggested several hours of wear, not the frantic untying that had occurred in Elizabeth's bedchamber. He must remember to raise Fellowes's wages ten shillings in the next quarter. This was not the first time the valet had saved him, and it likely would not be the last.

"This will do nicely." Jemmy turned this way and that, judging the exact dishevelment of his appearance and finding it most satisfactory. "You are to be commended, Fellowes."

"Thank you, my lord." The man bowed, took the soiled shirt, and disappeared into the dressing room once more.

Now for the hardest part of the evening—acting unconcerned about Elizabeth's disappearance without seeming too incurious or too interested. Perhaps he could help by volunteering the information that she'd retired with a headache. No one could fault her for that after the strenuous nature of the day they had all had.

He took one last look in the mirror and headed downstairs, determined to shield Elizabeth, in her absence, from the prying questions of the other guests. Tomorrow he would find a way to speak with her alone and query her about their future. As a gentleman, he would help hide her from everyone but himself.

Chapter 4

Next morning, dressed as though he expected to meet Beau Brummel himself, Jemmy straightened his shoulders and fixed a pleasant smile on his face before entering the breakfast room. From experience, he knew Elizabeth came down early, and he hoped to begin his campaign to woo her afresh over tea and toast. Disappointment wiped the smile from his face when he found the bright yellow room inhabited only by his sister, Georgina, seated at the table, peeling an orange.

"Jemmy." Georgie's eyes lit up, and her cheeks flushed. She patted the seat beside her. "Come sit by me. I must get my fill of you while I can. There's no telling when we shall be able to meet again." She frowned, her nose wrinkling comically as she turned the orange in her hands.

He made his way around the table, glancing about for any sign that Elizabeth had already come down. The tablecloth lay smooth, pristinely fresh, everywhere save the place occupied by his sister. Good. Elizabeth had not yet appeared. After nonchalantly brushing a kiss on Georgie's brow, he rounded the table and headed for the sideboard, loaded with gleaming silver warming pans.

Last evening's mix of wild passions, the stresses of mingling sociably with the house party company afterward, and
tossing and turning in his suddenly empty-seeming bed had
resulted in a voracious appetite this morning. Before he realized it, he'd heaped his plate high with smoked herring, cold
veal pie, sausages with mashed potatoes, rolls, and marmalade.

"Are you expecting a famine, Jemmy?"

He turned to find Georgie eyeing his plate before returning her attention to her orange.

"Can a man not be hungry in the morning without family
censure falling on his head?" Jemmy shot back, a little more
crisply than usual. He loved the banter he and his sister often
shared, but found himself too distracted this morning to continue it. "Have you had the table to yourself this whole
while?" He grabbed an orange for himself from the bowl at
the end of the sideboard.

"Yes, alas. No one has seen fit to come down and eat this
morning." Georgie dropped the orange peel, which she'd
managed to remove in one long piece, onto her plate. "I suppose all the excitement of the festival, with the drama that
unfolded with poor Sir Edgar, and Charlotte and Nash's announcement of their engagement last night has worn everyone completely out." Carefully, she dissected the orange
segments onto her plate, ringing the rim in bright color.

"It was quite an eventful night, I'll grant you." Jemmy
chuckled as he pulled out the high-backed chair beside her.
"I'll be surprised if the any of the company rises before
noon." He eased into his chair, the overly full plate balanced
neatly on one hand.

"Except for us and Elizabeth."

Jemmy froze, the plate now wobbling precariously. "You
said she hadn't been down."

Georgie shook her head. "I said she hadn't breakfasted.
She bid me farewell as I came down the stairs."

"Farewell?" The plate slipped from his hand and rattled

onto the table, spilling a little of the potatoes onto the clean white tablecloth. "She's left Lyttlefield Park?"

Staring at him warily, Georgie nodded. "At least half an hour ago. She said she needed to go home. Oh." She reached underneath her plate and produced a letter. "She left this for you."

Stomach twisting, Jemmy plucked it from her fingers. Feigning an air of indifference, he calmly broke the seal and slowly unfolded the sheet of cream notepaper. "Did she say why she needed to go home so suddenly?" She could have received a message from home in the middle of the night or early this morning, but a sinking suspicion told him his actions—or hers—had precipitated her flight.

"No, which is odd." Georgie frowned. "I asked if something had happened, and she said 'yes,' then paled and said 'no.' I couldn't get out another question before she thrust that into my hands and said to give it to you." His sister narrowed her eyes. "Did you quarrel with her last night, Jemmy? Don't tell me you have done something stupid."

"I . . . no, nothing I can think of." He hated lying through his teeth, especially to Georgie, for whom he'd always felt a special fondness. "She said she had a headache when I left her last night. That's all." Fearing the worst, he unfolded the piece of stationery.

"So you told us." Georgie picked up an orange section and bit it in half. "However, I did mark that the tips of your ears turned bright pink at the time."

"What?" He'd been staring at the letter, admiring the elegant swirls of Elizabeth's handwriting. His sister's words brought him back to the present with a jolt. "What does the color of my ears have to do with anything?"

"Oh, come now, Jemmy." Georgie gave him a withering look. "As if you didn't know that your ears turn the exact shade of the Rose de Meux in the gardens at Blackham Castle every time you lie about something."

"Leave my ears out of this, bran face. I was likely too

close to the fireplace." He busied himself with the letter, refusing to meet Georgie's eyes for fear his ears would betray him yet again. Drawing in a sobering breath, he forced his attention to the looping letters that sprawled thickly across the page.

Dear Lord Brack,

Christ. If she referred to him as Lord Brack after that wildly passionate interlude in her chamber last night, he was lost for sure.

By the time you receive this letter I shall be on my way back to my parents' home in London. I beg of you, do not follow me there.

Hell and damnation.

As I warned you last evening, I am not yet done with grieving my late husband. He is almost constantly in my thoughts, as you have become well aware.

A large blob of ink had pooled on the period of that sentence. Perhaps Elizabeth's pen had rested there over long as she reflected on the moment of which she wrote. He could certainly recall that scene vividly—her face pale, save for her cheeks flushed rosy in passion's grip as he gloriously spilled himself inside her, her one word marring the moment.

I find I am unwilling to consider such intimacies with another man while I am still constrained by my dear husband's memory. I am therefore removing myself from you, the company, and from society in general for an undetermined length of time, until my deep feelings for my late husband can be laid to rest. I feel it would be unfair to you to give you hope that I will change my mind soon. You should consider yourself free of any obligation to me that you might construe from our encounter last evening.

An icy hand gripped his heart. She meant to end their connection once and for all, without even giving him a chance to declare himself. He clutched the paper so tightly it tore. Had that impassioned interlude meant nothing to her, save the betrayal of a dead man? She had been embarrassed, true, but surely she knew he would never reproach her for that cry? He'd told her as much then and there. Perhaps she hadn't believed him. Should he have tried harder to allay her fears on that point?

Forcing himself to relax, he shot a glance at Georgie, who sat calmly eating another section of orange. Her gaze fixed firmly on the fruit, she nevertheless radiated a tension that would soon explode in a bevy of questions. If he knew Georgie, she'd demand to hear the contents of this letter, so he had better create a respectable version of it post haste. There remained but two lines left to read.

I truly wish you well, my lord, and hope for you nothing but the happiness which you so richly deserve. Thank you for all your many kindnesses to me during our brief acquaintance.

Sincerely,

Mrs. Elizabeth Easton

Wanting nothing more than to crumple the letter into a ball and pitch it into the fireplace with an oath that would singe his sister's ears, Jemmy instead breathed slowly through his nose and eased his death grip on the letter. His gaze fell again on her final sentence.

Thank you for all your many kindnesses to me . . .

Could he do her one more kindness and let her go?

If he chose, he could easily call attention to their tryst here. Everyone loved gossip, and Elizabeth's hasty departure would raise eyebrows if he were to drop a judicious hint or two to Lathbury down here, or even better to Lady Locke, the *ton*'s biggest scandalmonger in London. Widows could be compromised and forced to marry if their behavior became blatant, and she'd be expected to marry him, whether she wished to or not. The thought tantalized him, but he could not pursue it. He'd not force a woman to marry him, not even one he desperately wanted. No, he must do her that last kindness and create a reason for her precipitous flight.

He raised his gaze from the letter to the sharp green eyes of his sister, who had apparently eaten the entire orange and now turned her full attention on him, blast his luck.

"Well?" Georgie's eyebrows swooped upward.

"Well, what?" He must stall for enough time to come up with a plausible reason for Elizabeth to return to London so swiftly, before the party had officially broken up. Anything would do, except the truth.

"Well, did she say why she left so suddenly? Really, Jemmy, you can be such a chucklehead." Her green-eyed gaze had gone icy cold.

He longed to tell her the truth, to ask her advice on how to win Elizabeth, but that would certainly never do. Even though Georgie had been married, she was still his youngest sister, and he wasn't about to discuss such things with her. "She says only that she wished to go home to see the children." Such a sentiment seemed the most plausible excuse for Elizabeth. He breathed a sigh of relief, congratulating himself for devising the perfect explanation.

"There's nothing wrong with the children, is there?" Georgie grabbed his arm hard enough to make him wince. "She didn't receive a message in the night telling her to go home?" His sister fastened her gaze on the letter, and her hands shook.

He folded the piece of paper and stuffed it into his pocket before she could snatch it out of his hands. "No, nothing is wrong . . ." He cast his mind about, thinking swiftly. "Last night she told me she'd been missing them dreadfully." She'd been missing her husband dreadfully at least. "I suppose she decided in the night that she simply must see them." He stared at the plate of food, which had grown cold, and pushed it aside. No matter. A bite of anything would choke him.

Georgie sat back in her chair and released his arm with a little shake. "I suppose I can understand that." She slumped in her chair. "But I will miss her terribly. She is such a good friend to me, Jemmy. You have no idea."

He patted her hand. "I believe I do, my dear. She is a lovely woman, and I shall miss her company as well."

A footman in blue and gold livery had been hovering by the door for some minutes.

"Coffee, please, Robert." That he would welcome. He pushed his plate farther away and grimaced.

"Aren't you going to eat, Jemmy?" Georgie narrowed her eyes, her lips pursed in displeasure. "Don't let Elizabeth's departure spoil the rest of your visit." She tried to smile, but her mouth drooped. "We must make the most of our last few days together and be merry while we may."

"You are right, my dear." Chastened, Jemmy pulled his spirits out of the slough of despond into which they had been sliding ever since he had opened the letter. Georgie was right. He might not see her for some time to come after the house party broke up. He patted her hand, determined to be cheerful for her sake. "We shall continue to enjoy our visit, no matter what else has happened. Although I daresay Lady Cavendish would not be averse to having me down for the Christmas season, if you asked her." He usually spent the holiday in London but could manage several days here to be with Georgie. "I'm sure we could arrange for a lark or two then as well." As long as Father didn't catch on to why he kept going into Kent.

"But I won't be here, Jemmy, that's the thing." Georgie fiddled with her teacup, running her finger around the rim, producing a faint ringing sound. "After Charlotte and Nash wed, she will, of course, remove to Wrotham Park." Her eyes closed, and she bit her lip. "I cannot stay here."

"I'm sorry, Georgie, I hadn't realized." Her words startled him badly. Georgie had been so happy here. For her to have to return to her sister-in-law's house, where she was grudgingly welcomed and badly treated, would be intolerable for his sensitive sister. "Do you think Lady Cavendish would allow you to stay on for a while?"

He'd barely gotten the sentence out before Georgie started shaking her head, wisps of curls bobbing alongside her face. "I could not impose myself so, Jemmy. Charlotte has been too kind to me these many months. I would not ask such a thing of her, even if it were possible. I could not stay here without a companion, and I know of no one I could ask."

"I could hire a companion for you." That would work if only Father didn't find out. He currently lived off his inheritance from his mother, but Father would likely make life unpleasant for him if he found out he was helping Georgina after she'd been disowned for marrying against Father's wishes.

"Charlotte means to close the house and combine the households. I couldn't ask her to keep it running just for me." Head bowed to avoid his eyes, she continued to fidget with the cup in front of her.

Robert entered and poured his coffee, giving Jemmy time to think in silence until the footman left.

"It's a pity Aunt Fern is abroad in India. You could easily have stayed with her. What about the other ladies of your circle? Might you visit one of them for a time?" Not a very likely prospect; her friends were all widows, most with very limited circumstances.

"They are in situations perhaps not quite as dire as mine, but nearly so," Georgie confirmed his fears. "Elizabeth has the children and lives with her parents. Fanny lives with her brother-in-law, the Marquess of Theale. Jane has been a companion to Charlotte this past year, but she'll likely return to Theale's as well when Charlotte marries. Her late husband was the marquess's brother." She sighed, twitched her shoulders, and tried to smile at him. "I shall simply have to return to Mrs. Reynolds and the Kirkpatricks." She tugged on her bottom lip once more. "As long as I can make myself useful, she won't mind much."

The misery on his sister's face smote Jemmy's heart. Damn, but Father's decree had hurt her much more than the deed warranted. "You know I'd provide a place for you if Father allowed it, don't you, Georgie?"

"It's not your fault." She patted his elbow. "I disobeyed him by marrying Isaac. I knew the consequences, but I didn't care," she said, gazing at him fiercely. "I would do it again without a moment's thought to be with the man I loved."

She would, too. Jemmy absolutely had no doubt of that. He'd sneaked off to the parsonage to see Georgie married to the vicar's son, a regular chap who anyone could have seen adored Georgie. The glowing happiness on his sister's face as she spoke her vows in the crowded little room would remain with him forever. It hadn't been the brilliant match his father had wanted for his youngest daughter, but it had been a love match so obvious anyone could see it. Now, with Kirkpatrick dead at Waterloo, Jemmy wondered if Georgie would ever agree to marry again.

"Let me speak to Father, Georgie. Perhaps enough time has passed that he will allow you to return home." Unfortunately, such a reversal would likely come with a price—a marriage of Father's choosing—but it was the best offer he could make her. If he tried to set her up on an estate or in a modest house in London, Father had threatened to revoke all his funds. Although he lived off his inheritance, his father would be administrator of the trust until Jemmy reached the age of thirty. It was now less than a year until he would be free of the restraint, but they'd both be homeless if he displeased his father before that time.

"Well, you are welcome to try." Georgie leaned her cheek on her hand, as though too weary to care. "I cannot think that living with Father would be any worse than with Mrs. Reynolds. I'm amazed the woman considers herself a Christian after the things she's said to me. Always out of the hearing of the Kirkpatricks, of course. So by all means, ask him. He may say no."

"But he might just as likely say yes." Jemmy embraced her affectionately. "Although his terms might well make you think twice."

"Why?"

"He will likely take you back only so he can marry you off to a man of his choosing." Jemmy hesitated, then barreled ahead. "Perhaps you should have accepted Wrotham when you had the chance."

Her tinkly little laugh filled the breakfast room. "Nash did not want to marry me. He was only being gallant, and I knew that. He would never have been happy with anyone other than Charlotte, so that's as it should be."

"Your life would have been much easier, Georgie."

"My life is as I have made it, Jemmy." She folded her napkin with trembling fingers and laid it on her plate. "I would not change it one jot. Well, I would have Mrs. Reynolds not be so nasty toward me, but other than that . . ." She smiled, and her green eyes twinkled. "I think you should write to Elizabeth and let her know when you will next be in London."

"And why should I do that, Mrs. Meddler?" She knew how to change a subject, by God.

"If you have any affection for Elizabeth—and I'd wager any amount of money, if I had it, that you do—then you must pursue her. Don't allow her to get wrapped up in the children and forget you. Strike while the iron is hot, as Aunt Fern says." Georgie bounced up and kissed his forehead. "If you don't, I will guarantee you will regret it."

"Regret what?" Lord St. Just had entered the breakfast room on the tail end of Georgie's declaration.

"Good morning, my lord." Georgie bowed and threw a gay look at Jemmy. "My brother will regret his inactivity today if he does not mark my words." With an irrepressible giggle, Georgie sped from the room.

"Does your sister always speak in riddles, Brack? She's quite adorable, but a veritable Cassandra for making heads or tails of." St. Just grabbed a plate and began to load it down with an enthusiasm that made Jemmy rather ill. "What do you say to a ride this morning?" he asked, piling sausages on top of a mound of potatoes. "Fresh air always does one good. And Lady Georgina seemed to think activity was what you wanted today."

Sighing deeply, Jemmy nodded. "I believe you are right, Rob." He eyed his friend's heaping plate, now festooned with a ring of scones around the edge. "Good God, you're not going to eat that whole lot?"

A grin split St. Just's face. "A growing boy needs his strength."

"You're eight and twenty, Rob. Any growing you do will be outward." He eyed his friend's whipcord-thin frame. "Well, perhaps you could stand a bit of that."

With a snort, St. Just slid into a chair across from him. "I'm in better shape than you, old chap. This," he waved his hand over the huge mound of food, "will scarcely last me until luncheon." He speared a sausage and deftly cut it into thirds, the final third disappearing into his mouth.

As his friend chewed with gusto, Jemmy rose.

"Thought we were riding, old chap." St. Just cut into a slice of roast beef. The man's appetite had been legendary at school.

"Not this morning, I'm afraid," Jemmy said, eyeing the massive plate with distaste. "While you're occupied with devouring enough food to feed Bristol, I'm going to change and have Fellowes pack a bag." Georgie's words still echoed in his head, and his heart was inclined to listen. He'd even do her one better. "I'm for London as fast as the carriage can take me."

Chapter 5

Elizabeth drew a deep breath and mounted the steps to Worth House, her parents' town house in fashionable St. James Square. She'd had a long day of relentless soul-searching as she traveled through the countryside from Kent to London and could have used a distraction from her thoughts. Even her maid, Weller, never a chatty person, would have been better company than not, but Elizabeth had been obliged to leave her at home to see to her sisters. Oh, well, now she had arrived, she'd have more than her share of conversation. Bella and Dotty would likely provide that in the three minutes it would take her to enter the house and find them.

"Madam." Tawes opened the door as though he'd been expecting her today and not two days from now. "We are glad to have you home again." He took her spencer, hat, and gloves.

She sighed in relief to be home at last, with all its familiar sights and sounds. The pendulum clock in the foyer chimed the hour—five o'clock, enough time to change for dinner and perhaps have a quick visit with the children. Hothouse roses in a huge porcelain vase, edged in gold, scented the air. The red blooms were always there, their particular sweet scent a welcoming fragrance of home. A much longed-for peace descended on her.

As she started up the staircase, doors above banged shut, and shrill female voices drifted down from the landing that housed her sisters' chambers and their private sitting room, shattering the peace.

Still, it was good to be home. She continued up the stairs.

"Elizabeth, you are returned so soon?" Isabella called to her as she passed the second-floor parlor on her way to her own chamber. The dark-blond girl put down her book and rushed to the doorway. "How was the house party?" Then with an arch smile, "Was Lord Brack in attendance?"

Drat. Why had she made mention of his lordship to her sisters after the last house party at Lyttlefield Park in August? Nothing could remain a secret in the Worth household.

"Hello, Isabella. You are looking quite well this evening." Her sister was very much in looks indeed. Her cheeks pink, her lips shiny, her skin—prized for its creamy hue—fairly glowed in the lamplight. A sparkle of life in her big brown eyes told Elizabeth something had changed. Isabella had been in the doldrums ever since the end of the Season. What had occurred in the few days since her departure to cause this change?

"Thank you." Isabella preened, swishing her pale, pink-sprigged gown. "You look fagged to death."

"I've been rattling around in a carriage since before breakfast. You'd hardly look like you stepped out of a bandbox either." Elizabeth peered at her sister, giving her a more thorough scrutiny. The new pink gown, embellished with small tucks and pearls around the bottom, became her sister's coloring excellently. The delicate lace at the sleeves and neck was demure—and costly, to judge by the tiny, intricate pattern. Isabella's luxurious hair had been swept up into a stylish coiffure, quite like it had looked at assemblies during the Season. Elizabeth waved her hand, taking the girl in from top to toe. "Are you expecting someone to call this late?"

The girl smiled knowingly, then beckoned Elizabeth into the room before shutting the door. "No one knows but Papa, Mama, and Dotty." She drew Elizabeth down onto the chaise before the fire, hands fluttering, smiling like a china doll, as she bubbled with excitement. "Last evening, quite out of the blue, Lord Haxton proposed to me!"

"Goodness, Bella." Elizabeth blinked in astonishment. "Has he courted you since the end of the Season?" Mama had not said a word about such a thing; at least Elizabeth didn't think so. She'd been so distraught over Dickon's death and Charlotte trying to bring her out of mourning, she might have missed something.

"Not since the Season, no, but we did see one another during the Season's activities, and we went to Vauxhall twice with a large party." Bella's cheeks had turned quite as red as the room's Turkey carpet. "But nothing was ever spoken between us, although I did think him quite handsome and dashing."

Yes, Lord Haxton was both of those things; so Elizabeth had heard. She'd also heard from Jane and Fanny of his interest this past summer in the Marquess of Theale's daughter, Lady Anne Tarkington, while at the summer house party. Lady Anne, they'd told her, had led Haxton a merry chase the whole Season long, then accepted the heir to the Duke of Armondy, with her proud papa's full blessing. So if the Earl of Haxton could find solace with the daughter of a viscount instead, perhaps there was something to be said for him.

"Well done, my dear." She hugged her sister, praying for her happiness. "I wish for you all the happiness I had with Dickon."

"Thank you, Elizabeth. I'm sure we shall be very contented together." Bella beamed at her. "He's coming to dinner tonight." She fussed with her dress, smoothing its sleek lines. "I couldn't wait to dress for dinner, so I made Weller dress me ahead of time."

"Very ahead." Elizabeth rose, her weariness suddenly pressing upon her. "I must go see the children, then rest at least a little before dinner. Especially now that I am to meet your betrothed."

Grinning, Bella rose with her. "I do hope you approve of him."

"I am sure I shall, my dear," she said, taking her sister's hands and giving them a squeeze. "At least I will try very, very hard to do so." She laughed and hugged Bella. Only one more sister to wed now. The thought that both her younger sisters would soon have husbands and she none made her suddenly sober.

"You never said if Lord Brack was at Charlotte's party."

Her sister's words brought her up with a jolt. "Did I not? I am sorry. Yes, Lord Brack was in attendance this weekend." Heat rushed to her face as a vision of the two of them locked in a passionate embrace in her bed sprang up before her eyes.

"And . . . ?" Bella cocked her head, inquisitive as a sparrow. "Did he make his intentions apparent to you?"

Her head spinning, Elizabeth clutched the doorway, concentrating on remaining standing. "We . . . we spent quite a lot of time together." Dear Lord, what could she say? "But he made no formal declaration." That much *was* true at least.

"I am sorry, Elizabeth. I thought you said you liked him after your meeting in August." Bella's eyes held a touch of sadness. Was she sorry for her? "So why did you return early from this party? We certainly did not expect you home until Tuesday at the earliest." The girl sniffed. "I should have stayed and tried to bring him up to snuff."

So might she have done, and with very little insistence been successful, had she not fled like a thief in the night—or morning, as it turned out. She could not think of that. Would not think of Lord Brack in her bed. Nor of the horrible indiscretion she had committed.

"I fear I found myself poor company for anyone. I missed Colin and Kate so dreadfully, I simply had to come home. I really must go see them before they go to bed." Three steps down the corridor, and she had almost escaped. "I'll see you at dinner, and you can introduce me to your Lord Haxton," she called over her shoulder. Waving her hand, she fled down the corridor, only to realize she'd turned the wrong way. Well, she wasn't going back to be pulled into conversation again with Isabella. She took the servants' narrow staircase at the back of the house and climbed the steep stairs to the third floor. Drawing in deep breaths, she continued upward, panting as though she'd been running a race. Running away from memories she couldn't face. Not yet. Perhaps never.

As she neared the third-floor landing, she could hear squealing laughter from the nursery. Good, they'd not gone to bed yet.

"Good evening, my darlings." She swept into the nursery, catching the twins chasing one another around the nursery table.

"Mama, Mama!"

"Mama! You're home, you're home." Kate crashed into her left leg, just as Colin swarmed onto her right.

"Goodness! I left my two good children here and return to a brace of wild savages." Elizabeth knelt down and gathered them into her arms.

"We're not wild savages, Mama." Kate snuggled against her neck. "We were playing a game."

"A game? What game? And where is Nurse?" She looked about, but the new nurse her mother had engaged was nowhere to be found. Such a pity her own nurse had retired before the twins had been born.

"She tucked us into our beds, Mama," Colin spoke up.

"But then she was called away. One of the maids came and fetched her."

"So you took the opportunity to pop out of your beds like two jack-in-the-boxes?" Elizabeth gave her dark-haired son her sternest look.

"We've done it before, Mama." Without a hint of remorse, Colin looked her squarely in the face. "It does no harm, and Grandmama said exercise is good for us, didn't she, Kate?" He poked his sister in the arm.

"Oh, yes, Mama. She said we should run about, so now Colin chases me all the time." Kate's bottom lip stuck out.

"Do not poke your sister, Colin, and while exercise might be a good thing, running about just before bed is not part of any healthy program I've heard of."

"But, Mama . . ." Colin frowned, his small brows brooding, drooping over his eyes, darkening his face into an unbecoming countenance. She must nip this right in the bud.

"No, Colin, I am the one who says what you may and may not do, not Grandmama." Elizabeth took them by the hands, steering them back toward their beds. "Up you go, darlings."

Without too much reluctance, and no real grumbling, they settled down beneath the yellow and green covers, and Elizabeth bent to tuck them in. She had missed this routine, in truth.

"Did you have fun at the party, Mama?" Kate managed to speak despite the huge yawn that split her mouth.

"I did indeed, lovey." Elizabeth settled her daughter's cap more firmly on the pale blond curls. "We played cards and had dancing and a great festival called the Harvest Festival."

"What's a Harvest Festival?" Colin wormed his way into an almost sitting position. "Is it like the fair you and Papa took us to a long time ago?"

"Yes, my dear, very like that one. You were so small I didn't think you would remember it." Elizabeth busied herself smoothing his covers. She and Dickon had taken the children to a local fair the year before he'd been sent to Belgium. Suddenly, her whole body ached with wanting him again.

"What's wrong, Mama?" Both children were sitting up now, looking quizzically at her. Kate threw her arms around her mother.

"Nothing, my loves. I was remembering the fair with your Papa, is all. I still miss him very much." She tried to brush at her eyes to stem the flood of tears that threatened.

"Then who took you to the festival, Mama? You didn't go by yourself, did you?" Colin wagged his head at her, a perfect imitation of his grandfather that pulled her back from the brink and made her want to laugh. "That is not at all proper."

"You are correct, Colin. That would not be proper at all." She straightened her skirts to give her time to get her thoughts together. "An acquaintance escorted me, a gentleman I met at Lady Cavendish's party this summer past." She stopped and cleared her throat. "His name is Lord Brack, a very nice, jovial gentleman, to be sure." Admitting even that much seemed to open a floodgate within her. "One day another man may wish to marry me and become your new Papa. Someone like Lord Brack." She held her breath and waited.

"No." Colin sat straight up and crossed his arms. "I don't need another Papa. I have Grandpapa. And I will escort you to fairs and festivals whenever you wish, Mama. So you see, you don't need anyone else at all."

"But, Colin—"

"No, Mama, Colin is right." Kate climbed from under the covers and into her lap. "I don't want a stranger here with us, Mama. We just want you."

Elizabeth sighed and rubbed Kate's small back until she managed to coax her back beneath the coverlet. "It won't happen anytime soon, loveys, I promise you that."

"Good." Colin punched his pillow and settled down without further fuss.

Tucking the covers under Kate's chin once more, Elizabeth leaned down to brush a kiss on her sweet forehead. Once their regular breathing told her both children were asleep, she kissed Colin as well. He'd gotten to the "don't touch me" stage earlier this year. She whispered, "Good night, my love" in each one's ear, and rose.

At least, she knew now the children were not inclined to favor a new husband in her life, a new papa in theirs. She hadn't been unduly surprised at Colin's very vocal denunciation. Perhaps it was best to put all thoughts of Lord Brack out of her mind for the time being. The children shouldn't be upset so soon after their father's death.

She crept out of the nursery in search of Nurse.

It might be well and good to make such grand pronouncements, but unless she kept her thoughts from last night and Lord Brack's sleek, strong arms and supple, powerful body, all the good intentions in the world would be for nothing. Whether it upset the children or not.

Sipping her wine at dinner, Elizabeth wished with all her heart for the evening to be at an end. She'd hardly had time to change before dinner and now longed to crawl between her crisp sheets and close her eyes. Unfortunately, every time she thought of this, she also immediately remembered the tryst with Lord Brack and the gross impropriety of her reaction to him. Heat lit up her cheeks each time, causing her mother to ask her earlier if she had a fever. She'd shaken her head no and vowed to put that encounter behind her. It was done, and she would simply never see the man again. Of course, she'd likely have to eschew her friendship with Georgie and make an excuse not to come to Charlotte's wedding, although that idea pained her deeply. But she could not face Lord Brack, and that was all there was to it.

Dinner wound on, and she managed to keep her mind mostly on Lord Haxton's comments about his racing stable.

As her dinner partner on the left, she'd gotten to take his measure somewhat. A pleasant gentleman, to be sure, and when he glanced at Bella—which happened frequently during the meal—his brown eyes took on a decided gleam. Perhaps her sister's betrothed had been smitten with her despite his obvious attachment elsewhere this summer. For Bella's sake, she prayed it was so.

When her mother rose to leave the table, Elizabeth sighed with relief. Her father, brother, and Lord Haxton would likely remain for some time enjoying their brandy or port and talking about the settlements—the family property that formed a good portion of Bella's dowry in particular. Dickon had told her he'd been regaled with facts, figures, and a history of her dower estate for so long he'd prayed for a summons from the War Office to interrupt them. Papa could drone on and on about his various properties. She might be able to make the excuse of fatigue from her journey or headache to retire early before the men rejoined them.

Not for the first time, she longed for her quiet evenings alone with Dickon in their house in Russell Square. She'd had to give it up when he'd been killed, but the memory of their brief but happy time there was always warm and near to her heart.

After entering the drawing room, Elizabeth sank gratefully onto the lush green brocade chair beside the fireplace, sighing as the warmth seeped into her. If she wasn't careful, she'd fall asleep right here.

"Darling, you must tell us all about the house party," her mother said, lowering herself into the companion chair across from her. She handed Elizabeth a cup of tea. "You look completely fagged."

"I am, Mama." Elizabeth accepted the cup and eagerly sipped the hot, sweet tea. "I'd much rather hear about Bella's betrothal. How extraordinary that Lord Haxton would propose after so many months without a word."

"He was much taken with Bella this summer, I just knew it." Dorothea, her youngest sister, at eighteen, plumped down on the settee. "After Bella told me he'd danced twice with her at three different events in May, I knew he must be in love with her."

"Was he, Dotty?" Her mother's eyebrows rose like birds taking flight. "Why didn't you tell me this at the time? I daresay with that information I could have had Isabella married and in an interesting condition by now."

"Mama!" Bella blushed rosy red.

"Well, I didn't want to spoil it if by some chance he actually offered for that Lady Anne Tarkington." Dotty's lips curved upward. "Not the friendliest young lady of our acquaintance. Do you know her, Elizabeth? Always snobbish and stuck up because her father's a marquess."

"Don't be a cat, Dorothea." Their mother sat back sipping her tea, disapproval in her eyes.

"Well, he's my Lord Haxton now." Bella smiled like a cat with cream on its whiskers. "And I believe we will suit famously. He loves to ride, so we share that interest. I'm sure he told you about his racing stable. And at Vauxhall he mentioned a passion for Greek statuary, of all things. He's said as soon as the Elgin Marbles exhibit is opened, he will take me there. Perhaps in the new year."

"Likely married by that time as well," Mama said, adding sugar to her tea. "No reason in the world to wait. Short engagements are best. Marry on the Monday after the reading of the third banns. That would be three weeks from this coming Sunday. Oh, we have so much to do, girls. That may simply not be enough time."

"Well, you certainly seem to be well suited so far as I know, Bella. That is a very fortunate thing." Elizabeth smiled, remembering the early days of her marriage. She and Dickon had shared a passion for walks and touring the fine houses of England. They had spent their wedding trip in the Lake District, going through great house after great house, building castles in the air about their modest home in London. Did Lord Brack enjoy such outings, perhaps? She shook herself and gulped her tea.

"We really must think about setting the date, Bella." Mama returned to the subject of the wedding. "After Christmas, perhaps, but certainly before the Season. Then we can concentrate on Bella before all our time is taken up with chaperoning Dotty and making sure she makes a good match as well." Her mother leaned her head toward Bella and Dotty, and they all began an earnest discussion of the wedding details.

Elizabeth set her cup in her saucer, turning the handle this way and that. She didn't begrudge Bella the excitement of planning her day of glory, but she needed to also think about her own immediate future. The sobering fact was her life now would be very different than before Dickon's death unless she decided to set her cap at someone like Lord Brack.

His ready smile and jovial attitude would make him an excellent companion. They would certainly have no problems, no inhibitions about the physical side of marriage. The cup clinked into the saucer dangerously close to the edge of the table. How could she continue to think about a future with Lord Brack when she didn't know how she could ever face him again? Even worse, if they did marry, how could she be sure that such a shameful *faux pas* would never happen again?

"Is something wrong, Elizabeth?" Her mother's voice broke into her thoughts like a rock shattering glass.

"No, Mama. Why do you ask?" Hastily, she lifted her teacup, only to discover it was empty.

"You had a very odd expression on your face. Like your tooth ached." Mama raised her head from her conversation and peered at her. "Please be careful to have a pleasant, gracious expression on when Lord Haxton enters."

"Yes, Mama. No, I am fine. Just tired." She rose and took her cup to the tea tray. "Shall I ring for more tea?"

"Please do. I suspect we shall go through several pots before the gentlemen join us."

Elizabeth pulled the strip of tapestry-woven cloth. "Actually, I hoped to be excused, Mama. I am very tired, and I wanted to rise early and breakfast with the children. I thought we could spend the day together since I have not seen them since last week."

"Oh, no, my dear." Her mother shook her head and clucked her tongue. "The children have their own activities planned for tomorrow, and I insist you come with me to pay calls."

"But—"

"Elizabeth, you cannot continue to coddle Kate and Colin, especially not Colin. You don't want him to grow up cosseted like a lap dog, do you?" Mama fixed her with a gimlet eye.

"Of course not, Mama, but he's only six years old." Elizabeth looked to her sisters for support, but Dotty suddenly gazed intently into the fire, and Bella studiously inspected the bottom of her teacup. Precious little help to be had from that quarter. "He's still a baby."

"He'll be off to Winchester in less than two years' time. If you know what's good for him, you'll encourage him to be more independent now so it doesn't go badly for him later." Mama nodded vehemently.

A sinking feeling bloomed in the pit of Elizabeth's stomach. "Dickon and I had agreed to allow him to study with a tutor rather than attend boarding school so young."

"Nonsense." Her mother rose as the door opened to admit the maid with a fresh pot of tea. "Colin will go to Winchester, then Harrow, then Oxford, just as your father did."

"But Dickon said—"

"Your father and I have discussed the matter, Elizabeth." Mama waved her hand as though that were the end of the matter. "We have decided it is really in Colin's best interest to follow in this family's traditions, since his father is no longer here. Ah, there you are, Wentworth."

The maid scurried out as the gentlemen strode in. Everyone tried to talk at once, save Elizabeth, who retreated to the bay window overlooking the park opposite.

She mustn't let her parents' ideas upset her. Colin and Kate were her children, hers and Dickon's. No matter what, she would raise them as she deemed fit. As she and Dickon had discussed in the long, lovely evenings after the twins had been born.

The park, now touched by the light of the half moon, had been a favorite place to play when she'd been growing up. She'd hoped her children might enjoy that as well. However, if the only way to raise them correctly meant she had to leave Worth House, then she would do just that. The children were all she had left of Dickon. If she had to marry another man to see them raised as she wished, then she would do so without a second thought. Of course, she would have to trust such a man without qualm, for the moment they married, the children would be considered under his guardianship. Perhaps she should write to Georgie and ask about her brother's views on child rearing. Even if she never spoke to his lordship again, it certainly did no harm to ask. At least she would be prepared for that contingency.

Chapter 6

"That gold with a black lace overlay would look lovely on you, Elizabeth." Lady Stephen Tarkington—Fanny, to her friends—peered at the delightful shantung silk through her quizzing glass. "Very elegant, I think."

"You're right, it would give a perfect touch of splendor. However," Elizabeth paused, shaking her head regretfully at the bolt of fabric, "I simply cannot wear black to a wedding. Especially not Charlotte's. It would seem as though I were tempting fate. I wouldn't want to bring bad luck down on her for anything in this world." She sighed and reluctantly moved on. "Not even for such a perfect gown."

"I can't say that I blame you." Fanny hurried past three bolts of purple fabric, each one more hideous in color than the last. "Who in their right mind would wear this?" She touched the darkest of the three, a shade approaching the tones of an eggplant.

"I did when I went into half-mourning." Elizabeth stared at Fanny, who blushed, her pale face turning a rosy pink.

"I beg your pardon, Elizabeth." Her lips twitched.

"Don't." Elizabeth smiled and patted her friend's arm. "It was hideous when I bought it. The color of dark thunderclouds. See." She turned the fabric to and fro in the mid-morning light that streamed into Wilding & Kent, the fabric warehouse her family had always patronized. The deep purple looked dull and unattractive.

"Then why did you buy it, goose?" Fanny shuddered and moved toward the counter strewn with bolts in every imaginable shade of green. "Would this look good on me?" She fingered a brilliant emerald-green cut velvet.

"Oh, yes. It makes your eyes sparkle. On me, however . . ." Elizabeth sighed. She wouldn't wear green on a bet. It made her skin look like new cheese. "I got the purple because I was still grieving for Dickon, and I wanted to look hideous. I hurt so badly I wanted everyone who saw me to experience the hurt."

Fanny peered closer at the expensive material. "It does remind one of a bruise, now that I think of it."

Sputtering, Elizabeth turned back toward the gold. That would make a stunning dress for Charlotte's wedding. Not flashy enough to take away attention from the bride, but subtly rich and elegant. With the right design and accessories, it would turn the head of—drat. She'd promised herself not to think of Lord Brack.

"You could try a white lace overlay instead." Fanny had followed her back to the display of yellows and deeper golds. "Or perhaps gold on gold, if it's much deeper. That would cause a few heads to turn."

There was only one head she'd possibly want to turn, but even thinking his name brought on a blush. Only three nights ago, she'd made her disgraceful *faux pas* with Lord Brack. That humiliation still raw, she could scarcely contemplate seeing him face-to-face, much less speaking to him.

She'd wanted to hide away from the world, certain anyone seeing her guilty face would immediately know what had happened. However, when Fanny had sent round a note, asking her help in selecting dress materials for Charlotte's wedding in early December, Elizabeth had been curious about what might have been said about her precipitous flight from Lyttlefield Park.

"You may be right about the gold." She truly had little interest in this shopping excursion. Rather, she longed for a comfortable coze over a pot of tea to discover what had been said about her and, more importantly, what Lord Brack had said.

"To tell you the truth, Elizabeth, it won't matter a jot what you wear. I vow Lord Brack will not take his eyes off you from the moment you enter Lyttlefield Park."

A chill raced down her spine, and she shivered. "I'm sure I don't know what you mean, Fanny. Lord Brack has been very kind, but—"

Fanny snorted and shot her a look that silenced her. "You don't fool anyone, Elizabeth, least of all me. You and Brack were quite attracted to one another at both of Charlotte's parties." She narrowed her eyes. "I'm surprised he hasn't yet called on you to propose."

"I am certain he would do no such thing." A churning in her stomach made Elizabeth catch hold of the counter.

"Why else would he have left Lyttlefield Park for London the same day you did?"

"What?" Elizabeth grabbed Fanny's arm, dread descending on her. "Lord Brack did what?"

"He left for London on Sunday afternoon. I didn't see him, but Georgie told me."

Elizabeth closed her eyes. Lord Brack in London? Had he no respect for her wishes? Still . . . "He has not come to call on me." Pray God he did not. "Perhaps Georgie was mistaken."

"Oh, I doubt that." Fanny rocked back on her heels. "He will likely put in an appearance shortly. Trust me; he is smitten with you, my dear. Throughout the whole party, he might as well have shouted from the rooftops, 'I'm in love with Elizabeth Easton.'"

"Fanny, for God's sake, lower your voice," Elizabeth hissed, quickly glancing to see if other patrons nearby marked their conversation. Fortunately, everyone seemed absorbed in making their own purchases.

"Do you deny it? Or your interest in him?"

Staring at her friend, Elizabeth's heart sank. She'd tried to persuade herself that she did not miss Lord Brack's company. That this longing she could not deny stemmed from still missing Dickon, but deep in her heart, it wasn't true. "I did become very fond of Lord Brack when we were at Charlotte's."

The admission came slowly, painfully, and brought a rush of guilt with it. Her husband, whom she had loved very much, had been dead only a little less than a year and a half. Surely that was too short a time for her heart to heal?

"Very fond, is it?" Fanny gazed at her through lowered lids, reminding Elizabeth of a lazy lizard contemplating an unwary fly. "I'd say the kiss you two shared the night of the Harvest Festival spoke of more than fondness."

"What?" Panic seized Elizabeth. She glanced from side to side, once more afraid of being overheard.

"Lord Lathbury and I had repaired to the tree line ourselves. That demonstration by the Harvest Lord and the Corn Maiden had much affected Lathbury in an amorous way, shall we say?" A smile slowly spread over her face. "I did just see you two embracing before Matthew demanded all my attention."

"I . . . I didn't dream anyone had seen us." Elizabeth's heart thudded so loudly she feared it could be heard.

"Let us step over to Fitzroy's for some tea." Fanny peered at her. "You look as though you need something." She linked their arms and pulled Elizabeth out into the cold October rain. "Oh, dear. This shower came up unexpectedly. Here, use my umbrella."

Fanny popped the umbrella up, and they stepped briskly across the street to Mr. Fitzroy's tearoom. The warm, spicy smells of cakes and cookies immediately comforted Elizabeth, reviving her against the shock of Fanny's revelation. The homey little shop sported four small tables, one blessedly free. Fanny steered them to it.

Sinking gratefully into a wicker chair, Elizabeth clasped her hands together, staring at the spotless white tablecloth while she caught her breath.

"Tea, Mr. Fitzroy, if you please." Fanny nodded to the short, rotund man who hurried toward them. "The Lapsang souchong. And a plate of cakes against the chill, I think."

"Of course, my lady." An amiable nod to Fanny, and Mr. Fitzroy bustled away.

"Now," Fanny said, leaning forward to keep their conversation private. "Open your budget, Elizabeth. You've grown fond of Lord Brack, have you not?"

Swallowing painfully, as if she had ground glass in her throat, Elizabeth lowered her head and mumbled, "Yes."

"Then what is the matter, my dear?" She grasped her friend's hands. "Even if he hasn't declared himself formally, I am quite certain he has a great deal of regard and affection for you." Her smile made her blue eyes twinkle. "I could see that much in the dark and at a distance."

"Oh, Fanny, it's not that." How could she make anyone understand her continuing love for Dickon? "I believe Lord Brack holds me in high esteem and perhaps even affection." The memory of his passionate, hot body pressed against her naked flesh left no doubt of that whatsoever. The merest thought of that encounter at the festival turned her face red. "There is another impediment."

"Impediment?" Her friend's delicate eyebrows rose alarmingly. "What do you mean by that?"

Helplessly, Elizabeth stared at her, the events of that night replaying in her mind. The heat, the passion, the grand release that had sent her senses soaring until she had called him "Dickon."

"Indeed?" Fanny's perfectly arched eyebrows shot higher.

Elizabeth nodded, her stomach clenched, her gaze lowered

as she traced a faint tear in the tablecloth. She simply couldn't tell Fanny what had really happened. Didn't want to think of it, much less speak about it to another person.

Although, perversely, Lady Stephen Tarkington might be the only woman of her acquaintance who would understand the circumstances and what had occurred that night. Her husband, Lord Stephen, had taken other women to his bed during their marriage. Such a practice was not unknown in their circles, but Stephen had been careless of it, and his wife had found out. So Fanny was much more a woman of the world than any of the others in their circle, save perhaps Jane. Maybe Fanny could tell her if such a humiliating experience was likely to be overcome. "I cannot stop thinking about Dickon." She glanced at her hands, lying clenched in her lap. "Even when I'm with Lord Brack, I sometimes think of him."

With a shrug, Fanny sat back, and Mr. Fitzroy set cups, a fine bone china teapot, and the plate of cakes in the center of the table. "There you are, my lady." He carefully retreated.

Fanny added two lumps to her cup. "Milk?"

"Yes, please." Elizabeth added one lump, then drank gratefully. The hot strong tea touched a soothing chord deep within her.

"That feeling will likely go away as soon as you have a new man in your bed."

Elizabeth's hand jerked, the hot tea splashing over the rim into the saucer. "Fanny!"

"Don't be so missish, my dear. You are no stranger to the pleasures of the marriage bed any more than I." A self-satisfied smirk crept over Fanny's face. "You did your duty to Lieutenant Colonel Easton and mourned him properly. So your grieving should be past and done. He would not want you to linger in your sadness, but would wish you a new companion who could give you that physical joy again."

"So you believe Lord Stephen is smiling down upon you and the Earl of Lathbury?" Elizabeth couldn't help her arch tone. Fanny and Lathbury's affair had been the subject of many of the *ton*'s *on-dits* since Lady Beaumont's masquerade ball last June.

"Stephen lost all rights to complain about my behavior with Lathbury—or any other man, come to that—long before he died." Fanny squeezed the white napkin in her lap until her knuckles looked as though the bones would break through the skin. "I hope he looks down on Ella, and me, and Lathbury quite often."

"How has Ella coped with her father's death?" Fanny seldom spoke of her daughter. So much so that Elizabeth often forgot her friend had a child at all.

"As well as can be expected when she scarcely knew she had a father." The bitter words set Elizabeth's teeth on edge.

"Oh, Fanny."

"Stephen was a neglectful husband and father. Everyone knew that. However, Ella was quite taken with Lord Lathbury when he came to call. So perhaps she is capable of affection toward a . . . father figure." An odd, worried frown creased Fanny's brow.

"That's a good thing, isn't it, my dear?" Elizabeth paused to sip her tea and contemplate Fanny's puzzling expression. "If, of course, you are serious about his lordship. It is good that she seems ready to accept another man in her father's place."

Fanny shook herself, as if coming out of a reverie. "Yes, of course it is." Her face settled into pleasant lines once more. "Have you spoken to the twins about the possibility of your marrying again?"

With a sigh, Elizabeth poured another cup of tea and selected one of the pink sugar cakes. "Yes, and they were not happy with the suggestion." Their pinched, woebegone faces came instantly to mind. "They don't want another papa."

Her friend waved the objection away with a careless hand. "They are about the same age as Ella, are they not?"

"Maybe some months younger."

"Then they will come to accept it." Fanny shrugged. "They need not love the man, but if they respect him as a father, that should suffice. And if they see you are happier with him than without, they will be content. Losing a father at such a young age means they will remember little as they grow older. Another man in the house will seem natural and give them the stability they need." She gave Elizabeth a long look. "It will also give you a firmer place in society from which to launch them when they are older."

Sipping thoughtfully, Elizabeth pondered Fanny's words. It might sound like good advice when spoken of fleetingly in a tea shop, but she feared her friend simplified the very serious matter of bringing a new man into their lives. Then of course, there were her particular circumstances with Lord Brack. Would she ever be able to forget that horribly embarrassing scene? "I suppose I will simply wait and see what happens when and if we meet at Charlotte's wedding."

"I suppose so." Fanny finished her cup and leaned forward, a twinkle in her blue eyes. "Now, shall we return to Wilding's and purchase that delectable gold cloth and lace? You will need to look ravishing if you want Lord Brack to ravish you."

"Fanny." Elizabeth smiled ruefully and shook her head. Her friend acted like a dog with a bone, and was not going to let it go under any circumstances. "We will see when the time comes. However, I believe you are correct about the gold gown. It will be perfect for Charlotte's wedding, whoever sees me in it."

They rose, and Fanny shook out the umbrella and stepped out into the now misting rain. "I think three yards will be quite enough if you—"

"Fanny! Dear God. Turn around." Elizabeth dragged her friend to stand in front of her, facing her, shielding her from the few people hurrying their way down the sidewalk.

"Elizabeth, what is wrong?" Twisting her head to and fro, Fanny gazed about.

"Lord Brack!" Elizabeth nodded violently to her left, behind Fanny, where a tall gentleman, who could be taken for no one else but Lord Brack, had stopped to speak to an acquaintance. If only he hadn't seen her yet.

"Where?" Fanny turned all the way around. "Aha. I told you he would seek you out."

"Oh, do hush, Fanny. I cannot meet him."

"Why ever not?" Fanny peered at her suspiciously. "Is there something you're not telling me, Elizabeth?"

"Yes, but there's no time for it now." Elizabeth cast her gaze up and down the crowded street, searching for their carriage. Panic such as she had never known choked her throat. "I am going to run for the carriage. If he sees me and tries to pursue, please, I beg of you, detain him. I simply cannot speak with him."

"Very well." With a piercing look at her, Fanny nodded. "But I shall call tomorrow, and you will tell me everything."

Sighing deeply, Elizabeth nodded. "I promise. I shall send the carriage back for you directly I am home."

"I will return to Wilding & Kent; send Markson there." Her friend gave her a shove. "Now hurry. He just glanced our way."

Without a thought for the rain, Elizabeth darted down the street, dodging her way between pedestrians, praying her ankle wouldn't turn in the slippery mud that had washed up onto the pavement in patches. Why had Lord Brack turned up in pursuit of her against her wishes? And how was she going to avoid him?

Elizabeth spied the carriage in the next street and quickly clambered in as soon as the footman opened the door.

"Home and quickly, Markson. Lady Stephen has remained to finish her shopping. You must take me home, then return for her." Breathless, Elizabeth fell back against the familiar seats of the family landau.

"Are you ill, Mrs. Easton?" Markson peered down at her through the trap.

"A sudden megrim only. I will be fine once I'm at home."
And out of sight of Lord Brack. Oh, pray he had not seen her.
Though she assumed he knew quite well where she lived.

"Very good, madam." Markson dropped the trap, and immediately they began to move out into the traffic.

Elizabeth breathed a sigh of relief as Markson wound their
way homeward through the busy London streets, though her
thoughts spun from one subject to the next and back again.
Lord Brack had arrived in London. Sooner or later, he would
surely appear at a ball or a dinner party or call on her at
Worth House. She simply could not see him, not when the
moment she looked in his face she'd remember last Saturday night. No. She'd simply plead illness and refuse all invitations. Eventually, he'd understand she'd meant every word
of her letter.

That decision made, her traitorous mind spun back, and
her friend's words in the tearoom buzzed in her brain, like a
swarm of busy bees. People had noticed her and Lord
Brack's mutual attraction. Such a match would be perfectly
acceptable to the *ton*, even though they were rather close in
age.

She shifted uncomfortably on the black leather seat,
crossing her ankles, wanting to cross her legs. Their slight
gap in age might have had something to do with the intensity of the passion they had shared in bed the other night.
Why would her thoughts bend that way? More chilling to
ask, had she ever experienced that deep a connection with
Dickon? A disloyal question, perhaps, but her core throbbed
even now at the memory of Lord Brack filling her so intently over and over.

The mere thought almost set her body on fire, and she
leaned one cheek against the cool glass to try and calm herself. Lord, how could she have such wanton thoughts about
a man to whom she was not married? In the middle of the
day and in public? Did these wild fancies mean she wished
to marry him?

While she tried to wrap her mind around the absurdity of that last question, Markson stopped the carriage and opened the door. The cold air helped with her blazing cheeks as she climbed down, although images of Lord Brack's smiling face at dinner, at the Bull, and most of all, in her bed whirled around her head in a dizzying array. His kindness to his sister and her obvious adoration of him spoke candidly about his nature. No one since Dickon had ever been so attentive toward her in all ways. He was simply the perfect gentleman, if not for that one moment between them.

"Thank you, Markson. If you would return for Lady Stephen, please?" A shame she'd had to abandon Fanny, but it could not have been helped. Fanny would undoubtedly get her revenge when next they met.

"Yes, Mrs. Easton." The coachman touched the horses, and they trotted away once more.

Entering Worth House, she handed her pelisse to the butler. "Where is Mama, Tawes?" She stripped off her gloves and handed them to him as well.

"In the small drawing room, Mrs. Easton."

Elizabeth nodded as she started up the stairs to the first floor. A cup of tea would refresh and calm her jangled nerves.

"Mama, Mama!" Shrieks from the landing overhead rent the quiet air. The twins raced pell-mell down the staircase, hurtling toward her.

"Children! What is going on?" She made a grab for the banister just in time.

Colin seized her about the waist, while Kate flung herself at her left arm.

Elizabeth barely caught the child, pulling her body toward the banister, clinging to it for dear life. "Gracious, Kate." She set the girl down, automatically straightening her pale blue gown. "You could have knocked me down the stairs. We'd all have gone over like ninepins." Colin wasn't about to escape her censure either. "I will not have you running about like an ill-bred ruffian. Where is Nanny? You must never do that again, do you understand me?"

Colin's eyes brimmed with tears. "But I was so happy to see you, Mama. You haven't come to see us for ages and ages. I wanted you to play with us today, but Grandmama said you had gone out. You only come to kiss us good night sometimes." Two large tears rolled down his sweet face and plopped onto her hand. "Don't you love us anymore?"

Her heart lurched, as though a giant hand had squeezed it. "Oh, Colin." She sat right down on the stairs, pulling him into her arms. "Of course, I love you, my dear."

"You never tuck us in or read to us or tell us stories," Kate whimpered, clutching her closer. "When Papa was here, you did that every night."

"I'm so sorry, my loves." She rocked them from side to side, trying to stifle her own tears, which threatened to pour down any second. Since moving into her parents' home, she'd let her mother persuade her to spend less time with the children. A family tradition, to be sure, and the way she and her brother and sisters had been raised. But it had not been the way she and the twins' father had wanted it. They had been a true family while Dickon had been alive. With God's help, they would be so again.

"Well, my dears, I will remedy that, I promise you. Beginning tonight." She would too, so help her. Hugging both children close, Elizabeth sighed, imagining the fierce battle to come with her mother. Lady Wentworth always expected to get her way. Either she found a way to stand up to her mother, or she would need to marry again and set up her own household. Neither choice filled her with confidence, but the children had to be her greatest concern. She must be resolute for them.

Chapter 7

Plucking up his courage, Jemmy rapped smartly with the brass lion's-head door knocker at Worth House. He'd nearly turned back twice on his way from his lodgings, but faint heart never won fair lady, so he'd continued on today, despite yesterday's disappointment.

When he'd impulsively decided to follow Elizabeth to London, he hadn't formed any sort of plan of what to do; he'd just known it to be right that he pursue her. Arriving in London late at night, he'd taken up his old lodgings in Grenier's Hotel. The following day, he'd gone to Jackson's Saloon with an old friend, Lord Fendrick, whom he'd met at breakfast, and had emerged from that establishment to see Lady Stephen Tarkington standing in front of Fitzroy's. He'd hailed her, and when she turned toward him, he'd had the barest glimpse of a female figure running for a carriage, in a blue spencer with gold braid across the back that looked suspiciously like Elizabeth's.

By the time he'd caught up to Lady Stephen, the woman had gone. It had been on the tip of his tongue to inquire if the fleeing lady had been Elizabeth; however, the idea that she would run from him was so distasteful he instead turned the conversation toward Lady Cavendish's coming nuptials. After a few minutes' chat, he'd said good afternoon and left, determined to call on Elizabeth the very next morning.

After three sharp raps, he let the knocker fall, and immediately the door opened to reveal a thin, elderly butler with a ruddy face. "My lord?"

"Is Mrs. Easton at home this morning?"

"I am sorry, my lord. She is not."

Damn. So much for dithering. She'd likely gone out to pay calls already. With a sigh, Jemmy seized his card case, plucked out one of the smooth white cards, and handed it to the servant. "Please make certain she knows I called."

"Of course, my lord." The butler bowed and retreated, then shut the door.

As Jemmy turned to go, a movement of the drapes at a second-story window drew his attention. The poor light of the overcast day didn't allow him more than the glimpse of a figure; there was no way to tell who had watched his exchange with the butler. Nothing for it now but to return to Grenier's or perhaps his club. There'd be chaps at White's who could tell him what entertainments he should beg invitations to if he wanted to pursue Elizabeth. And he intended to pursue his widow until he could press his suit face-to-face.

Hemmed in on his right by two elderly dowagers and buffeted on his left by a bevy of young ladies giggling together, Jemmy peered around Lady Dalrymple's elegant town house in search of Elizabeth. To gauge by the crush of people present, the lady's rout was a stunning success. From the drawing room, where strains of harp music and a burble of conversation emanated, to the morning room, where card tables filled with players dotted the deep blue Aubusson carpet, to the glittering dining room he'd just slipped into, filled with delicious aromas, the *ton* had certainly turned out in force.

White's had indeed borne fruit. His friend, Lord Bolton, had informed him of Lady Dalrymple's rout this evening and had insisted he accompany him to the party. Bolton had assured him that most of the *ton* had been invited and would likely be in attendance at one time or another during the evening. Enough encouragement to keep Jemmy's hopes alive.

Now, having made his way to into the final room without catching sight of his quarry, Jemmy shrugged and picked up a plate from the sideboard. Might as well keep up his strength. The hunt for Elizabeth might take quite some time. He filled his plate with a smattering of route cakes, lobster patties, tongue, sliced ham, and a seed cake. No places being vacant at any of the tables in the room, he made his way to a corner, next to a pillar with a bust of Athena where he could rest his glass of wine, and set himself to eating the lot.

"Good evening, Lord Brack." Miss Smythe-Herringford smiled up at him from the tiny table in front of him. "How wonderful to see you back in London. We had quite given you up, hadn't we, Charles?" She nodded to her brother, Lord Penthorpe, also an acquaintance.

"Indeed, Brack. Where have you been keeping yourself?" Penthorpe forked an entire lobster patty into his mouth.

"Good evening, Miss Smythe-Herringford, Penthorpe. I didn't think I'd been away that long. I did go to Brighton for a time at the end of the Season and to a house party in Kent this past week." Jemmy glanced around, but no one new had entered the dining room. "I suppose I have neglected my duty here in London. My apologies, Miss Smythe-Herringford." He smiled at the young lady and took a bite of ham.

"I am so glad to know you are back. I'll be sending out invitations to my evening of cards next week. You will promise to come, won't you, my lord?" The lady's deep brown eyes widened, her pink bowed lips in a seductive smile. Miss Smythe-Herringford had made no secret of her admiration for him earlier in the Season. Apparently, nothing had changed in that regard.

"I will be delighted to attend if I am still in Town." Jemmy bit into a lobster patty, savoring the sweet, creamy lobster and the flaky pastry as a way to curtail his conversation.

"I shall count upon it, then, my lord." A smug smile spread across Miss Smythe-Herringford's pretty face. "You must sit down to whist with me and Charles first thing. Who can we ask to make up a fourth, Charles?" The young woman tried to catch her brother's eye, though he continued to be distracted by the rapidly disappearing contents of his plate.

Popping the final bite of the luscious lobster patty into his mouth, Jemmy glanced up at the doorway just as Elizabeth Easton stepped through, a beautiful smile on her lips. Gasping at the sudden manner in which his most earnest wish had come true, Jemmy promptly choked on the flaky crust. "Mrs. Easton," he croaked, coughing to dislodge the bits of pastry stuck in his throat.

Elizabeth raised her head, searching the room, then her eyes met his. Her face paled, her eyes widened, and she whirled around, fleeing the room in a swish of bronze taffeta.

"Mrs. Elizabeth Easton, do you mean?" Miss Smythe-Herringford asked, head cocked to the side. "I'm not certain she is on the guest list. Do you know, Charles?"

Jemmy lurched forward, thumping his plate on the table in front of the startled Penthorpe, and bolted from the room. Or tried to bolt. The crush of people seemed to have all gotten hungry at once and moved *en masse* into the dining room, blocking his access to the door. He twisted and turned, trying to press against the flow of guests. Grasping the doorjamb, he pulled himself into the card room in time to see Elizabeth, now in the music room, speak to an older woman, her mother perhaps.

The elder woman shook her head, and Jemmy took heart. Perhaps she would detain Elizabeth long enough for him to speak to her. He renewed his struggles against the horde of attendees. Buffeted to and fro, he at last gained the music room, where he peered about, looking for Elizabeth, but without success. He had lost her again. With forlorn hope, he made his way to the front door on the chance that she waited there for her carriage.

"Do you know if Mrs. Easton has left the party? The Worth family carriage?" he asked the footman on duty just outside on the porch.

"Yes, my lord. It did leave not two minutes ago. The lady must have been taken ill quickly. We hadn't even had a chance to move the carriage to the back mews."

The footman's elaboration gave Jemmy no joy. Elizabeth seemed determined not to see him, no matter the circumstances. Fleeing a party when she'd just arrived sent an eloquent message. She had meant every word of her letter.

"Will you have my carriage fetched as well, please?" Jemmy gripped the bannister as the servant motioned a young boy toward him. Perhaps he had been over hasty following Elizabeth to Town. The best course might be to give her some time to begin to miss him. He could remain in London, but not call upon her or try to meet her in the evenings. If she heard of his doings, perhaps even of his interest in other young ladies, might it cause a change of heart?

"Your carriage, my lord." The footman opened the door, and Jemmy climbed in. Doyle started the team, and Jemmy called, "Home, please."

A few minutes musing about the situation told him such a plan would never do. Not because it was not a good plan, but because he had grave doubts he could ever carry out such a scheme. If he continued to reside in London, someone would have to put him in irons to keep him from trying to meet with Elizabeth. And if he actually saw her at a ball or party, he would never be able to feign interest in another lady. At least, he knew himself well enough to admit such shortcomings. No, he must go back to Kent. Remove himself from temptation and let his absence begin to affect her. He hoped it would affect her as much as her continued absence affected him, both in body and in mind.

Chapter 8

"I daresay you will miss your comfortable home here once you marry, Lady Cavendish." Jemmy gazed around the beautifully appointed drawing room. He and Wrotham had just joined the ladies after dinner. His voice held more than a tinge of regret. He would miss the cozy room as well. The rich reds and golds in the Chippendale chairs set off the brilliant Turkey carpet but harmonized perfectly with the celadon-green walls. The elegant Robert Adams marble mantelpiece lent an elegance to the room, as did the delicate Queen Anne escritoire.

He had retreated to Lyttlefield Park after less than a week in London to lick his wounds and plan another strategy for wooing Elizabeth. He'd thought to return there before this, but dread of further rejection, coupled with his pleasant surroundings, excellent shooting, and the agreeable company, had persuaded him to lengthen his stay into a three-weeks sojourn in the blink of an eye. Not to mention that his sister had begged, pleaded, and wheedled him until he couldn't bring himself to leave.

"Not at all." Lady Cavendish produced a smile, turning toward Wrotham before it had reached the corners of her mouth. "I will make Wrotham Park even more comfortable for us when I arrive. We have agreed that I may decorate the entire house, save for the study, which is Lord Wrotham's sole domain." She laughed and grasped Wrotham's arm.

"That was the stipulation, my dear." Her betrothed's gaze never left her face. "I trust it is not too great a burden to bear, for I'll not change my mind on that point. Not a jot."

Laughing, she waved away his comment. "It is a small price to pay to be your wife and have the keeping of all of the Park, save that one square patch of it." Lady Cavendish rose. "I promise I will restrain myself in that room."

"And nowhere else, I trust?" Wrotham's mischievous tone made his bride-to-be blush, a sweet, deep pink brushing her cheeks. "Not if I have any say about it."

She rapped him sharply on his shoulder with her fan. "Wretch. What will dear Georgina think of us?"

"Just that you are the perfect couple, Charlotte." Georgie set her tea down and sat back on the sofa. "When you travel to London together, you will be the talk of the *ton*."

"Huh." Charlotte made for the teapot next to Georgie. "At least they cannot call me the 'Wicked Widow' any more. Not after we are married at any rate, do you think, Nash?"

"Quite likely, my dear. But one look at us together and the next *on-dit* will have you the 'Wicked Wife' instead." Wrotham laughed loudly and followed his lady to the tea tray.

"It is not amusing, Nash." She shook her head and poured more tea into new cups.

Not for the first time, Jemmy wished that he and Elizabeth could be so easy together. He supposed it must take time for such camaraderie to develop between a man and a woman. Still, Lady Cavendish had only met Wrotham for the first time at the August house party, the same time he'd met Elizabeth. Of course, Georgie had related the trials and tribulations the couple had to work through before arriving at this blissful state. Wrotham's courtship of Lady Cavendish had been largely unsuccessful for most of the autumn. Then, suddenly, at the Harvest Festival, they came to an accord and decided to marry that very night.

That very memorable night had affected more than one couple. Last week, Michael Thorne had married Nora Burns, his chosen Corn Maiden. That festival had proved as potent as a love charm.

"Will you be staying on for the wedding, my lord?" His hostess broke in on his daydream.

"I believe I shall run up to London and return for the wedding, Lady Cavendish. You will have so many details to attend to, I think you hardly need to worry about a guest." Jemmy sipped his tea, wishing it was more of the fine whiskey he'd downed in the dining room.

"Nonsense." Lady Cavendish shot him a no-nonsense look, eyebrows arched, nose flaring. "You must stay and be company for Nash while Georgie and I shop in London for wedding clothes." She settled next to his sister. "I thought we could go next week. Perhaps we might call upon Fanny and Elizabeth while we are there."

Elizabeth. Desire surged below, and he glanced away before his thoughts could be seen on his face.

"That would be lovely, Charlotte. I would enjoy seeing them again very much. I don't need to go shopping myself, but I will be happy to be company for you." The wistful sound of her voice pulled his attention back to Georgie, whose face wore a brave smile that smote his conscience.

Anger at their father welled within him, and he gripped the teacup, wishing he could fling cup and tea at the marquess. Georgie's estrangement from her family had taken its toll on his sister, both in her living arrangements and in her wardrobe. Elizabeth had confided to him that she'd made over several gowns of her own for Georgie for the first house party. Now here she was looking forward to going shopping for clothes, knowing she would be a bystander only.

Damn, but he would see to it that she was turned out as

befit the daughter of a marquess. And to do that—"I think Wrotham and I should accompany you ladies to London."

"The devil you say, Brack." Wrotham sat up so quickly his tea slopped out of the cup, missed the saucer completely, and landed on his trousers. "I'd planned for us to do some shooting while the ladies were away." He frowned as he wiped at the mess with his napkin.

"They'll need escorts while they are there." Jemmy paused, thinking furiously. "And the clubs in London will provide entertainment for us to rival any shooting expedition."

"Yes, do, Nash." Charlotte clapped her hands and beamed at him.

The man's firm will melted like one of Gunter's ices left in the sun. "Well . . ."

"It would be lovely if you would come with us. We can see some of London's sights. And the Little Season continues, so we will have entertainments to attend in the evenings. That is when we will need our escorts." Lady Cavendish took the cloth from him and continued to scrub the wet spot on his breeches. "Please, Nash?"

Wrotham swallowed hard and grasped her hand. "I think I am sufficiently tidied for the moment, my dear." His eyes burned into hers, and she blushed. "I blame you for this, Brack. As your penance, you must attend every ball and party with us. No shirking. I refuse to be left alone with all those women. There are never enough men, and I refuse to be danced to death by myself."

"Please do, Jemmy," Georgie squealed. "It will be so much fun to have you attend with us. Both you and Nash."

"Thank you, Georgie." Wrotham grinned at her and rose. "It is settled then, Brack?"

"Yes, of course." Jemmy nodded absently. Elizabeth would likely be attending at least some of the parties. It was the Little Season, after all, and she had one sister still out. Surely, she'd be accompanying her to some entertainments. Perhaps this time he could meet her at a ball, quite naturally, and then beg a dance of her and thus renew her acquaintance.

He'd written to her almost every day since he'd returned—and torn up every letter before he could post it, afraid it would be returned unopened. Her actions had made it pointedly clear that she did not want to see him, but if he could just meet her, face-to-face, perhaps they could get past the embarrassment she obviously still felt about their intimate encounter. Would she spurn his company again? Had she allowed another man to court her? He could find these things out if he went to London.

"If that is completely settled, I believe I will say good night, Charlotte." Wrotham slid his arm around Lady Cavendish's waist. "Good evening, Georgina, Brack." With a nod and a smile for Georgie, Wrotham ushered his betrothed from the chamber.

"Thank you, Jemmy." Georgie slid over the long sofa to sit beside him. "London will be much more fun with you there."

"I suppose, as your brother and escort, I shall have to look sternly down my nose at all the young bloods who will want to dance with you." Actually, he was rather looking forward to being her protector. He'd not been able to do so at her come-out for he'd been out of the country until just before she married. "I trust you'll want to attend several parties while we're in Town."

"Yes, thank you." She smiled, though her expression quickly drooped. "I haven't wanted to put myself forward in society, because of Isaac's memory. It seemed wrong of me to make merry when he was . . ." Her lips firmed, and her jaw set. "However, Charlotte's utter happiness with Nash has given me the will to continue on with my life, given me hope of finding another gentleman with whom I shall not mind sharing my life." Her smile returned, her eyes teasing. "You must promise me not to frighten away the good gentlemen."

"Am I to be the judge of who is good and who is not, or are you?"

Giggling, she patted his arm. "We must concur on that, dear brother, although I suspect there will be some differences of opinion there."

"Better me to concur with than Father." Jemmy stopped, the specter of their father glimmering in the light of the dying fire.

"Goodness, Jemmy. You can't be seen with me in London." Stricken, Georgie clutched his arm. "Father would cut off your funds and inflict who knows what other punishments on you for consorting with me." Fighting back tears, Georgie slumped back against the sofa cushion, all happiness fled.

Damn, he hadn't thought about their father when he'd proposed that trip to London. The Marquess of Blackham had decreed that no one in the family was to have any contact with Georgina after he disowned her. And with all the gossips in London, such as the notorious Lady Locke and Mrs. Stapleton-Worthy, his father would find out by the next post. He grasped the arm of the sofa, squeezing it as he fought to bring his anger under control. It just wasn't fair. He slid his arm around her shoulders and pulled her bright head onto his shoulder. "I'm sorry, Georgie."

"It's all right. I know you cannot afford to anger him." Hot tears streaked down her face, dropping onto his bare hand.

"I wish we could find some way to get you back into Father's good graces." Jemmy bit his lip. The older man had a steely will. Once he turned against someone, he seldom recanted.

Father's youngest brother had gambled away a family estate, long before Jemmy had been born. His father had broken with Uncle Roland to such an extent that Jemmy had discovered the man's existence only last year when he read a death notice in the *Morning Chronicle*.

"I wouldn't know how to even begin going about it,

Jemmy. He hated my marriage to Isaac, although I'm not certain if it was Isaac himself or my defiance of Father's orders that caused it." Georgie dashed the tears away. "I'm still not sorry I did it."

Lord, but she was a fighter. He patted her arm. "I'm not either. I know how happy he made you." Still, his sister's life had been hellish, to say the least, since her husband's death. If only they could entreat the marquess to forgive Georgina, her life would be a deal easier. "But you have the future to think of. And Father had no quarrel with you until you married against his wishes. If you could make a brilliant match, someone Father couldn't help but approve of, I suspect he'd welcome you back. Pity you turned down Wrotham. He'd likely approve of him."

"I told you I could never have married Nash." Georgie sat up, searching for a handkerchief in her pocket. She pulled out a button and a recipe for brandied peaches before she secured the scrap of white linen, edged in delicate pink lace, and dabbed at her nose. "As soon as I spoke with him, I knew he was in love with Charlotte. I could no more have married him than I could have shot him."

"Well, thank goodness you didn't do that." Jemmy chuckled. Georgie had a flair for the dramatic. Her acting skills had always impressed him. She'd regularly been able to fool their old governess with much more success than he ever had. "You need to give it some thought, Georgie."

"There is one vital flaw in your scheme, though." She tugged at the fabric of the handkerchief, tearing it a little. "If I made this brilliant match to please Father, to enable me to return to the family, I wouldn't need to."

"What do you mean?"

"I mean I'd be married and under my husband's protection. I'd have no real need for Father's blessing." Georgie smiled, smoothing the handkerchief flat on her lap.

A good point. Still, until she found someone to marry, she needed her place at home. "Think about it, Georgie. I will write to Father and tell him I will be watching out for you in London."

"Jemmy, don't. What if he cuts you off?" Georgie's face had shifted into its stubborn lines.

"I will word it so he thinks I do it only to ensure that the family's honor and reputation are preserved. I'll suggest to him that I should try to guide you into making a better match than before." If he wrote the letter just so, it might work. If not, he could find himself as destitute as Georgie. At least until he gained control of his inheritance when he turned thirty, in less than a year.

"There can be no better match for me than Isaac."

She was changeable as a March wind and twice as stubborn.

"I can also steer you away from some of the more notorious rakes who may still be lurking about. Introduce you to some capital chaps, like Lord St. Just. You seemed to get on with him rather well." That would be a brilliant match for Georgie. If he could arrange for her to become the Marchioness St. Just, his father would have to welcome her back to the family. Rob's wealth came close to his own father's. His friend was quite the eligible *parti*, though. It might be difficult to convince him to take his sister without some kind of settlement or dowry. At least he had an in with Rob. They'd been friends since school, so it was worth a try.

"Lord St. Just seemed very cordial at the Harvest Festival. He's amusing, but then he tries hard to be amusing."

The undertone of reproof sent a frisson of warning. For his scheme to work, Georgie must be amenable to it. He'd thought her quite appreciative of the marquess. "Did you not like him?"

"Yes, he was frightfully entertaining." Georgie nodded enthusiastically. "But he smiles a great deal. And I suspect he has a truly wild streak in him."

"Why on earth would you say that?" He'd always thought Rob the steadiest of chaps.

Georgie giggled. "Have you never really listened to the tales he tells, Jemmy? He grew up on the coast of Cornwall, near all kinds of smuggling activities, and seems very envious of their adventures."

"He grew up around tales of smugglers, that's all." Waving her concerns away, he rose to investigate his hostess's decanter, perched temptingly on a Queen Anne butler's desk. "I seriously doubt he wants to be one himself."

"I wouldn't be too sure of that." She shook her head, making her red curls dance. "The gentleman has more than a touch of the pirate in him. He may surprise you yet." Her eyes crinkled as she smiled, a sure sign she knew more than she was telling him. "But what else do you have planned to do in London? You won't need to chaperone me constantly." A sudden, but deliberate tilt of her head. "Do you plan to see Elizabeth?"

Caught in the midst of pouring whiskey into a glass, Jemmy jerked his arm, sending an arch of the pungent spirit cascading over the carpet. "Damn it, Georgina." He set down the dripping glass, inspecting his outfit to see if any had spilled on him. Leave it to Georgie to change the subject so violently. "Can you call for one of the maids to clean this up?"

Laughing softly, Georgie strolled to the wide strip of tapestry and pulled. "You didn't answer my question." Idly, she played with the tassel on the end, staring at him, waiting for an answer, damn her.

"Just pull the bell." Jemmy sipped the spirits left in the sticky glass, hoping it would settle him. He'd not discussed Elizabeth with Georgie since the day he'd returned. "I suppose I shall see her if she attends the same entertainments we do."

"You don't plan to call on her?" His sister's gaze speared him like the shaft of an arrow.

"I told you I tried that with no success." The bitter words were out before he could stop his mouth.

"So you should try again." She gave the pull a sharp tug.

"Because if you don't continue to pursue her, you're a fool." Sauntering back to the sofa, his sister wore the deeply satisfied expression of a cat who has killed an especially juicy mouse. "I am surprised you didn't return to London sooner. At least, you have written to her since your return, haven't you? You cannot take for granted that she understands the depth of your attachment to her."

Jemmy swallowed uncomfortably and sipped his whiskey. He'd not told Georgie he hadn't had the courage to send a letter. Gulping the last of the fiery liquid too quickly, he sputtered and coughed. "I should hope Elizabeth knows in what high esteem I hold her."

Of course, by not writing to her during the past month, she might very well think he'd acquiesced to her wishes and abandoned his pursuit. That had been cowardly of him. It would serve him right if she'd already accepted another man. That sobering thought brought him up short. Pray God that had not occurred.

"She might know it with her head, but not with her heart, Jemmy. You *have* written to her since?" Her innocent question made his heart sink.

"Since when?"

"Since your return, ninny. You told me you would write to her the day you came back to Lyttlefield Park, but you never said if she replied." She narrowed her eyes. "Did she?"

"No," he sighed. Time to pay the piper. "I haven't heard from her since I returned here."

"And you've done nothing this whole time?" She bounced up on the sofa, indignant. "You haven't written her a second letter? Honestly, Jemmy, why didn't you tell me?" Georgie's voice rose in shrill tones. "I could have mentioned you in my letters."

"Did she ever inquire after me in any of her letters to you?" he asked, hope rising.

"No, she has not. I would have thought that peculiar, but

I believed she had no reason to because she was correspond-
ing with you." The annoyance in her face made him draw
back.

"Perhaps she has done with me." His heart stuttered at
the thought, but it would serve him right for his cowardice in
not writing to her. How could he have simply accepted her
wishes at face value and done nothing to try and change her
mind? He'd been in limbo these past weeks, waiting for
some signal from her that he knew would not come unless
he goaded her to give it.

"Nonsense." Georgie rose, standing straight, eyes clear
and determined. "Do you love her, Jemmy?"

The question froze him. He'd scarcely thought past the
physical passion of their last encounter to the more eloquent
dealings in his heart. That he might never again hold her in
his arms, kiss her lips, behold a smile meant solely for him
was unimaginable. The consequences of his non-actions
crashed over him with the intensity of an ocean tide so cold
he ceased to breathe. He should have remained in London
and insisted she see him.

"Well?" Georgie stared at him, toe tapping on the wet
carpet, awaiting an answer.

"Yes, yes, I do love her. And I may have lost her." He ran
a shaky hand through his hair. "What a fool I've been."

"I suppose you are not the first man to come to that conclusion. However, you had best let that realization send you
to London first thing in the morning." Georgie grasped his
arm and propelled him toward the door. "Charlotte, Nash,
and I will proceed as planned next week. You may tell them
you've gone ahead for whatever reason you can produce,
but you must go immediately."

They sped out into the shadowy corridor, and she paused
to look into his face. "I only hope you have not left it too
late."

He hugged her close, thanking heaven for his sister and
sending up another prayer. "I hope not too."

Chapter 9

"This just came for you, Mrs. Easton. There's a gentleman downstairs says he'll wait for an answer." Weller handed Elizabeth a cream-colored sheet of folded stationery, inscribed with her name in a strange hand that sent a shiver of apprehension down her spine.

"A footman, don't you mean?" She took the note from her maid gingerly, as if it might shock her.

"No, ma'am. A gentleman, Mr. Tawes said."

Trying to stem her trembling, Elizabeth ran her fingers over the thick, expensive paper. A gentleman of quality certainly. "He gave no name?" She cut her eyes at the maid, not sure what she hoped to hear.

"No, ma'am. Mr. Tawes just gave it to me and said to bring it straight to you." Weller's long-suffering face made the prickles on the back of her neck rise.

"You didn't see him?"

"No, Mrs. Easton. I just brought the note." Weller gazed intently at her, tapping an impatient foot, eager to get back to her duties.

"I just wish I had some idea of who it is from." Elizabeth

turned the small square over, staring at the unfamiliar crest
in the blood-red wax.

"I daresay you'll know as soon as you open it, ma'am."

Elizabeth jerked her head up to meet the maid's eyes, but
the woman's face carried no tinge of impertinence. It had
ever been so with Weller. She spoke her mind with no
thought of how it would sound to anyone else, including her
mistress. Unfortunately, she suited Mama's tastes, and so
Elizabeth had no hope of hiring a more biddable maid anytime soon.

"I expect you are right in that, Weller." Elizabeth slid a
finger underneath the seal of wax and popped it off. She
traced the crest, then laid it on her writing desk. Gently, she
unfolded the creamy note paper.

My Dear Elizabeth

Dear God, was it—Her gaze flew down the page to the
signature, written with a brave flourish. Her whole body
flushed, heat sweeping from her face down to the tips of her
toes, as though she stood on a pyre set alight. She spun away
so Weller wouldn't see her red face. Ignoring her racing
heart, she scanned the few lines, drinking in every one he
had written at last.

Despite her refusal to see him or speak with him last
month, she had to grudgingly admit she had expected to hear
from him before now. She'd learned of his removal from
London, so she'd expected a letter or a note to arrive from
him. He had seemed so passionate, so taken with her, and so
persistent those few days he'd pursued her. Why would she
not have expected him to continue to attempt to see her? Or
to send a note to apologize for his conduct. Or to beg her to
reconsider her determination not to see him again.

As the tally of weeks had mounted with no further word
from him, she had grown used to the empty post, accepted
that he had acted the rake, and begun to regret their *téte-à-
téte* in earnest. Apparently, he had indeed seized the oppor-

tunity, brought on by that indecent pagan festival, to push his way into her bed for a momentary triumph that meant nothing to him at all, save a passing gratification of his lust.

Perhaps she had been wrong to snub his advances, but she'd been terribly ashamed of her behavior and frightened of how mortified she would feel if she had to speak to him again. Once he'd gone, however, she'd missed his attentions. So she'd resumed attending *ton* entertainments in hopes she'd find another kind gentleman to catch her eye. It infuriated her that none had done so.

Now, Lord Brack had finally written and apparently waited downstairs, demanding an answer. Without reading the note further, she crumpled it, her nails digging into her palms with a vengeance. "Weller, tell his lordship he can go—"

"Yes, ma'am?"

Breath heaving, Elizabeth paused. No, she should read it, then send him away with a very large flea in his ear. She carefully unclenched her fingers and smoothed the crumpled paper out as best she could. The ink had blurred a bit, but it was still readable. More light would help. With a sharp glance at Weller, Elizabeth turned the lamp on the table toward her and held the paper closer to the yellow circle of light.

My Dear Elizabeth

How forward of him to call her by her given name when she'd not given him leave. After so much time had passed since they'd seen one another, it didn't matter a jot that their last true encounter had been exceedingly intimate.

I pray this finds you well. Georgie has not spoken of any illness, so I have hope that you and your family are enjoying excellent health.

The very least the wretch could have done was send word by his sister, supposing he was still at Lyttlefield Park.

I have returned to London at last. Your friend Lady Cavendish, Lord Wrotham, and my sister will be arriving in

a few days' time, and I had hoped to renew our acquaintance
before their arrival.

So he wished to "renew their acquaintance" did he? How
civil of him. Why would he wish to do such a thing when he
seemed to have not a care in the world for her in the past
three weeks? Such neglect could not be mended with a simple "how do you do." Her hands trembled with her effort to
restrain herself from tearing the letter into a thousand pieces
and feeding it to a goat.

"Is anything the matter, ma'am?" She spun around to find
Weller eyeing her warily.

"No, Weller, thank you." Elizabeth breathed deeply, trying hard to calm herself as best she could. Much as she'd
like to slap the wretch's face, she could not see him, and
Weller could not act in her place and lay hands on the son of
a peer. Her reply must, however, voice her displeasure at his
cavalier manner toward her.

I understand Lady Braeton's Harvest Ball is this evening,
and I hoped I might ask for the first dance with you. We have
much to speak of, if you will be so kind as to grant me this
boon.

Your devoted servant,
Jemmy

Elizabeth dropped the letter onto the desk and sat down
heavily, leaning her head on her hands. What must she do?

She had indeed planned to go to Lady Braeton's ball this
evening. She and Dickon had always attended together.
Tonight, she wanted to attend in order to lay the ghost of
Dickon for good, then move on to another part of her life
with her late husband's blessing. What a muddle Lord Brack
had made of her plans. She most emphatically did not want
to see him, but neither did she want the rogue to prevent her
from attending. What to do?

"Weller, tell Tawes to tell the gentleman there is no answer. Just that. No answer. If he asks to see me, tell him I am
indisposed."

"Very good, ma'am." A fiendish glint of approval in the maid's eyes said Weller relished the answer she was about to deliver—and the havoc it would likely cause. The maid nodded and left the chamber.

Seized with a fit of pique, Elizabeth grabbed the letter and tore it into tiny pieces. With a cry of contempt, she strode to the fireplace and flung the bits into the flames. They flashed briefly, as they burned. So, she hoped, she had erased Lord Brack from her life.

Jemmy paced to and fro in the receiving room, each minute that ticked by seeming to spell doom for his effort to see Elizabeth once more. An eternity would have been shorter than the time it had taken for the butler to take his note and ramble up the stairs. Jemmy strode out into the foyer but found no one. Perhaps Elizabeth was taking time to write a note agreeing to his suggestion. Somehow, he doubted that, but he had to hope for something in the way of a miracle. At the sound of a step on the stair, he turned, hoping beyond hope that Elizabeth had decided to see him.

A rather plain woman, severely dressed in black, descended the staircase, looking up and down the foyer.

He gazed at her expectantly.

"I was looking for Tawes, the butler, to deliver Mrs. Easton's answer, my lord, but as I do not see him at present, I'll give it to you directly." Her impersonal eyes flicked over him.

"Thank you, Miss . . . ?"

"Weller, my lord."

"And what is the answer, Miss Weller?" Jemmy held his breath.

"There is no answer, my lord." The maid's stony face as she made this pronouncement sent a chill through Jemmy that settled like a block of ice in his stomach.

"No answer?" Had Elizabeth broken with him completely?

Cursing his own cowardice for not writing her sooner, he cast about for some other means of contact. "Then can you tell me if Mrs. Easton plans to attend Lady Braeton's ball tonight?"

"Mrs. Easton is indisposed, my lord." Not one jot of sympathy showed in the maid's frowning countenance.

"I see." How else might he find out her plans? He'd wager his horse Elizabeth was angry rather than indisposed. The question remained, was she going out for the evening? "In that case, I wish to speak to Lady Wentworth."

The maid narrowed her eyes, and her cheek twitched, but she said only, "Of course, my lord," before turning sharply on her heel and quitting the room.

Did she dislike everyone, or just him? He'd almost wager his was not a special case. Jemmy returned to pacing around the small, dim reception room to which the butler had shown him a quarter of an hour before. Though the fire roared in the grate, the room remained chilled, just like his heart. He had bent over to study a series of miniatures of children on a long, polished table when the maid returned, triumph in her smile.

"Her ladyship is indisposed at the moment as well, my lord." The servant stuck out her chin, as though she dared him to dispute her claim.

Jemmy sighed and clenched his fist behind his back. He'd be damned if he'd let the maid know his anguish at this news. Another avenue closed against discovering Elizabeth's plans for tonight. "And you are certain Mrs. Easton is indisposed? She doesn't intend to venture out this evening?"

"I'm sure I am not privy to all my mistress's doings, my lord. Only what she's told me." A gleam appeared in the tall woman's eyes. "Although, if I was the wagering sort, I'd lay my money on Lady Shoreham's masquerade ball. You find a lady dressed as Aphrodite, and you will have your answer."

So the minx had had plans to go out this evening. "I thank you very much, Miss Weller. I am in your debt for that advice." His mother had been related to Lady Shoreham, he believed. It would be the work of a few moments to beg an invitation to the gathering. "I wish you good day."

As she turned to go, Jemmy caught a self-satisfied smirk pass over the woman's face. That look of triumph again. As if he'd been bested.

He strode into the foyer, where the butler had put in an appearance and already had his coat and hat to hand.

"My lord," the elderly man held his greatcoat up, and Jemmy slipped his arms through.

The maid's actions continued to perplex him. She'd seemed well-satisfied that Elizabeth had refused to see him. Likely enjoyed the look of dismay on his face when she pronounced the words. So why would she then assist his suit by disclosing the entertainment Elizabeth planned to attend?

The butler settled the coat over his shoulders and held out his hat and gloves, the servant's lined countenance firm, but neutral. Could he elicit some sort of help from this man? Information about Miss Weller would not come amiss.

"I gather Miss Weller has been with Mrs. Easton for some time." Which might be true, even though she had not accompanied Elizabeth to Lyttlefield Park for either house party.

"Yes, my lord. She been the lady's maid to the Misses Worth for ten years now. And five years as Lady Wentworth's lady's maid before that. You'll not find another one so loyal to a family." The man's jowly cheeks rippled as he spoke, his chin raised.

"I could see her devotion to her mistress when I spoke with her." Devoted enough to lie for Elizabeth? He set his hat on his head, a nagging voice in the very back of his head urging him not to let it go.

The butler opened the door.

Damn, but he needed to be sure.

"A moment, Tawes?" Jemmy nodded and backed up into the foyer. He thrust his hat back at a footman and dug into his breast pocket for his card case. "Might I have a pen, Tawes?"

"Of course, my lord. Robert." He hailed the footman who held Jemmy's hat.

"Yes, Mr. Tawes?" The man stepped forward once more, back ramrod-straight.

"Fetch Lord Brack a pen, please. Do you require paper, my lord?"

"No, thank you. I believe my card will suffice." Jemmy drew the small white card from his case, engraved with a large, bold B.

The footman hurried into the receiving room Jemmy had just quit and returned swiftly with a pen and inkpot.

"Thank you. If you'd set them right there on the table." He indicated a long, polished high table that contained a vase of yellow roses.

"I think I will send up one more little note to Mrs. Easton, after all." Jemmy grabbed the pen and scratched two lines on the back of his card. *Hope to join you at Mrs. Shoreham's this evening. Looking forward to the first dance.* He laid the pen down and blew on the card for several seconds, holding it so the butler could plainly see the message. "You will see that gets to Mrs. Easton, won't you, Tawes?" Jemmy cut his plaintive gaze to the butler's face.

"Very good, my lord." Tawes turned the card over and bowed.

Jemmy cursed under his breath as the butler turned from him. He'd been so certain—

"My lord?"

A wave of relief surged through him. "Yes?"

"I thought I should mention that Mrs. Easton will not be attending Mrs. Shoreham's this evening."

"Ah, I did not know that." Jemmy clenched his fist. Miss Weller was a slyboots, after all. "I thought her plans had been fixed on the masquerade." He tried to look glum, all the while repressing the glee that made him want to kick up his heels and laugh. Miss Weller might serve her mistress well, but he would do his best to circumvent those efforts.

"No, my lord."

"She's decided on Lady Braeton's instead, has she?" Jemmy shook his head and pulled his best Friday face. "A real pity, for I am quite promised to Mrs. Shoreham. Old friend of the family, you understand." Why was he standing here prattling on to a servant?

"I do indeed, my lord. Shall I inform Mrs. Easton—"

"No, no. We shall have to meet another time." He held out his hand, and Tawes dropped the card into it. "Please do tell Mrs. Easton that I shall call upon her in a few days." Retrieving his hat and fixing it to his head, Jemmy strode out into St. James Square and breathed deeply. A narrow escape of a wasted evening, but he'd managed to finally get the truth.

If Elizabeth thought she could avoid him while they were in the same city, she would find him a persistent suitor. He'd been wrong to discontinue his courting of her but would beg her pardon with deep sincerity while they danced the first dance together tonight.

Chapter 10

"Good evening, Lord Brack." Lady Braeton all but cooed his name, her eyes a vivid blue that matched her gown.

"Good evening, my lady. My great thanks for your kind invitation." He'd managed to beg that invitation at the very last minute.

"Lady Joanna Knowlton, may I present Lord Brack? Lady Joanna is my next oldest daughter, my lord. She will officially come out next Season."

Ah, that explained his presence here tonight. Her ladyship was a matchmaking mama, still on the hunt. Her elder daughter, Lady Grace Knowlton, had married Lord Longford earlier this autumn, so apparently, Lady Braeton had her eye on him for Lady Joanna. Unfortunate, but he would have to disappoint both ladies. "I am delighted, Lady Joanna. May I claim a dance this evening?"

"Indeed, you may, my lord. Will the third set suit you?" The lady's low-pitched voice fell pleasantly on his ear from her delightfully bowed mouth. Jet-black hair, alabaster skin, and the family legacy of crystal blue eyes, all set off by an ice blue gown, made Lady Joanna a delectable future partner.

Alas, only for the dance. His heart was engaged elsewhere, and he'd be off to find his lady as soon as he did his duty to his hostess. "Such a charming room, Lady Braeton." He smiled, glancing about as if taking in the room's splendid appointments.

The gold-papered walls glittered in the light of a thousand candles. So much light should have banished the darkness completely; however, shadows still lurked in the corners. Did Elizabeth stand there, trying to hide? Or had she already marked his entrance and decided to pay him no mind at all? The possibilities pierced his mind like sharpened stakes.

"Lord Brack?" Lady Braeton tugged on his arm.

Startled, Jemmy tried to play off his momentary lapse. He fixed a pleasant expression on his face and said, "You should entertain more often, my lady. Lady Joanna and I could put this room to good use."

Her daughter didn't seem to mind his absentmindedness. "Oh, yes, Lord Brack. I have often told my mother that exact thing."

"That will do, Joanna. Perhaps you should go find your Papa. He was speaking with Lord Arrington, who is your first partner of the evening." Lady Braeton couldn't have made her feelings plainer if she had physically shoved her daughter away.

Lady Joanna bowed, then sped toward her father, a tall, distinguished gentleman sporting a monocle and a quizzing glass hanging around his neck.

"Shall I help you find a partner for the first dance, my lord? So you can make good use of my ballroom tonight. Where is Lady Amelia Bart?" She peered around the room, brows puckered in a look that did not become the lady.

"I shall seek her out, my lady; you may depend upon it." He tried to affect a look that said he'd like nothing better than to stand up with a girl who inevitably trod on his toes each time they danced. "But I must move on. I have quite halted the line." A bow and a grin as he made a swift escape directly toward the refreshment room. A fortifying libation was always a requirement after any encounter with Lady Braeton.

Skirting a quartet of young ladies, heads together, plotting, in their bright frocks near the doorway, Jemmy almost ran into the Marquess of Theale. "Ho, your lordship." He put out a hand to avoid an actual collision. Theale was splendidly outfitted this evening in a tailcoat so exquisitely cut it must demand everyone stare in envy. "Are you on the run or in the chase, my lord?"

Nose red, eyes blurry, Theale raised his quizzer to him, then nodded in answer. "Brack. Good chap. Trying to take one of my daughters off me, are you? Too late, too late. She's got her mind made up to outrank her sister. Nothing but a duke will do for her now." Theale swayed unsteadily on his feet.

"Here, my lord. Take a seat." Jemmy tried to steer the inebriated peer into a large, soft chair from which he hopefully would not rise before the end of the evening.

"Good lad." Lord Theale relaxed back into the seat, eyes closed.

Jemmy shot a look back at Lady Braeton. A foxed guest lay within her domain. She smiled brilliantly at him. Lord, now she would probably try to engage him to Lady Joanna in gratitude for scotching this little incident before it became a major disruption. Truly, no good deed went unpunished.

Glancing around the room again, searching desperately for Elizabeth, Jemmy spied Lord Wilton flirting with Lady Catherine Buckminster. Damn. He'd have to do his duty and speak a word in Wilton's ear. Lady Catherine was his cousin, just out last Season, and not someone to be trifled with. Life had certainly been simpler at Lady Cavendish's house for the past weeks.

"Excuse me, my lord." He bowed to Theale, who beamed at him and let out a whiskey-tinged hiccup and waved him off with another mumbled "Good lad."

Jemmy wove his way across the crowded floor as an alarming number of couples gathered for the first set. Good thing Braeton's home sported a ballroom larger than the usual terraced house. The crush of people had grown thick indeed. Half the *ton* must have turned out for the Harvest Ball.

Just as he reached Catherine's side, Jemmy glanced back to the entrance once more in the forlorn hope of finding that Elizabeth had appeared. Perhaps he'd been mistaken and she'd actually been indisposed. Curse his luck. He opened his mouth to greet his cousin and stopped, one hand suspended midway toward her.

Mrs. Elizabeth Easton, attired in a ravishing turquoise and cream evening dress, smiled and chatted avidly with Lady Braeton.

The room froze around him, the world reduced to his heartbeat roaring in his ears. All he could see was the vision of loveliness standing across the room, more breathtaking than he remembered. His whole world. Every detail of her seared itself into his memory—the small circlet of pearls nestled in her blond hair, the perfect bow shape of her red lips, her white breasts peeping from her daringly low-cut gown, the peacock feather fan dangling from her wrist. Even from this distance, he could recognize her voice as she took leave of her hostess and moved into the room.

"Lord Brack! What a pleasant—ouch!" Lady Catherine squealed as Jemmy clamped his hand around her wrist.

"Do pardon us, my lord," he called back at the shocked face of Lord Wilton. Towing Catherine as he hurried around the room, eeling them through the thickly packed guests.

"What do you think you're doing, Jemmy?" Catherine struggled to free her wrist, already recovered from her cousin's absconding with her. Her peevish tone registered loudly with Jemmy, though he cared for it not a jot.

"I am taking you, dear cousin, to meet a very good friend of mine." Thank goodness Elizabeth's bright gown stood out against the darker shadows of the room, else he'd have a deal of trouble finding her again. She'd stopped to talk to her sister, Miss Worth, standing beside Lord Haxton. So much the better. She'd hardly give him the cut direct before her sister's new fiancé, according to Georgie.

"Well, you needn't crush my hand into the bargain, Jemmy." Catherine pulled against his vice-like grip, and he eased it a trifle.

"I'm sorry." He glanced at her and grinned. "Good to see you, cuz. Even though I can't agree with your choice of partners." They had rounded the end of the ballroom and were within a few yards of his quarry. Elizabeth had not seen him yet, thank God.

"What do you mean? Lord Wilton—"

"Lord Wilton is a rake and a rogue, even if he does stand to inherit the third-largest estate in England. You should steer clear of him."

"Mama said—"

"I'm sure Aunt Augusta has said many fine things about Wilton. Your papa, however, would want to avoid the scandal if the scoundrel ruined you. He's done that to young girls before, so the rumor goes. Now"—he stopped and turned his back to Elizabeth and her sister—"I am going to introduce you to Mrs. Easton, her sister, and her sister's betrothed. You will be pleasant and cordial, and I will not tell your parents you were flirting shamelessly with a known rakehell."

"I was not flirting with him," Catherine protested. "He was flirting with me, and I was quite enjoying it!"

"Then we will find a less dangerous gentleman to flirt with you. Now, come and be introduced." Jemmy wound her arm through his and boldly stepped toward Elizabeth, a genuine smile spreading across his face. Lord, but she looked magnificent.

Laughing at something her sister said, Elizabeth looked up, straight into his face. Her eyes widened, two deep blue circles swimming in a sea of white for just a moment before she lowered her eyelids against the sight of him. Her neck flushed a deep pink that spread upward to darken her cheeks.

Miss Worth turned toward him, joy lighting her face. "Lord Brack. How do you do? I asked my sister about you just the other day."

"It was kind of you to think of me, Miss Worth." Jemmy tried to focus on the woman he was speaking to, but his attention kept straying to Elizabeth, like a magnet to its true north. "May I present Lady Catherine Buckminster, my cousin? This is Mrs. Elizabeth Easton, Miss Worth, and Lord Haxton."

They all murmured "how do you dos" as Jemmy held his breath, gazing at Elizabeth, who seemed even more lovely than he remembered, though her face had paled at the sight of him. The skin of her long neck had a creamy glow at least, her beautiful blond hair piled on top of her head, careless ringlets framing her face. When his gaze shifted to her full, red lips—he might never breathe again. Christ, he must find some way to make this stunning woman his.

"So pleased, Lady Catherine." Elizabeth threw one agonized glare at him. "But you must excuse me." She bowed and began to turn away, her mouth in a rigid line that broke the spell.

"Mrs. Easton." Jemmy dropped Catherine's arm, stepped toward the retreating woman, and boldly took her hand. He couldn't allow her to slip away. "I am particularly pleased to see you this evening."

"Thank you, my lord." With a glance around the company, she drew herself up, giving her wrist enough of a shake to signal her displeasure at his action.

Sighing, he released her, praying she would not bolt across the floor where the dancers were in the midst of "Maiden Alley." "I had hoped you might allow me to partner you in the next set."

Her lips thinned, though her cheeks had gained a spot of color. "I had not planned to dance tonight, Lord Brack."

"But plans may change, may they not, Mrs. Easton?" He smiled his most beguiling smile. "Surely one comes to a ball because one wants to dance." God, but he wanted to grab her and kiss her senseless.

"Then rather let me say I had not planned to dance with *you*, Lord Brack." Her blue eyes were cold as icicles and twice as hard.

"Elizabeth." This might be his only chance to plead his case. Catherine was chatting with Miss Worth. Haxton had carried himself off, most likely in search of a drink. Jemmy could certainly use one about now as well.

"I have not asked you to call me so familiarly, Lord Brack." Her nose flared, but deep in her eyes, a quiet pain lurked.

"I know you have not; however, I believe we are close enough in acquaintance to be termed intimates."

The color in her cheeks deepened to red, and she grudgingly nodded, though her jaw firmed. "Very well, in private you may call me Elizabeth, Lord Brack."

Stubborn woman. He forced a smile. "Thank you, Elizabeth. And I beg you to call me Jemmy."

A laughing couple bumped into him, almost throwing him into Elizabeth.

Lord, he could not do this in the middle of the room. "Come with me, please." He grasped her arm and steered her toward a quiet corner. "Elizabeth, I truly beg your pardon for not writing to you after I left London."

"That was quite all right, Lord—"

He glared at her, not wavering, until she sighed.

"Very, well. That was quite all right, *Jemmy*." The name came out grudgingly but landed sweetly on his ears. "I made it quite obvious I did not wish to see you. You were under no obligation to write."

"You know very well what I was obliged to do. And I did write, the very day I returned to Lyttlefield Park, but I tore it up." What a caper-witted lump he'd been. He should never have left. "I tore up a hundred letters in the past weeks, too cowardly to tell you what I feel. What I have felt since that night in October."

"I prefer not to speak of that, my lord." She tensed, glanced about, then slumped. "If that is all, my lord?"

"Devil take it, that is not all, and you know it." The last thing he wanted was to quarrel with her. A gentler road might make for a smoother ride. "May I have the next dance, Elizabeth? I would very much like to dance with you tonight."

Her mouth screwed up. Her lips opened.

He steeled himself for the "no" that was sure to come.

"Oh. Well, then, yes. I will dance the next with you, my lord." Surprised, as though she hadn't meant to say those words, she slowly closed her lips.

"They should be making up the set shortly. Shall I take you for some refreshments until then?" The more time they spent together, the better his chances to woo her back to him.

"No, thank you, my lord. I . . . ." She searched the floor. "I see Lady Stephen Tarkington just there. I should speak to her." She managed a small smile, so sweet it almost gave him hope. "I will wait for you there."

Bowing, he tried to ignore the havoc in his heart as the beautiful figure in turquoise swayed in a most alluring way as she made her way toward Lady Stephen. A vision he intended to see every day for the rest of his life.

Jemmy recalled himself—mustn't let everyone know how moonstruck he was over this lady—and returned to his cousin and Miss Worth. "Excuse me, ladies, may I fetch you some refreshments?"

"No, thank you, my lord." Miss Worth squeezed Catherine's hands. "Then shall I see you later this week, my lady?"

"Yes, Miss Worth." Catherine beamed. "I shall look forward to it."

Elizabeth's sister curtsied and sped off toward Lady Wentworth, who was in fervent conversation with Lady Braeton.

"Can you take me to my mother, Jemmy? I have such exciting news to tell her." Catherine's pink cheeks and sparkling eyes bespoke her excitement.

"You look like the cat who ate the canary, complete with feathers sticking out of your mouth, cousin. What are you about?" Jemmy presented his arm, wishing someone would offer him a strong drink. Between watching over his cousin, being accosted by a drunken lord, and trying to woo Elizabeth back, he was done in before the evening had scarcely begun.

"And a very tasty canary it was, too." Catherine hugged his arm as they continued around the dance floor. She seemed in the best mood and more animated than he'd ever seen her. "Miss Worth is betrothed to Lord Haxton, whose younger brother, Lord Christopher Stanhope, is about to be created the Earl of Anthorn-on-Pye for meritorious service to the Crown."

"I had heard of Lord Christopher's good fortune." Jemmy sighted his Aunt Augusta and steered them toward her. "Why does Stanhope's good fortune make you so happy?"

"Because Miss Worth has invited me to tea with her on Thursday with Lord Haxton and his brother." Catherine gripped his arm, digging her nails into him, even through the superfine. "I could not have hoped for a better introduction to his lordship. He doesn't frequent the *ton* gatherings, so it is rather difficult to scrape an acquaintance with him."

"Well, I certainly wish you luck, Catherine." Lord Christopher was a much better match for her than Wilton. As a third son, Lord Christopher Stanhope had been mostly overlooked on the marriage mart. No longer. He'd wager a considerable sum on that. "He's about to become the eligible *parti* of the

Little Season, so by all means, take any advantage you can, cousin."

"Take advantage of what?" Aunt Augusta, whose hearing at age sixty was much better than it should be, eyed him dubiously.

"Of all her good fortune, which I will leave her to tell you." He winked at his cousin. "Thank you so much for your company, Catherine. I hope it has been as advantageous for you as it has been for me."

"Why must you always talk in riddles, Brack? Your father should have taught you better. Come, Catherine. With what nonsense has Brack been filling your head?" Giving an imperious inclination of her head, his aunt captured her daughter's attention. "Thank you, Brack. If we need further assistance, I shall call upon you."

"Your servant at all times, Aunt." Jemmy bowed and swiftly took himself off. Anyone would know his aunt and father as brother and sister the moment they spoke. He pitied Catherine only a little less than he did Georgina. He'd always thought he and his sister must take after their mother in terms of temperament.

Wanting a drink even more desperately now, Jemmy headed once more for the refreshment room. Wine rather than whiskey tonight. He had to have a clear head when he finally got Elizabeth out on the ballroom floor and asked her to marry him.

Chapter 11

"Why, oh, why did I believe Weller?" Elizabeth muttered under her breath as she fled toward Fanny. An older gentleman stepped in front of her to let the Duchess of Granville pass. She hopped to the side to avoid one collision, and nearly cannoned into Lady Waterbury. She must keep her wits about her if she was to survive the coming encounter with Lord Brack. Her face had glowed with heat from the moment she looked up and saw him.

Weller had promised that she'd told the gentleman Elizabeth was indisposed and not attending any entertainments this evening. Then she'd embellished the tale, aiming for misdirection. Apparently, the maid had been less convincing than she believed, with Elizabeth paying the price of a most awkward engagement to dance with the one man she'd hoped to avoid for the rest of her life.

"Elizabeth, how do you do this evening? You seem rather out of breath." Fanny looked about, a knowing smile on her lips. "Is he very handsome?"

"Is who very handsome?" Elizabeth gulped in air, her heart racing. She spied Lord Brack moving across the floor. Good, he was taking his cousin to the Countess of Oundle.

"The gentleman who is chasing you."

"Don't be a goose, Fanny." Now he was heading toward the refreshment room. Perhaps he would forget when to return. "No one is chasing me."

"If Lord Brack is not chasing you, why are you fleeing him?" Fanny cocked her head and gave her a smug smile. "I saw him leave you just now, reluctance in every line of him. Did he write you that he was back in Town?"

"No, he never wrote at all." The bitterness in her voice surprised her. Had she truly wished Lord Brack to continue his pursuit of her? Time and her family circumstances may have shifted her desires, although the humiliation of that night still had her tied in knots. "You know I gave him to believe I didn't want him to continue his attentions to me."

"Then why are you upset that he abided by your wishes?" Fanny peered into her face, then grabbed her arm. "Let us go to the ladies' retiring room. I believe there is more to this tale than you have told me, and therefore not something that should be spoken where it might be overheard."

They strolled into the room set aside for the ladies, fortunate to find only two young girls there, just out and whispering together in a corner. They giggled, dipped a curtsy, and scampered out to the ballroom.

Fanny led Elizabeth to a bronze silk chaise and dropped gracefully down onto it. "Now, what exactly has been going on between you and Lord Brack?"

"Well . . ." Elizabeth gnawed at her lip. Could she admit to Fanny something so embarrassing? Truly, she needed guidance from someone, and if any of her friends could give her advice about something so intimate, it was Fanny. "Lord Brack . . ."

"Yes?" Fanny leaned toward her, eyes intent.

"Lord Brack and I . . ." She couldn't say it, not even to Fanny.

"Lord Brack did what, for heaven's sake? Kiss you and

slip in his tongue? Is that what has given you an attack of the vapors?" Fanny laughed.

Elizabeth pursed her lips. "Something more than that, although that certainly happened as well." It had been a part of their encounter she had actually liked. The trouble was she had liked all of it—up until the very end.

"Something more?" Fanny's eyes bulged. "You don't mean you . . ." She fanned herself briskly as though it were a hot summer's night, her mouth hanging open. "Are you telling me you ended up in bed with him?"

"Hush, for God's sake!" Elizabeth grabbed her peacock fan and plied it faster than Fanny. Her cheeks burned like they'd been seared by the sun. "Yes, if you must know. The night of the Harvest Festival. It was a very strange evening."

"Strange does not begin to describe it, Elizabeth, if you ended up in bed with a man." Fanny looked at her wild-eyed, as though she had grown two heads. "I'd have wagered a hefty sum you would be the last of our group to wed again. The thought you'd go to bed with a man without marriage never even crossed my mind."

What would she say to the next part of the confession?

"That's not the worst part of it." Elizabeth hung her head. "There's more."

"I am afraid to ask." Fanny gazed out into the empty room and clenched her fist. "Was he rough with you? Did he hurt you?"

"No, it was my fault." How on earth could she confess this to Fanny?

"Don't let him make you think it is your fault, my dear, no matter what it was." Grasping Elizabeth's shoulders, she shook her until Elizabeth finally met her eyes. "It was not your fault."

"But it was! I called him Dickon. How is that not my fault?" Elizabeth hid her face in her hands, too mortified to hold her head up any longer. How could she face Lord Brack for this dance? Perhaps she should try to slip out the servants' entrance and go home.

"You called him Dickon?"

Face still concealed, Elizabeth nodded, not daring to look up. "At the end," she whispered.

The silence lengthened until Elizabeth could no longer repress her sobs.

Fanny's hand touched her shoulder. "He's forgiven you."

She jerked her head up, tears still falling. "I'm sure he cannot."

"Then why is he still pursuing you?"

That question brought Elizabeth up short. She hadn't thought of that. He should have been angry at her for that slip, but that didn't explain why he pursued her to London last month, nor his behavior this afternoon or his insistence that they dance tonight. He could easily avoid her if he chose. Apparently, he did not.

"I forgave Stephen a similar transgression the first time." Hands clenched in her lap, Fanny gazed at a small, damasked sofa across the room. "And the second time. Not the third."

Cold chills raced down Elizabeth's back. "My dear, I am so sorry for you."

"It doesn't matter now." Arching her neck, her friend smiled, a chilling sight. "I've gotten my revenge." She shrugged and rose. "We must get you back to the ballroom so Lord Brack can claim his dance."

"Are men so truly forgiving?" Elizabeth stood, shook out her gown, and gripped her fan for courage.

"Usually more so than women in these matters. Follow me."

"What luck, my dear, to have drawn a waltz for our set." Lord Brack's twinkling blue eyes caught Elizabeth's attention. He used that distraction to pull her close to him and lay his hand flat on her back.

What had this roguish young man been up to while she'd been pouring out her troubles to Fanny?

"Indeed, I did not believe Lady Braeton one to court scandal." The intimacy of the waltz was said to be suited only to married couples. She now agreed wholeheartedly.

"Not scandal, surely?" Brack took the opportunity of a whirling step to draw her body closer to him, tightening his arm around her.

"Lord Brack!" How dare he?

"Jemmy, if you remember." Effortlessly, he steered them around the circle of dancers. Whatever he was, he was skilled on the dance floor.

"Jemmy, then. You are holding me much too tightly." Secretly, she found his nearness thrilling, though she couldn't let him know that.

"Nowhere near as tightly as I want to hold you." He inched her even closer. "As I have done in the past." He pressed his mouth close to her ear. "I remember holding you against me, all of you against all of me. Don't you remember how lovely that felt, Elizabeth? Don't you want to feel that again?"

Gasping for breath, Elizabeth fought the surge of passion that threatened to overwhelm her merely by his closeness. She vividly remembered their bodies entwined on her bed, kisses raining down all over her neck and breasts. Heat exploded at her core, and she fought to continue dancing as though her body had not suddenly been engulfed in those flames once more. If she was to continue the charade, she must steer the conversation into safer waters.

"I believe the past should remain in the past, Lord—"

His eyes threatened to cut her like a finely honed blade.

"Jemmy." She eased away from him a trifle. Enough room to let her take a deep breath. "Could we please walk about the room? I am not used to dancing so much nor so fast." She managed a cajoling tone and fluttered her fan before her face, both to conceal her eyes and to cool her as much as possible. The room itself seemed to exude heat.

"Of course, my dear." He immediately broke off the waltz and offered his arm. "Even though it took ten minutes of negotiating and a gold sovereign to arrange this dance with the orchestra leader."

"You didn't?"

"I most certainly did. How else could I guarantee I'd end up with you in my arms this evening?" He chuckled low in his throat and drew her arm through his.

"You are much more devious than I imagined. At Lyttle-field Park, I would have said you were the perfect gentle-man." Instead, Lord Brack was turning out to be one of those gentlemen Mama had warned her about. The trouble was, she was no longer a young, inexperienced girl. Maybe she no longer needed to travel the safe path.

"I can be your perfect gentleman, Elizabeth. A knight in shining armor who rescues you from an uneventful life—"

"My life is not uneventful, I will have you know." She rapped his arm with her fan so sharply feathers flew.

"I can guarantee I will make it more meaningful, more ex-citing than you ever dreamed." He stopped at the far end of the ballroom near a set of closed French doors. "I wish the night was not so cool. We could take the air out on the bal-cony," his voice became huskier, "and I could kiss you again."

"Lower your voice." Thrilled and panicked at the same time, Elizabeth drew him further into the shadow of a huge potted plant. "You should not say such things."

"Perhaps I should just do them, then." He grasped her head and pressed his lips to hers.

For a confused moment, she leaned against him, stunned by his boldness. His lips were as she remembered them, in-credibly soft, yet firm. Commanding. Caring. Then she pulled away, heart racing, unable to speak a word.

"You do remember that night, by God." Jemmy all but crowed.

"Of course, I remember it, you fool." Trembling, Elizabeth stepped back, her hands automatically going to her hair. If he'd mussed it, she would have to go home. She couldn't spend the rest of the evening looking like a hoyden. "That doesn't mean I wish to reenact it in the middle of a Harvest Ball."

"Does it mean you would you reenact it with me somewhere else?"

The hope in his raspy voice touched a chord deep inside her, a need she'd been trying to deny ever since it had happened. But she couldn't speak of such things in a public place. She could scarcely do so in the privacy of her boudoir. So switch to a safer subject and hope for the best. "Are you planning to attend Charlotte's wedding next month, my lord? Surely, they wish to have you present, along with all the house party, save only Lord Fernly, Maria, and Lord Kersey."

"Yes, I suspect they would be *personae non gratae* after that scandalous performance at the last party." He chuckled. "A very interesting evening for all concerned, don't you think?"

Drat. Here they were, right back onto the topic she wished fervently to avoid. She pushed on. "So you will be attending the wedding?"

"I believe so." He wove his fingers through hers. "Nash has asked me to stand as best man for him. I am proud to do it."

"I see." Elizabeth wasn't quite sure if that pleased her or not. "Georgina and Jane are to be Charlotte's attendants."

"Yes, Georgie told me. But you will outshine the bride, my dear." He squeezed her fingers, sending tingles up her arm.

"You mustn't say such things." Danger lurked in his eyes. She untangled her fingers and stepped away.

"What if it were true?"

"What?"

"What if you were a bride as well?" He grasped her

hands and drew her back behind the plant. "If you married me, we could share Charlotte's and Nash's happiness, or be happy on our own day."

Elizabeth blinked, her voice caught in her throat. The room spun a little, and she clutched at him with numb fingers. "Jemmy, you can't mean it," she said, when she could finally draw breath.

"But I do, my love."

"What about . . ." She clutched the fan so tightly the quills cracked. "What about Dickon?" It came out so low he had to lean forward to catch the word.

"Your late husband?"

She hung her head, blushing furiously. He had to know of what she spoke.

"I believe I told you at the time I understood these things. You loved your husband." He grasped her chin and raised her face to him. "I suppose that sort of thing must be expected sometimes when one marries a widow." He chuckled softly. "A hazard of the widow's bed, so to speak, but one I'm willing to risk if it means I can love you and be with you for the rest of my life."

"Jemmy." The sweetness of his voice, the warmth of his hands, the pleading in his eyes overwhelmed her until she feared she might swoon.

"Will you not even consider my proposal?"

"I would." Suddenly, she wanted to consider it with all her heart. But the niggling fear still rode her. "I would consider your suit if I didn't believe that my . . . lapse"—another furious blush set her cheeks on fire—"means I am not done with grieving for my late husband yet."

What she actually feared most was not that she still grieved, but that she was ready to let go of that grief. She didn't want to move on from Dickon, so kind, so loving, so familiar. Was she ready to leave him behind and step out into vast, uncharted territory of another man?

He sighed, as though the weight of the world had descended on his shoulders, but looked her clearly in the eyes. "Then I pray you, do not give me an answer yet. Think about me, think about us, think that I only wish to make you happy, and give me your answer when we meet again for Charlotte's wedding. Do you think you may be ready to give it by then?"

Elizabeth ducked her head and nodded. In the four weeks between now and then, she would search her soul and give him an answer. "Do you remain in London? Might we see you at tea tomorrow?"

Grinning, he wound her arm in his. "I was to return to Kent to shepherd Georgie here with Charlotte and Nash next week for a short shopping excursion. But I will arrange to meet them here instead, in order to avail myself of your excellent company at tea and perhaps another entertainment, before they arrive?" His countenance grew sober. "After the wedding, I hope to persuade my father to allow Georgie to return to Blackham. We've quite run out of options for her."

"I do wish my circumstances were different." A wish she'd made time and again. "I would love to have Georgie come to me."

"Perhaps one day it will be possible to have her in our home."

Always kicking up a lark, this one. She flashed him a rueful smile. "Perhaps one day."

They had reached the entrance to the ballroom. His gaze lingered on her face, as if memorizing every feature. "I shall hope and pray for your answer. Remember our night together, but also the other times as well. Our dinner conversations, our dances, our trip into the village, and the Wrotham ale."

She laughed, almost tasting that nutty brew.

"Remember all the times we have laughed together, and decide to live your life with me." With a kiss on her hand, he bowed and strode quickly away, leaving Elizabeth to look after his retreating figure, speechless and as uncertain of her answer as ever before.

Chapter 12

St. George's Church in Wrotham appeared vastly different to Elizabeth than it had that seemingly long-ago afternoon in August when she had first seen it. Then it had been a quaint empty stone building with lovely stained-glass windows and polished pews. Now it teemed with people from Wrotham village and the tenant farms, those pews tightly packed with faces eager to share in the joining of their beloved master and mistress as Charlotte and Nash wed.

Masses of hothouse flowers from Wrotham adorned the altar in a colorful display of bright reds, deep golds, and purest white. Candles in every window sent a glow throughout the sanctuary. Elizabeth took her seat next to Fanny at the end of the front pew, spots reserved especially for them. Both of them, as well as Georgina and Jane, who stood at the altar as bridesmaids, would be right there to support Charlotte as she took her first steps into her new life with Nash as the Countess of Wrotham.

It truly took a lot of courage to start life again, although Charlotte's life as a widow had been much better than as the wife of Sir Archibald Cavendish. To give up her newfound independence—after years of being under the thumb of first her tyrannical father, then an odious husband—had been her friend's hardest struggle. Her deep love for Nash, however, had finally won the day.

Everyone stood as Charlotte entered the church on the arm of her father. No small miracle that. The two had been at odds for years. This concession, to make him a part of her wedding, had been another struggle for Charlotte. Having decided that she owed him some little credit for making her match with Nash, she had finally acquiesced and invited him to the ceremony. As she neared Elizabeth, she smiled brilliantly at her friend, then snapped her attention back to the man who stood beside the vicar, waiting to make her happy at last.

Elizabeth feared her own problem would be the opposite of Charlotte's. Supposing Lord Brack could convince her that he had forgiven her disgraceful utterance and did indeed want to marry her, she worried that they could never achieve the stunning happiness she had known with Dickon. The radiant joy on Charlotte's face as she approached her soon-to-be husband spoke of the strong bond that already existed between them.

Her gaze strayed, naturally, from her friend to the man standing beside Nash. Lord Brack looked so elegant and dashing in his black morning coat, cut in excellent lines to show off his broad shoulders and lean build. The riotous mass of curly, honey-blond hair always made her want to smile. They made him seem so much a little boy, though in all other ways he was very much a man.

She must have been smiling then because he sent her a dazzling smile in return, just as Charlotte reached the foot of the altar, and he turned, with Nash, toward the vicar, Mr. Moore. Her cheeks heated, but she continued to smile as she sat and the service began.

"Dearly beloved, we have come together in the presence of God . . ."

The words transported Elizabeth back to her own wedding to Dickon, almost eight years before. An affair much different than this one.

He'd been Major Easton then, quite the dashing officer in his regimentals. Not that she'd fallen for a uniform, but he'd cut such a splendid figure the first time she'd seen him, she couldn't help thinking him the handsomest of men. It hadn't happened in a ballroom either, but on the parade grounds in Brighton, during an exhibition, where her family had gone immediately after her come-out Season. One look at him— sitting his horse like he'd been born in the saddle, chiseled features tanned by the bright sun, an air of dedication that bordered on a passion for a duty he loved—and her heart had been lost.

She'd managed to discover his name from an old family friend who had military connections, had begged an introduction from this same friend, and made her interest in Major Richard Easton known to him during the first dance he had asked for. His deep blue eyes had widened when she had squeezed his hand and told him he must ask her for a second dance, and then a third, for she never wished to partner with anyone other than him ever again.

A week later, with her father's reluctant permission and a special license clutched in her hand, they had married in St. Nicholas's Church in Brighton, before her family and Dickon's mother. After a blissful month as newlyweds, Dickon had left for Spain, leaving her uncertain and fearful that he would never return. Thankfully he had, though almost a year later.

"Charlotte, will you have this man to be your husband? To live together in the covenant of marriage?" Mr. Moore's voice suddenly brought Elizabeth back to the present, to the sight of Charlotte's face as she gazed at Nash. Her eyes sparkled, and her face glowed radiantly with an inner beauty born of true happiness. Surely, that was how she herself had looked when she had married Dickon. Would she look thus at Lord Brack if she married him?

A wave of heat rose from her neck into her face and even

into her head, until her hair felt like it was on fire. Lord, had someone lit a fire beneath her feet? She dug into her reticule for a fan, though it might seem inappropriate to fan herself. If she didn't get some relief, she would melt into the pew.

"What is wrong, Elizabeth?" Fanny whispered in her ear.

"Hot. I'm terribly hot all of a sudden." She found the fan, opened it as quietly as possible, and waved it as surreptitiously as she could toward her face. It helped a little, but the burning heat in her face continued. "Are my cheeks red?" she whispered back to Fanny as the vicar blessed the ring.

"A little." Fanny peered at her, a frown puckering her brow. "Are you unwell?"

Elizabeth abandoned conversation, concentrating instead on breathing slowly and keeping her fan going. The cool December air outside would be a blessing now. Soon she would be out in it, for Mr. Moore was about to proclaim the marriage.

"Now that Charlotte and Nash have given themselves to each other by solemn vows, with joining hands and the giving and receiving of a ring, I pronounce that they are man and wife, in the name of the Father, and of the Son, and of the Holy Spirit. Those whom God has joined together let no man put asunder."

The congregation rose, bringing Elizabeth gratefully to her feet. What had come over her?

Charlotte and Nash turned toward them, happiness radiating from their smiling faces.

Elizabeth tried to smile in return, tried to catch her breath, but the world had suddenly turned black, and she faintly heard Fanny calling her name before the darkness enfolded her completely.

"Oh, wretched smell!" Elizabeth jerked up into a sitting position. The horrible smell of *sal volatile* reeked in her nostrils still. She opened her eyes to find her circle of friends—

Fanny, Georgie, Jane, and even Charlotte in her beautiful blue wedding dress—gathered around her. Fanny had removed the small silver vinaigrette with the smelling salts from her face, though the scent lingered in the air. Georgie and Jane had their own small bottles in their hands, ready to step in if Fanny's didn't work. "What happened?"

"Goodness, Elizabeth." Georgie bustled forward to help her sit up. "You gave us such a fright."

"You swooned, my dear." Jane peered at her and felt her cheeks, her hands cool and soothing on her hot skin.

"Went over like a sack of potatoes, just before Charlotte and Nash started down the aisle." Fanny had capped her silver vial and slipped it back in her small, black reticule.

"Charlotte! I am so sorry." Elizabeth turned to her friend, mortified that she'd made such a spectacle of herself, ruining Charlotte's long-awaited wedding. "I don't know what happened. Can you ever forgive me for spoiling—?"

"Hush. You've spoiled nothing, my dear." Charlotte patted her shoulder soothingly. "I am just as married as I will ever be. But what happened to cause you to swoon?"

"I cannot think." That was true. Her head was in a whirl. Gingerly, she lay back down on what appeared to be a plain, cracked leather sofa. A swift peek at the room—small, plainly furnished, with a religious painting of Jesus addressing a mass of people—led to the conclusion she must be in the vicar's office.

"She complained that she was hot just before it happened," Fanny said, feeling Elizabeth's forehead, "though she doesn't seem to have a fever."

"Should I run and ask Jemmy to fetch the apothecary?" Georgie pocketed her vial and headed for the door.

"No." Trying to rise, Elizabeth's head spun even worse, and she dropped back onto the sofa. "Please. If I could be taken back to Lyttlefield Park and put to bed, I will be quite recovered by morning. I believe," she halted, then gathered her courage. "I was thinking about my wedding to Dickon, Charlotte. It must have upset me more than I thought. I believed I was over his death, but I see that is not true." She closed her eyes and sighed, fearing that might not be the reason at all.

"Of course, my dear." Jane stepped in to take charge. "Georgie, get your brother to fetch the carriage. Fanny, find Elizabeth's cloak, and Charlotte . . ." Jane stopped giving orders as the friends scattered. She grasped her cousin's hands. "You return to your husband and continue to Wrotham Park for the wedding breakfast. I am certain, after all the trouble to win his bride, Lord Wrotham will hardly heave without her."

"But Elizabeth—"

"I will see to Elizabeth." Jane hugged her cousin.

"I will be fine, Charlotte." Elizabeth raised up on her arm, which fortunately didn't make her head any worse. "Please, go and enjoy your wedding breakfast. Lord knows, you deserve it more than anyone else I know."

Brows puckered, Charlotte shifted from foot to foot, glancing toward the door. "As soon as the breakfast is over, I shall come to see you. If you are not better, I will go get Mr. Putnam myself." With that dire threat lingering in the air, Charlotte strode through the doorway.

"Now, my dear," Jane pierced her with China blue eyes. "What seems to be the matter?"

Turning a page in the tooled-leather copy of *The Monk*, by Mr. Gregory Lewis, that had been left in the room, Elizabeth shuddered at the alarming illustration of a monk pulling a young woman by her hair while raising a dagger to stab her. She snapped the volume closed. No further shocks today, thank you.

Laying it on the bedside table, she glanced away from the disturbing book. Who could have left such a work here?

Lord Fernley seemed a likely candidate. An extreme young man in every way. So fortunate he had not been invited to the wedding. He had quite set everyone's teeth on edge.

Of course, now she had nothing to read. She had quite recovered her senses and felt fine. All that fuss over her had not helped as much as good, old-fashioned rest. She glanced at the book again. It wouldn't take much effort to venture down to the library and choose something less sensational—preferably by Maria Edgeworth or Jane Austen. Somehow, though, she couldn't muster the energy to rise and go in search of something to read. Very well, then, a nap would insure that she would be ready to go down for dinner later. She yawned, and her eyes drooped shut. With a sigh, she turned on her side, wishing to shut out the whole debacle this morning. As she was just drifting off, a gentle tap, tap at the door jerked her awake.

Groggily she rubbed at her face and called, "Come."

The door opened and Charlotte popped around the walnut-paneled door, still attired in her wedding dress. "You weren't asleep, were you?"

"No, please come in." Elizabeth twisted around, her heart filled with dread. She might as well face Charlotte and get it over with. She'd ruined the wedding, and while her friend would forgive her, she would never forgive herself. Why was she doing this incredible number of horrible things?

"How are you feeling?" Charlotte settled herself on the side of the bed.

"I am truly well, save for being extremely tired. I cannot think why I cannot rouse myself more thoroughly." A languor did seem to have settled over her. Still, that was no excuse for her behavior at the church. She glanced away from Charlotte's face, filled with a concern and kindness that only stoked Elizabeth's guilt.

"I have found myself more tired of late as well." Charlotte gazed at Elizabeth's hand, as though unwilling to meet her eyes.

"Well, of course you are, what with all the wedding preparations, and readying Lyttlefield Park to close, moving your household into Wrotham Park. Anyone would be tired." Elizabeth twisted her hands. "I have no excuse, save an attack of the vapors."

"As long as you are well, Elizabeth. That is what matters most." Charlotte patted her hands and gently unclenched them. "Please don't—"

"No, Charlotte." Elizabeth moved restlessly beneath the covers. "I cannot excuse my . . . my disgraceful behavior at the wedding. God knows, you of all people deserved a perfect wedding day, and now I have spoiled it." Tears pricked her eyelids. She'd be weeping outright in a few moments. Why did she have to be a watering pot on top of everything else? "I'm so sorry."

"I said before you have spoiled nothing, my dear." She seized Elizabeth's fingers and shook them. "I am jubilantly happy to be married to Nash, and he is overawed in his new role of husband." Charlotte's face took on a serene beauty it seldom attained. "Husband. Never have I enjoyed saying that word more. Nothing you could have done, Elizabeth, save perhaps fire the church, could have taken the magic and joy from this day. So"—she fixed Elizabeth with eyes that suddenly glinted a vivid green—"what is the matter, my dear? Is there some illness I know nothing about?" She gripped Elizabeth's hands so tightly they ached. "Have you tried to spare me some ill news because of the wedding?"

"No, Charlotte, I swear to you, there is no illness." Elizabeth came to a complete stop, her earlier conversation with Jane weighing on her conscience.

"Nothing is wrong at home, or with the children?"

"Again, no, my dear. The children are fine, save that my mother has a tendency to try to raise them as she sees fit, rather than according to my wishes. Otherwise the children, my parents, my sisters are all very well."

"Only you, it seems, are not." The deepening concern on

Charlotte's face made Elizabeth's guilt grow. "I promise you can tell me anything, Elizabeth." Her friend took a deep breath, as though steeling herself for some unpleasantness, and gripped her hands. "Are you in love with Lord Brack?"

"Charlotte." Wanting to squirm like a worm washed out of the garden onto a pathway, Elizabeth tried to form an answer. "I . . . we . . ."

"I know you got on well together at the house parties, but when you went away so abruptly from the last one, I wondered if you had had a falling out." Charlotte worried her bottom lip, pulling at it with her teeth until Elizabeth feared she would draw blood. "Georgie swears she knows nothing, and Fanny refuses to speak, which makes me even more suspicious."

"Why would you say that?" Elizabeth eased herself up in the bed. At least Fanny had kept her confidence.

"Because you two have been so much in company in London. Fanny knows something, because if you had a secret she would pull it out of you quicker than a snake sheds its skin." She gripped Elizabeth's hands tightly. "I want you to trust me as much as you do Fanny."

"Fanny does know something," Elizabeth swallowed hard, "but she does not know everything."

"Surely, if there is a problem, I can help you now, Elizabeth. I am the Countess of Wrotham." Charlotte sat straighter, lifted her chin. "Whatever is wrong, Nash and I will do whatever it takes to make it right."

"I know you would if you could, but there is no help for it." Elizabeth lay back and drew the covers up to her chin.

"Would it help if Nash spoke to Lord Brack? If he has broken your heart, he will feel not only the wrath of Wrotham, but my personal vendetta against him as well." Eyes flashing, Charlotte jumped off the bed, her voice ringing out loudly as she began to pace the length of the room. "How dare he come here, like Lord Fernley with his advances, or . . . or make promises that he has no intention of keeping."

Aghast, Elizabeth drew back further into the soft mattress. Never had she ever seen her friend this frenzied, storming about like an avenging angel. The pose certainly became her—she'd become both terrifying and magnificent. Had Lord Brack actually done those things, he'd soon find himself at the unforgiving mercy of the Countess of Wrotham. But she had to step in and stop Charlotte from mowing a swath of destruction that would cut down anything in its path, including Jemmy.

"Charlotte, I assure you, it is not what you think." Her words arrested her friend mid-stride.

"What do you mean, 'not what I think'? Does it concern Lord Brack or not?" Deep green eyes glared at her.

"Yes, it does concern him; however—" She raised a finger to stop her friend's headlong push for vengeance. "He has made me no promises he is not willing to keep. He has made no unwilling advances." She sighed. "Quite to contrary."

"So all is well between you?" A perplexed frown marred Charlotte's face. "I don't understand."

"I have not spoken with him today, but I think I must. We had appointed today to settle things between us." Elizabeth shuddered to think how that coming interview would unfold.

"Why didn't you tell me?" Charlotte flopped onto the bed, her face now wreathed in smiles.

"I had not seen you, and I didn't like to write it." Sticking her resolve, Elizabeth looked her friend in the eyes. "But I will tell you now, and then I will see Lord Brack."

"And you will tell him . . . what?" Her friend's happy face smote her, yet she must continue.

"I must tell him I believe I am increasing."

Chapter 13

"**Y**ou believe what?" Color drained from Charlotte's face as her hand flew up to clutch her throat.

Elizabeth blinked back tears. Until recently, she hadn't given a thought to the possibility she could be with child. She and Dickon had been married a month, trying delightfully hard for her to become pregnant before he had to leave for the Peninsula campaign, but she had not conceived. So why would she have thought it could happen in just one night? "Yes, I believe I am going to have another child."

"And the father is . . . Lord Brack?" Charlotte whispered, as though she thought someone could hear her through the door.

"Of course, it is Lord Brack's child." Indignant, Elizabeth sat up in the bed. "Dickon has been dead for well over a year."

"No, no, my dear." A flustered Charlotte twisted the coverlet in her hands. "I only thought perhaps you had been attached to . . . or succumbed to an old friend in London. So of course, Lord Brack." Her brows knit. "But when did you . . ."

"The night of that wretched Harvest Festival." She covered her face. "When they crowned the Corn Maiden, something came over me, over us." Picturing the Harvest Lord kissing the Corn Maiden was all it took to make her blood begin to stir. "You really should ban that pagan ritual, Charlotte."

"You went into the fields at the festival and . . ." The excitement in Charlotte's voice jerked Elizabeth's gaze back to her friend, who was looking guilty herself.

"No, of course not." Indignation rose in Elizabeth once more. "Why would you think I'd do something *that* brazen?"

"Well, because . . ." Charlotte's face turned the exact shade of red of the apples in the still-life painting on the wall. "Nash and I . . ."

"Charlotte, you didn't!" Lord, she'd never have believed her friend could do such a bold thing. "My dear, how pagan of you." And Fanny had said she and Lord Lathbury had been in the shadows of the field as well. Perhaps the feeling of power that night hadn't been a product of her imagination.

"Nash said it was an ancient fertility custom. If the Harvest Lord and the Corn Maiden made a child in the field on that night, the spring crops would be plentiful. We had already agreed to marry, so . . ." Red now to the tips of her ears, Charlotte smiled and shrugged. "We even had a corn dolly presiding over us."

"A what?"

"A corn dolly. A little figure of a woman made from the last stalks of wheat cut this year. Also to insure fertility." Charlotte ducked her head. "Apparently it has worked, for I am certain I am increasing as well."

"Charlotte! Oh, my dear, how wonderful." Elizabeth hugged her friend, thanking the Lord for this good fortune. "Does Nash know?"

Charlotte nodded. "I told him as soon as I was certain, or fairly certain. I haven't had my courses since that night. I've also been tired lately and queasy in the mornings."

"Then I'd say you are almost definitely with child. My goodness. That makes three of us widows caught at your house parties, if you still count little Maria." That news had been the talk of the company even before the festival.

"Well, I suppose I must include the Countess of Kersey, because even though we cannot be certain she began increasing while she was here, she surely met the man here." A look of fleeting irritation passed over her friend's face.

"It seems you have already had practice as a matchmaking mama, Charlotte." Elizabeth laughed.

"Indeed, I have." Charlotte joined her, then quickly sobered. "So you will marry Lord Brack?"

Suddenly uncomfortable, Elizabeth sat up on the side of the bed. She had to come to terms with the only option she had left. "I suppose I must under the circumstances."

"You don't sound sure at all, my dear." Her friend's brows puckered into a deep V. "Do you not love him?"

"That is part of it, I suppose. There has been so much between us since that night." Oh, that wretched slip of the tongue. "He may be surer of his feelings than I am. But, Charlotte"—she grasped her friend's hand as though it were a lifeline—"is it possible to love two men at the same time? I do have very great affection and regard for Lord Brack, but I've never lost my love for Dickon." She hung her head. "What if I never do?"

"Will it matter very much? Dickon is gone, my dear. Are you afraid his spirit will haunt you if you are happy once more?"

A shudder rippled down Elizabeth's spine. "You have no idea. Perhaps it has already been haunting me."

"Nonsense." Rising from the bed, Charlotte released Elizabeth's hand. "Dickon would want you to be happy, not to pine for him for all the rest of your days. He was not a selfish man."

"No, he was not." She hadn't looked at it that way before. "And I don't believe he would want me to be sad and mourn him forever."

"Good. I hope that is settled in your mind." Charlotte

nodded and made for the door. "Why don't you remain in bed this evening? I'll send a tray up and make your excuses." She turned back, her hand on the door handle.

"That may be best." Elizabeth slid her hand over her stomach, flat for now, but not for long. "I will have the evening to practice how I'm going to tell him that I'm carrying his child."

The door bounded inward, pushing Charlotte and making her stumble backward.

Georgie fell into the room, her face red, her eyes round and wild. "I came to see how you were doing, Elizabeth. Jemmy sent me because he's been going mad with worry ever since you swooned, but . . ." Georgie halted mid-sentence and stared at Elizabeth's nightgown clad midsection. "I . . . I . . ."

"Georgie, it is all right." Charlotte put her arm around the distraught girl. "Elizabeth has just been telling me of her situation. She should tell you as well."

"I don't think I want to know, Charlotte. Not if it will break Jemmy's heart." Burrowing into Charlotte's shoulder, Georgie sniffed loudly.

"I truly hope it will not break his heart, Georgie." Trying not to smile at her friend's mistaken assumption, Elizabeth eased out of the bed. "Not if I tell him I am almost sure I am carrying his child."

"Jemmy's child?" Georgie's head popped up off Charlotte's shoulder, her mouth a large O. "But that is impossible. Jemmy told me you and he had had a falling out, that he didn't know if you'd ever speak to him again."

"That is only partly true." Elizabeth took her friend's arm and led her back to the bed, motioning her to sit. "We did fall out several months ago; however, this happened before that, when we had grown very . . . close." She eased over toward Georgie, who still stared at her with accusing eyes. "I would never dissemble about such a thing either to you or to Jemmy. I swear to you, I am increasing, and it is Jemmy's child."

"Elizabeth!" Georgie launched herself into her friend's arms. "I am so, so very happy for you. For Jemmy. I knew you couldn't stay mad at him. He's too wonderful for anyone to dislike for long." She continued to hold her in a stranglehold.

"I think I must agree with you, dear." Disengaging the enthusiastic Georgie and standing her on her feet, Charlotte came to the rescue before Elizabeth came to harm. "Lord Brack has been most charming to me and to Elizabeth all through our acquaintance."

"Shall I go fetch him, Elizabeth?" Georgie bounded over to the door. "You'll want to tell him straightaway. He's downstairs drinking with Lord Lathbury, and neither one looks particularly happy."

"I am not sure Elizabeth is up to any more excitement this afternoon." Charlotte put out a restraining hand. "She's had a most exciting day."

"As have you, Charlotte. It's your wedding day, don't forget." Elizabeth laughed as she slid back under the covers, thankful she could put off her meeting with Lord Brack just a little while longer.

"I suspect Nash will not let me forget that for one second once I return to Wrotham Park." Charlotte smiled and blushed. "I have vowed I shall have breakfast in bed tomorrow, as a proper married lady should."

"I suspect you will need your rest, Charlotte," Georgie piped up.

"Georgie!" Elizabeth laughed as the girl turned crimson-faced.

"Well, I have been married too, you remember." Poking the carpet with the toe of her green silk slipper, Georgie seemed to trace the blue and white pattern. "I know what men are like on their wedding night."

"I, however, do not, although I can make a guess." Charlotte laughed and opened the door. "Thank you for the warning, Lady Georgina." She winked at Elizabeth. "In any case, I am quite certain my husband will enlighten me shortly. Good night, Elizabeth. Georgie, I will see you at dinner at Wrotham Park." Charlotte left, still laughing.

"Do let Jemmy come see you, Elizabeth. He will be so thrilled. And you both will live happily ever after, just like in the fairy stories." Georgie sighed contentedly, her smile and shining eyes making her look like a character from a fairy tale herself. "I hope I will get another chance at one."

"If I can, you certainly can, my dear." Elizabeth hoped that was true. "However, I think I should let my news wait until the morrow. I would not want to overdo and have anything go amiss."

"Goodness no." Georgie flew to the bedside. "I agree, you must rest." Tucking the covers around Elizabeth, she continued to fuss over her. "I'll make sure they send your tray up immediately. You must keep up your strength. And I'll insist they send up hot soup. Nanny always gave us hot soup when we were under the weather. It was actually quite nasty stuff, but I daresay Charlotte's cooks are better than ours."

Suppressing a grin, Elizabeth bit her lip before replying, "Thank you, Georgie. You are a true friend and a comfort." She relaxed into the warm sheets. A good long sleep would do her worlds of good.

"Will you write a note to Jemmy before you sleep? He is truly worried about you." Georgie rummaged in the small writing desk in the corner and withdrew pen, ink, and paper, and returned to the bed looking like a hopeful puppy.

"All right. If I cannot see him, I can write, but only to say I am not ill, only fatigued, and he is not to worry." She took up the pen, using *The Monk* as a makeshift writing desk. "And I will ask to see him first thing in the morning," she said, scratching quickly across the creamy paper. "However, you must promise me you will tell him nothing of what I have confided to you. This news must come from me and no one else." She wafted the notepaper to and fro, then folded it in quarters.

"I promise, on my honor, not to say a word, even though it will be direst torture for me to do so." Georgie took the letter, that dreamy look coming over her face once more. "How peculiar that I know I am to be an aunt before Jemmy knows he is to be a father." Beaming at Elizabeth, she fluttered her hand and hurried out the door.

Elizabeth fell back on the pillows, quite as exhausted as if she'd danced every set at a ball. Something told her that feeling would not disappear for a very long time to come.

Staring into the amber swirls of his third whiskey since the wedding, Jemmy had to close his eyes against the dizzying speed. He'd be too foxed to go to Elizabeth if she did ask for him. Where the hell was Georgie? The clock ticking on the library's mantel piece read just after four o'clock. His sister had been gone at least an hour. He couldn't take much more of this waiting. The towering shelves of tomes that lined the room's walls seemed to be closing in on him.

His companion, Lord Lathbury, stared into the fire from the tall-backed leather chair across the room, a similar libation clutched in his hand. Probably his fourth of the afternoon. Lathbury hadn't said a word after the ceremony, although beforehand he'd been quite jovial. Jemmy had seen him talking very animatedly to Lady Stephen after they'd put Elizabeth into the carriage. He'd been distracted by Elizabeth's illness, but not so much that he didn't recognize an argument when he saw one.

Now the tall, square-shouldered earl sat in morose silence, drowning his sorrows, whatever they were, much like Jemmy. At least Wrotham had looked happy today, as a groom should. Jemmy only hoped he'd get the chance to find out himself.

Glancing at the clock again—only five minutes had passed, which had to be wrong—he swore he'd throttle Georgie if she ever made an appearance. At least those thoughts kept him from dwelling on what might be happening with Elizabeth.

His heart must have actually stopped when she collapsed into the aisle at St. George's. Wrotham had gotten to her first, sweeping her up into his arms and carrying her into the vicarage just behind the church.

Jemmy'd waited an hour in the cold until she emerged, pale but walking on her own, with Lady George Tarkington at her side. He'd tried to get to her, but Georgie had restrained him. Irritation had mounted when he had arrived at Lyttlefield Park, only to be banished to the library to drink and wait. He took another sip. At this rate, he'd be bedding down here in the library, unable to make it to his room, much less Wrotham Park for dinner.

The patter of running feet brought him to attention a moment before Georgina burst into the room waving a piece of paper.

"Jemmy, Jemmy, oh, Jemmy." She skidded to a stop in front of him. "I beg your pardon, Lord Lathbury. I didn't know you were still here." She curtsied to the brooding man, then looked to him expectantly.

Lathbury rose to his full six-foot, three-inch height, bowed to them, and stalked out of the room, glass still clutched in his hand.

Georgie's eyebrows rose to new heights.

"Don't pay him any mind. Love trouble, if I don't miss my guess. A hazard for this particular party, it seems." Jemmy shook his head. Mistake. He set the glass down on the mantle. "Is that for me?"

She nodded, eyes twinkling a fetching shade of green. "Do you want to know what it says?"

He held his breath and nodded, his heart in this throat.

"Well, I can't tell you."

"What? Why not?" Was Elizabeth playing games with him with Georgie as a go-between?

"Because I don't know what she wrote, silly." She held out the letter, and he snatched it, like it was a burning raisin in a game of Snapdragon.

"Brat. You should be sent to bed without your supper." He unfolded the note, trying to steady it enough to read.

"You had best go change if you want to dine, brother. Besides," her eyes twinkled mischievously, "I know more than what's in that note."

"You said you didn't know what was in it."

"I don't know the exact words, but I know the gist of it and more."

"You do?" Jemmy read the note, drinking in the words like a man dying of thirst, only to stop short of the first sip. "She says she cannot see me tonight." He had known she had not been well ever since that swoon.

"She needs her rest, Jemmy."

No, she needed to see him, dammit. Unwillingly, he came back to earth. "I suppose she does need that. Did Putnam see to her? Did you learn anything else about how she does?" He stopped reading, only now realizing his sister's earlier boast.

"No and yes." She put her hands behind her back, as though she was reciting in the schoolroom.

"Georgina Celeste Abigail Cross Kirkpatrick, I will take a birch to you if you don't tell me this minute—"

"Really, Jemmy, you are too easily baited." She laughed and plucked the letter from his fingers. "Did you see she asks to meet you in the morning? At breakfast."

"Yes, I saw that." Jemmy sighed and unclenched his hands. He must remain calm. "But what else have you heard, Georgie? You must know I am on tenterhooks. Did you speak with her? Is she truly ill?" Why would no one reassure him of her good health? Fear gripped him at the thought she had fallen gravely ill.

"I did talk with her, Jemmy." The teasing look vanished from his sister's face. "And I can assure you she had no illness. She is very tired and is taking dinner in her room, but that is all." She gripped his arm. "You can rest easy on that score, my dear."

The tension easing all through him, Jemmy suddenly found himself seated in the chair Lathbury had vacated. "Then why did she swoon in church?" There must be something more to it than that.

"Women swoon all the time."

"They do not." He thought back. Had he seen many women faint? Or had he paid no attention? "Do they? I don't recall ever having seen one do so. Have you ever swooned?"

"Oh, yes, lots of times." Plopping onto the chair across from him, Georgie nodded enthusiastically. "Sometimes for real, but quite often just for effect."

"For effect?" Deuced odd. "Whatever do you mean?"

"Ladies pretend to swoon sometimes to assure gentlemen that they are fragile flowers." She wrinkled her nose. "But then other ladies give you smelling salts, which are not nice to smell at all."

"They pretend?" Why had he never known this?

"Yes, but there is no harm in it." She shook her head, her face sober. "However, sometimes a lady's clothing will become too warm, or a day is hot, or you walk too fast and get out of breath and just, well, faint. It truly is a quite common occurrence." She cocked her head, slightly frowning. "You really have not seen a woman faint before?"

"Not that I recall." Perhaps he'd not paid attention to such things, or else . . . "Are you telling me the truth, Georgie?"

"Did you not see every woman in the church pull out her vinaigrette?"

That he remembered. He'd thought it odd at the time as well. Apparently, he'd been lucky up until now not to have seen a woman so indisposed. He hoped Elizabeth was not one to swoon often. Her collapse had frightened him as nothing else ever had. "Yes, I did see that. How interesting. I hadn't noticed ladies doing that before this either."

"There is a lot you need to learn about ladies, Jemmy." Georgie smiled and stood, bringing Jemmy to his feet. She rose on tiptoe to kiss his cheek. "Starting tomorrow morning." A swift embrace, then she ran nimbly out of the room.

With a sigh, Jemmy retrieved his drink and refreshed it from the library's cut-glass decanter. This might be the only way he would make it through tonight in order to face Elizabeth in the morning.

Chapter 14

For at least the twentieth time, Elizabeth turned over in the bed, trying to get comfortable. The clock on the mantle softly chimed the hour, the second time it had done so since she'd awakened from a curious dream about Dickon.

She'd dreamed about her late husband many times since the tragic day she'd learned of his death. Dreams where he acted courageously on the battlefield, dreams in which they'd danced at their first ball, shared their first kiss. In all the dreams she'd had, however, she'd never heard his voice. He would smile at her, and she could almost feel the touch of his hand, his lips. Every time, she'd awaken with tears trickling down her cheeks or discover her pillow cold and damp where they'd fallen.

This dream had been very different.

She stared up into the still blackness, her heart beating loudly in her ears, remembering. This dream had begun as many of her dreams did, on the battlefield at Waterloo. The acrid smoke of gunfire and artillery hung low, like a smudge, over the gouged and torn field, almost as thick as soup. Glimpses of men fighting appeared as though vignettes in a play, revealed by the capricious swirling fog. She was tramping across the battleground, clutching a dark red shawl about her shoulders, searching for Dickon. She'd had no fear for her own death—she was invincible in this dream—only of not finding her husband before it was too late. Directly ahead of her, the smoke cleared momentarily, and she saw Dickon, his red officer's uniform smudged with dirt and soot, standing amid a circle of blue-clad French soldiers, all dead. He turned to her, his sword bright with blood. With a crisp wave of his sabre, he saluted her, gave her the boyish grin she loved so much, then returned his attention to the next wave of blue-clad men attacking up the hill.

Even in the dream, she had feared she would see him wounded, struck in the head with the bullet that took his life. But the swirling mist covered the scene as the dream changed and a hand on her shoulder shook her awake.

She opened her eyes on the small rose garden she'd tended so lovingly in Russell Square. She was seated on the small stone bench under the trellis by the rear door, roses of all description riotously in bloom. Pinks, whites, reds, yellows—some roses she'd never planted there—were blooming everywhere.

The hand on her shoulder tightened, and she turned her head to find the warm, familiar gaze of adoration from Dickon's deep blue eyes. "Elizabeth, my love. Were you asleep?"

A thrill of hope surged through her. She had been asleep, been dreaming this whole time that Dickon had been killed. But now she must be awake, for she could hear him, hear the beloved voice, so deep and tender. Clasping his hand, she gave joyful thanks to God that her nightmare was finally over.

Her gaze shifted from his dear face to his uniform, torn here and there with cuts, stained with blood and dirt. She glanced down to her own ragged appearance, the blood-red shawl she had never possessed covering the black crepe gown of her early widowhood.

"Yes, my love. I have been asleep for a long time, it seems."

Tenderly, she cupped the beloved face, so strong and handsome, even streaked with sweat and grime and the hideous red. "But I am awake now. Oh, Dickon." She leaned her forehead on his, all her sorrow and hurt pressing against him. "I have missed you so much. Please don't leave me, my love."

He raised his head, his kind eyes crinkling at the corners as he smiled. "I am yours forever, my darling. I will be with you always. For as long as you continue to love, my love for you can never truly die."

He tried to lean away from her, but she pulled him back. "One kiss, my love. One kiss, I beg of you." The pain in her chest from unshed tears might crush her.

Dickon laughed and pulled her full against him. "You were ever greedy of our kisses. How can I resist you now?"

Lips, soft and warm, met hers. The spicy familiar scent he always wore assailed her as she urged his mouth open. Yes, she had ever been greedy of his kisses. Why would that change now? She drank him in, like an elixir of life, taking strength from him one last time.

She had opened her eyes on the darkness of her room at Lyttlefield Park and had known she was truly awake. She expected the crushing grief that always followed these dreams to grip her once more. Instead, she'd been seized by a restlessness, tossing and turning about dry-eyed in the soft bed. Sad, yet somehow content, for she had bid Dickon farewell at last.

The bedclothes suddenly weighed her down. She thrust them back and sat up to light the lamp. She prowled over to the window, her bare feet shrinking from the cold floor. No sight of dawn yet. It should be light by now, not the middle of the night. Likely she'd sleep no more tonight, though she would dutifully try. She climbed back into the bed, tucking the covers around her. Now what?

Shadows danced in the corners of the room as Elizabeth tried to settle down after that disturbingly real dream. What had brought it on was obvious even to her: the turmoil in her heart over wanting a male presence in her life—a very specific male presence, to be sure. One she must confront on the morrow—or later today, in fact.

Jemmy's handsome, boyish face and bright curly hair came to her mind's eye easily, as if he actually stood before her. Just as he had two months before in this very room. Good Lord.

She slid down beneath the covers, resisting the urge to pull the sheet over her face. This had been her room during the October house party. The copy of *The Monk* had been on the nightstand then, and she'd been curious about it. Which meant that the bed she'd been sleeping in, been dreaming of kissing her husband in, was the same one in which she'd— gracious! She didn't want to think of what they'd done in this bed.

Lord Brack. Jemmy. Though it was difficult, she must start thinking of him thus. The young gentleman had touched a chord deep within her when they'd melded their bodies. She'd no idea how hungry she'd been for a man's touch, and Jemmy's had been skillful, masterful. He'd been able to make her forget her grief for Dickon through the renewal of the carnal pleasures she'd enjoyed almost constantly when her husband had been in Town.

Oh, dear. The two experiences—passionate love with Dickon and equally passionate lust, stoked by that disgraceful pagan ritual—had begun to blend together, the one nearly becoming one with the other. Did she indeed wish to let go of the past? Did Dickon wish for their love to continue through her happiness? She had a high standard for any man to live up to in Dickon. Would Jemmy be able to take on such a daunting task? He seemed truly fond of her, magnanimously forgiving her for calling him by another man's name. If one thought about it in just the right light, Jemmy could take it as a compliment that he could be so skillful as to make her believe he was Dickon at that final shuddering release of emotion. In any case, like it or not, they had shared the ultimate intimacy, and from that had come a child.

A child who would, perhaps, have riotously curly blond hair and a sunny disposition to match. So she must do her duty, her duty to the child, and perhaps to herself as well, to be happy. For her, for Dickon, for the baby. Happiness had been a stranger to her for so long she couldn't admit that for her to be happy did not disrespect or betray her late husband's memory. Rather it was his benediction for her to live her life and make her peace with him.

Peace, like a mantle of softest wool, settled over Elizabeth, embracing her even as she enfolded it in her heart. She rather hoped the peace would aid her to sleep again, but no. Ten minutes later, she still tossed and turned, mulling it all over again in her head. If she remained like this, she would go mad.

In desperation, she glanced at *The Monk* and shuddered. Many books were an aid to sleep; however, Lewis's sensational volume did not have that reputation. On the contrary, if one wished to remain awake, some of the more lurid passages would certainly do the trick.

Throwing back the covers, she slid to her feet and thrust them into slippers. No one would be stirring at this hour. She would pop down to the library and find something more soothing to read. Donning her dark blue wrapper, she grabbed the big leather tome and the candle, and made her way downstairs.

The corridors were dim, shadows shrinking and growing as she passed through them. Thankfully, no one else seemed to be abroad, though the servants would be rising soon. Good. She could find her book and return upstairs without anyone seeing her and asking difficult questions she'd much rather not answer at the moment.

The door to the library stood open, its dark interior yawning before her like a great black mouth.

All the better to eat you with, my dear. Really, she must

stop these fanciful thoughts. What on earth had gotten into her tonight?

She hurried forward, the candle wavering, casting huge shadows that seemed to twist and sway. Perhaps it was the book. The gothic nature of *The Monk*, what little she'd read of it, had infused her with these ridiculous, irrational fears. Best to get it out of her hands at once.

Glancing about at the towering shelves of books, she saw no gap large enough in the tightly packed volumes to suggest where *The Monk* belonged. As she moved from shelf to shelf, the silence of the room began to weigh on her. Maybe she should simply put the book on the library table for a servant to return to its proper place. She could choose another book to read at a later time. That would allow her to make a swift retreat to her room before her imagination got the best of her.

She padded softly to the polished mahogany table in the center of the room, to lay the book on it. In her haste, the edge of the leather binding slid off her fingertips and thumped onto the table with a loud, hollow thud.

"Who's there?"

Elizabeth screamed, whirling toward the voice that boomed unexpectedly from behind the sofa that faced the cold fireplace. The candle flickered wildly and blew out, plunging the room into darkness. Who could be here at this time of night? Step by careful step, Elizabeth backed toward the door. If she could make it to the corridor, she could run for her room before the person could catch her.

"I say, don't be afraid."

The now-familiar voice stopped her as she reached the doorway. "Lord Brack?"

A quickly indrawn breath from the darkness. "Elizabeth?"

Relief washed through her, to be followed immediately by sheer panic. Jemmy was the last person she wished to see. What was he doing in the library in the middle of the night?

The scratch of flint and steel and a candle flared, revealing Lord Brack in shirtsleeves, blinking owlishly as he held the candlestick up. The flickering light illuminated his disheveled appearance—rumpled shirt, cravat hanging limply on either side of his neck, hair sticking up in unruly abandon.

Her heart thundered loudly in her chest.

"Elizabeth, what are you doing here in the middle of the night?" A concerned frown deepened as he set the flame down and strode quickly toward her. "Are you not well?" He grasped her hands. "Shall I fetch someone for you?"

Disarmed by his sudden nearness, Elizabeth reveled in the warm, strong hands on hers. The faintly salty male scent of him sent a wave of desire coursing through her, heating her from toes to eyebrows. Gasping at his touch, she whispered, "No, no, I am fine, my lord."

"I'm afraid I don't believe you, my dear." His frown almost reached his nose now. "Your cheeks are flushed, and you're trembling. You fainted in the church this morning. Obviously, you are not well."

"I swear to you I am not ill." She swallowed, trying to get moisture into a mouth gone dry as a desert. After so much time apart, the nearness of him quite went to her head. Dizzy with the excitement, she squeezed his hands and swayed toward him.

"My dear! You are *not* well. Here." He slid his arm around her shoulders and steered her toward the shadowy sofa. "Sit here, and I will ring for Fisk. He can send a footman for Mr. Putnam."

"Oh, no, my lord. I truly am well." She snared his hand as he grabbed his jacket. "I promise you. I came here to return a book and exchange it for something that would be more encouraging to sleep."

"What were you reading that was keeping you up?"

"*The Monk*." She pointed to the volume on the table. "Do you know it?"

Lord Brack chuckled as he settled his jacket over his shoulders.

Elizabeth wished he hadn't done that. The sight of his dishabille had set her pulse to racing rather pleasantly.

"I do. And I agree it is a book hardly conducive to a peaceful night's repose." He sat beside her on the leather sofa and ran a hand through his hair, standing it up on end with a rather appealing, rakish charm.

"So I thought I would find something by Mrs. Amelia Perriwinkle. Her books are always so amusing." Pulling her wrapper tighter around her, Elizabeth's awareness of the intimate nature of their situation increased. That she was more strongly attracted to him than ever became clearer every moment she spent in his presence.

"Yes, I believe they are." His gaze had strayed to her face, fixing on her mouth with a longing that made her stomach clench.

"And why are you here this time of night, my lord? Were you unable to sleep as well?"

He jerked upright, a hint of color in his cheeks. "Not exactly." A sigh escaped him, and he avoided her eyes. "I was concerned about your welfare when Georgina told me you would not be at dinner. When we returned from Wrotham Park, I was too restless to sleep and came in here for a drink." He grunted. "Several drinks, if you have not already guessed. Eventually, I took off my jacket to make myself more comfortable and lay down on the sofa. Until you roused me." He cleared his throat, his gaze shooting back to pin her to the sofa.

Elizabeth coughed, hoping for more time. She wasn't prepared for this tonight.

"I wish you would tell me the truth, Elizabeth. I am beginning to think you simply wish to avoid me. If it hadn't been for the episode in church." Gazing earnestly into her eyes, he ran his thumb gently over her knuckles. "I am worried about you, my love."

The sweet endearment melted her heart and the last vestige of her resistance. She must tell him. He must know, before they could go forward together. Gathering her courage, she clasped his hands. "I promise you, my lord, I truly am well. You are, however, correct that there was a reason for my swoon earlier." Drawing herself up, looking him straight in his eager, worried eyes, she said simply, "I am almost certain I am carrying your child."

Lord Brack blinked rapidly, his brows bunching together as his mouth dropped open. "I . . . I beg your pardon, but I was a bit foxed before. Did you say you are—" His gaze shot to her abdomen, though it was well cloaked by her wrapper. "Did you say you are carrying our child?"

Hearing him call it "their" child filled her with a sizzling warmth. A worry she hadn't even recognized as a concern—that he would deny the child—slid from her shoulders. "Yes, my lord, you did. I am."

"Oh, Elizabeth." He enfolded her in his arms and stood, lifting her off the sofa and crushing her to his chest.

"Oomph." He'd surprised a gasp out of her.

"Oh, Lord, did I hurt you?" He lowered her immediately to her feet and stepped back. The worry lines of his face were thrown into stark relief in the candlelight as he frantically looked her up and down.

"No, I am fine. A bit startled, is all." And a lot relieved.

"As am I." He turned away, walking in a circle, running his hand through his hair, rumpling it even more thoroughly. "I can scarce take it in. A child," he said, wonderingly. "And if a boy, my heir. Good Lord."

To her astonishment, he threw himself at her feet, grasped her hands, and looked up at her, beseeching. "Elizabeth, please, please do me the very great honor of becoming my wife."

She'd known he would ask again, even before her revelation. Their last encounter in London had all but assured her he was eager for them to wed. And she too was ready now. Gone were any reservations about her indiscretion in bed, and though they had not spoken of love, she could assure herself the passion that burned between them like a bright sun would one day transform into the deep, steady abiding love she had known before. "Yes, Lord Brack," she said, smiling down into his boyishly eager face, "I will marry you."

He leaped up, joy in his wide smile, and grasped her face, pressing her lips to his in a kiss that left no doubt about his passion.

His lips were soft as she remembered, but much more insistent, sweet with hints of the whiskey he'd drunk earlier. Delicious in every way. He ran his tongue along the seam of her mouth, and she eagerly opened to allow their kiss to deepen, to welcome him into her, into her life.

She relaxed against his hard body, enjoying the warmth spreading throughout her as she touched more and more of him. She would be greedy of this man's kisses as well.

With a groan, he pulled away from her, surreptitiously adjusting his breeches. "You have made me the happiest man alive, my darling, save in one thing."

Lost in the afterglow of that delicious kiss, Elizabeth smiled but shook her head. "I think we should display caution yet, my lord. We may be betrothed, but I do not believe the library is quite the place for more of a tryst than this."

Chuckling, he shook his head. "God knows, I desire you in every way, my love, yet that was not quite what I referred to."

"It wasn't?" She stared longingly at his mouth, hungry for it even now.

"No. What would make my happiness complete right now is for you to call me Jemmy."

The fire that shot to her cheeks surely warmed the library. She ducked her head to avoid his eyes. "I will confess I have thought of you that way for some time now, though I still feel strange addressing you as . . . Jemmy." The wretched blaze in her face increased. The name sounded strange on her tongue, but when she finally raised her head to him, his eyes shone with joy. He kissed her hands with a renewed fervor that touched her heart.

"Now I do claim to be happiest man in the world." The coiled excitement in him made her fear he might shout the house awake just to tell them the news. "Will you go with me tomorrow to my father to inform him about our intentions? He's at Blackham Castle in East Sussex, scarcely a half day's carriage ride from here."

"I think that would be lovely. Will Georgie accompany us?" She knew Georgie had been disinherited upon her marriage to a vicar's son, but her friend had hoped time and her widowed state might change her father's mind.

"No." He shook his head sadly. "That avenue is not quite open to her as yet, unfortunately. But while we are there, I will plead my sister's case. It is time Father relented and opened his arms to her again. Of course, if he does not, we will soon be able to make her circumstances better." He twined her arm through his, lit her candle, and started out of the library on an optimistic note.

Elizabeth sighed, contented as she had not been for more than a year. Perhaps her dream and that wretched book had led to a wonderful new chapter in her life after all.

Chapter 15

Jemmy's carriage rolled up to the front door of Lyttlefield Park at precisely nine o'clock later that morning. He'd already breakfasted early, in the company of Elizabeth, who stood beside him, looking fresh and pretty as a summer sky. Her pale blue spencer had a matching bonnet that framed her lovely face and brightened the blue of her eyes to azure.

They should have been weary and yawning after their late-night assignation, but he supposed the excitement of the moment kept him at least alert. However, there would be time to nap in the carriage during the long ride.

"Will you spend the night at Blackham, Jemmy?" Georgie had come out with them to see them off, the crisp air pinking her cheeks.

"Yes, it will take more than half the day to reach the estate." He handed Elizabeth in and turned back to his sister. "I wish you were coming with us."

"I do as well." Georgie wrinkled her nose and pursed her lips unattractively, making him laugh. "I wonder what would happen if I simply showed up on Father's doorstep? Do you think he'd make me sleep in the stable?" Her lips quirked into a smile, but her eyes were now sober.

"Doubtful; however, we will not tempt the fates today. I will speak to him, though, about your returning after Lady Cavendish removes to Wrotham Park. If you are very sure you wouldn't rather return to Mrs. Reynolds and the Kirkpatricks?" What a choice to have to make. Elizabeth had told him just how badly his sister had been treated by her sister-in-law.

"Rather like having to decide between Scylla and Charybdis. Live with a sea monster with six heads or a whirlpool that sucks you to the bottom of the sea." Georgie's rueful smile went straight to his heart. "I can see Mrs. Reynolds with six heads, and not one of them with anything nice to say to me."

His sister's woebegone face settled the matter. He must bring his father around and make him allow Georgie to return home at least for the short while before the Season began. Then, if she made a match Father approved of, she could marry and leave Blackham before the summer was out. Pity she hadn't gotten on better with his friend, the Marquess of St. Just, a very eligible *parti* in the *ton* right now.

"You'd best be off, Jemmy. Don't stand here staring like a mooncalf." She giggled as she playfully steered him toward the waiting carriage. "Give my love to Father, if he'll have it."

Jemmy nodded, bussed her cheek, and stepped up into the carriage. The door shut, and the coachman started the team.

Clutching her thick black shawl about her shoulders, Georgie continued to wave at him until the carriage turned into the long, tree-lined driveway and she was lost to him.

Settling back against the soft leather seat, he smiled at Elizabeth and took her hand. "I have hopes of mediating a reunion with Georgie and our father. After I've introduced him to you and he is secure in the knowledge that his heir is perhaps on the way, I'll wager he'll be in a more lenient frame of mind."

"I only hope he will not be shocked by the news." Elizabeth trembled at what Lord Blackham would think of her, already breeding before the wedding. It happened quite frequently in *ton* circles, even in the best of families. As long as the couple wed before the birth, nothing was thought about such situations.

"Father is seldom shocked by anything." Jemmy busied himself tucking the carriage robe more securely around Elizabeth. "Although his youngest child defying him may have done so. Disowning her has hurt not only her, but the whole family as well. My brother and other sisters have felt it keenly that they've not been able to see Georgina for almost three years now. Longer, I believe, for our sisters, who live rather far from central England."

"You have a brother and other sisters?" Elizabeth perked up. "Georgie didn't tell me. I shall have to scold her for that." She snuggled beneath the carriage blanket, looking at him with rapt attention. "Instead of dreading the meeting with your father, I can be your captive audience while you regale me with stories about your family. Georgie spoke only of her brief time with Isaac." Elizabeth glanced down to the rough, chilly floor of the carriage. "I must confess I sympathized with her decision to do so. However, I would dearly love to hear more about your family."

"One that you are soon to become a part of, my dear." He could scarcely believe it, though he spoke the words. "Yes, Emma, Countess of Ainnes, is the elder of the twins by approximately five minutes. She's that much older than Mary, Marchioness of Daverscombe, whose precedence now puts her several places higher than Emma, for which Emma has never forgiven her." He couldn't help chuckling. "They have ever been in competition."

"My children are much the same," Elizabeth sighed. "Both Colin and Kate have always wanted to win, no matter what the prize. An extra treat at dinner time or an outing to the park, each must be the one to win." She eyed him inquisitively. "I wonder if all twins are the same in that respect."

"Perhaps we will know in good time." He cast a glance at her stomach, well-hidden by her coat and her plaid carriage shawl once more. Even though he could see nothing—nothing to see at this stage of the game—he wanted that assurance nonetheless. He'd be more than thrilled to have two babies in the household. With Elizabeth's other two children, it would be quite the ready family. They must give some serious thought to where they would live.

"Since our family will be expanding quickly, would you rather live in Town this winter and remove to one of my father's country estates after the baby is born or leave immediately after the wedding?" Best they get this settled so they weren't at sixes and sevens when the time loomed large.

"There are merits to both schemes, my dear." She patted his arm, and hot desire shot through his veins at that merest touch. This short ride might be interminable. "In Town, my mother would be near when my confinement begins. That was a comfort when the twins were born."

The charming, perplexed look on her beautiful face made him ache to take her in his arms and smooth away her frowns. She should never feel distress at anything if he could find a way to remedy the problem. "As we have at least two weeks before the wedding, while the banns are read, why don't we consult your mother as well before we come to a decision? I will leave it totally in your hands, my love."

"Thank you." Frown disappearing, she relaxed against him.

He must find a way to prevent her worrying a jot, lest it harm the child. "For now, let us concentrate on this audience with Father."

"Audience?"

"Trust me, it will be an audience in all senses of the word." He smiled, raising her hand for a kiss. "But do not be alarmed. He will love you as much as I do."

"Really?" One well-shaped eyebrow rose.

"Actually, no." He pulled her face to his, touching his mouth to her soft, pink lips. "No one could ever love you as much as I do." Her mouth grew insistent, and his shaft sprang to attention. Perhaps he'd better purchase a special license instead. After such a long time, he wanted Elizabeth back in his bed as soon as humanly possible.

Sometime after noon, the carriage swept up the driveway of white crushed shells to the front door of Blackham Castle. Jemmy never failed to shiver at its imposing black stone façade, rising three stories from the ground. Half castle, half Tudor manor, Blackham had known William the Conqueror's boots, Henry V's footfalls, Henry VIII's lumbering tread, and, most recently, the Prince Regent's legs beneath his father's table. The castle had seen its share of triumph and tragedy, although today's entry had to be Jemmy's most personal victory. Bringing his bride to the ancestral home ranked higher than anything he'd ever done to give him both pride and pleasure.

Excitement making him rash, he jumped out of the carriage before the horses had quite stopped, then waited until it settled to carefully hand Elizabeth down.

She craned her neck back, gazing up at the forbidding edifice, and her face paled.

Best get her inside before she took ill or changed her mind about marrying him. The day had begun cold and had become progressively chillier as they had stopped to change horses. He offered her his arm, and they proceeded up the two short steps of the portico and rapped on the door. The hollow sound had scarce begun before the massive black door—stained, his father had told him, with a mixture that included actual human blood—creaked open.

"My lord." Quick, the butler who had been with his father since before Jemmy's birth, inclined his silvery head. "His lordship will be delighted to see you."

His father was never delighted to see anyone, but that was about to change. "Thank you, Quick. I believe that will be an understatement shortly. This is Mrs. Easton." He shot a grin at the older man. "You may wish us happy, Quick. Mrs. Easton, a war widow, has consented to marry me and make me the happiest man alive."

"My felicitations, my lord, Mrs. Easton." Quick's eyes had widened, but he seemed to recover. "His lordship is in his office."

"Naturally." Seldom did his father sit anywhere else, save the dining room table. "Please ready Lady Georgina's old room for Mrs. Easton. I trust mine will do for me once more?"

"Of course, my lord." They followed Quick down the familiar gray stone passageway, up to the first floor and into his father's sanctuary.

The Marquess of Blackham sat behind the black walnut captain's table—a spoil of war reportedly given to the Cross family by Sir Francis Drake in 1581—head bent as his pen scratched across the sheet of white paper.

"Lord Brack and Mrs. Easton, my lord." Quick bowed and hurried out.

"Hello, Father." Jemmy waited.

The marquess would naturally finish his business before greeting his son.

Jemmy patted Elizabeth's hand, secured in the crook of his elbow, and shot her a smile of encouragement. He'd tried to prepare her for his father's likely gruff reception. She seemed serene standing beside him, a small tilt to her lips. Her hand on his trembled, however, and he prayed Father would not upset her further. There was the welfare of the child to think about.

Some minutes later, his father straightened his shoulders. The pen that had been scratching across the paper continuously slowed. A final period, and the marquess stabbed the pen a final time into the inkpot. With a flourish, the old man signed his name, leaned back, and raised his head.

Father hadn't changed much since he'd last seen him—in September, was it? The deeply grooved lines around his mouth were a bit more heavily shadowed than when last he'd been here. Had they gotten deeper? Thick gray eyebrows rose over dark brown eyes that scrutinized first him, then flickered to Elizabeth.

Dropping his arm, Elizabeth straightened, her mouth firming, though she still maintained a pleasant demeanor. Even though he could no longer feel her trembling, he knew it continued. Father often had that effect on people.

After some moments, Father rose and bowed, though his face retained its perpetual grim visage. "I wondered when you'd find it convenient to return home, Brack. To what emergency do I owe this visit?"

Sighing, Jemmy stepped forward, bringing Elizabeth with him to the foot of the table. "Mrs. Easton, may I present my father, Lord Blackham? Father, this is Mrs. Elizabeth Easton, my betrothed."

"Pah." Drawing his lips in as though they had purse strings attached, his father spat out the word. "Knew it had to be something like this the moment I saw you had a woman with you."

"Now, Father—"

"You are not betrothed until I say you are betrothed." The wizened man glanced first at him, then at Elizabeth. "Thought to snare yourself a title, did you, Mrs. Easton? A marchioness, no less?"

Jemmy opened his mouth to protest, but Elizabeth leaned toward his red-faced father.

"I am pleased to meet you, my lord. And no, I have no thought for a title. I did not marry for one the first time. Why should I do so now? I love your son. That is the only consideration I had when I accepted him."

Hearing those words sent a thrill of love coursing through Jemmy. She'd never professed it to him before. Now she had stated it boldly before his father. She loved him.

"Huh. Fine words, young woman." Father harrumphed and nodded to a small, narrow sofa to the side of the room. "Sit. I have no intention to continue standing." He plopped back down into his chair.

Jemmy and Elizabeth sank onto the well-oiled leather settee. "Father—"

"I am in the midst of negotiations for your marriage to the Duke of Buckleigh's daughter. A much more advantageous match than Mrs. Easton, I presume." His father cast a sharp eye at Elizabeth. "Unless you are also the daughter of a duke?"

"No, my lord, I fear not." Elizabeth met his stare evenly. God, she was fearless. "Merely the daughter of a viscount and the widow of a man who gave his life for king and country."

"Indeed." The marquess leaned back. "He was . . . ?"

"Lieutenant Colonel Richard Easton, late of His Majesty's Coldstream Regiment, under the command of Major General Lord John Byng. Killed in defense of the Château d'Hougoumont."

"Commendable." His father tapped a finger on the table. "Do you have children, Mrs. Easton?"

"Yes, my lord. Twins. A boy, Colin, and a girl, Katherine. They are six years old." If his father's questions disturbed Elizabeth, she did not show it. She sat calmly, her fingers rubbing the edge of her reticule.

"That speaks well of your ability to produce an heir for my son."

"Father!" Outraged, Jemmy jumped to his feet. "That is totally uncalled for."

"On the contrary, my boy"—his father speared him with a cold glance—"it is an issue very much to the point of marriage. In some ways, marriage to a widow with children gives a sense of security to the continuation of the line not possible with an innocent girl just out." His face darkened. "I have firsthand knowledge of this."

"Father." God, his father was impossible. He could throttle the old man when he got off on this perpetual bee in his bonnet.

"No, my lord." Elizabeth stayed him with a look, and he sat down. "Of what knowledge do you speak, Lord Blackham?"

"I was married for twelve years to a woman—sterling qualities, excellent bloodlines—who could not give me children. I spent twelve years thinking my line would die with me." The old man's eyes lit up. "Then God granted me grace and she died of influenza. I married Brack's mother, who gave me five children in as many years before she died producing the last child."

Elizabeth had paled a trifle during this tale, one Jemmy had heard all his life, but she only raised an eyebrow. What a perfect countess she would make and later a magnificent marchioness. If his father didn't dissuade her, nothing ever would.

"So your ability to bear my son an heir speaks more highly of you than your pedigree, which I now come to." Father leaned forward again, peering intently at Elizabeth.

Jemmy gripped the arm of the sofa. He'd be lucky if Elizabeth ever spoke to him again after being subjected to this inquisition.

"You have given me your late husband's *bona fides*, at least his military ones." His father laced his fingers together. "I assume he was a second or third son of the nobility? The daughter of a viscount would hardly settle for less."

"I did not 'settle' at all, my lord." Elizabeth's jaw tightened, the first indication of displeasure Jemmy had seen since their arrival. "I chose to marry him because I loved him, not because of his family or connections." She took a breath so deep he could see her chest expand. "However, yes, Lieutenant Colonel Easton was from Shropshire and of gentle birth. A younger son of the gentry who had to make his way in the world."

"I see." Nodding, his father continued to watch her as keenly as a cat at a mouse hole. "And your father? You are the daughter of . . . ?"

"Viscount Wentworth of Dorset." Elizabeth tipped her head back, pride in every inch of her. And this beautiful woman was all his.

"Wentworth?"

At the sudden icy tone, Jemmy snapped his attention back to the figure behind the desk.

Elizabeth shifted uneasily on the seat, her eyes suddenly wary. She must have heard that change in tone as well, and for the first time, she seemed rattled. "Yes, my lord. John, Seventh Viscount Wentworth."

Father's face had paled. Now it flushed bright red, and his eyes narrowed to slits.

Jemmy leaned forward, and fear shot down his spine as he put an arm out instinctively to protect Elizabeth from the evil that now looked out of his father's face.

"No."

"I beg your pardon, my lord." Elizabeth clutched her reticule to her, her fingers crushing the dark fabric.

"I forbid it." The marquess rose to tower over the table, hatred, dark and hot, infusing the clipped words. "You will not marry my son, Mrs. Easton. Not now, not ever."

Chapter 16

The floor melted beneath Jemmy's feet. The odd sensation he sometimes had in dreams—of tumbling over and over down a long, dark hole—overwhelmed him now in broad daylight. He shifted his weight, and the firm gray stone floor arrested his headlong fall into madness. He hadn't heard his father aright. "Father, did you actually just forbid us to wed?"

"You're a quick one, Brack. Always knew you'd live up to my expectations of you." His father glanced at him, a mirthless smile on his lips.

"I don't understand, Lord Blackham." Elizabeth stared straight ahead, eyes seemingly focused on the shiny mahogany desk. A pirate's desk. "You say we cannot marry?"

"Well, you've certainly picked a good one, Brack. Next time, make sure she understands the King's English. Of course, the next one will be a duke's daughter and of my choosing." His father sat and took up his pen, drew out a fresh sheet of paper and dipped the pen in the inkpot.

"The hell it will." Jemmy clenched his hands into fists so tightly they ached. "How dare you dismiss Elizabeth out of hand? She's done nothing to you." Jemmy shoved his hands behind him to keep himself from throttling the old man. "Why would you do this?"

"I have forbidden this marriage, and you will obey me, Brack. You will cease connection with this young woman and marry Lady Maude Aston without further discussion." Father started the pen skittering across the expanse of snowy white paper.

"I will do no such thing." Straightening his shoulders, Jemmy threw back his head. Stubbornness ran in the family, straight from their sire. "What possible reason could you have to refuse to allow this marriage?"

"I will tell you nothing I don't want you to know, boy. My reasons are none of your business." His father finished writing his sentence in a hand so shaky it looked like a spider had crawled across the sheet on spindly legs.

"It is my business, Lord Blackham." Elizabeth had managed to break the spell and now stared at his father with cold contempt. "If you are impugning my name or my family's, my lord, I assure you, you will answer for it. I do not care what your age may be or whether this accusation comes from some illness or madness. If you will not tell me why you refuse to allow me to wed your son, I will inform my father. He or my brother will demand satisfaction of you."

"Elizabeth." Jemmy slipped his arm around her shoulders. She was trembling so hard he had to grip her tightly. "No one wants a duel," he whispered. "I would likely end up having to meet your brother, and we don't want that, do we?"

She shook her head. A tear dripped off her cheek, falling onto his hand as he clasped her closer.

He met his father's eyes, and a wall of ice descended on him. "I do not care what you say or what slight you perceive Elizabeth or her family has made against you. I reached my majority years ago. Elizabeth is of age and a widow. You cannot force me to marry someone against my will, and I tell you now, this instant, I will *never* marry Lady Maude. I will marry Elizabeth, and there is nothing you can do to stop me."

Father laid his pen down beside the paper, a dangerous smile on his lips. "Oh, but there is, Brack. There is indeed something that I can do to stop you from making this foolhardy decision." He steepled the tips of his fingers.

"Don't listen to him, Elizabeth." Sending his father a defiant glare, Jemmy drew her tight against him. "I will marry you no matter what he says." They turned for the door.

"If you do, I shall cut you off without a farthing."

The sharp words arrested them as Jemmy grasped the latch. He whirled around to face his father.

"Every cent. You will not have a penny to light your way across the road."

"I have Mother's inheritance—"

"That is in a trust until you are thirty. And I am the guardian of that trust until that time. Had you forgotten that?"

The light in the study seemed to dim around the edges until all Jemmy could see was his father's triumphant smile. Father would hold the purse strings of that account until August of next year. His mother's settlement had come to him more than three years ago, to provide for him until his father died and he assumed the marquessate. But according to the terms, his father administered the funds as he saw fit. The very reason he had not been able to help Georgie.

Glee shone in his father's face. "I see you had. The terms are quite plain, you know. Those funds become available to you at your discretion only when you attain the age of thirty. Not a day before. Until then, I disburse them as I see fit. If you have cause to doubt me, you can ask your uncle, Lord Richard Makepeace. He was there when the settlements were drawn up."

A giant hand seemed to squeeze the air from Jemmy's lungs, not allowing him to breathe.

"So you see, Brack, you will dance to my tune or you won't have a penny to pay the piper."

"Does Georgie have funds from your mother as well?" Elizabeth whispered her question in his ear. "Money from any settlement would have been transferred to her husband upon her marriage."

"I'm afraid not." Jemmy clenched and unclenched his hands, itching to plant his father a facer or two. "Her money would have gone to her when she married, except for the provision that Father must approve of the marriage. Ergo, Georgie's continued plight."

Elizabeth's face drew in upon itself, her eyes haunted. "When will you turn thirty?"

"Not until August." A lifetime in their circumstances.

She closed her eyes and swallowed hard. "Then you must not disobey him. If he cuts off your funds, how will you live?" She bit her lip, but otherwise her face was deathly calm. "We must return to Lyttlefield Park immediately. There is much preparation I must make before leaving for London."

"No, my love, we will not give in." Jemmy grabbed her hand, needing her touch desperately. "We must tell him about the—"

"No." Elizabeth peered over at his father, waiting patiently behind his table. He'd finished the first page of his latest missive and had started on the second page. "Swear to me you will tell your father nothing. If he were to tell anyone about my condition, I will never be received in polite society again."

"But if he knew this child very well might be my heir, he might see sense. He wants the line to be secured."

Tears starting from her eyes, Elizabeth shook her head. "No, not even for that will he allow us to wed. He has concocted some slight against me or my family. Remember, he became unreasonable when he found out who my father is."

She bit her lip. "I will go directly to London and confront my father. Perhaps it is something from long ago, and the two men can settle it now so we can wed."

Such calm courage. She was the most magnificent woman he had ever met. Raising her hand for a kiss, he grazed her soft skin with his lips. "I pray it is so with all my heart, my love." Turning to his father, he rose and bowed stiffly. "The time is late. We will stay the night and leave early tomorrow morning." He glared at his father, daring him to object.

The man merely waved a hand at him and continued his spidery writing.

He had opened the door and handed Elizabeth through when the thin, reedy voice stopped them once more. "Once you return Mrs. Easton to wherever she currently lodges, you will immediately return here. I expect word from the duke any day now, and with this letter"—he slowly waved the pages he'd just finished before his face, drying them—"I believe the offer will be too sweet for His Grace to pass up. Lady Maude is not in her first bloom of youth, but she will make you an admirable marchioness and the duke a strong ally for us."

Rage descended over Jemmy until the edges of his sight darkened once more. He started toward the man, his only thought to put an end to the hideous imp of hell.

Elizabeth's firm hand on his shoulder stayed him, but it was a near thing. Swinging for his father's murder, justified though it might be, would not help him or Elizabeth's plight. She tugged at his arm.

With a parting glance of abhorrence at his father, Jemmy headed toward the door.

"When you return"—the hateful voice filled the room once more—"bring Georgina with you. The chit can stay here until I can arrange matters for her satisfactorily."

Resisting the urge to retort back, which would serve no purpose save his own gratification, Jemmy jerked his shoulders back and grasped Elizabeth's hand. "I will tell her, Father," he said as he escorted Elizabeth away from the vile man. Under his breath he added, "May God have mercy on her soul."

Automatically putting one foot before the next, Elizabeth clung to Jemmy's arm as they snaked their way through the narrow corridors of Blackham Castle. She neither saw nor heard anything for the spinning in her head that threatened to make her swoon.

Jemmy could not marry her.

The devastation had scarcely begun to sink in. Her whole body was numb as from a blow. She managed to steal a glance at him—jaw tightened, lips in a grim line, teeth clenched—as he escorted her deeper into the bowels of the castle. Gone was the carefree, boyish man she had come to love and admire. Also gone were her dreams of a new, happy life once more. Blasted asunder by the cursed words of a bitter old man. She stifled a sob.

"Here is your chamber," he said at last, stopping before a solid walnut door. "This was Georgie's old room." His words broke the silence, though not the awkward constraint that lay between them. "I will be just around the corner in the next corridor."

"Thank you," she whispered, unwilling to meet his eyes.

"I love you, Elizabeth." He grazed her hand with his lips. "Believe in me, my love; this is not the end of it. I swear I will marry you, no matter what he plots and plans."

Noble words and spoken with sufficient passion that they brought a measure of balm to her heart. However, the truth lay elsewhere, and she knew it. If Jemmy's father controlled his money, they could defy him at their peril. Without funds for simple necessities, such as food and lodging, they would be little better than destitute. She tried to smile, but the effort hurt her heart. She must begin to withdraw her newfound affection for Jemmy and find a way to assuage the hurt that cut deeply, even though she saw its necessity. "I love you, too. However, I fear we must face the harsh reality of the situation."

"Then we shall face it together." Squeezing her hands a bit harder than necessary, he gave them a little shake. "Do not despair, my love. We will find our way through this. At dinner tonight, we will examine our options and talk strategy. Elizabeth," he cupped her face and tears slipped from her eyes.

He was so kind, and loving, and she couldn't have him. She buried her face in his shoulder.

"My love, my love." He cradled her, rocking her gently. "Shhh. Do not cry. We will be together as man and wife, if I have to move heaven and earth to do it." He kissed her, lightly, sweetly, devastatingly. "Dinner is at six in the winter months." He rubbed her back, and she nestled closer to him. "I will have Quick send one of the maids to help you dress." He pulled away from her and peered sharply into her face. "Trust me?"

"Yes, my love, I do." Sniffing, she tried to pull herself together. He sounded more sure and confident than she had ever heard him before. Pray God, he had a plan to defeat his father's wishes.

With a final brush of his lips across hers that melted her heart all over again, he pushed the door open, sent her his best boyish grin, and bounded off down the hall. She gazed after him until he turned the corner and was lost to her sight.

The chill of the hallway caused her to hurry inside, where her battered soul could perhaps renew itself in the warmth of the fire. Gazing about Georgina's room, she smiled despite her shocked and reeling senses. Whimsical pictures of gardens with riotous blooms dotted the walls, a bouquet of silk violets perched on the writing desk, and a collection of embroidered pillows—the embroidery done by a not-so-skilled hand—made the room speak in Georgie's enthusiastic voice. A friendly, comforting voice that would help get her through the worst hours, in which she would have to come to terms with the fact that she was now with child, but without the prospect of a husband.

Sarah, the young maid sent to help her dress, had just clasped a locket encrusted with amethyst around her neck when a knock at the door made Elizabeth jump.

"It's all right, mum. You look a treat now." Sarah smiled at her in the vanity's mirror and hurried to the door.

Elizabeth rose, brushing at her skirts, touching her locket to make sure she was presentable.

Grinning broadly, Jemmy stepped into the room and offered his arm. "May I escort the fairest in the land to dinner?" His gaze took her in, his eyes lighting with approval.

"Indeed, you may, my lord." In spite of her heavy heart, she smiled back. That grin was too infectious to fight against. And if Jemmy seemed determined to fight his father's plans to marry him to Lady Maude, and optimistic that they would succeed in thwarting the marquess, then she should allow herself to hope a little while longer.

The shadowy dining room held an extremely long, polished cherry table laid with three places, one at both ends, and a third in the middle. The huge polished expanse, a raised gilt design running around its edge, would easily seat twenty. How on earth could they converse normally at such a distance?

"I'd suggest eating in the kitchen, but Mrs. Harmon would probably pull my ear completely off." A ruddy-faced young man, who looked like a taller, blonder version of Jemmy, melted out of the shadows and into the stronger light afforded by the three candelabras that lined the table.

"Hal!" Jemmy bounded forward to shake the young man's hand. "What the devil are you doing here? You are never home from Cambridge so early."

Hal grinned, a charming, lopsided smile that, paired with

his unruly curls and sparkling blue eyes, was immediately endearing.

"Bit of a stramash over another chap landing in the duck pond." Hal bounced on his feet, as if he were a child's ball come to life.

"You never!" Jemmy chuckled and shook his head.

"Did I not? Bloke had put it about I fancied one of the most unappealing young ladies I'd ever seen in Town. If that had gotten back to her, I'd never have got rid of her or her father." He eyed Elizabeth, an approving appraisal to judge by the grin on his face. "I see you've fetched up a likely prospect."

"I'm sorry. Mrs. Elizabeth Easton, may I present my brother, Lord Harold Cross? Hal is my younger brother, a year younger than Georgina and a bit of a bounder." Despite his words, Jemmy looked rather proud of the young man.

"It's good to see you too, Jem." Lord Harold sent a glance of mock scorn to his brother. "But I am delighted to make your acquaintance, Mrs. Easton." He bowed charmingly and raised her hand for a kiss. "You are a friend of our sister, Lady Georgina?"

"I am, my lord." To her astonishment, the young man then grabbed the silverware and plate and strode to the end of the table.

"I intend to eat down here with the lovely Mrs. Easton." Lord Harold turned an innocent stare on her. "You don't mind me monopolizing your time, do you, ma'am? Unless you wish to join us, Jemmy?" Pulling out Elizabeth's chair, Hal grinned down at his brother, who was standing, hands on hips, glaring at them both.

Elizabeth lowered herself into the proffered seat, glancing from brother to brother, torn between dual desires to laugh and weep. The presence of another person had been expected, but she'd anticipated a stiff, unpleasant dinner with Lord Blackham. A brother was a welcome change of dinner companion; however, the subject she needed to discuss with Jemmy couldn't be broached, not before this stranger.

"Mrs. Easton is my betrothed, Hal, so mind your manners." Jemmy had piled cutlery and napkin onto his plate, grabbed a wineglass, and joined them at the end of the table.

"Ah, come to get the old man's blessing?"

"Quite." Jemmy unloaded his plate, setting the items next to Elizabeth's place.

"So I may wish you happy?" The eager face lit up again. Such a jovial young man. Elizabeth quite liked him. It was hard not to.

"Not quite yet, it seems." Jemmy glanced at her, raising an eyebrow.

If Jemmy wanted to ask his brother's opinion of their situation, it would likely do no harm. He'd know eventually if the wedding never occurred. She gave a very slight nod and sat down, her appetite suddenly vanished.

Chapter 17

Lord Harold lived up to his promise of being a charming if somewhat roguish dinner companion. He possessed a quick wit that put Elizabeth at her ease immediately. Stories of his escapades at university had her laughing in spite of her circumstances.

"You have been at Cambridge how long, my lord?" Elizabeth set her knife and fork down, astonished to find the plate completely clear. She'd feared she'd have no appetite, but Lord Harold's engaging stories had managed to take her mind off her own woes.

"Only since this fall. Before that I was at Oxford off and on for two years." He cut his gaze at Jemmy, who snorted.

"My brother, while a brilliant scholar when he wishes to be, usually spends his time at university getting into and out of scrapes. Hal, you've been sent home four times in the past three years?" Jemmy sipped his wine, eyes wide and innocent.

With a large, false sigh, Lord Harold slumped in his seat. "Alas, yes. I had actually hoped it would be five by now. I'm in a race with Lord Barger to see who can get booted out of school the most times before our fathers stop sending us. Currently, Barger is one up on me with five."

Despite herself, Elizabeth had to laugh at the long, unrepentant face. The situation wasn't crushing, really. Lord Harold, as a younger son, had to make his way in the world, and education would help that. But his *joie de vivre*, irrepressible as Jemmy's, made it hard to censure him. "Certainly, you will settle down to your studies eventually, Lord Harold?"

He drained his wine and signaled for more. "Highly unlikely. I've my own inheritance when I reach thirty. And then I can always find a pretty girl with a substantial dowry to marry. If I play my cards right, I may never have to do anything with my life save get myself out of scrapes and marry well." Wagging his eyebrows in rakish glee, he sent Elizabeth into peals of laughter. "Which brings me to the subject of marriage in general and your marriage in particular, Jemmy. You have obviously betrothed yourself to a lady with a keen discernment for wit. I commend you." He raised his glass of burgundy to Jemmy. "So why may I not wish you happy?" Do you fear Mrs. Easton means to jilt you?"

"Nothing so dramatic as that." Jemmy's laughing face sobered at once.

Reminding her anew of her own plight, his words made Elizabeth's spirits plummet.

"Father has forbidden us to marry." Jemmy drank deeply from his wine goblet.

"Does he object to your bride-to-be?" Lord Harold cocked his head toward her, twirling the stem of his wineglass between thumb and forefinger. "You are suddenly much more intriguing, if I may say so, Mrs. Easton. I love a puzzle." His infectious grin made it impossible for her to take offense.

"I am happy to provide you with a new challenge, my lord. You may call me Elizabeth, as I hope we are all to be related soon." She drank the last sweet drops of the burgundy, feeling suddenly useless. If they did not wed, what would such a familiarity matter?

"And you shall call me Hal. All my friends do." He shot a look at Jemmy. "Even some of my relations."

"I have no idea why he objects to the marriage. He refused to say." Jemmy stared into his final swallow of the blood-red wine. "Then we could at least come up with a counterargument. It's impossible to argue against 'None of your business.'"

"Perhaps if you could prove her connections grand enough?" Hal's eyes brightened. "Please tell me you are a duchess in disguise." His wistful tone made Elizabeth laugh in spite of herself. Lord knew, there was nothing amusing about her situation.

"I fear not, Hal. I am the widow of the second son of a somewhat prosperous esquire, a lieutenant colonel who died at Waterloo, and the daughter of a viscount. Quite ordinary in fact." Her laugh sounded like a fox's yip. "Perhaps that is the objection. Likely, he has grander aims for his son and heir."

"That I can believe." Hal frowned.

"Still, he didn't sound unreasonable when you spoke of your late husband." Jemmy's brow puckered as he poured them more wine. "I even thought he believed it rather noble that your husband had died for his country."

"So did I." The marquess had seemed rather sympathetic at that point in the interview. She twirled her glass by the stem, staring at the candlelight dancing off the crystal. "He didn't seem inclined to refuse the marriage until I mentioned my father's name."

"What's that all about?" Hal leaned toward her, his eyes sparkling with interest.

"I have no idea."

"Do they have some feud between them?"

"Not that I have ever heard." Elizabeth shrugged. Until she

met Jemmy, she'd never heard of the Marquess of Blackham. "My parents certainly have never mentioned such. Has your father ever spoken about Wentworth or the Worths before? Or the Kelcotts? That is my mother's family."

With a sigh, Jemmy shook his head. "Never. Well, not to me. Hal?"

His brother threw up his hands. "My conversations with Father always center around my shortcomings, not his. But I can tell you this. If there's bad blood between the families, you and Elizabeth are going to have to find a way to overcome it on your own. Father would willingly march into hell and gladly roast there rather than give in to anyone."

Hal's sober face at this pronouncement made Elizabeth's heart stutter. She clenched her fist around the glass's stem. Surely that wasn't true? Hesitantly, she turned to Jemmy, praying he would refute his brother's bleak statement.

Avoiding her eyes, he grasped her hand in both of his. "Unfortunately, that is true, my dear. If Father is set against the marriage, he will not change his mind."

A cold chill ran icy fingers down her spine. What on earth were they to do? Her situation could be hidden only for so long. If they could not marry . . .

"Then Father be damned." Hal thumped his glass on the table, and the dishes danced. "Marry without his consent. You are both of age. Who will stop you?"

"Father. He holds my purse strings for eight months, so he has just reminded me." Jemmy growled and his face darkened. "My funds are in trust until I'm thirty." He shot his brother a piercing look. "The same is true for your portion, I believe?"

"Gads." Hal's ruddy face paled. "I'd thought the age was twenty-five. I'd banked on tapping into that lot next year. I'll send to Connors in the morning to find out the lay of the land." He rubbed his eyes and groaned. "If it's to be five more years of facing down Father, I may just enter the church and be done with it."

Jemmy snorted. "You'll become a clergyman when pigs fly in the air with their tails forward."

A grin split Hal's face. "The 'tails forward' part is the sticking point, I'll grant you."

Quickly sobering, Jemmy chaffed her hand. "What he has done is tie my hands where Elizabeth is concerned."

The caress was sweet, but his words brought the reality of their situation sharply into focus. They truly might not be able to marry in time for the child to be born legitimately. Her stomach dropped with sickening force.

"Defy the old curmudgeon and marry anyway." Hal's eyes sparkled, as if spoiling for a fight not his own.

"Easier said than done." Jemmy downed the rest of his wine and wiped his lips on the back of his hand. "How would we live? With Elizabeth's parents? They'd not want their daughter married to a man who is almost destitute. What would that say about me as a provider for her and her children? She has two small children who must be cared for. Not to mention we would not want to live in their pockets." Jemmy signaled the footman for more wine.

"I will be no help at all," Elizabeth said quietly. She'd been mulling over her financial situation as well and discovered it to be bleak as a cold midwinter's day. "I shall lose my widow's pension from my late husband when I marry. It is not much, but it has made a deal of difference to my limited independence." She toyed with her glass but refused the offer of more wine. She needed her wits about her from now on.

"Then I propose we drink some more." Hal grabbed the bottle from the astonished footman and shooed him away. "Let's get foxed and drown our sorrows."

"I fear I must retire, gentlemen." Elizabeth rose, glad to be moving at last. "We have an early start and a long journey tomorrow."

The men catapulted to their feet, Jemmy grasping her arm as if it were a lifeline. "Allow me to escort you to your chamber, my love." He turned to Hal. "Don't wait for me, brother. Saying good night to this lovely lady will likely take some time."

"Huh." Hal grunted. "More wine for me, then."

"Good night, Hal." Elizabeth squeezed his hand. "I am truly glad to have met you."

"I hope to see you at your wedding, Elizabeth."

She smiled wanly, doubting now it would ever take place.

"Good evening, brother." Jemmy called as he followed her out the door. "That's one less hurdle. Hal likes you."

"I wish it had been as easy with your father." Elizabeth swallowed hard, fighting to keep her composure. Perhaps she should trust that Jemmy would devise some remedy for this catastrophe that they had not already come up with. If she thought any more about the possibility of them having to part, or worse, having to marry someone else, she wanted to dissolve into a puddle of tears. Let her retire to water her pillow alone. Alone. Surreptitiously she touched her belly. It was ironic that she actually was not.

Elizabeth sat at the carved ebony vanity table, brushing her hair, trying to think of anything other than the possibility that Jemmy might no longer be in her life. Though she had been slow to admit her feelings—too slow, if truth be told— now, faced with the stark reality that she might lose him, she finally understood the depth of her love for him. Her life, which had been devastated by the loss of Dickon, had been renewed slowly but surely by Jemmy's persistent pursuit of her—a decorous chase that had culminated in complete capitulation by his prey. To now think of life without him was abhorrent.

She pulled the brush though her hair briskly, the sting on her scalp invigorating.

Yes, she loved him. Deny it thought she might try, she loved Jemmy with a depth that astonished her. Just the thought of being with him sent shivers and tingles down her spine. His warm smile, his merry disposition, his understanding and forgiving nature, and his devotion to his sister made him the perfect gentleman, in her estimation. Very similar to, yet very different from Dickon. Perhaps the one man who could take his place in her heart, the one other man she could love for the rest of her life.

To think one embittered old man could take him from her wasn't to be borne. She banged the brush on the table and stood, ready to do battle like a legendary shield maiden, but not quite sure how to meet the enemy.

A sudden grating noise behind her made her spin around to face the bed. A dark wall panel next to it shivered, as if coming to life. She blinked, unsure if her eyes were playing tricks on her or if this was actually happening. A scene from *The Monk,* when a ghost materialized before the heroine, flitted through her mind, and she backed up a step at a time until she was pressed against the vanity chair. Dear Lord, what was going on?

Grabbing the candlestick off the table, heart racing like a runaway carriage, she approached the wall. The grating sound had stopped, but a low hum seemed to be coming from behind the panel. She touched the smooth, cool wood, seemingly just like all the others around the room.

Sudden vibration beneath her fingertips made her jump back. The grating noise resumed, louder than before, and with a loud "pop," the panel swung open into the chamber.

Elizabeth screamed as Jemmy emerged into her room, bedaubed with cobwebs over the shoulders of his dressing gown.

"Jemmy?" Confusion swirled around her head as she peered first at him, then into the inky black recess behind the panel. "What . . . what is going on?"

Instead of answering her, he set his candlestick down, grasped her face, and kissed her. His warm, full lips pressed her passionately, his tongue immediately seeking access.

Melting against him as her tension drained away, she

gladly opened her mouth to welcome him in. As though his touch gave her sudden strength, she pressed her own attack, wrapping her arms around his neck and invading his mouth in return.

He groaned, clasping her bottom, pulling her into him until she could feel his hardness pressing into her. Tighter and tighter they strained into each other until she could not breathe and reluctantly broke the kiss, panting.

Leaning his forehead against hers, he whispered breathlessly, "If that is the welcome I will get, I vow I will install a secret passageway in the master's chamber on each estate we own when we are wed." He chuckled and kissed the tip of her nose. "I didn't frighten you too badly with my grand entrance, did I?"

Still out of breath, Elizabeth stepped back, wobbling just a bit. "You did give me quite a start, Jemmy. All I could think of was that wretched book *The Monk*, with its castles and secret passages and ghosts." She peered around him at the black hole in the wall. A stale, musty smell crept from its depths. "Is this truly a secret passage?"

He grinned and gathered her into his arms. "It truly is. Georgina and I discovered this loose panel when we were young. We explored behind it—she was fearless, as you may have already guessed, even at age seven—and if you thread your way through the timbers, you arrive at the back wall of my chamber, just to the side of the wardrobe. It took us weeks to carve a hole big enough for me to slip through and to cut the paneling and disguise it, but we managed to make a true secret passageway so we could visit one another when we had been sent to bed or locked up as punishment."

"You were locked in your room?" Appalled, Elizabeth hugged him more fiercely.

"I think you can see that my father's word was not to be gainsaid. Locked in your room with no supper and no breakfast was the standard penance. Of course, once we created this passageway, Georgie would sneak food up to me." He shook his head and held her away from him. "We, however, will never resort to such punishment with our little ones, will we?"

Elizabeth's heart sank. "Jemmy, don't speak of what will likely never be."

"Oh, it will come to pass, my love." Gently, he placed his hand on her stomach and looked deeply into her eyes. "Our child is already on the way. Do you think I will allow anyone to keep him or her from bearing my name?" The firm resolve in his voice gave her sudden hope. "Do you honestly believe I would allow an old tyrant to lock me in a financial prison and force me to abandon you? You underestimate me, my dear." He kissed her lips again. "I am quite as stubborn as Father, and I have something to fight for that he does not. Love."

"I so want to believe that, Jemmy, I truly do." She laced their fingers together, binding them as they should be forever and ever. "But if we wed without his consent, how will we live?"

"I will go to my mother's family. My grandfather is still alive, though very frail the last I heard. Still, I don't think he will deny my request if he knows the cause."

"What will you ask of him?"

"A loan of a modest amount. Enough to keep us safe and happy in a small home in London until my inheritance is truly mine. He would want that, I'm sure. And as soon as I reach thirty, the money will be returned to him, with interest." He raised their hands and kissed their joined fingers. "We will need to live quietly, but we will be together."

The crushing weight of loss slid from Elizabeth's shoulder with an almost audible thud. Tears pricked her eyes. "That will be quite enough for me, my love."

"Then let us celebrate our coming union." He grinned, and his eyes flashed black with sudden desire. Pulling her by the hand, he led her, step by step, toward the tall poster bed.

"Jemmy! In your father's house?" Scandalized and ex-

cited, Elizabeth trembled with a wave of longing to be with
him once more.

"What better place to affirm our love? I admit I'd rather
have you in my bed, but I don't want to subject you to that
passageway. It is a bit dusty and small. I can't have the
mother of my child crawling through the walls of her future
home." He seized her lips as he deftly drew off her wrapper.
When the kiss ended, she stood naked before him; both
wrapper and nightgown lay in a puddle at her feet. Eyes
large as black almonds, he beheld her, and his breathing became a ragged panting. "Oh, Elizabeth. You are even love-
lier than I remember."

Desire rushed through her from her very core, radiating
outward through her body. Under that hot gaze, she might
burst into flame. Her own breath came short and sharp, her
need to feel him inside her rising to a painful peak.

A deep shrug of his shoulders and his dark silk banyan
slid to the floor, revealing his perfect, naked body in the soft
candlelight. As though a Greek sculptor had made him just
for her. Hard muscles in his torso, arms, and chest rippled
with his labored breathing as he stepped toward her. His jut-
ting member, long and thick and hard, could also be a piece
of ancient art, though it was scalding hot as it pressed the
cool flesh of her stomach.

He cupped her buttocks and lifted her onto the bed, laying her down on the crisp sheets. Running his hands along
her body, trailing his fingers over her breasts, stomach,
through the thicket that covered her sex, he ignited a fire in
her soul.

She moaned with need as he slid them into her, panting
aloud at the exquisite feeling of him stroking her heat, building an inferno that threatened to incinerate her before he
could join with her. "Jemmy," she cried, tugging at his head.
"Now, please, all of you now."

His fingers vanished, leaving her wanting until the hot
flesh of his cock pressed against her, seeking entrance. He

leaned over her, pinning her shoulders to the bed with fierce possession. "I am yours, Elizabeth," he said, kissing her neck, making her squirm and moan anew, totally conscious of him poised at her opening.

The musky male scent of him filled her head, increased the ache between her thighs. She strained toward that heat, longing for it inside her.

"I am yours," he repeated, his voice urgent. "Are you mine?"

"Yes, Jemmy, yes. I am yours, my love." She almost wept with the joy of the confession. She belonged to him in every way.

With her admission, he smiled and thrust forward, filling her completely, seating himself deeply within and making them as one. "Do you trust me that we will be together as man and wife?" He rocked slightly back and forth, a tanta-lizing promise of more to come.

"I do," she panted, wild with the joy of having him in her. "I do believe it, Jemmy. Yes, yes, my love." She thrust her hips toward him as he slowly drove in and out, bringing her to the brink of that incredible pleasure she'd been longing for. Wrapping her legs around his buttocks, she encouraged him to move further within her, to go faster to reach the heaven that hovered just out of reach.

He leaned in to kiss her, fierce and hard as their bodies rocked together. When he raised his head, he stared into her eyes. "You are mine, Elizabeth. Mine forever. I pity the man who tries to keep us apart."

"Ahh, Jemmy! Jemmy!" she cried as the rapture took her, and she flew apart, gripping him inside her over and over again.

"Mine!" he shouted as his hot seed spurted deep into her.

She sagged into the mattress, his weight pleasantly heavy on top of her. Completion was very sweet, and never so much as now, with him. With Jemmy.

Too quickly, he rolled off of her and lay beside her, his panting harsh and wonderful in her ear. Her own blood was calming, though her heart still raced. Her bones had gone on holiday. It was more than enough simply to contemplate the dark ceiling, his presence large and warm and comforting.

She snuggled against him, her buttocks pressed against his member, limp at the moment, but showing faint signs of life already. For tonight, to be here together was more than enough.

Chapter 18

Disgruntled, but trying not to show it, Jemmy joined Elizabeth in the front hall next morning as the carriage was brought around for their departure.

"I missed you at breakfast," she murmured as Quick assisted her with her dark blue spencer.

"An early audience with Father. I'm truly sorry to have missed your company." He adjusted his hat and offered her his arm. "Shall we?"

The journey back to Kent, while pleasant because of his nearness to Elizabeth, seemed too quiet as the day wore on, as if a pall had been cast over them. They talked of mundane pleasantries, rather than the fear most pressing to them. How were they to marry—and they must marry soon if Elizabeth was to escape ruin—without Father's consent?

His scheme to enlist his maternal grandfather was their best course; however, it was far from certain. Jemmy and his brother and sisters had had little contact with their mother's family all their lives. To go begging now might secure the funds they needed, but it might very well not. He hadn't mentioned that to Elizabeth, nor would he until forced to by necessity, if it came to pass.

So he had approached his father early this morning, and the conversation turned quickly into argument. He might as well have saved himself the aggravation and breakfasted with Elizabeth. The time would have been better spent. Father simply refused to budge on his decision. And now he demanded that Jemmy escort Georgie back into the old man's web as well. He stared out the window at the cold dead countryside, his own outlook as grim.

Elizabeth seemed to sense his mood, and they lapsed into silence, though they held hands the whole way, parting only when they stopped to change horses.

They pulled up before the columned façade of Lyttlefield Park as the afternoon shadows had just begun to lengthen across the pale marble steps of the portico.

"I will call for my carriage to be readied," Elizabeth said, smoothing the folds of her rumpled dress. "I think I should leave immediately for London. If I can talk to my parents, they may be able to tell me what is behind your father's refusal of our marriage." Her lips trembled, cutting his heart to the quick. "The more information we have, the better our chances to overcome your father's objections."

"I swear it will not prevent me in the least from marrying you, my darling." He grasped her hands and kissed them as the groom opened the carriage door.

She smiled, and his heart melted. "I pray so, my love."

He jumped to the ground and handed her down, loath to let her go even for a moment when they were to be parted so soon. "Let me order you some tea."

She shook her head as they entered the foyer. "I must pack immediately if I am to leave within the hour."

"I will send it to your room with some sandwiches. You haven't eaten anything since breakfast." He leaned closer to her, the heady feminine scent of her making him weak. "You must keep your strength up, you know."

Her cheeks pinked prettily, though that may have just been the cold. "Thank you, my dear. That would be lovely."

Handing Fisk their coats, he paused to soak up the blessed heat. He rubbed his hands together briskly. He could use something hot as well. "Fisk, please have some tea and sandwiches sent to both my and Mrs. Easton's rooms. And make haste. The lady leaves in an hour."

"Very good, my lord." The butler handed the coats to a footman and hurried toward the kitchen.

"As I will not see you for some time, may I at least see you to your room?"

The liquid blue eyes she turned on him made his heart pound.

"Of course, you may." She grasped his arm, and they started up the polished front stairs. "Will you come to me in London? After you take Georgina back to Blackham?"

Stunned, he stopped in mid-step. "You wish me to come to London?"

"If we are to wed, I think you should become acquainted with my parents and the children, don't you?" Her smile held back laughter.

"I didn't think you'd want me to . . . yes, yes, of course. I will come immediately after I deliver Georgie." Unfortunately, that had sounded as though his sister was a parcel. He clutched her arm, suddenly a trifle giddy.

"I hope I shall have good news by the time you arrive. Perhaps my parents can shed some light on your father's dislike of them." Taking his hand, she led him the rest of the way to her room, where she paused delicately. "I will miss you so much, Jemmy." She leaned in and kissed him softly on the lips.

His body throbbed, the aching need for her seizing him again. When they married, they must go away somewhere alone and devour one another for at the least a month or two.

Grasping her face, he kissed her deeply, igniting a fire within him that demanded he claim her just once more.

As if sensing that need, she gently withdrew from him, though her eyes glowed with a like desire, her cheeks awash with the red of crisp fall apples. "When you come to me in London, and we are married, then we will continue this moment."

"Most assuredly." Breathing deeply, he kissed her hand, and she slipped into her chamber. With a groan for his aching parts, he hurried toward his own bedroom, Fellowes, and a hot, soothing bath.

Jemmy entered the drawing room that evening determined not to mope over Elizabeth's absence. He'd managed to see her off in the early afternoon, with another soul-stirring kiss and the admonition to write to him once she arrived and spoke to her parents about their impending marriage. She was not to speak of their imminent parenthood—Jemmy had promised on his life to follow her to London as soon as he had settled Georgie at Blackham, at most in a day or two. Then they would make that announcement together.

He had just greeted Lady Wrotham and assured her of Elizabeth's good health when Georgie bounded into the room, bringing, as she always did, a breath of vitality and *joie de vivre* with her. She made for them directly.

"Charlotte, I have such news! Jemmy, did you tell her?" Georgie smiled broadly, hopping from one foot to the other, like she was six years old again. She certainly acted a child much more often than she acted a grown woman and a widow.

"I fear you have interrupted me asking after Lady Wrotham's health, dear sister. I've not had time to tell her more. Besides"—he fixed her with a stare of false sternness—"I haven't seen you to tell you anything."

"I talked with Elizabeth before she left." She raised her chin triumphantly.

"What news is this, Georgina?" Looking from Georgie to him, Lady Wrotham raised her perfectly arched eyebrows.

"Father has sent for me!" Georgie burst out and hugged

Jemmy's arm. "He's forgiven me and wants me to return to Blackham."

"That is wonderful news indeed, Georgie. I am so happy for this reconciliation." Lady Wrotham hugged her, though the puckered frown on her face was less enthusiastic.

Unless he missed his guess, his hostess feared the summons to Blackham had ulterior motives. Those fears would likely prove correct. Georgie had told him of Lady Wrotham's history with her own father, who seemed even worse than their parent, if such a thing were possible.

"We must leave your kind hospitality tomorrow, my lady. After three years, our father is anxious to see Georgina again." That final interview this morning had convinced him that their father still harbored resentment over Georgie's first marriage and her defiance of him. Sadly, she was now out of options. Lyttlefield Park would be closed shortly, leaving her nowhere to go save home or to the Kirkpatricks. Apparently, his sister had decided Father was now the lesser of two evils.

"I am happy you will be going home at last, Georgie." Lady Wrotham released her, peering closely into her face. "However, you do know that you are always welcome at Wrotham Park? If you ever find your circumstances as difficult as before, you must come to me and Nash. Promise me you will."

"Of course, Charlotte." Georgie beamed at her friend. "I don't suppose Father has actually forgiven me. And I suspect I am in for a great deal of lectures and admonishments about being a defiant child. But I shall withstand him and write to you to put your fears at rest once I have seen him. Jemmy will be there in the beginning, so I don't suppose Father will beat me again."

"Georgie!" Lady Wrotham had turned quite pale.

"Georgina." Jemmy stepped in before his sister could cause a scene. "Father has never struck you in his life."

A puzzled gaze, wrinkled nose, and knit brows met his

eyes. "Well, of course he hasn't done it in your presence, Jemmy. I just said he wouldn't do that with you there."

"Georgina, when did he strike you?" Lady Wrotham's ashen face grew even grimmer.

"When I was six years old."

"What?" Jemmy's jaw dropped. He shook his head to clear it. She didn't actually mean—

"You must remember, Jemmy. I was six, and I had gone into Father's study looking for Lucy." Georgie nodded gravely at Lady Wrotham, whose color had come flooding back. "My King Charles spaniel. She roamed all over the castle, and I had a terrible time keeping up with her. So one day she had wandered into Father's study—"

"Georgie, do you really think—"

"I am telling this story, Jemmy."

"Perhaps we should go in now?" Lady Wrotham asked hopefully.

"Brack." Lord Wrotham appeared beside the countess as if by magic. "Good to see you back." The tall, dark-haired earl smiled easily. "Thank you so much for your assistance the other day, both with the ceremony and with Mrs. Easton. I trust she is well today?" He peered around the room.

"She left for London this afternoon, Wrotham." Lady Wrotham placed a hand on his arm. "I was just saying perhaps we should go in to dinner?"

"What about my father beating me?"

In the shocked silence that ensued, Jemmy cursed under his breath. His sister might yet make an actress with her perfect sense of the dramatic.

"I beg your pardon, Georgie." Wrotham seemed to land on his feet first. "Your father did what?" His mouth drew into a straight line so taut his lips disappeared.

"It's not what it sounds like, my lord." Jemmy shot a stern glance at his sister. He must take control of the situation before his father's reputation was sullied needlessly. The marquess was guilty of many things, but not this one.

"Did your father beat her, Brack?" The narrowed dark gaze sent a qualm of unease down Jemmy's spine. He'd not like to meet those eyes over a brace of dueling pistols.

"No, he didn't."

"Oh, yes he did, Jemmy." Georgie flew at him, insistent as a sparrow.

"When did this happen?" Wrotham's face had darkened like a thundercloud.

"When she was six years old." Jemmy sighed. Georgie was currently more in danger of him beating her than their father.

"Six years . . . I thought you were away to Blackham yesterday?" The earl's face had cleared into a confused frown.

"Mrs. Easton and I were. Georgina has not seen our father for some three years. The incident of which she was speaking to Lady Wrotham occurred when Georgie was six. It was a mere nothing."

"He beat me." Georgie's insistent voice had the complete attention of Lord and Lady Wrotham.

"He swatted your derriere once, Georgie."

"It still hurt very badly, and Lucy had to defend me."

"Lucy?" Wrotham looked as though he wasn't quite sure if he should laugh or growl.

"My King Charles spaniel." Georgie smiled brilliantly. "She was the sweetest thing. No one could raise a hand to me while she was around or she'd growl and snarl and make a proper fuss."

"And this occurred when you were six?" Wrotham looked doubtfully at Georgie.

"Yes, I found Lucy in Father's study and was trying to get her to leave with me. I pulled her collar, and it slipped over her head. I fell against Father's worktable. A bottle of ink spilled, and he spanked me. The once." She nodded at Jemmy. "That's when my brother came in and took us out of the room."

The exact same look of disbelief mixed with repressed

laughter on the Wrothams' faces made Jemmy want to laugh even more. "As you see, my lord, hardly a dire matter." He tried to school his face, but a chuckle escaped him.

Lord and Lady Wrotham joined him, leaving Georgie miffed.

"It may not have been a proper beating, but it did hurt," she said indignantly.

"I believe it is now time to go in." Lady Wrotham took her husband's arm and led them from the room, her shoulders twitching.

Jemmy followed, with Georgina on his arm. "You had best beware, bran face. I will make that little smack seem like a feather's stroke if you don't stop telling that story."

"Then you will be the one to rue the day, Jemmy. One of Lucy's great-grandpuppies is still at Blackham." She smiled sweetly up at him. "And I've heard tell she bites."

The journey to Blackham, Jemmy's second in three days, had been more pleasant than expected, given his and Georgie's confrontation the evening before. His sister had started the day bravely cheerful; however, the final hour of the trip had seen her grow pensive, her front teeth worrying her bottom lip. As they swept up to the castle, she gripped his hand.

"It will be all right, my dear." He squeezed her hand back and helped her down from the carriage. "We can rest and dine before facing Father." Something he wanted to do as little as she. "Hal is home, at least he was yesterday. You never know how long he will light here."

Quick met them at the door. "His lordship requests your immediate presence in his office, my lord, my lady." The older man's face split with an unaccustomed smile. "It is very good to see you again, Lady Georgina."

"Thank you, Quick. It is good to see you as well." Georgie smiled as she relinquished her green wool spencer. "You haven't changed at all." She peered round the foyer, at the heavy ancestral weapons hung around the room. "Nothing has."

The butler bowed. "I will have Charles fetch your things to your old rooms."

"Thank you, Quick, but I will be staying the night only. Fellowes will see to my personal items. The rest can remain in the carriage. I leave at first light tomorrow."

"Very good, my lord."

Jemmy offered his arm, and Georgie placed a very small, very cold hand on it. "Don't worry, my dear. I will see you through the first interview with Father."

"Yes, but then you will leave me." She puckered her brows. "I shall have to go seek out Lulu."

"Lulu?"

"Lucy's great-grandpup."

Jemmy chuckled as they strode down the corridor. Georgina would be all right despite Father. He'd wager a year's income on his sister's resilience. At last, he stopped before the office door. "Are you ready?"

Raising her chin, she nodded and gripped his arm afresh.

Their father sat, behind the captain's table, in the exact same posture—hunched over, writing a letter—as Jemmy had left him in yesterday morning. Had the man not moved at all? What a wretched existence he must lead. When he inherited the marquessate, he'd be damned if he let the running of it consume his life like that.

They waited several moments before the older man raised his head, his dark eyes betraying an interest in Georgina. "Well, step forward, let me have a look at you, child." He rose slowly, his face flinching as though he'd not done so in many hours.

Georgie bit her lip but dutifully stepped toward the table, giving him a slight smile. "Good afternoon, Father."

"Hmm. Turn around please."

Obediently, Georgie turned in a circle with a sigh, the small steps making her bob.

"You have turned into a lovely young woman." The marquess sounded surprised. "I commend you on making the most of yourself, despite your disobedience and subsequent dire circumstances."

"Thank you, Father. I have had the good fortune to make friends who have been very kind." Georgie clasped her hands, squeezing them together.

"You'll not need those friends any longer. I have arranged a very advantageous match for you, despite your previous disrespect to me and to the family." Father's brows dipped almost to his nose. "You are to marry within the month. I have had a letter just today that confirms the arrangement."

Georgie turned deathly white and staggered backward.

Jemmy leaped forward to steady her. "You could have told me, Father. I would have broken the news to her better than this."

His father shrugged. "The news should be a pleasing prospect to Georgina. Not only will she be received by the family once more, but she will finally be aiding the family's future. I was fortunate that Lord Travers was still in need of a wife and heir. It has been over three years since I had to break off negotiations with him because Georgina ran off and contracted that *mésalliance* with Kirkpatrick."

"Lord Travers?" Two spots of color rose in Georgina's cheeks. "That pompous, overbearing, popinjay with the nasty smile?" She shuddered and clutched Jemmy.

"I would not cast such aspersions on my betrothed were I you, Georgina. The man is respectable and, for some reason, still retains a fondness for you. He was quite eager to discuss settlements when I contacted him last week."

"He used to leer at me when I first came out," she whispered to Jemmy. "I hated attending parties and balls because Lord Travers was always first in line to ask for a dance. His hands were so moist I could feel it through my gloves."

"Is there no one else you could marry her off to?" Jemmy glared at his father as he helped Georgie to a seat on the leather settle, then stood behind her, trying to lend her as much strength as possible.

"Why need I look further?" His father sounded genuinely surprised at the question. "The man's an earl, has more than sufficient property and income, and a great desire for the match. Your sister should be grateful that I offer this as an olive branch. If she does not care to avail herself of it, I will wash my hands of her for good, and she can find a husband on her own. One who will take her with no dowry or connections." His smile had an evil glint. "Not an easy task for a widow with not a penny to her name."

"I will have Mother's inheritance." Georgie spoke up, though she didn't look at her father. "A man might take that into consideration."

"Perhaps. Although so much might happen in the six years before you come into that money. Some men may not desire to gamble on such a thing." Father's tone suggested he certainly would not.

Jemmy dug into Georgie's shoulders with a convulsive grip. "Do you care nothing for your children, Father, other than to use us as pawns to further the family's wealth and connections?"

"What other reason should there be other than to serve the family?" His father watched him with cold eyes. "You forget yourself, Brack." He drew another letter from a pile of correspondence and waved them away. "I will see you in the morning."

Narrowly holding his anger in check, Jemmy helped Georgina to stand, then escorted her from the room. How could Father do this to Georgie? He should have expected the man to continue to exact revenge for his sister's disobedience, but marrying her to a man she actively disliked was carrying it too far. Perhaps he should remain at Blackham for a few days to support his sister. If he could come up with an alternate plan for her, she wouldn't need to make this odious marriage to Travers, a profligate rake with a scandalous reputation no amount of money could make acceptable for a sensitive woman like Georgina.

He'd write to Elizabeth and explain the circumstances. A second letter, to his friend Robin, Marquess of St. Just, might be in order as well. Two heads were better than one, they said, and Rob always had an outrageous plan of action to offer. Right now, the outrageous might be his best hope.

Chapter 19

This time, the half day's journey to London felt like a week. Alone in the carriage again, with a fresh set of worries and only her own thoughts for company, Elizabeth could have sworn time stood still.

Her last look at Jemmy, waving cheerfully as the carriage pulled away, would remain seared into her memory. Even now she longed to see him again. A hollow space in her heart ached to have him hold her once more. She would not have thought it possible, even two months ago, but Jemmy had captured her heart, and Elizabeth had been powerless to stop it.

Didn't want to stop it. Perhaps she had unconsciously wanted a man in her life again, not because she no longer loved Dickon, but because she herself needed to be loved. Now the sobering reality that she and Jemmy would have to fight to marry had made her wary and put her on edge. The baby could be kept a secret for another few months, until she began to show. By then her options would be few indeed, so she didn't want to think of that at the moment.

Unfortunately, her mind was being as stubborn as the marquess himself, shifting back to Jemmy and the plight of their marriage rather than ordinary subjects, like her children or the coming Christmas holidays. By the time she reached her parents' town house in St. James Square, she had worried her handkerchief so it lay in tatters on her lap. Clutching it to her, she descended the carriage, straightened her shoulders, and marched up the steps.

"Good to have you back, Mrs. Easton." Tawes took her wrap, a hint of a smile on his lips.

She'd always gotten on well with their butler. "Thank you, Tawes. Where are Mama and Papa?" she asked, stripping off her gloves and flexing her chilly fingers.

"Her ladyship is in the upstairs parlor. Lord Wentworth is in his study."

"How much time before dinner, Tawes?" She needed to speak to her parents together. Lord knows she didn't want to have to repeat Lord Blackham's hateful words more than once.

"A little more than an hour, madam."

"Good. Would you ask his lordship to attend us in the parlor?"

"Very good, ma'am." Tawes accepted her gloves, and she headed up the stairs.

The cozy green and gold parlor, with its dainty furniture, gilt and white picture frames, and generous fireplace was usually her favorite room in the house. Today, however, it seemed colder, less welcoming somehow, as she approached her mother, who sat at one end of the green and gold striped sofa, a well-filled tea tray next to her.

"Elizabeth. Goodness, we didn't expect you home until at least tomorrow. Come kiss me, my dear." Her mother set her teacup into its saucer and presented her right cheek.

"Hello, Mama." Elizabeth dutifully bussed the proffered cheek but cast a curious gaze around the room. "Where are the girls? Surely they are dining in tonight?"

"Sadly no, my dear." Patting the cushion beside her, her mother smiled invitingly then picked up her cup once more.

"Since I didn't expect you to return so soon, I gave permission for them to dine with Lady Mary Callon-Gorge." Mama kept chattering while she rang the bell and ordered more tea. "Why have you returned so early? How was Lady Cavendish— I mean, Lady Wrotham's wedding? Did you bring a piece of the wedding cake home for Dotty?"

"No, Mama. I am sorry, but I completely forgot to bring it." Best sit across from her mother while delivering her news. Elizabeth sank down into the green wing-backed chair opposite the sofa.

"Well, dear, Dotty will be so disappointed. She has talked of nothing but dreaming of her future husband." Mama shook her head and paused for a sip of tea.

"I am sorry, Mama." Elizabeth seized the moment to take the conversational reins. "I will explain it to Dotty when she comes home tonight. But I wanted to tell you my news."

"News?" Mama's eyes grew round, glee spreading across her face. "Tell, tell! One says nothing ever happens in the country, but Lady Wrotham's parties seem determined to break that rule."

"I've asked Papa to join us. He will want to hear this as well." Elizabeth turned anxiously as the door opened, but it was only the maid with fresh tea.

"Oh, dear. I do hope it is not bad news." After pouring, her mother dropped four large lumps of sugar into her own cup.

Elizabeth shuddered as always at so much sweetness, adding one lump to hers. "That may well depend on what you and Papa can tell me. There is a sort of mystery afoot, and I dearly hope you can enlighten me about it."

"Mystery? Elizabeth, please tell me you have not gotten yourself mixed up in some intrigue down in Kent, of all places. First, it was those robbers you told me of, now something different has occurred?" Her mother's eyebrows swooped upward, alarmingly close to her hairline.

"No, Mama. Not intrigue. At least, I don't think so." She

sipped the hot tea, and the tension in her shoulders lessened. "But it does apparently concern you and Papa."

"What concerns Papa?" Her father came through the doorway, a cherubic smile on his handsome face. "Good afternoon, darling. Did you just now return? We have missed you." He strode forward to kiss her cheek. "I am so used to having you back with us I don't quite know what to do when you are gone anymore."

She must seize this perfect opportunity to tell them. "That is what I wished to tell you about." Elizabeth set her cup down and squeezed her hands together. "Papa, Mama, I am to be married again."

"What?" Her parents spoke in unison, her mother suspending her cup before her face while her father froze in the act of reaching for a piece of bread and butter.

"Married again?" Mama rattled her teacup into its saucer. "But you have just put away your mourning, Elizabeth. I assumed you would grieve for Dickon at least a little while longer. You seemed so heartbroken when he died."

"I know, Mama." Heartbeat speeding up, Elizabeth set her cup down before she spilled it. Indeed, it seemed strange to say out loud that she would marry again. Only the image of Jemmy's dear face gave her the courage to continue. "I did not believe I would ever love again, but it has happened."

"Is it that chap you sisters were talking of the last time you came home? Lord Brack?" The bread and butter continued into Papa's mouth. "Afraid I don't know him."

"Did you meet him at Lady Wrotham's party? You never said a word about him to me." Mama turned a cool eye to her husband. "When did Bella or Dotty speak of this Lord Brack to you?"

"In October, I believe. About the time Bella's betrothal was announced. Perhaps you were distracted by Lord Haxton's presence." Papa gave her an arch look that was ignored.

"Well, I must say you have been a slyboots about this, Elizabeth. Now"—Mama settled back again, hands crossed over her stomach—"who is this Lord Brack?"

"I believe you know his father, the Marquess of Black-ham?" Elizabeth sipped her tea, keenly interested in her mother's answer. At last, she would find out the reason for Lord Blackham's rejection of her.

Her mother gave a strangled shriek and clutched her throat.

"Blackham!" Papa spat the name as if it was poison. "You wish to marry the Marquess of Blackham's son?"

"Ohhh . . ." Her mother had slumped over on the sofa, moaning in a low, guttural voice. The usually serene expression on her face had flown, leaving wild staring eyes of vivid blue in a stark white face, held in the grip of an unspeakable horror.

Shocked and confused at this totally unexpected reaction, Elizabeth carefully set her cup down once more. "Yes," she answered, shakily. "His eldest son, James, is Lord Brack." The suspicion that all was not well, based on yesterday's interview with Lord Blackham, had erupted into full-blown fear. What in the world could have happened to provoke a reaction such as this from her parents?

"It is out of the question, Elizabeth." Her father drew himself up, tall and forbidding.

"But, Papa—"

"No, Elizabeth." Her mother had sat up and recovered her voice, though she still clutched her throat. A wash of pink had suffused her face, so perhaps she would not faint after all. "He is a cruel, cruel man. You must not marry him."

"I'm not marrying Lord Blackham, I'm marrying his son. Jemmy is nothing like his father from what I have observed." Fear flooded her mouth, leaving a sharp, coppery taste in its wake. She'd clung to the hope her family would be supportive of her marriage to Jemmy, even if his father was not. They might have been able to live at Worth House for the time before Jemmy came into his inheritance. Without their assistance, however, their marriage would hinge solely on Jemmy's grandfather, a completely unknown factor. The impossibility of it ever taking place began to loom larger in her mind.

"He must take after his poor mother, then." Groping in her pocket, Mama produced a handkerchief and pressed it to her streaming eyes.

"You knew his mother?" Elizabeth seized on this smidgeon of hope in the swirling chaos. "Then surely you must believe me when I tell you Jemmy is a wonderful man who will make me as happy as Dickon ever did."

"His mother, God rest her soul, was a sweet girl. So he may be all you say he is. But if he's got Blackham's blood in him, well . . ." Her father shook his head, his face grave. "I warn you, he could change."

"What did the man do to make you say such a thing?" Fear bubbled in her veins. Jemmy was nothing like his father, but dear God, could he become so in the future? The marquess had struck her as being stubborn and rather harsh, but not the monster her parents seemed to loathe. "You must tell me."

"He killed Louisa." Her mother broke down completely, sobbing with such anguish Elizabeth flew to her side and threw her arms around her.

"Oh, Mama, certainly not." She held the shaking woman, her own confidence shaken to the ground. "Who was Louisa?"

"Lord Blackham's second wife and your mother's best friend." Her father clenched his teeth and abruptly strode to the bell and rang.

"I'm so sorry, Mama." Elizabeth hugged her mother tighter, tears starting from her eyes. Lord Blackham must be a fiend to have done such a thing. But what had he done? How had he managed to escape justice? Even a peer could not kill someone outright and not expect to be arrested. Last century, Earl Ferrers had found that out to his dismay. And why had she heard nothing of this from Georgie or Jemmy? Did they not know? "What did he do? Are you certain it was not an accident?"

"No. It was no accident." Hiccupping, her mother sat up, wiping her streaming face. "He knew she should not have any more children, yet he insisted on keeping her breeding. My poor Louisa."

"Oh." Elizabeth sat back as well, less certain of Lord Blackham's villainy. A woman entered marriage knowing her duty was to bear her husband children, with the attendant risks that childbirth entailed. "Then he didn't mean to kill her, Mama. Childbirth is always uncertain. And I'm sure it was sad for you to lose her as she was your bosom friend, but Lord Blackham—"

"Lord Blackham knew so many children so quickly would kill her. The doctor told Louisa she should wait for at least a year after her last child was born or it could go badly for her. But she would not listen and refuse Blackham her bed."

Such blunt talk before a man froze Elizabeth. Surreptitiously, she glanced at her father, whose stony face held no sign of blush. Most gentlemen would have run from such a conversation. She cleared her throat and sipped the now-cold tea.

"Do not be shocked at my frank speech. I have hated Lord Blackham these twenty-five years since Louisa's death." She waved a hand at her husband. "You needn't mind your father. He's heard this all before."

Another shock, but before she could quite take it in, the door opened, and a footman bearing a decanter and glasses entered.

Elizabeth stared at the dregs in her teacup while the man deposited the tray on the sideboard and disappeared out the door. Certainly, she sympathized with her mother's sentiments; however, she was not quite as convinced as Mama that Lord Blackham had intentionally meant to kill his wife. Neither could she understand Lord Blackham's refusal to allow her to marry his son. Her mother and perhaps her father might have an objection, but Jemmy's father should bear her family no ill will. Some piece to the puzzle was still missing.

"Mama, even if this is true, I still do not understand why Lord Blackham will not allow Jemmy and me to wed. Your friendship with his wife and your accusations of his . . . killing her, unless you did so publicly, shouldn't have caused such a refusal." Raising an eyebrow deliberately, Elizabeth stared at her mother. "Is there something you are not telling me?"

"Yes, my dear, there is." Her father drained his glass and poured another. "What she is not telling you is that Lord Blackham offered for your mother before he offered for her friend."

Elizabeth gripped the handle of the cup so tightly she feared it would snap. Mama almost married Jemmy's father? The very idea made her skin crawl. She shivered and sank back on the sofa. "Obviously, you refused him."

"My family wanted the match very badly. Wanted to have their daughter a marchioness. And I dutifully met his lordship at balls and parties." Mama's face was blank as she sat lost in the memory. "He was older, but not too objectionable. Very distinguished-looking, I thought at the time. I could perhaps have made the match, but then . . ." She turned to Papa and held out her hand.

He took it and kissed her fingers.

"I met Wentworth at Lady Gill-Abbot's ball, and I knew, I just knew I could never marry anyone else. My father called me a fool, but he agreed to the match and refused Blackham's suit. The marquess was livid." She narrowed her eyes at the remembrance. "Why he would think all he needed to do was make an offer and his title would do the rest, I'm sure I don't know."

"Having met the man, I can understand it." Grimly, Elizabeth recalled the marquess's haughty tone and demeanor. He would certainly think his title reason enough to marry him.

"After I met your father, I didn't encourage Blackham at all." She swallowed hard. "But Louisa did." She clutched her husband's hand. "I was never quite sure if Louisa had come to care for Blackham, or if perhaps she felt sorry for him. Or if the idea of being the Marchioness of Blackham turned her head. Blackham had made no secret of the fact he wished to wed again, and quickly. He'd not been out of mourning for his first wife a week before he appeared at Almack's, trying to court me. After I refused him, Louisa set her cap for him."

The pieces of the puzzle were beginning to sort themselves out in Elizabeth's mind. Her mother had been the marquess's preferred choice. And the marquess always got what he wanted, according to Jemmy. Only this time he hadn't. So he had married Mama's best friend as revenge? "Did you see your friend much after her marriage?"

"No. I never saw her again." Tears glistened in her mother's eyes. "And that . . . fiend she married refused to even let her write to me." Her head came up, a triumphant smile on her lips. "But we managed to outsmart him. Louisa was not forbidden to write to her sisters, so she wrote to Mary, her next youngest sister, and would sometimes enclose a letter for me as well that Mary would send on. So I knew when her first child, the heir, was born, then a pair of twin daughters, and another daughter." She squeezed her eyes shut. "At last, came a letter from Mary without one from Louisa, telling me that my friend had died during the birth of her fifth child. Five children in as many years." Wiping the tears away, her mother lapsed into silence.

"Of course, there were the two that were twins," her father added, as if to keep the facts of the matter straight.

"Still, there were too many, too close together. Even the doctor said so."

"He'd waited twelve years with a barren wife, he told me." Elizabeth shook her head, deeply saddened. "So I suppose he meant to have as many children as he could as quickly as he could. I can see him wanting that above all else."

"That may have had something to do with it." Her mother sniffed, drawing in ragged breaths. "But I believe he did it to spite me, to get back at me for my refusal."

"Mama!"

"I slighted him. He knew Louisa was my best friend in the world. Everyone knew it, for we were constantly together. So he married her. But when he discovered that hadn't hurt me, he took her off to the country and wouldn't let her see me or correspond with me, or so he thought. Then he killed her and . . . and it's all my fault." Weeping as though her heart would break, Mama covered her face. "If I hadn't rejected him so harshly . . . if I had tried harder to discourage Louisa from marrying him, perhaps she would be alive today."

"There, there, my dear. I have told you time and again, it was not your fault. And I doubt you could have swayed Louisa, no matter what you said." Her father patted her mother's arm, then commenced pacing back and forth before them, looking like he could use another drink.

"And if you had done so, Mama, neither Jemmy, nor Georgina, nor their brother and sisters would have been born." Grasping her mother's hands, Elizabeth peered into her face. "Neither do you know if your friend would have wanted such a thing." If Jemmy's mother had wanted the match, even Mama would not likely have deterred her. "You cannot change the past, Mama." She shook her head sadly. "If anyone knows that, it is I. All we can do is make the best of the present and look to the future." Elizabeth grasped her courage. "I love Lord Brack and will marry him, no matter what."

After a long silence, during which Papa seemed to peer into her soul, he sighed. "She is right, Amelia." He moved beside Mama, his hand gently resting on her shoulder. "I've told you time and again, my dear; you must find it in your heart to let this hatred go. Nothing at all is served by it, and it tears you to pieces each time you think of it." He shifted his gaze to Elizabeth, clenched his jaw, then nodded. "Especially if Elizabeth is determined to marry Blackham's son."

Thank goodness, Papa had come around. He'd always taken her part in any conflict with Mama.

"I just don't know if I can, Wentworth." Mama sniffed into her handkerchief.

"You must try, Mama." Elizabeth held her mother closer. "You must find a way to forgive Lord Blackham instead and help to persuade him to allow Jemmy and me to marry. If not, Jemmy will be cut off without a farthing until he turns thirty and inherits his mother's money. It is not a long time, true, but we simply must wed well before his birthday in August." They absolutely could not wait.

"His birthday is in August, you say?" Her father's puzzled frown deepened. "Eight months is truly not the end of the world, Elizabeth. I know short betrothals are the fashion these days, but it is by no means an unreasonable time for an engagement. Have you given this due consideration?"

"Your father is correct, Elizabeth." Wiping her face and fanning it with her limp handkerchief, Mama raised her gaze and nodded emphatically. "You can wait that short a time easily. You will stay with us, and Lord Brack can keep his bachelor rooms in Town and have a long, decorous courtship."

"I am afraid we cannot wait, Mama." Elizabeth sighed. This would not be easy. "In fact, waiting is quite out of the question." She must write Jemmy at once, asking him to come to London and meet her family. Once he met them, Mama and Papa must love him as much as she did. They could be married from St. George's and live here quietly at Worth House until he received his inheritance.

"What is the rush, my dear?" Frowning, Mama sniffed and added another lump to her tea.

Steeling her courage with a final sip of ice-cold tea, Elizabeth drew a deep breath. "The rush is to mask the fact, as best we can, that our child will be born a bit too soon after the wedding." She stared into the shocked faces and stiffened her resolve. "Now, how can we get Lord Blackham to consent?"

Chapter 20

"Where is Hal?" Jemmy glanced around the breakfast room the next morning as he sat down to a plate of eggs and sausages. The table's sole occupant was his father, who sat cracking the top off an egg with military precision.

"I have no idea." Father waved away his second son. "The puppy wastes my money flitting from school to school, returns here for a day or two, then takes himself off God knows where. I should put a stop to it, withdraw his funds. But then he'd likely move in here permanently, and that I would not stand for. Let him disrupt someone else's household."

The top of the egg popped off, and Father methodically scraped the tiny scrap of meat onto his plate before discarding the shell.

"Sons can be so inconvenient." Jemmy signaled the footman for coffee and tucked his napkin into his lap. Hal seemed to lead the charmed life.

"Quite." His father sipped his tea, then resumed hollowing out his egg. "I have written to Buckleigh this morning about the settlements for Lady Maude. Once they are satisfactorily completed, we will proceed with the wedding plans."

"What?" Startled by the outlandish suggestion, Jemmy narrowly missed spilling the coffee the footman had just set before him. Father had gone too far this time. "I told you, Father, I will not marry anyone other than Elizabeth Easton. I do not care that you will cut me off. Do your worst. In eight months, I will have Mother's inheritance, and that will be an end of it."

"I think you will marry Lady Maude without any fuss, my boy. You may have misjudged what my worst can be."

A tickle of apprehension hit Jemmy right between his shoulder blades, the exact spot a knife might be inserted. True, his father was capable of cruelty, as witness his treatment of Georgie, but what more than cutting off his funds could the old man do? "I will take my chances."

"Will you? I wonder." Lord Blackham smiled, and Jemmy's stomach roiled.

His father never smiled.

"You may find it interesting that I have also written to Lady Locke this morning." A quick glance at Jemmy before he continued scraping industriously at the almost empty eggshell.

"You have been busy this morning, I see." With an effort, Jemmy managed to maintain his nonchalance, though his mouth suddenly dried as though filled with sand. Lady Locke was the most notorious gossip in London. Whatever Father had written would be the talk of the *ton* hours after the lady read the contents of the letter. The woman had a cadre of gossipmongers at her command, ready to spread true tale or vicious rumor in an instant.

"You should not lie abed so late. You miss the best part of the day. The one thing I approve about your sister is her habit of rising and breakfasting early. She was here hours ago." He stared pointedly at Jemmy. "I, too, am an early riser. I had just sat down to a cup of tea when Georgina appeared."

Foreboding exploded into full-blown fear. Father's intense stare, coming from that smug face, could only mean he thought he'd got the better of Jemmy. Pray God it wasn't true.

"Your sister has always been a chatty creature, and while it is not a habit I approve, it did prove quite enlightening this morning."

Swallowing to clear his throat, Jemmy's tongue stuck to the roof of his otherwise dry mouth.

"She prattled on about the Countess of Wrotham's wedding and happened to mention that the bride was in an interesting condition, despite the fact the wedding took place only a few days ago."

Confused, yet wary still, Jemmy allowed himself to hope Georgie had been more discrete with Elizabeth's similar condition.

"Her confession about Lady Wrotham meant nothing to me; however, it occurred to me that Mrs. Easton might very easily be in a similar situation. Young people have so little restraint these days."

Fighting to maintain absolute control over his face, Jemmy tamped down the fear that would give him away, should it become evident to his father. "So unfortunate for you that she is not." The lie came easily to his lips. To protect his beloved, he'd lie to God himself.

His father shrugged. "That is one of the problems with society today. They care so little for the truth. A lie will do just as well—and sometimes better if it will make a rumor that much more juicy. So they will be shocked, but oh so pleased, to find that you were stopped from making the grave mistake of marrying Mrs. Easton, who was trying to foist her bastard off as yours." Father patted the table beside his plate, where a long letter lay half hidden.

Why hadn't he noticed that letter before?

"After Georgina left, I wrote to Lady Locke, who would certainly want to know about Mrs. Easton's perfidy and your timely escape." Father sipped his coffee, then wiped his smug lips.

"You are the bastard, Father." Jemmy shot to his feet, banging the table and making the dishes rattle. "Elizabeth is—" Some deeply instinctual voice warned him not to confess about the child. Don't give his father any further leverage. Clenching his fists, he took a deep breath, bringing himself back under control. "Elizabeth is innocent, yet you will cause her to be ruined for what? Why will you do this to her? To us?"

The evil smile that curled his father's mouth would have struck terror into anyone who saw it. "As the saying goes, 'Vengeance is a dish best eaten cold.' I have waited a very long time for this particular dish."

The horror of the situation began to sink in. "Vengeance for what? What slight—real or imagined—is worth ruining Elizabeth?"

"Oh, the slight was real. Very real indeed." Father clenched his hands where they lay on the table. Grasping the letter to Lady Locke, he waved it tantalizingly before Jemmy's face. "If you do not give up this mad quest to marry Mrs. Easton, I will put this letter into Lady Locke's hands by the next post."

Slumping into his chair, Jemmy shielded his face with his hand, thinking furiously. Should he tell his father that Elizabeth was indeed carrying his child? Would the hope of an heir be enough to make him change his mind? Jemmy feared not, and so could not risk that revelation. So that damnable letter must be prevented from finding its way to Lady Locke at all costs. He would have to pretend to acquiesce to his father's demands, then as soon as he left the breakfast table, ride hell-bent for London. If the weather held, he could be there in a day.

He could procure a special license and marry Elizabeth immediately. It was not the way he had hoped they would wed, but with his marriage, his father's threats would become harmless. Or almost harmless. There might still be talk, but pray God, when the child was born, it would favor him, with a bit of Elizabeth thrown in for good measure. Still, enough to put paid to any speculation it was not his child.

Now to the dilemma at hand. How to prevent that blasted letter from being sent. "Of course, I do not want these false rumors spread." He raised his head to meekly face his father. "The main thing is to keep Elizabeth's reputation spotless. I will give you my word I will do as you ask, if you pledge me yours that you will not send that letter."

"You will marry Lady Maude?"

Swallowing down the bile that choked his throat, Jemmy nodded. "If that is what you wish and Elizabeth is not harmed." There was no honor in this blackmail; therefore, he did not consider himself bound by his word in this case.

"Buckleigh should arrive later this week. The settlements will be agreed upon and a date for the wedding set. As it is close to the Christmas holiday, I will suggest the week between Christmas and New Year's. You will meet with Lady Maude, marry her, and give our line an heir of whom to be proud."

"Of that you may be sure, Father." Jaws clenched so tightly they ached, Jemmy bowed and strode from the room. Now to act, while his father was lulled into a sense of security. Taking the stairs two at a time, he made his way up to Fellowes's chamber and rapped on the door. "I need you."

A faint "Yes, my lord" came through the valet's door.

Jemmy continued down the corridor to his room. He must avoid the appearance of leaving. Sadly, that meant abandoning Fellowes for a time. No matter. He would compensate the man well. Jemmy popped the door to his chamber open and hurried inside. His steps slowed as other implications surfaced.

He had no money, save for a handful of coins. That would scarcely do to get him to London. If only he'd thought to draw from his account before coming to Blackham, but that avenue was now closed to him. Did Georgie have any money? Likely not, given her circumstances, but it never hurt to ask. She was a very resourceful girl. Something might turn up.

With a sigh, he pulled at his cravat. Where the devil was Fellowes? The man had been right behind him. Jemmy strode back to the door, unbuttoning his waistcoat. He grasped the latch and pushed down.

Nothing happened.

Frowning, he rattled the handle, but it simply wouldn't move down. He rapped on the door again. "Fellowes? Fellowes. What's going on here?"

"Mr. Fellowes has been taken to the village, my lord, and will be put on the eleven-thirty mail coach to London." The voice of a footman answered him with dreadful precision.

"Why? And why is this door locked?"

"The marquess's orders, my lord."

"Damn you." Jemmy pounded on the door, then ran a hand through his hair. What the devil was he going to do now?

Georgina.

Backing away from the door, Jemmy rushed to the secret panel and carefully pried it away. The inky black hole gaped open, and he sighed in relief. A glance over his shoulder, and he sprinted back to the door, pressing his ear against it, but heard nothing. He rattled the latch.

"Yes, my lord?"

So Father had posted a permanent guard. He was taking no chances on him escaping. "Tell my father this was hardly necessary." The old man knew him extremely well, but perhaps not well enough.

"Very good, my lord."

Silence returned, but whether from the footman's lack of conversation or his absence, Jemmy couldn't tell. As long as no one tried to come into the room, he was safe. He slipped into the secret passage, pulled the panel closed behind him, and threaded his way through the narrow, dark space. At last, he scratched lightly on Georgie's panel. It opened to reveal his sister holding a candlestick, her face pale.

"Jemmy. Do you know what is going on? The door to my chamber is locked." She backed up as he strode in, going immediately to the door and rattling the latch.

"Shhh." Georgie darted forward.

"Yes, my lady?" Another footman's voice. Damn.

"Nothing, James," Georgie called through the wood. "I just wanted to keep you on your toes while you guard me." She beckoned Jemmy toward the window that looked out toward the back of the estate. "I was coming to see you. To tell you that I had been locked in again. What do you think it means?"

"It means our father is a right bastard and about to force me to marry Lady Maude." The words steeled his resolve. He was not going to marry anyone except Elizabeth.

"I don't know what, but something happened at breakfast. I had been telling him about Charlotte's wedding—not that I thought he was interested, mind you, but one must talk of something—and I mentioned that she and Nash were to expect their first child in the spring. I didn't think he was actually listening to me, Jemmy, but he must have been because he looked up and, oh, Jemmy, he *smiled*." She gulped, her eyes widening in horror. "It was the most terrifying thing I'd ever seen. If he'd smiled like that at Waterloo, the French soldiers would have run screaming back to Paris without firing a shot."

"Huh." Jemmy snorted, even though the situation was not funny. "I just saw a demonstration of that myself. It does put one's teeth on edge."

"But Jemmy, why? Why did he smile like that and then lock me in my room?"

"You gave him an idea, bran face. An idea of how to make me agree to marry Lady Maude." The man's mind was fiendish, make no mistake about it.

"What?" Georgie's hand flew to her mouth, shocked into a large O.

"When you told him about Lady Wrotham increasing, he decided to blackmail me, threatening me with sending a letter to Lady Locke saying Elizabeth was increasing and she was trying to make me marry her when the child wasn't mine."

"Oh, Jemmy." Georgie sank down into a chair, her eyes staring. "Lady Locke." Her eyes widened impossibly large. "She'll be ruined. You'll be ruined. Lady Locke will—"

"I know. I've soothed Father with the assurance I will marry Lady Maude to gain time to thwart him." He gazed about the room. How could he escape?

"But you're going to marry Elizabeth, Jemmy. You can't break her heart!" She grabbed him by the shoulder and shook him like a dog does a rat.

"Nothing in heaven or earth will keep me from marrying her, my dear." He stilled her hand, then cocked his head at the door. "He locked my door, so I had thought to escape through yours, but that way is blocked as well."

"Father is quite the tyrant, isn't he?"

"Quite." He strode to the one window in Georgie's room. His chamber was inner-facing, without any windows. His sister's room, however, overlooked the kitchen garden. Looking down at the frostbitten cabbages and straggling rows of wilted lamb's lettuce, he cursed under his breath. The two-story drop would likely kill him.

"You're not going to jump, are you?" Clutching his arm, Georgie peered out the window beside him.

"No. I don't have a death wish." He shook his head, craning his neck to look down the black face of the wall. "I do wish this blasted wall had something growing on it. I could shimmy down that, I suppose."

A scraping noise at the door had Jemmy diving under the bed, skinning the heels of his hands on the floorboards. No one knew of their secret passage, and he preferred to keep that secret.

"Do not worry, Jemmy. It is only a letter . . . from Charlotte." Tedium turned to excitement as Georgie grasped the letter more firmly and popped the blob of red wax off the paper as Jemmy pulled himself out from beneath the bed. She unfolded the sheet of fine white paper with flourished writing across the page. When she did so, a smaller, folded piece of paper fell to the floor.

"What's this?" Jemmy grabbed the square of paper and rose from the floor. Glancing at the scrap he froze, the handwriting at once familiar.

"It's a letter from Elizabeth," they said in unison.

"Charlotte writes that she received this letter for you from Elizabeth yesterday." Georgie waved her letter under his nose. "She feared neither of us would be allowed to receive letters from her but prayed a message from Charlotte would pass through unsuspected."

"Clever woman." Jemmy unfolded the tiny letter as carefully as he could, though his hands shook with the restraint.

"My dearest love . . ." Head reeling at the impact of her endearment, he vowed they would be together always if he had to burn the house down to escape to go to her. He continued to read, frustration and fear mounting with each word on the page.

He glanced up at Georgie. "She begs me to come to her. Christ!" Crumpling the edge of the letter in a convulsive grip, Jemmy stared at his sister, frantic. "How can I escape, Georgie?"

"If only I were Rapunzel, I would let my hair down out the window and you could climb down." She patted her bright auburn hair, smiling sadly.

"Hair?" No, but what else could support his weight? A glance around the room, and his gaze lit on the bed. He rushed to the window, doing a rough calculation of the height. God, he hoped he was accurate enough. "It could work."

Georgie backed away from him. "But, Jemmy, my hair is much too short to—"

"Not hair—bedsheets. We can knot them together and toss them out the window." Excitedly, he searched the room for other cloth that could be employed in a similar manner, but quickly gave it up. "We'll have to anchor it to something." The dressing table was too light, the door latch way across the room. The near leg of the bed was closest, so it would have to do. Time was of the essence. "If we tie it to the bedpost, that should serve." He patted the post. "This bed is solid oak, so it should do fine. "Now, how many sets of bed linens do we have?"

"I think only the ones that are on the bed." Georgie trotted to the clothes chest and peered into the bottom. "No," she sighed after sticking her whole head inside the wardrobe.

"I pray two sets will be enough, for we have the sheets on my bed as well. If we pull them crosswise it should give us more than enough length." Jemmy threw back her covers and grasped the edge of the top sheet.

"Wait." Georgie grabbed his hand before he could pull it free. "What will you do once you get out? Can you steal one of Father's horses?"

"I may have to bribe a groom. Do you have any money?" Cold hard coins would be an asset right now.

"No, not a farthing."

Damn. Well, stealing the horse would likely not be a huge problem, especially if he waited a few hours until most of the grooms were asleep. The journey to London would be difficult, however, if he couldn't stop along the way to purchase food and drink. He ran his hand through his hair, pulling the short strands. "I'll manage somehow."

Georgie had been standing still, a perplexed frown on her face. "Let me see if I am allowed to write to Charlotte. If so,

I can ask to borrow a few pounds." Her cheeks turned pink. "I can tell her it's because of the coming wedding to Lord Travers. I'll tell her I fear Father won't give me money for wedding clothes, so I want to at least purchase some new ribbons."

"The perfect excuse, my dear." His sister had ever been a master schemer.

"I'll put in about your plight with Lady Maude as well, so if Father does think to read it, he will think you are resigned to it and won't suspect the money is for you."

"Another clever woman in my life. What would I do without you?" He hugged her and kissed her forehead. "You start on your sheets, and I'll grab mine."

Georgie stayed his hand. "If I'm allowed to write, it will take at least until tomorrow to receive Charlotte's reply and the money. Until then, we must act as though nothing is amiss, so our linens must remain on the beds until tomorrow after they bring dinner." She licked her lips. "Unless they mean to starve us into submission."

"Father wants our obedience, not our deaths. We are much more valuable to him alive than dead. But you make a good point about everything needing to seem the same as usual." The next twenty-four hours would try his patience to the bone, but it must be endured. Better to take this time now than risk not getting to London at all. "Let me return to my room in case Father comes up to talk about the settlements with His Grace." He grunted as he opened the secret door. "I almost wish he would. I'd truss him up like a guinea fowl ready for roasting and spirit us both off to London and safety."

"As long as you escape his clutches and get safely to Elizabeth, it will all have been worth it." She patted his arm, and love for his sister welled up within him.

"I swear to you, Georgina, I will find you some husband other than Travers. You deserve much, much better than him. Once I'm in London, I'll write to St. Just again, ask him to please come up with another plan. Rob's a great one for making plans." He grinned at her, and she wrinkled her nose.

"Do not do me any favors on that account, Jemmy."

Apparently, there really was little love lost between his sister and his friend. "Still, keep a lookout for him. You don't have to like him to accept his help."

Jemmy grabbed the candlestick and ducked back into the dusty tunnel between their rooms. Pray God, this harebrained scheme would work. He'd keep an eye on the footmen when they brought his dinner. If he could overpower them, he'd run for it, steal a horse, and be gone. At Blackham Castle, it was always prudent to have a secondary plan in mind.

Chapter 21

"Oh, dear Lord!" Sinking onto the sofa in the family sitting room, Elizabeth let Charlotte's letter flutter to the floor like a dying sparrow. Spasms of pain gripped her stomach so badly, she feared she might cast up her accounts.

"What is wrong—" Mama looked up from her book of Lord Byron's poetry. "Elizabeth! Are you quite all right?"

"Charlotte writes that Jemmy is being held captive at Blackham Castle, under lock and key, by his father." Fantastical words Elizabeth could scarce comprehend. She stared straight ahead, seeing nothing. This explained why the letter had arrived by special courier. Hot and cold shivers wracked her body so violently she could barely sit. She could only gasp in air and try not to swoon.

"I told you his father was a fiend. Elizabeth? Elizabeth!" Her mother let Byron drop onto the sofa, bounded to her feet, and rushed over to her. "Your face is paper white."

The world tried to turn dark, and Elizabeth struggled to remain conscious as she slid over onto the cushion. No, this couldn't be happening.

"Elizabeth. Here, breathe."

The *sal volatile* fumes rocked her into an upright position. The stuff was vile, but it worked.

"What is wrong, my dear? Lord Brack is not injured, is he? Merely detained?" Mama patted her cheeks with little stinging slaps that annoyed rather than hurt. "Blackham cannot hold him forever."

"But Charlotte says he will hold him long enough for him to wed the duke's daughter." Elizabeth's heart hitched, beating fast, then slow, aching as though a phantom hand gripped it. "She had it from Georgie. The marquess will keep Jemmy locked up until he agrees to marry Lady Maude Aston."

"Lady Maude? Oh, dear. How unfortunate a match," Mama tsk-tsked. "She must be thirty if she's a day. Very brave about never being asked, but she has had that unsightly scar on her lip from childhood. Poor thing." Shaking her head, Mama turned her attention back to Elizabeth. "What can we do to help, my dear?"

"Can you speak with Lord Blackham? Plead for us? You could persuade him to allow us to wed, Mama." Seizing her handkerchief, Elizabeth pressed it to her streaming eyes. This was the end. If Jemmy could not get free, this was the end for them. They must marry, and soon, else she would be the scandal of the day in matter of weeks.

"Blackham could never be swayed by anything I said to him." Mama returned to the sofa and proceeded to pour tea. "Else I could have persuaded him to allow Louisa to write to me. He despises me. I am the reason he forbids the marriage in the first place." Mama plopped lump after lump of sugar in her tea. "At least, he cannot compel dear Lord Brack to marry her."

"He can, however, keep Jemmy locked in the castle until it is too late," Elizabeth sobbed. "Until everyone knows I am ruined." The hatred in Lord Blackham's heart must be deep indeed if he would revenge himself on an innocent woman and her unborn child, to get at the woman who had scorned him. Little wonder she did, if he always behaved in this manner.

"It will not come to that, Elizabeth." Mama's gaze dropped to her teacup. "Your Papa and I will let nothing ruin either your reputation or that of our other daughters."

A pang of guilt struck Elizabeth's heart. Bella's betrothal could be broken off if Haxton got wind of this predicament. If one sister was tainted with scandal, all were suspect. Poor Dotty might never even have a Season if her eldest sister was brought to ruin. So what could be done other than try to reason with Blackham?

"What can any of us do if Lord Blackham won't even let Jemmy out of the house? Stage a rescue?" A desperate measure, but really, what else could they do?

"You can marry someone else." Mama's lips were firm, her unflinching gaze now on Elizabeth.

The incomprehensible words sounded as if in a foreign language. Marry someone else? "No." Elizabeth shook her head, tears flying. She'd rather for her life to be over if she and Jemmy could not wed. "How can you think of such a thing?"

"To save your reputation and your sisters' prospects, you will do it. Your father has already spoken to one of his friends from Eton, Lord Robert Naylor, the youngest brother of the current Duke of Penburthy."

"A friend of Papa's?" How ghastly. "I cannot do that, Mama. I love Jemmy. I'm carrying his child. I simply can't marry another man." Would the nightmare never end?

"Women have always done what they must to preserve their family, their honor. If love is sacrificed for this, so be it. It will not be the first time." Mama stirred her tea. Silent. Waiting.

What could she do? If she held out for a miracle, for Jemmy to come to her, she would jeopardize not only her happiness, but Isabella and Dorothea's as well. Her hands clenched of their own accord, until she forced them to relax.

"Can we not wait a little while, to see if Jemmy is able to escape?" She might be clutching at straws, but better that than an action she would regret every day for the rest of her life. "Circumstances will not be dire for another month at least."

"All the more reason to marry now, before anyone has the barest hint you are increasing. Then you can pass the child off as Lord Robert's more easily, and there will be no talk at all. These things happen all the time. The trick is to be married before anyone suspects a thing."

"But Mama, I can't—"

"Elizabeth, you will." The command in Mama's voice would brook no demur. "It is through your fault that the family is at risk. Therefore, you will do your duty and marry Lord Robert if he'll have you."

Her fault, her duty. When put that way, it was hard to argue otherwise. She had let her passions carry her away, and now she must pay for that whirlwind evening. Nothing to be done save make herself go through with the marriage, for all their sakes. Little matter that her heart was breaking. "Has Papa written to Lord Robert already?"

"Even better." Her mother beamed and slid closer to her on the sofa. "Lord Robert is in Town for the funeral of one of his brothers. Not the duke, and anyway Lord Robert is far down the line of succession. Still, that does put him one step closer to the dukedom." Mama shook her head. "Don't worry. The old duke had twelve children. Only one died in infancy, and that one was a girl. So Lord Robert has eight older brothers, most with sons of their own. Barring some biblical disaster, your child will never stand to inherit the dukedom."

Elizabeth cared not at all for such things. Jemmy's child should be Jemmy's heir, no matter what. Except that likely would not happen now, unless some type of miracle occurred. Tears had started again, and she wiped her eyes with the back of her hand, the handkerchief being too sodden to be of much help. "When would you wish me to meet Lord Robert? I assume we will not intrude on his grief—"

"Your father has invited him to dinner this evening. Take him to meet the children, see how he gets along with them. See if you think you will suit."

"That seems to matter not a jot," Elizabeth mumbled.

"I hope you find you will suit tolerably well." Mama pierced her with a keen glare. "Few men these days have the instincts to rescue a damsel in distress."

"I must write to Jemmy. Tell him . . ." Elizabeth couldn't control a sob. "I must tell him I am forced to release him from his promise."

"Elizabeth, I am truly sorry, my dear. We must hope it all turns out for the best." Mama hugged her briefly and straightened. "I will advise you to send your letter, as I did to Louisa, through the countess to your friend, Lady Georgina, if you wish it to reach Lord Brack. Blackham never found out about my and Louisa's correspondence." Mama's smile held a hollow triumph. "You may take some slight comfort in thwarting the marquess at least once."

Jemmy wound his way through the passage to Georgie's room, batting at cobwebs that threatened to catch fire from the candle he carried. Just his luck he would set the house afire. Of course, if he did, they would have to let him out of his room. Rather drastic, but he filed away the notion in the event the bedsheets didn't work.

He scratched on the back of Georgie's panel, and it moved instantly. "That passageway is as cold as midwinter's day," he said, rubbing his hands busily in front of her crackling fire.

"That's because it is midwinter's day, silly." Georgie rubbed her hands before the blaze as well.

"Did the letter get off yesterday to Lady Wrotham?" He hated to think what they would do if the letter had not been sent. But no matter what transpired, he would leave for London on the morrow even if had to turn horse thief of his own horse.

"As far as I know, it did. James, the footman, seemed rather relieved to take it after I talked his ear off about needing Lady Wrotham's opinion about a dress for my wedding. I put that in the letter too, just in case Father read it. I think it best he believes that I am consenting to his plans as well."

"But secretly you are not?" Jemmy strode to the window, once again trying to judge the distance to the ground. He itched to put their plan into action, but understood the necessity of waiting for Lady Wrotham's reply—hopefully containing the bank notes that would not only bribe the groom but would see him swiftly to London.

"Well, if there is another way, I would certainly prefer it to life with Lord Travers." Georgie shuddered. "I suspect he would be as faithful to me as Fanny's husband was to her." Wrinkling her nose, she turned around to face him. "I know one should not speak ill of the dead, but why shouldn't you if the dead person wasn't very nice in life? We speak ill of the living who do wrong. Why do the dead deserve less honest treatment?"

Jemmy chuckled and returned to the fire. "You are one of the most unexpected philosophers I know, bran face. I have no answer for you, other than to assure you I will write to St. Just as soon as I reach London. He'll have some idea of how to keep you out of Travers's hands."

"You must also write and tell me all about your wedding, Jemmy. I am terribly sorry I won't be there. I should have loved to see you marry your own true love." She sighed, drawing her shawl more securely about her shoulders. "But I think you must marry her as soon as possible. Take no chances. Father cannot do anything once you are wed, save take away your funds."

"That is enough," Jemmy said, despair stealing over him. "Although if I have Elizabeth as my wife, I could manage

any number of privations." It was killing him to simply wait
and do nothing. Never had he experienced so great a sense
of urgency to take action, yet he must stand idly by, talking
calmly with his sister before the cheerful fire. As soon as
Lady Wrotham's letter arrived, the sheets would be off the
bed and down the wall. He'd get to London the day after tomorrow, the good Lord willing, and put this nagging sense
of foreboding to rest as he lay once again in Elizabeth's
arms.

Lord Robert Naylor turned out to be surprisingly cordial,
if somewhat aloof. Elizabeth supposed that was to be expected when meeting for the first time the woman one had
agreed to marry who was carrying another man's child. A
tall man, with a pleasant, though narrow face and a patrician
nose like the bust of Caesar that stood on a pedestal in their
library. His brown eyes seemed kind, though fine lines criss-
crossed his skin all around them.

"Lord Robert was top of the form in classics, Elizabeth,"
her father said, handing his friend a glass of Madeira as they
sat companionably in the family parlor before dinner. "He
reads Latin, Greek, and some form of ancient Sanskrit, isn't
it, Robert?"

"Yes, the *daksini* dialect. I have always had a fondness
for languages." Lord Robert smiled bashfully and sipped his
sherry. "Your father was a fair hand with Latin."

"But not with Greek, by God," Papa laughed. He seemed
to be quite enjoying the company of his friend. Perhaps he
arranged this marriage to assure himself of more frequent
visits from his old school companion. "You saved my bacon
there many's the time. Never would have gotten through my
examination in Greek if not for your excellent tutelage."

"Always glad to help you out, Wentworth. Any time."
His gaze fell on Elizabeth, and spots of pink appeared in his
cheeks. He tossed back the remaining sherry too quickly and

began to cough. The rest of his face slowly turned red, until Papa pounded him on the back.

Lord, don't let the man expire right in front of her. Elizabeth sat beside her mother, despair over the whole affair suddenly assaulting her. Lord Robert might be a good man and a rather pleasant companion, but he wasn't Jemmy. He would never be Jemmy. They'd had little time together, and it should have made this decision easier, but that was patently untrue. Her heart knew whom she loved, and she wanted him with an intensity that threatened to make her ill. It simply wasn't fair. To lose first Dickon, and now Jemmy, was grossly unjust. Didn't she deserve happiness for more than a little while?

Lord Robert had ceased choking and had drawn her father into a far corner, talking earnestly, to judge by the sober aspect of his face.

"You seem to be getting along well with Lord Robert," her mother leaned over to whisper.

"I have no choice, do I, Mama? And I have scarcely spoken two words to him." Hoping to convince herself of the possibility of some affection between the two of them, Elizabeth eyed the man she would soon call husband. Life would be completely intolerable with a man of whom she was not even fond.

"Before dinner, you should introduce Lord Robert to the children. They have not yet retired, and they need to meet their new papa before he becomes part of the family." Mama smiled and gave a little wave to the gentlemen.

The suggestion made Elizabeth cringe, but it was practical, as her mother's advice often was. The children must know, and she could then gauge better how Lord Robert felt about Colin and Kate as well. "I believe you are right, Mama."

Beaming, her mother sipped her sherry, her self-satisfaction glowing all around her.

With a sigh, Elizabeth set her glass on the table and rose,

steeling herself and forcing a smile to her lips. "Lord Robert, I thought it might be good to introduce you to the children. We have time before dinner, and I believe they should meet you and know our plans."

Her betrothed paled a trifle but nodded. "As you wish, Mrs. Easton. I think it best as well." He offered his arm solicitously.

"We will return directly, Mama, Papa." Elizabeth took Lord Robert's arm and led him to the staircase to the third-floor nursery. Touching his arm set off no alarms. She didn't revile him, thank goodness. Neither did his touch fill her with dread; she felt merely sadness at what was not to be. Resolutely, she continued up the stairs.

As they approached the nursery, all seemed quiet, and Elizabeth breathed a sigh of thanksgiving that her children would make a good impression on Lord Robert. This was such a huge undertaking for a bachelor who had never been around young children. She pushed the door open and met with the angelic sight of Kate rocking her doll to sleep, and Colin holding a colorful book of maps, absorbed in the world of Cornwall.

"Children." Elizabeth slipped her arm out of Lord Robert's.

"Mama, Mama." They raced toward her, throwing their arms around her and burrowing into her.

"I'm so glad you're back." Kate hid her face in her mother's skirts. "I missed you."

"I missed you as well, my love. Let me look at you."

The petite form stood straight, blue eyes front, arms at sides, her white nightgown making her face look pink and rosy.

"Me too, Mama." Colin stood beside his sister, pulling himself up to be taller than Kate.

"I see you too, Colin. You are growing taller every day." Where had his babyhood gone so quickly? She swallowed hard. "Children, I would like you to meet someone."

A wary look crossed Colin's face as he stared up at Lord Robert. Kate's brows furrowed immediately.

"Lord Robert Naylor, these are my children. Katherine and Colin Easton. Children, this is Lord Robert. He is a friend of your Grandpapa's and"—Elizabeth bit her lip—"and a friend of mine as well." No harm to do this gradually. "Will you say good evening to him?"

"Good evening, Lord Robert." Kate bobbed a quick curtsy, then rushed into her mother's arms.

"Good evening, my lord." Colin continued to stare at the stranger, suspicion in his drawn brows and puckered mouth.

"Good evening, children." Lord Robert's voice had changed.

Startled by the deeper tone, Elizabeth glanced at him to find his hands clasped behind his back, almost defensively. His tall frame seemed to lengthen until he towered over Colin.

Colin in turn stretched upward, trying his best to be as tall as possible. "You don't scare me, Lord Robert." He puffed his chest out, for all the world like an admiral on the bridge of his ship staring down a French captain trying to board her. "And I can take care of my mother all by myself."

"Colin." Elizabeth leaned down to peer into his belligerent face. "You must not be disrespectful to Lord Robert. He is here tonight as a particular friend of mine."

"I don't care. I don't want him to take you away." Colin flung his arms around her.

"Why do you think Lord Robert would take me away?" She pried him loose from her and stared into his blue eyes. Dickon's eyes.

"Because Nurse said so." He sniffed and wiped his nose on the sleeve of his nightshirt. "I overheard her talking to Meg, the housemaid. That you would be marrying Lord Robert if you knew what was good for you, and going away." Tears threatened to spill from his glistening eyes.

She really must speak to her mother about Nurse.

"But my loves," Elizabeth said, gathering them into her arms, "it would not be just me. You would come with me. Lord Robert would take us all to live with him in his home."

"And leave Grandmama and Grandpapa?" Kate clutched her tighter.

Casting an apologetic look at Lord Robert, Elizabeth discovered empty air where his lordship had stood but a moment ago.

"Don't marry the stiff man, Mama." Colin squeezed her tighter. "I don't like him. Why can't we stay here always?"

If not for her folly, they could have remained with her parents until the children were older. Until she and Jemmy could marry properly. Now she would never know the joy of playing together with her children and Jemmy. He would have been a wonderful father to all her children. Lord Robert, she feared, would never be a favorite in the nursery. She would have to make it up to the children as best she could. "When a lady marries, she must go live with her husband. I, for one, believe we will all come to like Lord Robert very much as time goes by."

Pray God she spoke the truth. "We shall give him a chance and see if things don't turn out just fine." Elizabeth smiled brightly and took the two children by the hand to deliver them to their beds. She wasn't sure which of the three of them needed the most convincing.

Chapter 22

"So you have never married, Lord Robert?" Elizabeth sipped her fortifying wine, a delicious Bordeaux now. The white they'd had with the fish was her favorite, but at the moment she wasn't about to be choosy. The Bordeaux went down smoothly and kept her pleasantly numbed to Lord Robert's revelations. More and more information had come to light with each course, so she'd found herself imbibing much more frequently than usual during dinner.

"No, Mrs. Easton, I never did." Lord Robert ate robustly, but politely paused to answer her.

Did he have regular meals when he was at home? The man ate like there was no tomorrow. Neither was he a large individual. Where on earth was he putting it all?

"Are you fond of children? You have nieces and nephews, perhaps?" Hopefully, the man had had some contact with children.

"Well, I do have many nieces and nephews. My parents had twelve children, and as they got married, of course, they produced ample progeny. However"—their guest paused to savor one of cook's potatoes *a la russe*—"I was away at school when most of the girls married and moved to their husband's houses. My eldest brother, then Lord Sedgewick, married when I was a mere child, so I grew up with his sons. More of a friend to them than an uncle. Two other brothers married but had no issue."

Elizabeth shot a glance at her parents, who pretended not to see it.

"The book you are currently working on, Robert, how is that going?" Her father jumped into the conversation, changing the subject with all the grace of a goose landing on ice.

"I've worked on it for the better part of this year, Wentworth. It's been slow going, I'm afraid. Too many distractions." He shook his head sadly as he popped creamed carrots into his mouth.

Leaning toward him, Elizabeth furrowed her brows into a grim frown. At least, she hoped it was grim. "I wonder if you will be able to work properly with a new family underfoot, my lord." If she could convince him they would be a noisy bunch, perhaps she could get him to reconsider the marriage. Although she couldn't begin to imagine what else she would do if she didn't marry Lord Robert, it was becoming rapidly apparent to her that she truly did not wish to marry him. Perhaps she could retire to one of her father's country estates.

"I have given that very question considerable thought, Mrs. Easton." Lifting his wineglass, Lord Robert nodded gravely at her. "I cannot work unless I have most of the day to myself in the library so I may write and conduct research at will."

"You are very dedicated, my lord." Glee bubbled up within Elizabeth. Her children, while tolerably well behaved, were still children. She opened her eyes wide and innocent, just as she'd watched Georgie do. "Do you not fear my children and myself might distract you from your studies?"

"That was the question, Mrs. Easton, the very question I had to ask myself when Wentworth here approached me about this business." Lord Robert smiled at Papa.

"What conclusion did you arrive at, Lord Robert?" Elizabeth gritted her teeth but smiled anyway.

"Of course, since I am here, Mrs. Easton, I assumed you understood that I am willing to go through with the marriage." Startled eyebrows raised first at her, then at her father, Lord Robert leaned over to her father. "Did you not inform her of this, Wentworth?"

"I most certainly did, Robert." Papa glared at her. "Perhaps she was having a little joke with you."

"I am sorry, Lord Robert, I do understand; however"—she attempted a concerned countenance—"I wanted to make absolutely certain you were prepared for life with small children. They are well behaved, but they are, nevertheless, children. Sometimes *noisy* children." If the man was going to take them, by God, she'd make sure he knew exactly what bargain he was getting in exchange for whatever dowry her father must have offered to entice this man to marry her.

Lord Robert leaned back in his chair, his cravat seeming to relax about his throat. "You are very conscientious, Mrs. Easton. I commend your sense of fairness to assure yourself of my understanding of the situation with your children. Put your conscience at ease, my dear. I have weighed the prospects and believe, almost to a certainty, that I shall be able to manage quite tolerably."

"Indeed." How lovely to know she and her children could be tolerated.

"Yes, I believe I will be able to work despite the din for the short time before the boy is sent to school. Your father informed me that your son will be at Winchester shortly. Quite a good school. I went to Eton after a series of tutors, then finished at Oxford, where I met your father. I assume your boy will end up there as well. That is satisfactory."

"*If* he goes"—Elizabeth glared at her father—"he will come home for holidays. I'd want him to bring his school chums home as well." She turned her attention to Lord Robert, who sat transfixed, a spoonful of liver soufflé poised before his mouth.

"Holidays?" The soufflé quivered.

"Of course, Colin could come to us for his holidays, couldn't he, Wentworth?" Her mother broke in smoothly. "Elizabeth and Kate could come as well." Solution found, her mother beamed about expectantly, a bright smile on her lips. "No need for Lord Robert to be disturbed at all."

Lord Robert's shoulders relaxed, and the soufflé continued into his mouth. "That is a splendid idea, Lady Wentworth, if it will not disoblige you too much. Then the girl would only need a governess to keep her occupied until her come-out; then she would be married and out of the house as well."

Opening her mouth to disabuse him of these plans for Kate, Elizabeth got not a word in before her mother hastily rose. "Come, Elizabeth, I am certain your father and Lord Robert have much to discuss over port. I will ring for tea, and we can settle the details of the wedding while we wait for them." She grasped Elizabeth's arm with fingers of steel and urged her from the room.

They made it to the family parlor before Elizabeth exploded. "What are you doing, Mama?" She jerked her arm free and sailed across the room to stand rubbing her it before the fireplace. She'd likely have a bruise there tomorrow where Mama's fingers had gripped her so intently.

"Trying to keep you and this family from ruin." Mama's gaze cut her to the quick. "You have presented us with an impossible situation, Elizabeth. Bella's betrothal, while announced, could still be broken if a scandal of sufficient intensity should taint the family and come to the ears of Lord Haxton. Then there is Dotty to think of, poor thing, who is to come out this Season, if you and your by-blow do not make her unmarriageable." Mama pulled the bell, flounced over to the chaise, and lowered herself onto it.

"I did not do this on purpose, Mama. I am perfectly willing to marry Jemmy if you will kindly produce him. He also wishes to marry me. It is the man you angered a lifetime ago who has locked Jemmy up and is forcing him to marry someone else," Elizabeth shot back, overwhelmed again at the monumental contrariness of life. "You married the man you loved. Why am I not allowed to do the same?" Her chest hurt abominably from unshed tears. "I do *not* want to marry Lord Robert."

"You may not have another choice, Elizabeth." Mama smiled and nodded as the door opened, her signal always to stop speaking when servants were present. "Tea, please, Tawes."

"Very good, my lady." The butler withdrew.

Mama's smile fled. "You chose to dance, my dear, and I am sorry to say, you are going to have to pay the piper a hefty sum."

Tears spilled down Elizabeth's cheeks. How could she marry someone, anyone, who was not Jemmy? "I could go into the country until the child was born. We could place it with someone, somewhere. Anywhere it would be cared for and loved."

Rising from her seat, Mama pulled Elizabeth into her arms. "You know that would not be possible. People would find out, Elizabeth. They always do. Then you would be ruined just the same."

"They will know anyway. No one is going to believe that I have married Lord Robert because I love him. Nor will anyone with a grain of sense believe I was overcome with a fit of passion for him and bedded him before we were wed. No one will believe this is Lord Robert's child." Not one single person would believe the lie. Why, then, tie her forever to a man she did not love?

They paused a moment while a footman set up the tea things and left.

"The *ton* may not believe, but they will accept and forgive because you have done the correct thing. They will not penalize you or your sisters for your folly." Mama sat her down on the chaise and handed her a handkerchief. "You must try to make the best of the situation you can. Lord Robert does not seem a bad man. Your father speaks very highly of him. And likely he will not mind you traveling to London next year, after the child is born, to spend time with your family. You will miss Bella's wedding, of course, but it would not do for you to attend and flaunt your condition. Best to remain in the country for some time after the birth. Allow people time to forget exactly when you married. Then they will just say, 'Oh, it was born in the early autumn,' and no one will count inconveniently." Calmly, Mama poured and handed Elizabeth a cup.

"But what am I to do in the country, Mama? Do you think there is some village near him in whose life I might take part?" Miserable, Elizabeth sipped her tea and almost choked. Hastily, she put the cup down.

"I am sure there will be some way to fill your time while you are there. The children can occupy much of it, especially with a new baby. When Colin goes to school, it may be harder." Sighing, Mama tasted her tea, added a lump, and moved on. "You will have Kate and an infant to care for. I am sure as long as they don't disturb Lord Robert, he will let you keep them with you. As you say, there may be village events—bazaars, charities, that sort of thing—to occupy you." Doubt clouded Mama's face. She had never been one to take an interest in the home village at Worth. She'd always persuaded Papa to take them to Brighton after the Season.

As Elizabeth thought about it, they had not spent three summers together at Worth in all her life.

"And of course, Lord Robert will let you come to us whenever you wish."

Elizabeth tore at the handkerchief, wishing to rip something apart, anything at all. All her sorrow and frustration would disappear if she could tear a hole in time and go back to last summer. She would do so much differently.

"Dry your eyes, my dear. Your betrothed will be in shortly, and you may not look the eager bride, but you will look pleasant and cordial to him. He is doing us a great favor. We will be forever in his debt." Handing her a fresh handkerchief, Mama patted her hands before serenely pouring more tea.

Elizabeth blotted her face, hoping it didn't look too hideous. She wouldn't want to turn her betrothed to stone.

The door opened almost immediately, and Elizabeth straightened up, the semblance of a pleasant smile plastered on her face.

Deep in conversation with her father, Lord Robert seemed not to notice. He walked absently toward the sofa and sat beside her. "But the translation should have read, 'We thank you greatly,' not 'We thank your Greatness.' Totally different meaning all together, don't you know?"

"How clever of you to have seen the discrepancy, Lord Robert," Elizabeth said, picking up the thread of the conversation instantly. She smiled and placed her hand on his arm and caught her mother's approving nod.

"Not a'tall." He cleared his throat and looked away.

This would be a tedious courtship, but mercifully short. The marriage, however, would likely last an eon. "Mama and I were discussing the possibility that I might make myself useful in the local village. Your estate is in . . . ?"

"South Shropshire. Near the village of Ditton Priors." His furrowed brows made him resemble a worried beagle. "There may be some charitable work you can do about the parish, but I seldom venture to the village. My studies and the running of the estate itself occupy almost all of my waking hours."

"So you do not attend church regularly?" The scope of her new world was shrinking by the minute.

Lord Robert shook his head. "Got away from it after Oxford. Never seemed enough time for my studies when I was managing Lord Craigmont's affairs. The only time I had to myself was Sunday mornings, so I took advantage."

"But you would have no objection to my taking the children to services each Sunday?" Only once a week, but she'd take the escape it offered her.

"No, oh no, my dear." He blinked at her father. "I would not dream of preventing Mrs. Easton from attending worship if she so chooses."

"Of course not, Robert. I am sure Elizabeth didn't mean to imply such a thing." Papa glared at her, but she stared straight back at him, defiant.

"No, indeed, Lord Robert. I was merely attempting to define the parameters I may expect once we are . . . wed." The words almost stuck in her throat, and Elizabeth swallowed convulsively. Could she truly be thinking of doing this? "Do you come to London often, my lord?"

"Heavens, no." Lord Robert looked so alarmed at that prospect he shrank from her as though she had said she had the plague. "The journey alone takes two days in good weather. I find all my wants provided for amply on the estate."

"You do not come even for the Season, my lord?" The shocked look on Mama's face made Elizabeth smile to herself. Finally, something about Lord Robert had displeased her.

"I do not hold a seat in Parliament, nor would I wish one, my lady." He shuddered. "Therefore, I see no reason for traveling so far. I am only in Town now because of my brother's funeral."

Arching her brows pointedly at her mother, Elizabeth returned her attentions to her suitor. "I am so sorry for your loss, Lord Robert. It must be very difficult to lose one's brother."

A fleeting spasm of grief passed over his face, then Lord Robert shrugged. "I had not seen him in over ten years. Our family, though large, is not close. Still, I did think it my duty to attend the funeral."

"Quite the right thing," her father said, then added, "Brandy, Robert?"

"Why yes, thank you, Wentworth." Lord Robert perked up. "Quite a lucky thing to have seen you at White's right after the funeral. I'd have left Town immediately after, if not for your request. I'm in the midst of a manuscript, a translation of Ovid with some really exciting new interpretations of the works." His face flushed with the excitement of his work, he took a pull at the brandy, his cheeks turning almost red. "We will leave directly after the wedding, if that is quite convenient for you, Mrs. Easton. I simply must get back to my work, you understand."

Gritting her teeth, Elizabeth summoned a smile. "I am sure that can be arranged, Lord Robert." She narrowed her eyes at her father, who hastily dropped his gaze to his glass. "When do you wish to wed?"

"Tomorrow."

"What?" Elizabeth bounded to her feet.

"That is rather sudden, my lord." Her mother pulled her back down. "I was hoping you would stay through Christmas with us."

The scandalized look on her betrothed's face almost made Elizabeth chuckle. And Mama looked as put out as she'd ever seen her.

"At least let us have time to arrange a proper wedding breakfast. It would only be family and some of Elizabeth's friends, so it would take but a day or two."

"I am afraid not, my lady. We must leave for Ditton Priors no later than the day after tomorrow. We will have a day to marry, the wedding night . . ." Lord Robert mumbled the last of that sentence, his face turning bright red to his hairline. "Then we will leave the following morning."

"I cannot possibly have everything packed and ready in—"

"We will see to it, Lord Robert, that Elizabeth is ready to

travel day after tomorrow." Her mother nodded emphatically, daring Elizabeth to contradict her.

"But the children—" Elizabeth tried to bring the voice of reason to bear on the proceedings, but her mother had the bit in her teeth and would not be gainsaid.

"I will oversee the maids in packing up all the children's belongings, my dear. So there will be no question of when it can be done. It must be done by tomorrow night." Mama glared at Papa, who hastily nodded assurance to Lord Robert.

"You'll find the air so bracing in Shropshire, Elizabeth, that once you arrive, you will never want to leave it either." Papa beamed largely at her. "I daresay after a year of two up there, you will come to enjoy the solitude as much as Robert does. Country estates are a challenge at first, but I know you will rise to the occasion beautifully, daughter." He raised his glass. Mama and Lord Robert did likewise. After a long moment, feeling like nothing so much as a traitor to herself and Jemmy, Elizabeth raised hers as well. Sometimes one simply had to embrace the inevitable.

Chapter 23

Elizabeth sat before the crackling fireplace, uncomfortably aware of the man sitting beside her on the chaise longue. Mama and Papa had retired after the toast to her coming marriage, citing the need for her and Lord Robert to become better acquainted. A prospect she dreaded on several fronts.

Straightening her shoulders, she smiled tentatively at her companion. She really must pull herself together and accept that Lord Robert would be her husband. He didn't seem a bad man, only rather self-absorbed and set in his ways. Of course, having been a bachelor all his life, he would be. Still, perhaps she could change those ways so they could be more comfortable together. To that end, she needed to learn more about him.

"Why have you never married, my lord?" She flicked her gaze from the fire to his startled face. "Surely, the son of the Duke of Ardlow would have been a most eligible catch."

His quick smile held a rueful touch. "The first son and heir absolutely was, Mrs. Easton. The twelfth one, much less so."

"Please call me Elizabeth." She swallowed hard but kept

speaking. "I think we should try to become more comfortable with one another."

"I thank you, Elizabeth." He sipped his champagne and visibly relaxed against the chaise. "And you must call me Robert." With a sigh, he drained the last of the bubbling wine.

"Your father had twelve sons?" Goodness. She'd never heard of such a thing. Fervently, she prayed Lord Robert did not wish to follow in those footsteps.

"Well, there were twelve children, several girls in the mix, of course, but eight sons, of which I am the youngest." His brows furrowed. "There are but three of us left now. James, the late duke, died ten years ago, Charles died as a child of the whooping cough, Henry in action during the war, and now Alfred." His eyes took on a saddened aspect. "He was closest to me in age, two years older at fifty-one."

"I am so sorry for your loss, Robert." She carefully placed a hand on his arm. "You needn't speak of it if it makes you sad."

He covered her hand with his, patting it absently. "Thank you, my dear. It does make one reflect on one's life. And as you can see, given the circumstances, I had very little to recommend me as a husband. I was always more interested in my studies, and then, of course, I had to make my way in the world. I truly had no means for taking a wife."

"What did you do?" He had managed to touch a chord in Elizabeth, making her suddenly interested in this lonely man.

"My father's influence got me a position with the Earl of Craigmont, in Shropshire, as his man of affairs. We rubbed along well together, and when he died several years ago, he left me a small, unentailed estate of his, not far from the primary residence. My inheritance, though small, is sufficient to maintain me there." His face brightened. "So I've been able to devote myself to my studies at last."

The fervor in his voice, the eagerness that leaped into his face when he spoke of his work, told her exactly where this man's passions lay. He would never feel that way about a woman of his choice, much less her. Still, he was willing to sacrifice his hard-won solitude to rescue her reputation. The action spoke equally well of Lord Robert's character and of his fondness for her father.

Stiffening her resolve, she vowed she would do her best to make him a comfortable home and see to his needs in exchange for the respectability he would give her and the name he would give her child.

"And here I am to come in and disrupt your well-ordered life. You are very good to do this. Why did you agree to my father's proposal?" She hadn't taken time to wonder at his motives, only her own circumstances, until now.

"Wentworth has been my closest friend for some twenty years. How could I say no?" He knit his brows, seeming quite puzzled that she would ask such a question.

Swallowing several times, she squeezed her hands together. "Did he explain my circumstances, Robert? Completely?" Assuming Papa had told the man would not do. She must make certain he knew everything before they wed. "He told you that I am . . . with child?" The shame of the words seeped into her soul, forcing her to close her eyes. "I was weak. I fell in love and then . . . he could not marry me." Lord, she sounded like one of those lurid romances Bella liked so much.

"Do not distress yourself, my dear." Lord Robert patted her arm, and she opened her eyes to find his kind. "Of course, your father told me of the predicament. Wentworth would never have kept such information from me. He also assumed, quite rightly, that if I could not have accommodated his request, the information would have gone no further. I have always kept his confidences and he mine."

That brought her up short. What confidences could this man have ever had? Again, the feeling that there was more to Lord Robert than met the eye pricked her interest. "So you will have no qualms of raising the child as your own?

He or she will be yours in the eyes of the *ton* and the eyes of the law, no matter if the truth eventually comes out." She lowered her gaze. "If it is a son, he will be your heir."

Robert shrugged, seemingly unconcerned. "Then he will be more of an heir than I would have had if not for our marriage." He peered intently into her face. "I am under no illusions about this marriage, Elizabeth. It is a true marriage of convenience, although I hope we will eventually rub along as well as most couples. Your child will be treated as any other child we may have."

Elizabeth tried to stifle the gasp that escaped her. Of course, she had understood that her marriage to Lord Robert would not be in name only, but the sudden realization that they would indeed be intimate—possibly by this time tomorrow night—hit her with the power of a blow to her stomach. She blinked several times, hoping to force herself to expel the breath she held.

"Elizabeth? Is something wrong?" Lord Robert ducked his head to peer into her face. He grasped her hand and chaffed it. "Are you quite all right?"

Slowly, she drew breath in and nodded vigorously. "I am well, my lord. A sudden faintness that I've been plagued with of late." And would be for some time to come. "I'm certain you understand a woman feels differently at times like these."

"Ah, well, yes." Sounding like an exotic bird, Lord Robert cleared his throat. "I have heard such things from friends who have families. Nothing to worry about, though?"

"No, I shall be fine." She would too. As soon as she could accept the idea of intimacies with this stranger. Odd that she'd thought the same thing of Jemmy after they'd first shared a bed. Perhaps it was a normal reaction, though she strongly doubted she would ever feel for Lord Robert what she'd felt for either Jemmy or Dickon.

"Once you are no longer unsettled by all this fuss, you will hopefully regain your full health. The house in Shropshire has quite the reputation for peace and quiet, which I'm certain you will enjoy and take full advantage of." He rose and offered his hand. "Shall I see you to your chamber?"

Elizabeth nodded, grateful to think of the solitude her room promised for the night, although it would likely be her last night alone. Still, Lord Robert seemed very willing to accommodate her. Perhaps she could put off their "wedding night" for a time. He had lived alone for years, so the deprivation would be slight. They could get to know one another before taking that next, fateful step toward physical intimacy. "Thank you, Lord Robert. That would be very kind."

"Robert, my dear." Quite suddenly, he drew her to him. "You must call me Robert when we are alone." Without any further warning, he pulled her flat against him, wrapping his arms around her, crushing her to his chest.

Stunned, Elizabeth could scarcely catch her breath before he tipped her head back. A sense of dread at what must be coming enveloped her.

His muscles were solid, hard as granite, in fact. Surprising, since she'd assumed his studies would have rendered him softer. Lord Robert obviously had kept his body as well occupied as his mind. Staring into her face with blue eyes almost black with desire, he whispered, "You are a very beautiful woman, Elizabeth. That was also a consideration when your father suggested we marry. I was a guest at your first wedding, though I doubt you remember me." He ran his hand through her hair, gentle yet firm.

Did she remember him? The shock of his close presence now had abated somewhat, but her mind refused to focus on anything other than the press of her breasts against his jacket and his obvious hardness rubbing along her thigh.

"I hope our union will be long and prosperous." His ragged breath brushed her face before his mouth descended onto her.

Shocked at this complete reversal of his studious, almost absentminded nature, Elizabeth opened her mouth to protest, and he thrust his tongue inside, then quickly withdrew and thrust again, like a woodpecker at a tree.

Fortunately, disbelief had stopped her from making any loud protest. It wouldn't do for the servants to rush in to find them grappling in the family room. Really, the man was too gauche. Conquering her revulsion, Elizabeth tried to back away and close her lips. After all, the man was a complete stranger to her.

On the contrary, he now pressed his suit, grasping her head and keeping it still while he kissed her more thoroughly than she had ever wished to be kissed. Had she liked the man, it might have been quite enjoyable; however, Lord Robert needed time and a more willing partner to perfect his technique.

She was barely willing, even if she had agreed to marry him.

Still his tongue thrust in and out.

Shifting her stance, forcing herself to calmly endure the kiss, she wished once more that this could be Jemmy. The thought conjured him up, his tousled blond curls riotous after she'd run her fingers through them. Slim, but muscular build and always impeccably dressed. Oh, but she longed to touch him, to plunge her tongue into his willing mouth and explore every inch of it at her leisure.

The daydream ended when Lord Robert began to urge her toward the chaise again, his hips bumping hers, his member pushing as eagerly as his tongue.

Bringing her hands to rest on his chest, Elizabeth gave a mighty shove.

He staggered backward, confusion in his eyes. "But, Elizabeth, we will be married this time tomorrow night. I am sure no one would fault us for anticipating the wedding by a few hours."

She stared at his red face, her stomach churning. He thought her no better than she should be, and the circumstances from her past bore this out. Still, she couldn't do it, especially not in the family room. "I am certain I would not feel comfortable, Lord Robert, doing so in my parents' home without the benefit of marriage vows between us. Look what happened to me the last time I so let my guard down."

Breathing in short, ragged bursts, Lord Robert stared longingly at her. "But we will be married—"

"That gentleman had every intention of marrying me until he was prevented." She blinked back tears. What use was it to deny him? It would all come to the same pass tomorrow night. Still, a niggling voice in her head urged her to wait. Have one last night to herself before taking up her wifely duties with this man, in a marriage which she now understood would not be postponed. One short, final night of freedom. She backed toward the door. "I will say good night, my lord. We shall see each other in the morning at the church."

"At the church?" His eyes were large and round as an owl's.

"Yes, of course." Elizabeth had gained the door frame. "It would be bad luck for you to see me before we are wed."

"You believe such pagan poppycock?" Lord Robert looked entirely offended and somewhat displeased with her.

Elizabeth's heart struck a wild beat, hoping that such an irrational belief might be too unorthodox for this scholarly man.

Instead of an explosion of displeasure, however, her betrothed merely sighed deeply. "Very well. I will see you at the church. However, we will have a discussion about your reliance on such animalistic claptrap instead of good, sound logic. A discussion that will begin tomorrow night."

"Yes, my lord. Until tomorrow, then?" Not the usual wedding night conversation, but then this would not be a usual wedding nor marriage, she would wager. Elizabeth sped through the doorway, turned right down the corridor, and fled toward the staircase. Her first thought was to flee to the stable, order the carriage, and demand to be taken back to

Lyttlefield Park. Her heart fluttered faster at the thought of such a sanctuary. However, it would do no good, save to embroil Charlotte in her troubles. Neither would marching into her father's chamber and announcing she could not marry Lord Robert.

Father could, perhaps, be persuaded, despite his fondness for Lord Robert. She had always been able to wheedle him down, given enough time. Mama, however, would hound her worse than a beagle after a fox, until she was assured the scandal was put to bed. Of course, she would disregard the fact that Elizabeth would be put to bed as well, and with a man not of her choosing.

Fighting to compose herself, Elizabeth mounted the stairs, willing herself to calm. On the second floor, she still hurried down the silent hall. How had it become so late? No light shone underneath her sisters' doors. They must have retired long ago. Time was flying past, racing toward her wedding day. She shuddered as she opened the door, a sudden chill skittering down her spine.

The well-appointed room was warm and inviting. The fire had been made up, crackling and hissing in the grate. The bed had been turned down, and her night rail laid out for her. A pity she could not take the maid with her, but Weller must remain to attend her sisters. Would Lord Robert allow her a maid? So many things one wanted to know but did not think to ask. The biggest question still remained to be dealt with: How was she to actually force herself to marry Lord Robert tomorrow?

Arms clutched across her chest, Elizabeth paced to the window, looking out into the inky blackness, every ounce of her being urging her to go, to try to get to Jemmy. The sheer impossibility of it weighted her down like a boulder, and an overwhelming grief poured through her. She stumbled back and sank into a chair before the fire, tears streaming down her face. How could she marry Lord Robert—or anyone, for that matter, other than Jemmy? She would be utterly miserable for the rest of her life, trapped with a man she did not love.

Schemes bloomed like a summer garden. Could she run away somewhere to have the baby where no one would know? Had she unlimited funds, perhaps. She could go to the Continent. Was it too late to discuss this with her parents? Perhaps it would work if they gave out that her grief for Dickon had become so overwhelming she must leave England, and all its memories, for some undetermined time. The *ton* would believe that. Her devotion to Dickon had been unquestioned in society.

But what of Colin and Kate? She slumped as another impediment to her scheme surfaced. Could she manage them by herself through the final stages of a pregnancy and the early days of her child's infancy? It would be hard enough if she stayed here at home with the help of Mama and Papa. She couldn't handle anything without the support of her family.

Hopeless. It was utterly hopeless. Her sobs renewed, her chest hurting so badly she cried harder just to push the tears out and rid her of the pain. A wrenching pain she feared she would face for the rest of her life.

Chapter 24

Frantic knocking at the secret door brought Jemmy up off his bed, where he'd been lying, moping, for the better part of the day. Furious with himself for not being able to break out of his room, he'd finally paced himself into exhaustion and thrown himself onto the mattress.

Hurrying to the panel, he cursed their father once more. If such things had real teeth, the man would have died a horrible death before now. Jemmy shoved the panel aside, and Georgie stumbled in, clutching a candlestick, a cobweb draped over one ear and plaster dust speckling her blue gown. One look at her face, eyes wide and frightened, and he gripped her arm. "What has happened?"

"Jemmy, oh, I am so sorry." Her face had blanched whiter than snow as she held out a folded piece of paper. "The afternoon post just arrived. Charlotte sent it in a letter to me."

He snatched it from her hand. "It's not opened. How do you know—"

"Charlotte's letter." Tears leaked from Georgie's eyes. "Elizabeth . . . Elizabeth's . . ."

"What?" His heart turned to ice.

"She's marrying a friend of her father's to give your child a name."

Like a physical blow, the words took the breath away from him, rendering him dumb. He stared at Georgie as she continued to talk but could hear nothing she said. Elizabeth to marry someone else? Why in God's name would she do such a thing so quickly? They'd parted not quite a week ago, convinced they would find a way to wed. He caught his breath, and Georgie's voice penetrated his shocked senses.

". . . only thing that could have happened. I never dreamed Charlotte would tell her that."

"Tell who what?" Staring at the folded square in his hand, dread filled him once more.

"That you were locked up and Father wouldn't let you go until you married Lady Maude."

Georgie wrung her hands and sniffed. "I was only trying to make sure, if someone opened my letter, that they'd be reassured we were cowed by Father's order and not trying to escape. I never imagined Charlotte might tell Elizabeth that, but, of course, she would believe Elizabeth needed to know. I knew it was false, so I guess I thought she'd know it was false too, although I don't know why she would think that." Georgie stopped and looked at his letter. "Aren't you going to read it?"

Shaking his head to clear it, Jemmy carefully unfolded the little square of paper. The dear handwriting—elegant loops swirling across the page—was tragically brief and spotted with watermarks where, it seemed, tears had dropped.

Dearest Jemmy,

Charlotte has informed me of your change in circumstances. I am bitterly heartbroken at the news of your betrothal to Lady Maude as well as your detention at Blackham Castle. If your father will have his way, with total disregard for our lives and feelings, then we must bow to the inevitable, much as it breaks my heart to do so.

By God, when this was over, he would beg Elizabeth on bended knee never to send him another letter as long as he lived. The ones she had sent him so far had borne nothing save bad news.

I hereby release you from your promise and pray you will do the same for me. My parents insist I marry to keep scandal from our door, else I would never betray my love and trust in you.

Farewell, my love.

Elizabeth

"I have to go." Jemmy flung the letter to the floor, brushed past Georgie and into the secret passageway. He bumped into beams and stumbled over the clutter of plaster and lathing that littered the floor. Cursing himself for not grabbing Georgie's candle, he pressed forward toward the light from Georgie's room where she had left her panel ajar.

He shoved that panel aside and strode directly to the window. The drop from the second floor looked as daunting as ever, but he'd attempt it or die trying. No way in hell would he allow Elizabeth to marry someone else.

After pushing up the window, he peered down to check for activity below, then leaned out, assessing the height and possible softness of the ground. A cold breeze ruffled his hair as he estimated the drop. At least twenty-five feet, maybe thirty. Perspective could be devilishly deceptive. High enough to break his neck in any case. Or any other bone in his body, for that matter. The rough black stone that composed the castle wall was sheer, nothing even to grab hold of.

"What are you doing?"

A hand on his collar jerked him back, causing him to hit his head on the window frame and making the old glass chatter.

"Have you gone totally daft, jingle-brains?" Georgie scowled at him as he rubbed his head. That had smarted.

"I was checking the drop."

"You were planning to jump." Her green eyes filled with outrage.

"No, I was assessing—"

"You were getting ready to climb out that window, Jemmy. I saw it in your face when you read Elizabeth's letter." The fear in her eyes told him she had believed it. "Getting killed won't stop her from marrying someone else. You must wait and stick to the plan."

"How can I wait, Georgie? She's getting married to someone—"

"Lord Robert Naylor. Charlotte's letter said so. But not until tomorrow."

"Tomorrow!" God, he'd never get to London in time.

"They couldn't marry today because of the funeral."

"What funeral?" He stared wildly at her. Had his sister gone mad?

"Lord Robert. His brother died. So they had to wait. And so do you." She waved a finger at him. "Just until dark. You must stick to the plan. If we had one more day before the wedding, we could just send to Charlotte, telling her to stop it, but of course, it could be intercepted." Georgie frowned. "Father is so inconvenient."

"You have a talent for understatement, bran face." He tried to chuckle, but it hurt his throat. "What's the current plan if not to leap out the window?"

"Twist your sheets and mine together and lower you out the window after dark this evening. Thank goodness, the light begins to go around three." Shivering, she closed the window. "That only gives us a couple of hours. We must make haste." She tugged at his arm, leading him back toward the secret passage. "Let's start with your sheets, since you won't be using them anymore after this."

"Just how am I to get to London? The mail coach has already gone. I suppose I can overcome one of the grooms and steal a horse." Jemmy lit the candle before entering the passageway once more.

"Or bribe them." Georgie darted to her writing desk and produced her letterbox. "Charlotte's letter contained yours and this." She waved a sheaf of bills before his face. "Ten pounds. That will get you to London with change to spare," she crowed gleefully.

"You do have the most delightful friends, Georgie." He took the bills and shoved them into his pocket.

With a quick grin, she motioned him into the passageway once more. "Come on, chucklehead. We have work to do."

Two hours later, as the light was beginning to fade, Jemmy flexed his aching hands. They'd been twisting and knotting sheets nonstop until his fingers were almost numb. In order to make the makeshift rope sturdy enough to hold him, they'd had to twist the sheets over and over, then knot them at intervals while still twisting. Trial and error had finally yielded an efficient method that allowed them to generate sheet-rope at a cracking pace—until they ran out of sheets.

Jemmy cursed as he opened the window once more and was met with a blast of air even chillier than when last he'd checked. Ignoring it, he made a quick survey of the garden below. No one stirring. Good so far. "All right, Georgie. I'm lowering it now."

"Wait." She rushed to the mantelpiece and grabbed a tall, brass candlestick. "It's very windy. Tie this to the end to make it hang properly."

"Genius." After a moment of awkwardly tying the tail of the sheet-rope around the candlestick, he opened the window once more.

"Shouldn't you wait until it's properly dark?"

Daylight still shone brightly, though the castle's shadow had lengthened considerably, covering the garden, and spreading across the lawn beyond.

"I can't wait any longer, Georgie." The fear he'd been holding at bay crept up to whisper that if he didn't leave this instant, he'd arrive in London to meet Elizabeth coming out of the church on the arm of her new husband. His fists clenched of their own accord. He wasn't about to let that come to pass.

"Is there a moon tonight?" Georgie peered out the window, where a ghost of the moon already hung low in the sky.

"I think there will be some moonlight at least. And once I get to the post road, it will be much easier going. I can follow that all the way to London." He lowered the candlestick out the window, feeding it briskly over the sill. The wind banged it against the wall, and Jemmy winced. Pray God no one heard that below.

"Try not to make any noise. We don't want the servants to come out and investigate. My room is directly above the kitchen." Georgie danced on her toes, trying to peer around him as he continued to lower the rope.

He shot her a grin. "You sound as if we're both going down this rope." He stopped, a crazy notion seizing him. "Come with me, Georgie."

"What?"

"Come with me to London." He leaned against the rope to stop its descent. The wind had picked up, and the temperature seemed to have dropped. It was deucedly cold all of a sudden. "You could stay with Elizabeth in London and with us after we are married."

She reached up on tiptoe to plant a kiss on his cheek. "That is very sweet, brother. But no." Georgie shook her head and motioned him to continue lowering the sheets. "I cannot ride as well as you. I'd only slow you down, and if you didn't get to her in time because of me, I'd want to kill myself." A shudder shook her. "No, I will stay here and pray for your safe arrival. As soon as you can, send word to Charlotte, who will send to me."

"But, Georgie." Stricken, he stopped again. "What will Father do to you when he discovers I'm gone?" Damn, but he should have thought of that before now. Father had always

been fiendish in his machinations, but rarely had he resorted
to physical punishment, save Georgie's "beating." However,
when he found out he'd been thwarted with Jemmy's escape, would he take more drastic measures in revenge?
Might he actually beat her?

"I don't really want to think about that, but I have been."
She bit her lip but raised her chin. "It doesn't matter. You
have to go, and I have to stay. We'll worry about it when it
happens."

"Georgie." He couldn't leave her here to face the tender
mercies of Father's wrath. "Then I'm not going."

The set of her jaw as she planted her feet made granite
look soft. She reared back to eye him with a coolness that
did credit to their sire. "You are going to leave if I have to
bash you over the head with the other candlestick and throw
you out the window. I will be fine."

"You can't know that." God, what was he to do?

"Yes, I do, because he won't know I've helped you."
Pushing him aside, she continued feeding the sheets over the
windowsill. "As soon as you're down, I'll pull the sheets
back up, untwist them and put them back on your bed. I'll
smooth everything over, then come back through the passageway, do the same thing for my bed, and no one will be the
wiser."

"Except I will be gone. How will you explain that?" Perhaps it could work, but only if their secret passage remained
secret.

"I won't need to. How could I know anything? I wouldn't
have had contact with you for four days." In the waning
light, he caught a flash of her teeth as she grinned. "I will,
however, advance the possibility that the footman who has
been bringing your meals must have forgotten to lock the
door at some point." She bent to tie the tail end of the
sheets to the leg of her bed, then straightened. "Time to
go, brother."

Impossible situation. However, the tug of his heart to go

to Elizabeth had to win out. Their future would be dashed to pieces if she married this Lord Robert. Georgie, on the other hand, might be able to play innocent and avoid the worst of their father's wrath. An abominable risk, but one he had to take.

"Go immediately and take the linens back, then shut the panel and wedge something behind it so it won't open from my side. If they don't discover the passageway, you may be all right." He pulled on the rope, but the bed outweighed him by a hundred stone at least.

Time to go.

The wind whistled through the open window, cutting through his coat and making him shiver. It would be a cold ride through the freezing temperatures of the night. At least the horse would be warm beneath him. "Wish me luck, bran face. I'll come back for you as soon as I can."

"Wait." She scurried back into the passage.

Jemmy groaned. It would be midnight before he was away.

"Here." Georgie had returned with the blue wool blanket from his bed. "So you don't catch your death."

With a grateful smile, he slung the blanket over his shoulder, its warmth immediately shielding him from the frigid air. "And you took it from my room, so nothing will be missing from yours. As I said, genius."

Georgie smiled and hugged him. "Go save your damsel in distress. Just be careful!"

He nodded and grasped the rope. "I will." Peering into her eyes, he said simply, "I love you, Georgie."

"I love you too. Now go, before I freeze."

Barking a laugh, he eased himself up onto the windowsill. The sensation of nothing beneath his feet was strange and disconcerting, not at all pleasant. Grasping the sheet-rope in a death grip, he wrapped it around his hand and lowered himself carefully below the sill.

The wind buffeted him immediately, blowing his blanket

away. It sailed off like a kite without a tail. He paid it no mind, his sole focus was on not falling to his death. His arms strained to take his weight as he tried to stop himself from plummeting down the rope. Glancing up, he brushed his foot against the wall, finding a purchase in a small crevice that decades of wind had carved out. He leaned back and planted the other foot. Could he walk down like this?

Easing one foot down a few inches, he adjusted his grip on the rope and lowered himself slowly. The other foot slid down, and the ground came closer. Foot by foot, he descended as darkness fell. At last, he ran out of rope with about ten feet to go. Clinging to the knot tied to the candlestick, attempting to avoid bashing his head on it, Jemmy took a deep breath and released the rope. He dropped to the frozen ground, the shock reverberating up his legs in painful streaks. Pins and needles shot through his feet, and he dove forward but remained standing.

Immediately, he looked up to see the sheets and candlestick rising rapidly. At last they disappeared altogether, and his sister's slender, white hand, stark against the dark stone, waved him away before she shut the window with a bang.

The light had gone to deep purple in the shadow of the castle, but he located the dark blue blanket quickly enough. Pulling it around his body, he savored its warmth and hurried to his left toward the stables.

Chapter 25

Deep twilight cloaked Jemmy by the time he reached the main stable block, where his own horse, Pharaoh, was kept. Gripping the blanket against the cold, he inched along the gray stone wall surrounding the stables, head cocked for voices from within. If he could catch one or two under grooms, he might be able to buy their cooperation and their silence.

Moving slowly, he raised his head to peer into one of the curious round windows cut into the stone. The only person in sight was a young groom, sitting astride a bench, polishing a harness. Perhaps good fortune would shine on him after all.

Inching toward the door, he listened but heard no conversations. He eased the door open and popped his head around the door frame.

The young groom, barely twelve years old if he was a day, glanced up, then jumped to his feet, his hat immediately in his hand. "Beg pardon, milord. What can I do for you?"

The lad's flushed face with serious eyes gave Jemmy hope anew. "Where are the other grooms, lad?"

"They're all gone in for their tea, milord, but I can run

fetch 'em for you right quick." He started to bolt toward a door along the wall to the right.

"No, no need, lad." Jemmy eyed the door the boy had started for. "I've come to get my horse. Thought I'd ride down to the Whyte Harte for a pint or two."

"Very good, milord. D'ye want me to fetch me da for ya?"

Jemmy had already sized the boy up as a sturdy, eager sort. "I'd wager you could saddle him for me, couldn't you, lad?"

"Oh, yes, milōrd." The boy's brown eyes shone with pride. "I know how to do it right quick, I do. Which horse is yours?"

"Pharaoh. The roan stallion." Jemmy could see the horse just two stalls down. "That one there, sticking his nose over the stall door."

"Yes, milord, right away, milord." The boy rushed down the aisle. "He's a grand horse, he is." He disappeared into the tack room and returned to sight a minute later laden with Jemmy's saddle slung over one arm, bridle in hand. "Just two shakes of a lamb's tail and I'll have him ready for ye." The boy trotted toward Pharaoh's stall and ducked inside.

Jemmy eyed the door to the stable's kitchen. If the boy was fast enough, he might just make it out of here. Fidgeting with the blanket, Jemmy tied the ends together, fashioning a cape of sorts around his shoulders. The boy hadn't seemed to notice the odd article slung around him, thank goodness.

Time ticked away. If the boy didn't hurry, the grooms and coachman would be out, and then he'd either have to run for it or try to bribe them all. While ten pounds might be a fortune for one man, it became less appealing when shared among ten, especially when it would likely mean getting the sack from the marquess.

The door to the kitchen opened, and Jemmy ducked back into the shadows. A middle-aged man, Mack, one of the grooms who had been here when Jemmy was a boy, ambled toward the outside. Probably to relieve himself. Damn it, where was that boy?

The slow clop-clop of shod horses' hooves on stone began as the boy emerged from the stall, leading Pharaoh toward him. Thank God.

"Here he is, milord." The boy looked around, face pinched into puzzlement.

Jemmy darted forward, grabbing the reins and vaulting into the saddle in one swift movement. He transferred the reins to one hand and dug into his pocket. "What's your name, lad?"

"Tom Redman, milord." The boy flashed a look up at him, worry in his eyes.

"Here you go, Tom. And many thanks for a brave night's work." Jemmy leaned over to hand the boy a one-pound note. "You earned it lad."

"What the devil's going on here?" The door to the kitchen opened, spilling grooms and coachmen into the aisle, blocking Jemmy's path to freedom.

"A cold ride for a pint of ale, Harper," Jemmy called to one of the grooms he knew. He gathered the reins and tensed his calf muscles, ready to dig into the horse's flanks.

"Aye, you've a frosty one ahead of you if you're for the Harte tonight, my lord." Harper didn't move, his gaze flicking from Jemmy to Tom. "What've you got there, Tom?"

"A small token for service rendered, Harper. Now if you don't mind . . ." He urged the stallion forward. Only a few more yards, and he'd be through the door and out into the night.

"It's a pound note, Mr. Harper." Wonderingly, Tom held it up. The bill probably represented half a year's wages.

"What?" Harper strode toward the boy. "A pound?" He looked suspiciously at Jemmy. "What'd you give him a pound for?"

"All right, lads, back to work now. Tea's over." Mack had returned from the yard. He stopped, taking in the scene, and his eyes narrowed. "His lordship gave instructions regarding you, Lord Brack. I'll thank you to get down off that horse now."

"Just going to the Whyte Harte for a pint, Mack. I'll be back in time for dinner." Jemmy smiled and dug his heels into Pharaoh's sides.

The horse shot forward, scattering the men as he made for the open door. Mack made a grab for his reins as he sped by, but Jemmy kicked out, connecting with the groom's stomach and tumbling him to the ground.

Pharaoh cleared the door, and they were out in the cold night air, cantering down the driveway as if a pack of hell-hounds were nipping at their heels.

Jemmy raised his face and shouted victoriously into the dark sky, peppered with stars and the half-moon, now hidden behind a cloud. He'd made his escape, though not as secretively as he'd hoped. That mattered much less now he was free. At the end of the driveway, he slowed the horse to a trot and turned him for the village. Once there, he'd pick up the post road, and if the clouds didn't continue to hang over the moon, he'd have a clear path on 'til dawn.

There would be pursuit, no doubt. Father would try his best to get him back, but he had a head start and a determination, borne of desperation, to evade his father's men. Add a trick or two up his sleeve to throw them off the scent, and he just might win home to Elizabeth.

Suddenly, the moon sailed from behind the veil of clouds, shining a dazzling light onto the shadowy road. Perhaps their fortunes *had* changed. He urged Pharaoh back into a ground-eating canter. So far, so good.

"Hold on, Elizabeth," he said grimly into the night. "I'm coming."

Chapter 26

The vestibule of St. George's Church, London, had absolutely no heat. Elizabeth stood shivering, white puffs of breath showing as she clutched her father's arm, wishing herself anywhere but where she was. She peered through the tiny window of the vestibule door into the church proper, empty save for Mama and Lord Robert. The rector had gone to retrieve the registry and thaw the inkpot. "I still do not understand why this wedding had to be performed so quickly, Papa."

"It will be over in a few minutes, Elizabeth. Then you can get on with making a home with Robert. I daresay he's not the most eligible man in your eyes, but he is a good man." Papa looked down his long nose at her, as if she were impugning Lord Robert's sterling reputation.

"I understand that he's a good man, Papa. I truly do. What I don't understand is why we have to marry on only one day's acquaintance. Why can't we wait to have the banns read? That would take only two weeks. There would be no greater scandal than there will be now." She needed time to make her peace with the fact that she would be marrying a man she didn't love and that the man she did love,

256 *Jenna Jaxon*

and who loved her, would be marrying someone else as well. Did no one else understand that her feelings mattered as much as the reputation of the family?

"Do you believe a longer acquaintance will change your opinion of Robert?" Raised eyebrows said her father sensed this was not her true argument.

"Perhaps." If she went to hell for lying in church, then so be it.

Papa sighed and stamped his feet. Hers had frozen long ago. She could no longer feel her toes in her blue slippers. If only her heart were so conveniently icy.

"I know you do not feel for Robert what you felt for Easton or even what you may have imagined you felt for this Lord Brack." His lips drew inward, displeasure in every line. "However, you are fooling yourself, Elizabeth, if you think by delaying a day, or two or three, you will be more accepting of this marriage. 'Tis best done quickly, as Shakespeare put it. Once it is done, you can begin to learn to get along together."

Her father, however, would not be the one to share his life, or his bed, with a complete stranger. With a man she feared she would respect but never come to esteem. Lord Robert had wonderful qualities, she was sure, but he wasn't Jemmy. And that made all the difference.

The mere thought of his name made her weak. How could she live if she could never see him again? Even if she couldn't marry him, she would be free to continue to love him. She might break her vow to Lord Robert, to cleave only unto him, as soon as it was made, but she could not stop loving Jemmy.

What if she rebelled? What could they actually do to her if she refused to marry Lord Robert? The rector would refuse to marry them if she did not willingly agree to the marriage. Did she have the courage, when the time came, to say "no"?

"Ah, here is Reverend Newcastle now." Papa tightened his grip on her arm. "It'll be all over soon, now."

Mouth dry, Elizabeth swallowed convulsively, then opened her mouth to tell Papa she couldn't do this, but he was already propelling her through the door and down the aisle.

Lord Robert turned to look at her, and her feet became unruly. They seemed to stick to the floor rather than want to send her down the aisle toward what she suddenly understood was the worst mistake of her life. Her groom smiled as she approached, and her heart thudded faster.

"Pick up your feet, Elizabeth," Papa hissed, almost pulling her along. "I don't want Lord Robert to think I'm dragging you to the altar."

Well, that was exactly what he was doing. Dutifully, Elizabeth straightened her shoulders and quickened her pace. What she would do when she reached the smiling rector at the end of the aisle and the time came to take her vows she had no idea.

On her father's arm, she passed her mother sitting in the first row, her green spencer a splash of color against the severe, dark wood of the pew. Mama had bespoken a new hat for the occasion, cream-colored, with lace and tiny flowers scattered all over it. She peeped out from beneath the brim of this frothy confection, to pierce her with a steely eye. If Elizabeth jilted Lord Robert now, Mama would likely disown her. Biting her lips, Elizabeth walked on.

At last, they stood before the rector and Papa handed her over to Lord Robert. She took his blue-clad arm gingerly, suddenly unwilling to touch him. This uncertainty would drive her mad. Best to get it over with and try to make a life somehow. She looked up into his face, and Jemmy's mischievous grin smiled back at her.

He was here! The unruly golden curls, the straight nose, merry blue eyes, broad comforting shoulders. They were to marry after all. Her heart sung with joy.

Elizabeth blinked and the beloved features melted into the affable but older, less familiar face of Lord Robert. She bit her tongue to stifle a cry of disappointment. Batting her eyes rapidly several times to stem the tide of tears that threatened to cascade in a torrent down her cheeks, she swallowed the lump in her throat as the rector began the service.

"Dearly beloved. We have come together in the presence of God to witness and bless the joining of this man and this woman in holy matrimony."

Time seemed to slow down. The rector's voice droned on and on. Surely, he would soon get to the crucial point, yet she still didn't know what to do when he did. Her stomach trembled, and she gripped Lord Robert's arm tighter. What must she do?

Loud banging in the vestibule snapped Elizabeth out of her lethargy. Who was making that frightful noise?

Angry voices rose over Mr. Newcastle's quivering, quiet tones. "Who gives this woman to be married?"

"I do." Papa kissed her forehead. "You'll be fine, my dear," he whispered, then frowned as he gazed toward the door at the back of the church.

The disturbance had not abated.

"Excuse me, Mr. Newcastle. I'll just have a look. Please, continue." Papa hurried toward the vestibule door. He'd not gotten halfway down the aisle when the door burst open, so forcefully it hit the wall behind it and bounced back.

Hair gloriously disheveled, a fine blond stubble on his cheeks, eyes streaked with red, jacket and boots stained with mud, Jemmy strode through the doorway.

"Jemmy." Never had anything looked so wonderful. Elizabeth dropped Lord Robert's arm.

"I demand that you stop this wedding." Jemmy strode down the aisle, brushing past Papa with a look that would have frozen a lesser man. He reached Elizabeth and grabbed her hand. "This woman is betrothed to me."

"That betrothal was broken when you contracted to marry another lady." Papa waded into the thick of things.

Lord Robert stood unmoving, his eyes wide, leaning backward as if he intended to flee.

"I never contracted with her." Jemmy drew himself up to his haughty best. "My father advanced the marriage, but I am long past the age when he could command me. Neither can he compel me to marry anyone against my will. And I swear before God it *would* be against my will if my bride was anyone other than Elizabeth."

"See here, my lord—"

"Mr. Newcastle, proceed with the wedding." Mama's commanding voice cut above the lower registers of the men. "Elizabeth will marry Lord Robert. She has agreed to it."

Mr. Newcastle eyed Jemmy dubiously but dutifully opened his mouth.

"I, however, have the prior claim, my lady." Jemmy glared at her mother, and his hand gripped Elizabeth's arm tighter. "Mr. Newcastle, you would do well to desist, sir. I am the Earl of Brack and as such demand that you hear me out." He glanced around at the little gathering, his bright blue eyes wild. "I'll have you know that, since last night, I have crawled out of a window, shimmied down twenty feet of twisted sheets, stolen a horse, come close to being shot, ridden all night long—getting lost twice—and have finally arrived here to claim my bride." Sliding his gaze directly to Mama, he fixed her with an unyielding gaze. "Or shall I give Mr. Newcastle another, more *personal* reason why Elizabeth should wed me instead of Lord Robert?"

"How dare you threaten us with some made-up scandalous rumor about my daughter?" Papa stepped forward, standing in front of Jemmy, his chin thrust out and puffing out his chest.

"Scandalous perhaps, but truth all the same." Jemmy gave him a withering look, and Papa stepped back. "Shall I tell the truth and shame the devil?"

Enough was enough. Elizabeth rolled her eyes back in her head, let her legs buckle, and hoped Jemmy would catch her.

"Elizabeth!" Jemmy's reflexes were excellent, thank goodness. He nimbly caught her against him and lowered her to the floor.

"Elizabeth! Fetch some water." Papa's voice held an urgency she'd seldom heard.

"Smelling salts." Mama would, of course, be practical. "I have some in my reticule." Lord, she hated that smell but steeled herself for it.

"Elizabeth." Jemmy patted her hands. "Can you hear me?"

She continued silent, limp as wilted lettuce.

"Stand back." Suddenly, she was borne into the air in Jemmy's strong arms. Through slitted eyelids, she could see the church pews speed by as he carried her back down the aisle, through the broken door to the vestibule, heading outside.

As soon as the cold air hit her face, and she could assume they were away from her family, she fluttered her eyelids open.

Jemmy stopped, concern etched on his brow. "Elizabeth? Are you all right?"

Her smile spread so broad she feared her cheeks would crack. "Jemmy, oh, Jemmy!" She flung her arms around his neck and kissed him, never wanting to let him go.

"Elizabeth. My God," he said when he could speak again. Gently, he lowered her to the ground, disentangling them until she stood on her feet again. Passing his hand over his face, he sighed, looking like he wanted to drop down in the street. "Are you all right?"

"Perfectly fine, now." She pulled him into her arms, lacing her fingers together behind his back. Let someone try to take him from her. "I know how to stop a wedding, don't I? The swoon was a false one this time, however." She cupped his cheek, the prickles of a day's growth of beard scratching against her fingers. "Oh, Jemmy, was all that true that you said in the church? Did you really climb down the castle wall at Blackham and ride through the night?"

"I did indeed." Leaning his head against her forehead, he stroked her arm tenderly. "And I'd do it again and much, much more if I was assured of such a wonderful outcome." He straightened, and his face took on a hollow, haunted look. "Elizabeth, I was terrified I'd be too late. I pushed the poor horses until they were almost lame." With a sheepish grin, he raised his right hand. "I swear I will go back along the way and pay for good feeding and care for every horse I rode between Red Hill and here."

"Bless every one of them." She dove back at him, wrapping her arms around him and squeezing him tight. "I cannot believe you are real. I told myself you couldn't come." Tears of relief trickled down her cheeks. "I almost lost you."

"It was a near thing, I grant you. I did hit upon a piece of luck. Georgie had told me your father's house was in St. James Square, but she didn't know the number. When I rode into the square an hour ago, I was looking to and fro, fearing I'd never find the right house, when a maid out on some errand stopped and asked if I needed help. She pointed out the correct establishment." He grinned and wiped her cheeks with his thumb, his touch like silk on her skin. "I knocked and, when it opened, hurriedly told the butler I was Lord Robert's brother in search of the wedding, and he directed me here. If I'd had to knock on several doors . . ." He kissed her again. "I arrived not a moment too soon."

"No, you did not." Relief finally began to spread through her. The nightmare was almost over. "So when can we be married, my love? I don't want anyone or anything to ever come between us and our happiness again." The mere idea of what could have happened had Jemmy been delayed at all made her truly faint.

"We'll discuss it with your parents." He moved away from her as the door to St. George's opened, spilling out Mama and Papa and poor Lord Robert, looking dazed.

"I'll write when I arrive in Shropshire, Wentworth. I wish

you and your family a Merry Christmas." Lord Robert bowed to them, then turned his steps toward her.

A fluttering fear—born of guilt, she supposed—lodged itself in her breast. What would she say to the man?

Jemmy fell back a pace but remained behind her, a staunch support.

That she had acted badly had already occurred to her; that she could have acted in no different manner at all had also crossed her mind. Still, Lord Robert had been willing to come to her aid. She owed him her thanks, and an apology.

"Lord Robert—"

He held up a hand and shook his head. "You need say nothing, my dear." He eyed Jemmy, then returned his gaze to her. "Our marriage was always a matter of convenience, and now I find it is for the best if our arrangement come to an end. Lord Brack seems perfectly willing and capable of taking care of you." He shuddered. "More than capable, I would say. And if one's heart lies elsewhere, then it is a disservice to all if that call is not answered."

"Lord Robert, you are a true gentleman. I thank you from the bottom of my heart for your gallant offer of marriage, although I find it is not required after all." She dragged Jemmy forward. "Lord Robert Naylor, may I present Lord Brack. Lord Robert was prepared to come to my rescue when we believed you unavoidably detained."

"My lord." Lord Robert bowed slightly.

"My lord." Jemmy made a more formal bow. "I am in your debt for the care and assistance you have rendered to my betrothed." There was an ever-so-slight emphasis on the word "my" that thrilled Elizabeth to no end.

"Not a'tall, my lord." Lord Robert nodded, a bit more cordially. "I am glad if I could render my services to Mrs. Easton. She is a lovely woman." His blue eyes intensified as he gazed at her.

Heat rose to Elizabeth's face under such scrutiny.

"You are a very fortunate man, Lord Brack." Another

piercing stare at her, and she lowered her gaze. "Very fortunate indeed. Should you ever require my assistance again,
my dear, your father knows how to find me. Good day, Mrs.
Easton, Lord Brack."

Sighing deeply, Elizabeth took Jemmy's arm as Lord
Robert's tall, straight figure wound its way toward his carriage. "He is a very good man. I will pray each night that he
finds the happiness he deserves, whether that is alone with
his books and studies or with a good wife who will be fond
of him and take care of him as he writes his manuscripts."

"Well, I give you leave to pray for Lord Robert, and even
to be fond of him, as he did attempt a very chivalrous deed
for you and your family. However"—Jemmy paused and
trapped her hand in both of his—"a fondness is as far as it
may go."

Elizabeth laughed, a great weight rolling off her shoulders. "I agree, my love. You shall hear no argument from me
on that particular."

The approaching figures of Papa and Mama, faces sullen,
said Elizabeth's trials were far from over. She quickly
dropped Jemmy's hands but raised her chin and set her jaw.
She'd not antagonize them, but neither would she allow
them to sway her from her chosen path. "Mama. Papa, I
would like to present—"

"Come, Elizabeth." Glancing first at her, then briefly at
Jemmy, Mama took Papa's arm and urged him toward the
landau. "Please get into the carriage before we become even
more of a public spectacle."

Lord, more battles to face. But with Jemmy here, they
could face them together.

"I would like to present—"

"You heard your mother, Elizabeth." Papa's tone was as
cold as the two stygian pools that were his eyes.

Puffing out the frigid air, Elizabeth set her shoulders
back. If her parents wanted this fight here and now, so be it.
They would not give her beloved the cut direct, not after

everything he had gone through to get here. She'd walk every step of the way home if she had to. "I'll not enter that carriage until you agree to the introduction. I do not care that you disapprove of my choices, Mama. They are mine to make. And I will not allow you to slight the man I love, the man I am going to marry."

"Elizabeth," Jemmy spoke quietly behind her. "Perhaps we should—"

"No." She raised a forbidding finger to him. "They will acknowledge you this instant, or I will walk every step of the way home. I am done being told what I shall and shall not do." Swinging back around on her parents, she almost gasped to see their mouths hanging open. Good. At last, they were paying attention to her. "Who I shall and shall not marry."

Papa coughed, and Mama sent him a familiar sideways look, one of her standards that said, "I'll take care of this," when their eyes met.

Sure enough, lips pursed, Mama finally nodded. "Very well, Elizabeth. We will meet Lord Brack, but for God's sake, allow us to do it at home out of the cold. Wentworth, assist me into the carriage before my feathers freeze."

As Papa helped her in, Elizabeth turned to Jemmy, whose eyes twinkled a bright blue. "Do you think you can manage one more turn on a horse today? It is not far, as you know."

Jemmy grasped her hand and raised it to his lips. "I would ride to hell and back just to see you perform in such high dudgeon. It quite becomes you, my love." He released her hand and bowed to her father. "I will see you shortly, my lord." With a flash of his grin, he hurried toward a tired-looking black stallion, tied to one of the church's posts.

"Elizabeth." Her father called her back to the waiting carriage, and with a sigh, she gave him her hand and stepped up into it. This short ride would be accomplished in deathly silence or with Mama's noisy recriminations. Either way, it didn't matter, as long as Jemmy was there at the end of it.

Chapter 27

The quick ride home was silent, thank goodness, though Mama's glare could have melted the Sphinx. Papa had opened his mouth once, but she had fixed him with her fiery eye, and he subsided into a fit of coughing.

They had scarcely pulled up in front of Worth House before the door opened, and there was Jemmy, reaching in to hand her down. He still looked windblown and rough, but he'd managed to remove most of the clumps of mud from his jacket.

Brimming with joy, as though she was really returning from church duly wed, Elizabeth took his arm and led him into the house.

Tawes's eyebrows nearly disappeared into his hairline when he opened the door, but he speedily recovered. "Mrs. Easton"—a subtle pause—"my lord."

She smothered a giggle as she relinquished her spencer to the butler. Jemmy had presented himself as Lord Robert's brother. No wonder poor Tawes would be flustered, wondering why she would leave to marry one brother and return on the arm of another.

"Come into the family room. There's a small wedding

breakfast laid there that we may as well eat." Elizabeth took his arm and led him up the stairs, her steps so much lighter than when she'd come down them an hour before.

"So we shall anticipate the wedding yet again?" Jemmy whispered, his grin widening.

Smothering a laugh, Elizabeth ducked her head, her cheeks heating, remembering the last time they had done so. "We've done more scandalous things than almost any couple I know."

His face sobered instantly.

"What's wrong?" Fear clutched her heart. He was precious to her, now more than ever. She couldn't bear to contemplate anything else going amiss.

"Nothing, my love. At least, nothing that won't keep until we speak with your parents."

A niggle of unease continued to nag her, but his strong, warm presence beside her dispelled any lingering worry. As long as they were together, nothing else mattered.

They entered the family drawing room, the sideboard laid with savories and a cake, decorated with pink and white icing.

Bella and Dotty, sipping tea with their heads together, looked up at their entrance.

"Elizabeth! How was—" Bella stopped, her cup midway to its saucer.

"Who is that?" Dotty whispered loudly to her sister, her own cup also suspended in the air.

"I don't know." Bella set her teacup down carefully and rose. "Elizabeth, what's going on?"

Dotty's cup rattled into its saucer as she followed Bella toward them.

"Isabella, Dorothea, may I make known to you Lord Brack? These are my sisters, my lord. Miss Worth and Miss Dorothea Worth." Elizabeth's heart beat strangely. She did so hope some of her family approved of Jemmy.

"This is Lord Brack?" Bella's eyes lit up. "How do you do, my lord? Elizabeth has spoken of you to us quite often this past fall." Her pleased smile faltered. "But, Elizabeth, I do not understand." She peered behind Jemmy at the door. "You left this morning to marry . . ." Blushing, Bella clutched her throat and looked away.

"Weren't you supposed to marry Lord Robert?" Dotty's shrill voice broke in. "Whatever has happened, Elizabeth?"

"She's taken leave of her senses, girls." Mama strode into the room, imperious as always. "Bella, ring for more tea. I am in dire need of something hot. Dotty, fetch me two of the lobster patties."

"Aren't they for the wedding breakfast, Mama?" Confusion mounting, Dotty looked from her mother, to Elizabeth, to Jemmy. "Was there no wedding?"

"There was not." Mama glared at Elizabeth before settling into her accustomed gold jacquard wing-backed chair. "This is now a festive luncheon, although I see no cause to celebrate."

Shooting her sister a look of utter bewilderment, Dotty threw up her hands and headed to the loaded sideboard.

"Circumstances may not be as dire as you fear, my dear." Her father entered the room and made straight for the decanter on the desk. "At least Lord Brack has put in an appearance, eleventh hour though it was. I suggest we reserve our judgment until we hear the whole story."

"But, dear Lord Robert—" Producing a lace handkerchief that matched her blue sprigged gown, Mama dabbed her eyes, even though no tears seemed evident.

"Do not distress yourself over Robert." Pouring until his tumbler was half full of his favorite cognac, Papa paused to sip his drink. "He is quite content to return to Shropshire unencumbered by a wife and two children." Her father shook his head, looking sheepish. "I should never have brought him into this affair in the first place. But I wanted Elizabeth settled quickly, and when he suddenly appeared at the club, I took the chance."

"Still, he seemed so much more suitable than . . ." Mama shot an unrepentant glance of dismay at Jemmy.

"My dear, let us meet the gentleman before you disparage him. Elizabeth," Papa ambled over to stand beside Mama's chair. "Won't you introduce us to your friend?"

Gratitude toward her father flooded Elizabeth's heart as she brought Jemmy forward to stand before Mama's chair. Introducing him to the queen would be easier. "Mama, Papa, may I present Lord Brack? Lord Brack, my parents, Lord and Lady Wentworth."

"My lord, my lady." Making a crisp bow, Jemmy smiled broadly, bringing out a dimple in his left cheek Elizabeth somehow hadn't noticed before. "I am so pleased to meet you at last."

Mama had the grace to blush at that.

"Get you a drink, Brack?" Papa raised his glass.

"I'd be obliged, my lord. It's been a long night." Jemmy followed her father over to the sideboard.

"So, Mama." Elizabeth sat on the sofa beside Mama's chair, eager for this conversation. "What do you say now?"

Pursed lips wavered as her mother struggled with some strong emotion. At last, a tear rolled down her cheek, and she dashed it away. "He is very, very like Louisa," she whispered. "Not at all like Blackham."

Sighing in relief, Elizabeth took her mother's hand. "He is a wonderful man, Mama. I love him. I am certain you will come to like him as well if you can just give him a chance."

Her mother nodded and squeezed her hand, her lips still trembling. She sent another glance at Jemmy, then wiped her eyes once more.

The girls slid next to Elizabeth, all atwitter.

"He's very handsome, Elizabeth." Dotty cast a glance over her shoulder at Papa and Jemmy. "Such nice curly hair. Just like Lord Byron's. I must marry a man with curly hair. I adore it so." She clasped her hands together over her bosom, her eyes bright.

"We will see about that this spring, young lady." Mama's no-nonsense persona had apparently resurfaced. "You will do as you are told, and perhaps you will find a gentleman willing to marry you, curly hair or not."

"Don't be a goose, Dotty. A man's hair doesn't matter a fig." Bella lifted her chin, nose quite in the air. "I'm sure I don't care at all that Haxton's hair is straight and black."

"What you do care about is that you are to be Countess of Haxton." Dotty stuck her tongue out at her sister.

"Girls, please." Massaging her temple, Mama groaned softly. "My poor head. Bella, did you ring for tea? This day has been trying enough as it is without you and your sister fussing over nothing."

"And will likely become more trying, my dear." Papa and Jemmy reappeared from their conversation by the decanter.

"What on earth do you mean, Wentworth? Oh, thank goodness." Mama relaxed back in her chair as the footman entered with a fresh pot of tea and cups. "Do pour for me, Elizabeth. And don't stint on the sugar. I fear I will need fortification for your father's next revelation."

"Not mine, my dear." Grim lines etching his face, Papa sipped his drink. "I'll let Brack tell you, as it is his tale."

"What is it, my lord?" Elizabeth dropped four lumps into her mother's cup, contemplating dumping the whole lot in. Best not. She might find herself needing something to strengthen her as well by the time Jemmy had finished.

"Before my father locked me in my room at the castle—"

"He locked you in, my lord?" Dotty bounced up on the sofa, her eyes shining with excitement. "Do you mean like Emily St. Aubert in *The Mysteries of Udolpho*?"

"Dorothea, calm yourself." Mama fixed her youngest child with a stern eye. "If you cannot learn to comport yourself in a more unexceptional manner, you may find your Season postponed for a year or more."

Lips poked out in a pout, Dotty sank back onto the sofa. "But he said he was locked in a castle, Mama. I should think that called for an exceptional manner. It sounds terribly thrilling."

"It may sound thrilling to you, Dorothea. And it may have been thrilling for Lord Brack, but you simply cannot shout about it as if you were still ten years old. Now, my lord"—Mama turned her attention back to Jemmy—"pray continue."

He smiled at Dotty and winked conspiratorially. "Well, escaping was rather thrilling, I must admit, but the confinement was most inconvenient. I had no means to tell your sister I was coming for her. But by the grace of God, my sister, and Lady Wrotham, I managed to arrive here in time. Thank goodness, you hit upon that clever method of sending your letters through Lady Wrotham, my dear. It quite saved the day, I tell you."

"It was my mother's idea, my lord." Elizabeth turned from her beloved to beam at Mama.

Jemmy's jovial face softened. "Then I am truly forever in your debt, my lady. I would never have known of Elizabeth's plans were it not for her letters."

Pulling a Friday face, Mama grasped her tea but gave a nod of thanks before sipping it and sighing.

"Now, Miss Dorothea," Jemmy returned smoothly to Dotty, who sat across from Elizabeth, staring at him, quivering like a coiled spring, "I will tell you all about the daring escape; however, I must relay my unfortunate news first." His smile fled as he seated himself next to Elizabeth.

She grasped his hand, steadying herself with his touch. "Go on, my lord."

"Father has written a letter to Lady Locke, denouncing you as a scheming minx trying to foist a child off on me that is not mine."

"Dear Lord." Elizabeth's stomach dropped. This could ruin not only her, but her entire family. Lady Locke would relish such a tale, no doubt. Truth rarely mattered in her pursuit of the latest scandal. And to be the first to know such information would certainly be a feather in her cap.

"This is outrageous, even for Blackham." Mama had gone as white as the teacup clutched in her hand.

"He said he'd waited a long time for his vengeance." Jemmy turned to her, an eyebrow raised. "I assume you know to what he was referring."

"I do." Mama's lips pressed together, a red slash across her pale face. She rubbed her temple with short, rounded strokes, a sure sign of one of her headaches. It had been a day of stresses, to be sure.

"I will elaborate on that situation later in private, Lord Brack." Elizabeth wanted to spare Mama from reliving that painful experience yet again, especially in front of her younger daughters.

Jemmy nodded, but his attention remained on her parents. "As soon as my escape was reported to him, we must assume he sent the letter to Lady Locke. The post had already come by that time yesterday, so either he put it in today's post or he sent it by one of his footmen, with directions to put it directly into the lady's hand. In any case, she will likely receive it today or tomorrow at the latest."

"How could he say something so . . . so horrible about you, Elizabeth?" Bella's pinched face had paled as well. Her betrothal might well be thrown into jeopardy should this tale be spread about. "It is wicked, wicked to tell such lies. Does he not know you would never do something so shameful?"

"Can't you simply inform Lady Locke that Lord Blackham is lying, Elizabeth?" Dotty turned a trusting face from her sister to her mother. "Won't people believe your word over that of Lord Blackham?"

Shifting uneasily, Jemmy ran a hand through his already unruly hair.

Elizabeth's face heated until she had to fan herself with her hand. Oh, what a thing to have to admit to her innocent sister.

"They might believe for a while, my dear." She cleared her throat and forced herself to continue. "However, when our child is born two months early, the *ton* will think back, and wonder, and whisper."

"How do you know your first child will be born early?" Dotty's pink face was screwed into a frown.

"Because . . ." Elizabeth gazed down at her lap, unable to meet Dotty's puzzled expression.

"Elizabeth!" Bella's hushed voice sounded loud in her ears. "You aren't . . ."

"Yes, I am." Still keeping her head down, she forced the admission out from between clenched teeth.

A sharp gasp from Bella, and Elizabeth wanted to bury her face in her lap.

"Will someone tell me what's going on?" Dotty's voice was a mixture of exasperation and bewilderment.

In the silence that followed her question, Elizabeth raised her head to find her sister scowling first at her, then at her mother. It was her fault. She must be the one to explain. "I am already carrying Lord Brack's child, Dotty."

The shock in her sister's face was almost comical. "Elizabeth! You can't do that. You're not married to him yet!"

"Hold your tongue, Dorothea." Mama snapped at her. "This is not a discussion for the ears of a girl betrothed, much less one not yet out. However, as it could well affect your prospects, I suppose you must hear it." Marshaling a calmness she certainly must not feel, Mama stared into Dotty's face. "A woman does not have to be married to have a baby. She is ruined if she does, so take note of that, miss, but the fact remains that it is not impossible to do so. Elizabeth and Lord Brack will marry soon, so we hope it will be of no consequence for us. However"—Mama pinned her youngest daughter with an evil glare—"you should not take their somewhat special circumstances as an example to follow."

"Oh, no, Mama." Dotty scooted away from Elizabeth as though she might contract leprosy.

"Lord Brack," her mother turned her keen gaze toward Jemmy, "do you know the direction of your father's letter to Lady Locke?"

"No, I'm afraid not, my lady."

The smile that touched Mama's mouth had an air of triumph to it. "Well, even so, I am thinking that perhaps we are not quite lost after all." She sat back and took up one of the lobster patties.

"How so, Mama?" Elizabeth grasped her teacup and added another lump of sugar. After this conversation, she needed some fortifications of her own.

"Yesterday, when I was visiting Lady Gant, I learned that Lady Locke, who is her cousin, has left London and gone to her daughter's home in Northumberland. So if Lord Blackham isn't possessed of this particular piece of news, and likely he isn't, he will have sent the letter to either the lady's London address or to her late husband's estate in West Sussex. In either case"—her mother's voice took on that triumphant sound reserved for her particularly satisfying coups—"it will languish for at least a month, unless she's left instructions to have her mail sent to her. Should that be the case, we should still have a week or more, what with the holiday and the state of the post roads in this weather. As soon as you are married, we can put it about that your father was trying to discourage the match, Lord Brack. Then when Lady Locke's letter comes to light, we will have already sown the seeds of doubt."

"Whatever the case, we should marry as soon as possible, to help dispel any rumors that might pop up." Jemmy came forward again and sat beside Elizabeth. "The problem remains that I will not inherit the bulk of my mother's money until I am thirty. That is only until next August, but it will be a hardship until then."

"So you propose to marry my daughter when you have no means whatsoever of supporting her?" Mama drew herself up from the depths of the wing-backed chair like a dragon emerging from its lair.

He raised his chin and looked her parents squarely in their faces. "I intend to lay the problem before my mother's father after Elizabeth and I marry. He may feel inclined to assist us for the few months it will take to get past this obstacle."

"And at this point, my dear"—Papa hastened to deflect her mother's wrath—"I think they have very little choice." He nodded to Jemmy, kindness in his eyes. "I believe we can accommodate you and Elizabeth here at Worth House, Brack, until August. This is not the time for Elizabeth to be any more distressed than she already has been."

"Thank you, my lord, for that generous offer, but I am in the process of working out a solution on my own." Jemmy's lips were set in a very firm line, but his ears had turned a disturbing shade of pink. Did that happen when he was under duress?

"I understand your wanting to provide for you family yourself, young man," Mama came back at him, determinedly, "but my daughter is in a delicate condition. She has two children who should not be uprooted higgledy-piggledy. I insist that you remain with us after the wedding and until the child is born. Then you may set up your housekeeping wherever you wish and move them all into it. Not a day before." Her gimlet eye made even Jemmy squirm.

"We needn't settle every detail this instant." Elizabeth rose, hoping to spread a soothing oil on the roiling waters. "But we will need to discuss plans for the wedding over dinner. And since Jem—Lord Brack—has had a rather tiring two days, I suggest he be allowed to refresh himself before dinner." She smiled at Jemmy. "Let me show you to your chamber. The Alexander Room, Mama?" Decorated with pictures of Alexander the Great and many military hangings and artifacts, it was the most important guest room in the house.

"Yes. I think that will serve well for Lord Brack."

Jemmy bowed. "Thank you, my lady. My lord."

"Tell Porter to see to him," her mother called as they left the room.

"Well, that went much better than I had anticipated." Jemmy laughed as they headed down the carpeted corridor and turned to the right.

"Indeed, it did, considering that two hours ago Mama wanted to give you the cut direct. Now she's got you in the best guest room and is practically forcing us to live with her." Elizabeth sighed. "That may be a mixed blessing. Dickon and I lived with my parents for a short time after we married. It was difficult to be . . . intimate while under my parents' watchful eye."

"Considering the alternative, I believe we will learn to live with the arrangement, my love." He took her hand and kissed it.

"What was the alternative solution you spoke of just now? Is that something we should still pursue?"

He chuckled and tucked her arm back into his. "A bluff, pure and simple. I had no plan in mind other than the one to ask my grandfather for assistance. But I have found that if you claim to have one, people take you more seriously."

"Jemmy." She smacked his arm, eliciting a yelp from him. "No wonder your ears turned pink."

"You have found out my best secret." His eyes were merry, despite their tired appearance. "Whenever I tell a falsehood, my ears turn the color of one of the roses at Blackham."

"I hope I shall have little occasion to see that display, my dear." Elizabeth laughed as she stopped at his chamber door. "I'll tell Porter, my father's valet, to come see to you."

"Lord, I shall have to track down Fellowes and send him to Lyttlefield Park to fetch the rest of my things. Thank goodness I didn't take everything to Blackham or I'd never get them back." He drew her to him, and she reveled in his nearness. Had he not appeared when he did, she'd now be Lady Robert Naylor. A shudder wracked her.

"Are you all right?" He cupped her face and her fears fled.

"Now I am." She grasped his face and melded their lips together, sinking into him once more, like coming home. When she finally broke the kiss, his eyes were dark, eager to continue. "I'm afraid we shall have to wait until after the wedding for anything more, my love," she said with a rueful smile. "Unfortunately, this house has no secret passages."

Chapter 28

Next morning, Christmas Eve dawned chilly and overcast, with a promise of snow in the damp air. Given her current circumstances, with Jemmy under the same roof and her marriage to him imminent, Elizabeth gazed out the window at a beautiful world. She finished brushing her hair, smiling to herself, and turned for Weller to pin it up in a simple style for the day.

It promised to be a busy day. She must get Jemmy to take her shopping, for with all the distractions recently, she had no Christmas gifts for the children or her family. The prospect of doing something so domestic with him filled her with an inner happiness that she'd sorely lacked in the past week.

Her toilette complete, she headed down to breakfast, hoping Jemmy might be there by now. Her heart lifted as she heard his rich baritone voice in the breakfast room as she approached.

"So I was dangling from a rope of twisted sheets—"

"You never did, Lord Brack. Weren't you terribly frightened? Didn't you think you'd be killed?" Dotty held Jemmy captive, apparently, as he told her about his recent adventures.

"I was more afraid I wouldn't be in time to keep your sister from marrying another man." Jemmy looked up as she entered, his face brightening as if the sun had emerged from behind a cloud. He bolted to his feet and hurried over to her. "How are you, my love? Did you sleep well?"

"Better than I have since I left you at Lyttlefield." That was certainly true. She'd retired shortly after dinner and slept like the dead, awakening refreshed this morning.

"Then I declare we must never part, for you must always enjoy a full complement of rest." He escorted her to the place next to his. "I'll be most happy to assist you with that, my love."

Elizabeth cast her gaze down at her lap and slipped a napkin onto it. Her body tingled with the thought of his next to hers again in her bed. Soon. Very soon.

"Why are you turning red, Elizabeth? Is it too hot for you in here?" Dotty peered at her with concern.

"No, dear, I'm fine. Perhaps I came downstairs too quickly." Lord, she hadn't had these kinds of problems when she and Dickon had lived here. Of course, her younger sisters had been in the schoolroom then, not often seen at all. She would have to learn to control her face better.

"What may I get for you this morning, my dear?" Jemmy hovered over her, a smile playing over his lips.

"Just tea and toast this early, thank you."

"Nonsense, Elizabeth. You must keep up your strength." He strode away to the sideboard.

She sighed and motioned to a footman. "A pot of tea, George, please."

"Is he always so forceful?" Dotty whispered to her behind her napkin.

"Sometimes." Elizabeth shot a glance at her betrothed busily piling a plate high. "It depends. Good Lord, Jemmy, I couldn't eat all of that if I tried."

He set the plate, brimming over with poached eggs, ham, beans, muffins, and a smattering of potatoes, in front of her.

"And where is the toast?"

"No room for it." He grinned. "Finish that lot, and I'll go back for more." He seated himself between her and her sister and dug into his own half-finished plate, as full as her own.

"If I finish all this, I won't be able to move for three days." Elizabeth contemplated the food items with distaste. She could rarely stomach more than toast when she was first pregnant before. This time the nausea had been less distressing, but if she ate more than the salty ham, she'd be fleeing the room in search of a chamber pot. "I'll make a bargain with you," she began, cutting a small piece of the ham. "I will eat this piece of ham and then you will go shopping with me. Won't that be a more pleasant way to spend the day than hearing me groan in misery?"

"Come again, love?" He cocked his head, making him look like a puzzled beagle.

"We can have luncheon out, and I will be happy to eat more after noon. Before will make me ill, Jemmy. Trust me on this." The ham, with its salty taste and chewy texture, was good, though she'd have preferred her toast instead. "I thought we would start out at the Pantheon Bazaar, since we have but little time, and if I cannot find everything there, then we can try Howell's. I have a list upstairs."

"How terribly efficient you are." He grinned approvingly at her.

"She's like that all the time, Lord Brack. You just see if she isn't." Dotty finished her tea and rose. "I shall leave you to your shopping. Good morning." She drifted out of the room, leaving them quite alone.

"Before we leave I must send 'round to Fellowes's old rooms to see if he has come up from Surrey or is still there waiting for me." Jemmy continued to chisel industriously at the mound of food on his plate.

True to her word, Elizabeth finished the ham, taking small bites and drinking plenty of tea to soothe her stomach. "I hope you find him, soon, my love. I know you will get tired of this same suit day in and day out."

"Porter did a splendid job of refreshing it overnight, but I sent to Lyttlefield Park by the morning post to have my things brought here, though I expect they cannot arrive before the day after Christmas. Everything stops for Christmas Day. Which reminds me." He set his knife and fork down. "I must go to the Archbishop of Canterbury's office this morning to procure a special license. We can't be married until the twenty-sixth, most likely, but we shall have everything in place to go as soon as we can."

"Apparently not before the twenty-seventh to procure a license or be married either, Brack." Papa strode in briskly, heading straight for the sideboard.

"Good morning, Papa."

"Good morning, my lord." Jemmy looked up at her father. "Have you tried the Archbishop's office already?"

"First thing this morning. Thought I'd steal a march on you, surprise you with it. Dashed awkward too, as I'd just gotten one three days ago for Elizabeth and Lord Robert. But the offices are closed, not to reopen until the twenty-seventh. Depending on the whim of the Archbishop, you may not be able to wed until then—or the twenty-eighth, if he decides to make very merry for the holiday." He raised his eyebrows at them. "Why such glum faces? You shall have the license in three days and wed shortly thereafter. What's wrong with that?"

"Nothing, Lord Wentworth, although I'd like to have Elizabeth secure as my wife as quickly as possible." He patted her hand, sending a warm glow up her arm.

Of course, there were other reasons to wish they were married. Her lonely bed last night had made her yearn for a secret passageway more fervently. But they would be together eventually; that was all that mattered.

"Well, there's nothing for it. Can't use the license I already have, so we will all have to find a way to pass the time." Her father sat down opposite them and began eating with the same fervor Jemmy had shown.

"We thought we would go shopping this morning, Papa. May we have the carriage? I must buy some presents for Christmas." Hopefully, their excursion would keep their minds off their troubles.

"Good plan." Her father popped a boiled quail egg into his mouth. "Best for you to be seen about together. Then the *ton* won't be shocked when they find you have married without an announcement. The more groundwork now, the less footwork later."

"That seems settled." Jemmy swallowed the remainder of his coffee and set the cup down. "Shall I meet you in half an hour?"

"I will be ready." The prospect of a wonderful day with Jemmy all to herself brightened Elizabeth's spirits immeasurably. This Christmas holiday might prove to be her best one in years.

When Elizabeth entered the Pantheon Bazaar, she stopped dead and simply stared, drinking in the sights and sounds of London at Christmastime. The Bazaar bustled with last-minute shoppers wandering in and around its lavish stalls decorated with sparkly tinsel and bright red and white ribbons wound around fresh greenery. She couldn't remember the last time she'd come here. Last year, she'd been in deep mourning and hadn't had the heart to go shopping at all. Now the festive air of the place, coupled with Jemmy's solid presence beside her, made her all bubbly inside. The brightly lit stalls carried everything from expensive jewelry to books, to sweetmeats, to tea, to children's toys and more. Ropings of cedar, bayberry, and pine gave the airy venues a crisp, outdoor scent, in keeping with the holiday. The throngs of people, chattering, laughing, and calling words of holiday cheer to one another gave Elizabeth the feeling she'd rejoined the human race at last.

"Where does your list say you need to start, my love?" Jemmy surveyed the mass of people and grinned, looking too charming for his own good. "I await with baited breath to see your plan in action."

"You may laugh now, Jemmy, but you will bless me and my efficient list, for it portends an equally efficiently managed home." Her exuberance faltered. "When we have one."

"Now, now." He took her arm and started them into the crowd. "No melancholy today. As an ambassador from Father Christmas"—he deepened his voice, and she laughed in spite of herself—"I forbid it at this merriest time of year. Here," he continued in his own voice, pulling her toward a stall that sold candied fruit and nuts. "Let me buy sweets for my sweetheart."

"Jemmy." She couldn't help but smile at his high spirits. So like a puppy, bouncing with excitement at every turn.

He handed her a cone of candied cherries, figs, and chestnuts, then grabbed one and popped it into her mouth before she could protest.

As she bit down, the candy exploded in a burst of sugary goodness, mingling with the tart meat of the cherry itself. She savored it but handed the cone back to him. "You may keep charge of this, please. I told you, no more food until this afternoon."

"Whatever you wish, my dear." Grabbing the paper cone, he fished out a sweet and tossed it up in the air, catching it in his mouth, grinning at her all the while.

"We must get down to serious shopping, Jemmy, or I shall have nothing to give to anyone. Here, we must stop here for Bella and Dotty." Halting before a stall that sold silk shawls, gloves, and other ladies' accessories, Elizabeth happily searched for presents for her sisters. She'd already decided what she wanted; she simply had to find the perfect items. With several judicious comments from Jemmy, she found them with more ease than usual. The happy stall keeper obligingly wrapped up her purchases: a silk paisley shawl of pale green and gold and a pair of white gloves, embroidered with flowers and vines in white.

"Dotty will love the colors of this shawl, and it will go with her best ball gown and several of her dresses for her Season. The gloves are for Bella, who can wear them as her 'something new' at her wedding."

"What will you have for your 'something new' in three days' time?" Jemmy handed the parcels to the footman, George, who followed them for that express purpose.

"I hadn't even though of that." Elizabeth laughed. What indeed would she wear for her "something old, something new, something borrowed, and something blue"? She'd not bothered with the fun superstition when she believed herself marrying Lord Robert, though she'd have needed all the luck she could have gotten then. "I suppose I shall wear my blue silk gown I had made for Charlotte's wedding. That will take care of 'blue.' Mama's lace handkerchief, made from Great-Grandmama's wedding gown, will be something 'old.'"

They walked through the jostling multitude of shoppers toward a bookseller's stall Elizabeth remembered. Papa would enjoy a new volume of Sir Walter Scott to read.

"I can borrow Bella's pearl necklace. Now I'll just need something new myself."

They arrived at the bookseller's, and she began to avidly search the many volumes. "Do you know of any new works by Sir Walter Scott?" she asked Jemmy. "Papa was quite entertained by *Guy Mannering* last year." She hailed the stall keeper. "I wondered, has Sir Walter Scott brought out a new volume this year?"

"Yes, ma'am." The older man with gray and white hair reached behind him to retrieve a two-book set. "This is the latest by Sir Walter—his new series Tales of My Landlord;

this is the very first subset of that series. Both bound in lovely calfskin." He handed the set over to her.

Before the books touched her hands, Jemmy had swooped in and grabbed them "I'll take those, my dear. Too heavy for you to lift both at once." He handed her a single volume.

The maroon leather tooling was exquisite, embossed with gold and black. So soft in her hand. She rubbed the spine lovingly.

"What do you think, my dear? Will your father enjoy these?"

"I believe he will." She smiled at Jemmy. How pleased Papa would be with these volumes. "He will sit right down and begin the first one after dinner tomorrow if we give him leave." They had all teased Papa dreadfully about reading novels, but it didn't deter him one bit. "I will take them both."

Another parcel wrapped and handed over to George.

"You are an efficient manager." Jemmy took her arm and patted it. "I will relish turning my household over to you."

The praise warmed her heart. She had been a good manager of Dickon's small household, and she missed running it. Always she had loved making sure the accounts balanced at the end of the month, refurbishing items when necessary. Not that there'd been much of that. They hadn't been together long enough to wear out carpets or draperies. She squeezed Jemmy's arm, drawing a grin from him. Pray God, they would be married long enough to wear out many sets of household furnishings.

"Where to next?"

"The toy stall is just around this corner unless they have moved. No, here they are. Oh, Jemmy, look at the wooden horse!"

It stood at least a foot and a half high, a slender maple-colored leather horse with wheels and a seat that doubled as a handle. It was elaborately carved to make the mane and face look as real as possible. Colin would love this. He rode his rocking horse all the time in the nursery. She ran a hand over the polished body.

"I don't even have to guess who this is for." Jemmy chuckled.

"Am I being too extravagant?" Biting her lip, she debated the merits of the purchase. She had been more indulgent of the children after their father had died. Did this go a bit too far?

"Extravagant?" Jemmy scoffed. "Wait until our child is born. You will declare a new meaning for the word once I begin to acquire things for him. Or her," he hastened to add.

Elizabeth sent up a fervent prayer that this child would be a boy. All men needed to secure the succession, and it would make her feel proud to accomplish her duty so efficiently.

Not stopping to count the cost, Elizabeth paid for the horse, and George left to cart it to the carriage. His shocked face proclaimed he hadn't a clue where it was going to go.

"Now we must find something just as fine for your daughter. Young ladies should be spoiled just a trifle more than boys. They are the most special, after all." Jemmy started off to explore the tables and displays of children's toys.

Before he had gotten too far, Elizabeth called to him. "I think I've found it, Jemmy." She pointed to a porcelain doll with eyes that opened and closed and clothing that small fingers could remove and replace as often as desired, down to her tiny black boots. "Isn't it perfect for Kate? It even looks a bit like her. She will love it."

"What little girl wouldn't?" His voice turned wistful.

Perhaps she had been mistaken that he would want a boy first. A fire spread throughout her, warming her toes and fingers—indeed, every inch of her was flaming with desire for him. Goodness, she must get hold of herself.

"Now I wish to find the jewelry stall," she said as the stall keeper carefully wrapped the beautiful doll. George had failed to return, likely still wrestling with the horse, so the man handed it to Jemmy. "I'd like to purchase a necklace for

Mama. And then I believe we shall be finished. We will have certainly earned our tea and scones." She giggled as she dragged him through the ever-swelling throng of shoppers. "Almost there."

The jeweler's stall glittered with trays of trinkets, rings with paste stones, necklaces of exotic beading, bangle bracelets, colorful earrings with glass stones. A mouthwatering display. Excitement coursed through Elizabeth at the sight of such a wealth of possible gifts. She faced Jemmy and threw her hands up. "However am I to decide?"

"If this is for Lady Wentworth, you must think of a favorite color of hers or a gown and choose a necklace to compliment it." He watched her keenly. "I had no idea you were so fond of jewelry, Elizabeth. I shall have to order the Blackham jewels for you to wear as soon as we are established. They have been languishing at Richardson's since my mother died." He chuckled. "I do not even know what they look like."

"I am certain they are beautiful, Jemmy. I shall be proud to wear them." Thrilling to the idea of wearing his family's jewels, Elizabeth happily went about choosing the necklace for her mother. As Jemmy suggested, she searched for a piece that would complement her mother's favorite green gown, with the ecru trim. She would likely wear it during the holidays and could show off the necklace then.

A string of green, white, and black glass beads, with small clusters of beading strung to resemble flowers, lay in a tray to the side. "How pretty." She lifted them up, and the light struck them so that the beads turned iridescent. "These will be perfect."

She handed the string to the shopkeeper and turned to find Jemmy looking at a tray of gold rings.

His brow furrowed in concentration, he picked up first one, then another ring. They were a variety of widths, all solid gold, but some with fancy carvings. He glanced at her and smiled. "Will you come help me choose your wedding ring? We will have need of one shortly."

Heart swelling with love, she blinked back a tear and nodded. Her gaze fell on a narrow band, carved with vine leaves. She picked it up, and he slid it on her finger, where it fit perfectly. Looking into his eyes, Elizabeth wanted him to hold her and never let go.

Jemmy kissed the ring and drew it off her finger. "Now I believe we are done, until two days after tomorrow, when this ring will never leave your hand again."

Chapter 29

By the time they arrived back at Worth House, Elizabeth's feet were aching, and she had to stifle a yawn as Jemmy helped her out of the carriage. Shopping had never worn her out like this before. Perhaps the new life within her had begun making demands on her body's strength already.

"Why don't you nap until time for dinner, my dear," Jemmy suggested as they mounted the steps to the house.

"That does sound like a lovely idea." She was quite drooping with fatigue. A long nap would revive her for dinner and Jemmy's introduction to the children. Lord knew what they'd say about him after the fiasco with Lord Robert. "I will see you at dinner, then, my love."

He grazed her cheek with his lips, sending warmth all through her. "Rest well."

Slowly, she made her way up to her room, undressed, and lay down, thankful for her bed. If she could just stop the ideas whirling about her head, she could sleep.

Elizabeth sat up, momentarily confused about where she was. Then the calm blue and white furnishings of her childhood room became familiar once more, and she lay back down, relishing the warmth of her nest.

Scratching at the door announced Weller, who strode in with Elizabeth's gown in her hand. "Time to get up, Mrs. Easton."

But she wanted to linger. If only Jemmy were here with her, she'd like nothing better than to stay hidden in this bed, not leaving it for days. A smile played over her lips at what they might do to occupy their time. Yes, they needed to arrange that as soon as they were wed. With a deep sigh, she pushed back the covers and sat up, her hair swirling around her shoulders.

"Goodness, ma'am. We'll have to put your hair to rights. It's come right down." The older woman clucked and fussed over her as she stripped and dressed her, the rhythm of the movements lulling Elizabeth into a peaceful state.

Her toilette finished, with the addition of a strand of pearls and matching earrings, Elizabeth rose and donned a cream-colored silk shawl that complemented her deep salmon-colored gown. She was looking forward to the family's traditional Christmas Eve celebration after dinner. There would be music and dancing, Papa's special rum punch, and fruitcake. Tomorrow, with the children, they would have presents in the morning, the Punch-and-Judy Show in the afternoon—the children always loved seeing the silly puppets argue—and crackers and a snapdragon in the evening.

Her conscience suddenly smote her. She hadn't seen the children in two days. With the wild antics of yesterday and Jemmy's arrival, she'd simply not thought to visit the nursery. Well, she could take a few minutes now to pop upstairs and see them before the longer visit tomorrow. So she turned her steps toward the staircase that led to the third-floor nursery, running lightly up them, suddenly excited to see Colin and Kate and tell them of her change of plans.

Approaching the nursery door, she was startled to hear the high-pitched laughter and chatter of the children, punctuated by a deeper male voice. Had Papa come up to see

Colin and Kate? She drew near the open door and popped her head through it just as Kate hit a high squeal of laughter.

Colin wielded a toy sword at his sister, who battled him valiantly with a whirligig as she rode on Jemmy's back. Down on all fours, he made an admirable steed.

"Mama! Mama!" Dropping his sword, Colin rushed to her.

"Mama. Put me down, horse." Kate commanded, swishing the whirligig over Jemmy's head.

"Of course, my lady." Jemmy held still as Kate clambered off his back and threw herself into Elizabeth's arms. "Mama! I missed you." She burrowed into Elizabeth's chest.

"I see you did, my loves." Elizabeth hugged them, all the while eyeing Jemmy's transformation.

He rose from the floor, in shirtsleeves, cravat askew, curly hair sticking up all over his head, completely unruly. He could have been one of the children, with his face flushed bright pink, his eyes sparkling.

"We've made a new friend, Mama." Colin pointed to Jemmy. "He said he knows you and he wanted to get to know us. Nanny Fields said it would be all right this once."

"He's ever such a good horse, Mama," Kate said, nodding her approval as if she were royalty. "I didn't fall off, not once. And I used my magic wand to slay the dragon."

"And the dragon had a sword?" Elizabeth tried to keep her composure, but they all looked so pleased with themselves, she had to smile.

"We thought it only fair, my dear, as the dragon couldn't breathe fire, that he have some way of defending himself." Slapping his legs to shake the dust off, Jemmy grinned at her and slipped on his coat, which had been abandoned onto a chair.

"Ah, quite right." Elizabeth sat down between the children, unmindful of her gown. "One must have a fair fight, mustn't one?"

"Exactly." Kate waved her whirligig wand over the

dragon's head. "You must stop being a dragon, now, Colin. I'm very tired." A huge yawn split her face, and she stretched her arms up in the air.

"I believe it is past your bedtimes, loveys, and tomorrow will be a very busy day, don't you remember?"

"Christmas Day!" they sang out together.

"Come on, Colin. Let's go right to sleep so it will come ever so fast. Good night, Mama. Good night, Lord Brack." She hugged Elizabeth, made a dainty little curtsy to Jemmy, and scampered toward her bed.

"Good night, Mama. Good night, Lord Brack." Colin kissed her cheek and whispered, "Can he be our new Papa instead of the tall, stiff man? Please, Mama? He's ever so much more fun."

Smothering a smile, she appeared to think about it. "I think that can be arranged, my love. If you are very sure, I think we may manage it." She hugged him before he ran to his bed, jumped into it, and flung the covers over his head.

"One moment," she whispered to Jemmy before heading into Nanny Field's room. She gave orders to Nanny about waking the children in the morning, then returned and took her beloved by the hand, leading him out of the nursery. "You just made two huge conquests and have been invited to join the family. What possessed you to come up here? You would have met them tomorrow; then you wouldn't have been quite so rumpled."

As if he'd just realized his appearance was anything other than perfect, he held out one creased arm of his coat and tsked. "Fellowes can put me to rights in ten minutes before dinner. I found myself with some time to spare before dinner, and I was curious about the children." He gave her a sheepish grin. "I'm sorry I didn't wait for you to introduce us, but I am glad I made a favorable impression. Kate is going to be a beauty, just like her mother." He took her arm. "And Colin has a very sharp mind—he was immediately thinking strategy as the embattled dragon."

"Then you like them?"

"Very much.' He patted her arm. "And soon we will have our own as well." A quiet look at the empty corridor, and he stopped, putting his arms around her. "As many as we like." He smiled, joy in his eyes. "I wouldn't mind a houseful as long as they take after their mother," he said, nuzzling her neck.

"I would like the boys to look like their Papa." Breathing deeply, Elizabeth leaned her head back, baring herself more openly. He caressed the curve of her throat, sending tingles down to her core. "Curly blond hair, blue eyes, and ears that turn pink, so we'll know when they are fibbing." Lord, he made her want to abandon herself right here in the hall.

"We will see if that can be arranged." Continuing to kiss his way across her neck, he turned and went up behind her ear.

Shivers wracked her, then she flushed with desire.

He walked her backward until her bottom hit the wall, and he pushed himself against her, settling into the V of her legs as though he was a missing part of her. "I would say we could start now, but we already have."

Seizing her lips, he thrust his tongue into her, and the heat exploded all over her.

She relaxed into his arms, drinking him in as their tongues tangled. With an effort, she slid heavy arms around him, pulling him closer, urging him to give her more. Was there an unoccupied room on this floor?

A floorboard creaked, and Jemmy leaped back.

Panting to catch her breath, Elizabeth peered first one way, then the other down the corridor, but no one appeared. With a groan, she pushed herself away from the wall and took Jemmy's hand once more. His touch still seared her, but the sudden fright of discovery had cooled her ardor for the moment. "Let us go repair ourselves before we join the others." She eyed Jemmy, whose cravat was coming loose and jacket hung slightly askew. She suspected she looked rather frowsy herself. "At least once we are married, we won't have to sneak about so much."

Jemmy chuckled, his eyes twinkling mischievously, and tucked her arm into the crook of his. "My love, that is part of the fun."

Christmas Day seemed a gay party to Jemmy, whose remembrances of Christmas from his youth were rather austere in comparison. At Blackham Castle, the day was kept with good food and drink, presents for the staff, and, when he and his brother and sisters were young, toys for them as well. The celebration he witnessed at Worth House, however, was extravagantly lavish to say the least.

Presents after breakfast brought squeals of delight from the children, and oohs and aaahs from their elders as well. Elizabeth's sisters seemed well pleased with their gifts, and rushed to try them on and display them. Her parents were equally complimentary, and Jemmy smiled when Lord Worth quietly retreated to a corner chair with the first volume of Tales of My Landlord in his hand.

Later that morning, he and Elizabeth had stolen a few moments of their own to exchange gifts. He'd been thrilled when he'd managed to surprise her with a garnet necklace and matching earrings. Her shining eyes, as she asked him to fasten it around her neck, had touched his heart deeply. That this woman's merest glance would delight him for the rest of his life at last began to sink into his mind, and a contentment he'd never experienced before sent a hush through him.

In turn, he'd been amazed when she'd presented him with a gold watch fob, engraved with the initial B in a flourishing style. "That letter B will serve you both now and later," she'd whispered as she placed a soft kiss on his cheek. When she'd had time to secure his present he had no idea, but he was now convinced the woman was a marvel at efficiency.

Those stolen moments had been few that day as the family continued with what were obviously their accustomed Christmas Day activities. After presents, they had all bundled up and walked three blocks to a Punch-and-Judy Show. The crisp air had done nothing to dispel the crowd gathered around the puppet booth, and Jemmy and Lord Worth had been obliged to lift the children up on their shoulders so they could see. The twins thought this marvelous fun and squealed with delight at their vantage points. A brisk walk back home, in the nick of time to avoid his toes freezing clean off in his boots, ended with a glass of hot rum punch, another family Christmas tradition, he'd been told. They made merry at dinner as well, with the children joining them for crackers and a snapdragon, everyone shouting and laughing as they snatched at the burning raisins.

"When we are married," Jemmy remarked, having paused from kissing Elizabeth beneath a sprig of mistletoe, "every Christmas will be just like this one."

Boxing Day brought its own style of hilarity. Lady Wentworth served Tawes tea, Lord Wentworth drove the female servants a turn in Hyde Park, and that evening, at the Servants' Ball, Jemmy danced with Mrs. Cates, the housekeeper, while Elizabeth partnered a bright-red-faced Fellowes, who had turned up midafternoon with Jemmy's trunks from Lyttlefield Park.

The morning of December 27 dawned at last, crisp and cold, with a few random flakes of snow in the air. Jemmy bounded down the stairs, hurrying a trifle and pulling at the sleeves of his gray suit, freshly pressed by Fellowes. Jemmy could have wished for no better Christmas present than the return of his valet. He'd just left the man glowing with praise for his timely entrance yesterday, and a newly minted half-guinea as a token of his appreciation.

Unfortunately, Lady Wrotham's ten pounds had decreased alarmingly over the holiday, but he patted his breast pocket, Elizabeth's gold ring always on his person. It had cost him dearly, as it should. Now he knew of her penchant for jewelry, once he inherited his mother's fortune, he would dress her in pearls or diamonds, if she preferred them. For now, however, they would be happy with this small token of his undying love.

He signaled a footman and left orders for his horse to be brought around, then strode into the breakfast room, where everyone had congregated save Lord and Lady Wentworth.

"Good morning." He addressed the company with a pleasant smile, then turned to the business of heaping his plate full of sausages and potatoes from the warming pans lying companionably side by side. "I trust you are all recovered from yesterday's unaccustomed work?"

"Good morning."

"Good morning, my lord."

"Good morning, my love." The last came from Elizabeth, seated at the head of the table, eyeing him brightly.

He grabbed silverware and quickly claimed his place to her right.

"I hope you will excuse Mama today, Jemmy. She is always totally incapacitated by Boxing Day." Eyes twinkling with amusement, she sipped her tea. "Actually, having to wait upon Tawes each year brings on an attack of the vapors the magnitude of which you simply would not believe. Although I suspect the strain is equally great on Tawes, who has always been most proper."

Jemmy chuckled at that. Fellowes had seemed unusually overwrought after his dance with Elizabeth last night. "Do not fret yourself, my dear. I do quite understand. And if you will give me leave, I will head to the offices of the Archbishop of Canterbury for the special license that proclaims we can be man and wife without further delay."

"I think that is terribly forward-thinking of you, Lord

Brack." Bella spread marmalade on her toast, then crunched into it with gusto. "So long and drawn out to have the banns read." She wrinkled her nose. "I do wish I could convince dear Haxton to get a special license so we could marry immediately. Mama wants us to wait until the new year." With a huff that sent her wisps of hair flying, Bella pulled a Friday face. "Or we could run away to Gretna Green."

"Bella." Elizabeth shot her sister a stern look and shook her head, her eyes flashing a warning. "Dotty, be a dear and run fetch my reticule. I have a letter to post."

Unconcerned, her sister nodded and left the breakfast room.

"Isabella," Elizabeth hissed as soon as Dotty swished through the door, "I very much doubt you would ever run off to Scotland to be married. Lord Haxton would not hear of it, I am sure. But to put such ideas within the hearing of Dotty, a flibbertigibbet if ever there was one, is dangerous, to say the least. Given half the chance, I'm sure she'd be across the border at the first opportunity and think it a grand lark."

Even with the little acquaintance he'd had with Elizabeth's youngest sister, he feared her words were nothing but the truth. The family must keep a close check on Miss Dorothea Worth during her coming Season, lest they have another problem on their hands the like of his and Elizabeth's.

"Your sister is correct, Bella." Lord Wentworth entered with the *Times* tucked under his arm, his brows lowered to a severe level over his eyes. "We must keep Dotty's mind focused on a respectable marriage this coming year, else I will never hear the end of it from your mother."

"Then I will hasten on my way and return with as little fuss as possible." Jemmy swallowed an extraordinarily large mouthful of coffee, so large it hurt his throat.

"Would you like some company, Brack?" Wentworth folded the paper and laid it on the sideboard. "I believe I could do with some fresh air before sitting to my breakfast."

"I'd planned to ride, my lord."

"Splendid. Just the thing, bracing air." Lord Wentworth headed for the door. "Let me change, and I'll be right back."

Jemmy clasped Elizabeth's hand. "I will not be more than an hour, my love. Once I return, we may be married at any time, any place."

"Here and now would suit me fine." She squeezed his hands, though it might as well have been his nether regions, the desire for her burned so bright.

"Your wish, my dear, as well as mine." He'd have to bring a clergyman back with him so they wouldn't waste a single minute before they could wed. He kissed her hand, wanting to draw her closer, yet daring not with Isabella in the room. He shot a glance at his soon-to-be sister-in-law, who had the good grace to smile.

"I should go see what is keeping Dotty with your reticule, Elizabeth. You don't want to miss the morning post." She rose, bringing Jemmy to his feet. "Excuse me, my lord," she said, gaily tripping out of the breakfast room and pulling the door almost all the way shut.

"Courtship is often made or sabotaged by one's well-meaning relations." He drew her up to him, slipping his arms around her waist, and nuzzling her neck in the tenderest spot.

"I am very glad to have the former type of relation." Elizabeth settled against him, and sighed. "Very glad indeed."

Frantic knocking at the door woke Elizabeth from a much-needed nap. After two hours of waiting, she'd given up on Jemmy and Papa and retired to her chamber. She must not be such a lie-abed, even if she was carrying a child.

"Come in."

"Oh, ma'am. Miss Elizabeth." Clearly disturbed, as indicated by the unconscious slip with Elizabeth's name, Weller wrung her hands. "You must come quick. His lordship is asking for you."

"Papa? Where is Lord Brack?" A trickle of icy fear slid down her back.

"He is there as well, ma'am. They are in the family parlor." Weller bobbed her way out, obviously sent somewhere else as well.

What had happened? She slid out of bed and reached for the yellow sprigged gown, one of the simple ones that she could don herself. Quickly, she pulled it on, collecting herself so she could face whatever crisis awaited, and made her way to the family's favorite room. No matter whether joy or sorry, the Worths faced it there.

Chaos had erupted when she entered.

Shouting and waving a fist at no one in particular, Papa was terribly red in the face. Bella and Dotty, wide-eyed, cowered on the gold sofa, Dotty also clutching a cup of tea and her sister. Jemmy stood at the sideboard, a tumbler brimful of brandy in his hand.

"What is going on, Papa?" Elizabeth darted toward her father. "Why are you railing at no one?"

"I will not brook this insult, Elizabeth." He banged his fist on a table, toppling a china figurine onto the floor with a crash.

"Oooh," Dotty jumped and screamed, tea flying in an arch through the air, landing on her sister.

"For heaven's sake, Dotty." Scrubbing at her ruined gown, Bella grabbed the cup from her and set it on the tea table. "Now see what you've done."

"Goodness, Papa!" Elizabeth stared at her father's face and neck, now an alarming shade of red. "What has happened?"

"We cannot get married, Elizabeth." Jemmy took a large slug of the brandy, his eyes squinting closed at the burn as it made its way down his throat.

"What?" She clutched her throat, her stomach sinking to her toes.

"The Archbishop of Canterbury refuses to issue a special license for our marriage."

Peering first at Jemmy's bleak countenance, then at her father's livid one, Elizabeth gathered her wits and pursed her lips. She had had enough of waiting. "Why won't he issue it?"

"Because . . . because . . ." Papa couldn't quite spit out the words.

This inability to speak frightened her more than his blustering, which she'd dealt with all her life.

"Because, apparently, His Grace the Archbishop is the cousin of Lady Maude Aston." Jemmy stared at her, misery in his eyes. "He refuses to issue the license and has sent instructions to all the parishes under his diocese forbidding them from reading the banns for us."

"Why would he do such a thing? Cousin or not, he's a man of God." Elizabeth had to catch hold of the back of a chair, as her knees threatened to buckle.

Jemmy leaped to her side and lowered her into the chair. "He must have received instructions from—"

"Wentworth!" Lady Wentworth swept into the parlor, her eyes blazing like a demon. "What has Blackham done now?"

Chapter 30

Her mother strode over to her father, outrage and anger in every seething movement. All eyes followed her progress in silence until she stepped beside Papa, whose lips were firmly sealed.

"Well? I was summoned from my nap by Weller, who hurried me into these most inappropriate clothes"—she waved her hand to indicate a serviceable, but plain, day gown of deep purple—"and insisted you must see me at once." She narrowed her eyes. "I do not do anything 'at once,' unless I myself deem it necessary. So I ask again, Wentworth"—her gaze speared her husband—"what has Blackham done now? Only his didoes could cause this much to-do."

"You are very astute, my dear." Papa's face had returned to mostly a normal hue from the vivid scarlet of a few moments before. "Lord Blackham is indeed behind the latest outrage. Here, please sit." He ushered his wife to her usual wing-backed chair, then downed his whiskey and returned to the sideboard for a refill. "You tell her, Brack. I am liable to break something else if I try to tell it."

"We went to obtain the special license from the Archbishop of Canterbury, who we discovered is the cousin of

Lady Maude Aston, to whom my dear father is endeavoring to engage me. We were therefore sent away with a large flea in our ears." Patting Elizabeth's hand, Jemmy continued to try to sooth her. Unfortunately, it helped not at all.

"I see the Archbishop is not above petty family loyalty. So unexpected in the highest clergyman in the land." Mama sniffed and rang the bell. "His mother was Bridget Sutton, as I recall. Well, Wentworth, what is our next option?"

"For tuppence, I'd go down to Blackham Castle and speak a word with his lordship." Her father growled, beginning to pace like a tiger in a menagerie. "That he refuses to allow Elizabeth to wed his son is an undeserved disgrace on her and an insult to our entire family."

Choking back tears, Elizabeth sank further into the chaise. Would she and Jemmy ever be able to wed? Doors to their ultimate happiness kept slamming shut at every turn. There seemed few options left them. Time was running out before scandal overtook them.

"I doubt that would have any effect at all, my lord." Jemmy rose and went to refresh his glass. "Lady Wentworth, did you ring for tea? I fear Elizabeth needs something against this shock."

"Here is the footman now."

The man entered, tea service in hand, and set the tray down beside Mama.

"Thank you." Immediately, Mama poured tea and dropped in five lumps of sugar. She passed that cup to Elizabeth, who took it without a murmur. "What are our other options?"

"Well, we could attempt a common license." But Jemmy shrugged almost before the words got out. "However, it needs to be in your home parish, and I am certain the vicar at Blackham would refuse us as well."

"And apparently all the parishes of London are closed to us as well." Papa's color had returned.

"On what grounds?" Elizabeth raised her head. Surely the clergymen had to have a reason to deny them to wed.

"Pre-contract with Lady Maude. My father was supposed to sign the settlements with the Duke of Buckleigh the day I escaped Blackham. The Archbishop would not let me marry one woman when I am contracted to another." Jemmy sighed and seated himself next to Elizabeth. "I am so sorry for all of this, my love. You deserve none of it."

"No, she does not, Lord Brack." Mama sipped her tea, her mouth pursed as though the tea had no sugar. "I was against this match from the beginning because of the machinations of your father, who I remember quite well. You take after your mother, thank the good Lord, or I would forbid it still." She sniffed and sat back in her chair. "However, the current circumstances, plus the imminent possibility of scandal should Lady Locke return to Town soon, lead me to suggest a course of action I really cannot believe I am saying."

Grabbing Jemmy's hand, Elizabeth sat up and took a deep breath. "What, Mama?"

"Go to Gretna Green and marry in Scotland." Mama's head snapped with military precision toward the sofa, where Dotty and Bella sat, their mouths opened in perfect Os. "You did not hear that, girls, and if you did, you will forget the name at once."

"Yes, Mama," they said together, looking askance at one another.

Gretna Green. The Scottish border town that had seen hundreds of elopements since Lord Hardwicke's Marriage Act had been put into law last century. Never in her life had she considered eloping to Gretna Green. Girls from nice families did not do that.

"That would do the trick, my lady." Jemmy gazed fondly at Mama. "We can be there in four or five days."

"If the weather holds," her father put in as he moved to stand behind Mama's chair. "If not, it may take longer."

"As I see it, Wentworth, it is our only option." Mama reached up to take his hand. "All other avenues seem closed to them. We must think of Elizabeth's reputation as well as the other girls. If everything comes to light, it will still be better if they are already married. Blackham will not be able to put aside a marriage."

"What about the—" Elizabeth cut her eyes toward her sisters, then sighed. It just hurt to say the words aloud, even if the girls already knew. "What about the child? Five days banging along in a cold carriage cannot be good for him."

"Have you decided it's a boy?" Jemmy grinned at her.

She smiled back and squeezed his hand. "I might as well dream I carry your heir until I find out differently."

"We will go slowly, my love. Take perhaps six days to travel the distance and stop to rest each night," he said, trying to assure her. "I will keep you both safe."

"Yes, *we* certainly will." Rattling her teacup into its saucer, Mama set a beady eye on Jemmy. "Wentworth and I will accompany you in the carriage so no new scandal will rear its head regarding your lodgings on the way."

"You will go with us, Mama?" Stranger things could happen than having one's mother accompany one to be married at Gretna Green, but very few she'd wager. Especially as her mother hated traveling.

"There seems absolutely no other way for you to be wed, and wed you must." Mama raised an eyebrow at Papa. "You agree with me, don't you, Wentworth?"

"Uh, yes, yes, of course, my dear." Papa's face reddened as he tugged at his cravat, suddenly too tight, perhaps? "We should go to offer chaperonage and advice."

"It is settled then." With an imperious air, Mama nodded so fiercely her coiffure toppled, bringing her hair down over one eye.

"What about us?" Dotty, who had been silent up until now, suddenly found her tongue. "We want to go with you and see Elizabeth and Lord Brack married. I daresay it will be the closest thing I ever see to an elopement."

"Indeed, you will not go." The words were snapped so

quickly they could have cut like a knife. Mama's glare fixed Dotty like a bug on a pin. "This family chamber is the closest you will ever come to Gretna Green if I have anything to say about it, Dotty. And Isabella"—quick as a March hare, Mama turned her attention to her second daughter, who sat calmly drinking tea on the corner of the chaise—"you will not accompany us either. I shall have Aunt Dorothea, your namesake, come and stay with you and the children while we are away." A triumphant gleam appeared in her eye. "No one will find fault with my sister's chaperonage. She will keep you company and out of mischief while your father and I are from home."

"But, Mama!" Both girls cried in unison, and Elizabeth's heart went out to them. Aunt Dorothea's ideas about strictness made Mama look positively lenient.

Holding up her hand, Mama stopped them from saying another word. "I will not have you gadding about as unchaperoned girls. Else we shall have to take up permanent residence in Gretna Green. It simply is not done, no matter the circumstances."

Her sisters subsided back onto the chaise to mull the turn of events over with sober countenances.

"Then it is settled?" Elizabeth gazed expectantly from Jemmy to her parents.

"Yes, my love." He kissed their entwined fingers. "It may take a week, but we will wed in the end. Then my father will have to cease with his infernal plotting. Perhaps, in time, he will come to accept you as my wife and this child as his grandchild."

"It will be a cold day in hell when Blackham gives up one of his schemes." Mama rose, and Jemmy shot to his feet. "However, I will be glad of the chance to ruin this one. Come, Elizabeth. I shall oversee the packing for the journey. Weller will be awash in trunks if we are not careful. We must leave at first light."

Getting slowly to her feet, Elizabeth was overcome with

weariness beyond belief. All this turmoil was wearing her out. Once she and Jemmy were married, she wouldn't leave her bed for a week. Snickering, she shot a glance at her betrothed and caught a confused face. Perhaps Jemmy would feel the same way when the time came. A thoroughly pleasant prospect.

The morning dawned clear and cold, an icy gray sky giving way to brilliant pinks and oranges as the sun rose. It caught Elizabeth yawning as Jemmy helped her into the sleek family landau. She'd gotten very little sleep, for Weller's lack of ability to pack silently could not be underestimated. Coupled with her own worries and fears, the stealthy noise of rustling linen and thumping chests had kept her tossing and turning in her bed. Pray God, she could nod off when they were safely out of London.

"You do not look well, my love." Jemmy seated her in the forward-facing seat, himself across from her.

"Merely fatigued with the activities of the night. I scarcely slept a wink." She settled down into the comfortable black leather seats, relaxing at once. As soon as Mama and Papa arrived, they could leave and perhaps she could nap.

"I will try to persuade your parents that the haste can be spared a bit." His worried frown was endearing. "If Lady Locke has not yet received my father's letter, then we shall be married before the lady can slander you or me. Therefore, we must take the journey in easy, but quick, stages."

"We must not alter our plans, Jemmy." She nodded toward her parents, approaching the carriage.

"Bricks, Wentworth. We must have hot bricks at our feet, else we will freeze, just as Lot's wife did." Mama cast a baleful glance at George, the footman. "Hot bricks, George. At once. I'm sure I don't know why they are not already here."

Elizabeth shuddered at that particular tone of voice, always reserved for their journeys: to visit relatives, to Papa's northern estates, to his seat in Gloucester. Anywhere they had ever gone, the journeys began in the exact same way, no matter if they traveled in summer, winter, or fall: a call for hot bricks, followed by a virtual sermon upon the ministry of keeping your feet warm.

"As you have been told for years, Mama, the bricks are kept heating until the last possible minute. That assures that they are comfortable for the duration of the journey or until they can be replaced at the first change of horses."

"Well," Mama humphed as she sat heavily beside Elizabeth, "as we are now in the carriage, they had best send them out immediately if we are to be off in good time." She patted Elizabeth's hands. "We will not stop until we are quite outside of London, your father tells me. So the sooner we begin, the sooner we will end."

As she could scarcely argue with that statement, Elizabeth merely nodded and sent up a prayer of thanks as the bricks, wrapped in flannel, were tucked in at her feet, the heat drifting pleasantly up under her skirts to linger around her knees.

"Place your feet on either side of mine, Jemmy. Then you will have some warmth as well." She eagerly shifted her legs to give him room.

"No touching of the limbs, Elizabeth." Her mother's voice cracked in the small enclosure.

"Mama." Elizabeth gave her parent what she hoped was a withering look. "I am on my way to my wedding. My second wedding, mind you. And I am already carrying his child. I do not think his touching my limbs will make the slightest bit of difference at this point. I would rather he not catch an ague."

"That's as may be, my girl. You have not married him yet, however, so no inappropriate behavior, if you please." A wag of Mama's finger, a gesture of admonishment Elizabeth remembered well from her childhood, was interrupted as the carriage hit a rut that set Mama's crimson bonnet to bouncing. She shrieked and clutched the brim.

Elizabeth risked a glance at Jemmy, whose mouth twitched suspiciously. "You have nothing to say, my lord?"

With a sideways glance at her mother, he leaned forward to whisper, "I was calculating if my remaining funds would extend to hiring a separate carriage for the return journey to London. Then we could linger as we liked as we retraced our steps. There would be no hurry then, and a carriage to ourselves would be much more enjoyable, don't you think?"

"I believe you are correct," she whispered back, sighing at the thought of having Jemmy all to herself for the five or more days' journey.

The dawn light had become brighter, bathing the carriage with a pearly glow. Her gaze fell on her mother's skirts, covering her heated bricks. A slow realization that her father's feet had entirely disappeared underneath those skirts as well sent somewhat of a shock through her.

Jemmy let out a snort as he quickly shifted his gaze out the window.

Elizabeth followed suit, biting her tongue to keep from commenting to her mother about "sauce for the goose."

The carriage slowly wound its way throughout the early-morning bustle of London. Hackney cabs lined the streets, their horses snorting out great plumes of white steam. Shops were beginning to open, ready for the day's custom. They passed a baker's shop just as an early customer entered and the delicious aroma of yeasty bread, fresh baked, wafted into the carriage.

A loud growl rumbled from Elizabeth's stomach. She clamped both hands over the offending organ and met Jemmy's laughing gaze.

"Did you eat nothing before we left, my love?" His lips twitched in suppressed mirth.

"You know we had no time for breakfast." She lay her heated cheek against the cold windowpane, gazing longingly at the baker's shop. "I do hope we can stop and remedy that once we are out of the press of the London traffic."

"I shall insist upon it, my dear." Jemmy squeezed her hand and turned toward her father. "Will that be acceptable, Lord Wentworth? Elizabeth did not break her fast this morning, which cannot be good for either her or the child. Can we stop as soon as we pass through Islington?"

"Better to wait until we've reached the Great North Road and left London completely." Papa's gaze rested on her thoughtfully. "I'd say about another hour unless the traffic gets worse."

Not at all what she'd wanted to hear, but Elizabeth nodded, hoping her stomach would stay quiet until then. She'd not felt hungry until that wonderful bakery smell had assaulted them. Catching Jemmy's eye, she smiled at him, trying to reassure him. His face, however, now wore that determined look she was coming to know well—brows furrowed, eyes narrowed, lips a thin straight slash across his face.

He glanced out the window again, then pounded frantically on the trap. "Stop the carriage!"

"What the devil?" Papa grabbed the strap beside the door as the carriage lurched to a stop.

Elizabeth and her mother clutched each other to keep from sliding off the seat.

Jemmy threw the door open and bounded out into the street.

"Jemmy!" Elizabeth called as he dodged through the thickening traffic until he was lost to her sight.

"You are marrying a lunatic, Elizabeth. I hope you are satisfied." Mama straightened her bonnet again and glared meaningfully in the direction Jemmy had disappeared.

"I am sure he has a good reason for this behavior, Mama. He is hardly a lunatic, as well you know." Although she spoke with conviction, privately Elizabeth entertained the possibility that Mama's pronouncement might have a grain of truth. Without a doubt, Jemmy was impetuous. Was that a virtue or a failing in a man?

Markson had moved the carriage to the side of the street, where they sat for some minutes, Mama tapping her hand rhythmically on her knee. "I will certainly speak to Lord Brack about this behavior as soon as—"

"Look." Papa pointed down the street toward Jemmy, dodging his way back toward them laden with several parcels that stuck out helter-skelter. "Apparently he did have a plan." Papa opened the carriage door, and Jemmy thrust the packages into Elizabeth's lap as he scrambled in.

Immediately the carriage filled with the most mouthwatering scent of fresh bread and sweet rolls. Almost tasting the smell, Elizabeth licked her lips and beamed at her beloved.

"No need to wait to eat, my love, my lady," Jemmy nodded to her mother, "when there was food to be had for ready money."

"Why indeed." Elizabeth tore the brown paper from a loaf of crusty, hot bread, tore off a chunk, and popped it into her mouth. The explosion of warm, sweet goodness in her mouth made her groan with pleasure. "I love you, Jemmy."

"Well done, Brack." Papa tore off a piece and offered it his wife. "Have some, my dear."

Mama rolled her eyes at him but took the offering and bit into it with gusto. "My thanks to you. Lord Brack. I believe you will do, after all."

"There is fresh butter and a pot of marmalade as well." Crossing his arms, Jemmy settled back in his seat, a satisfied smile on his face.

"Bless you, my love." Elizabeth unwrapped the rest of the parcels, and little was heard for the next half an hour save "Pass the butter, please," and "My, but this is sticky."

Sated at last, Elizabeth sank back against the seat, relaxing into a wonderful, drowsy state. "I believe I shall nap until we reach the first changing post. How far do you think it is, Papa?"

"We've just now turned onto the Old North Road proper," he replied, surreptitiously licking marmalade from his fingers. "We will come to the tollbooth at Whetstone shortly. After that, perhaps a mile or so, there's an inn, the Turtledove, where we can rest a bit before pushing on."

"Lord Wentworth."

They all gazed upward at the trap.

"Was that Markson?" Papa frowned. "Why is he slowing?"

The carriage had gone from its goodly pace to a trot and now had slowed to a crawl. Elizabeth peered out the window, looking for a reason for the change in speed, but they were in a wooded area, and there was nothing to see. "Jemmy, I do not like this."

Papa stood up and opened the trap. "What is going on, Markson?"

"It may be nothing, love." Jemmy patted her hand, but his eyes had narrowed, and he glanced from side to side out the windows, obviously on alert.

"Is it highwaymen, Wentworth?" Mama's tone held nothing but disgust. "They are usually not so bold in daylight. If it is, however, mark my words, they will rue the day they stopped my carriage."

"Mama, hush." Elizabeth grasped her mother's hand and gave it a shake.

"Well, Markson, why have we stopped?" Papa sounded testy. Perhaps there wasn't any danger, only an overturned carriage up ahead or a tree downed over the road.

Muted voices filtered down through the trap, then Papa lowered the trap and opened the door. "Of all the days in the year for a carriage to lose a wheel." He clambered out and headed toward the front of the carriage.

Uttering a sigh of relief, Elizabeth closed her eyes. Delay she could accept, although she did long for a bed and a good nap at the Turtledove. She leaned against the carriage door, tempted to fall asleep here and now.

Suddenly, the door opened, and she was falling out into the cold, crisp air. Jemmy saved her, grasping her arm and hauling her back inside as a big, burly man, dressed in dark coat and pants, gold braid decorating the edges of the jacket, leered at her.

"Ahhhh," she screamed, struggling toward the opposite side of the carriage.

"Damnation." Jemmy shoved her into her startled mother and thrust his foot at the stranger, kicking him backward. He swung the door closed, then reached over to close the door Papa had left open. Before he could grab the handle, a similarly attired man grabbed his arm and hauled Jemmy out of the carriage.

Elizabeth shrieked and tried to follow him.

"Help! Help! Robbers! Thieves!" her mother screamed, to no avail, as the ruffian slammed the door shut.

"Go, Grieves," he shouted up to someone on the coachman's seat.

The carriage started with a thump, sending Elizabeth and her mother jouncing against the seats as the landau careened away.

Chapter 31

Cursing like a tavern brawler, Jemmy picked himself up from the frozen grass where he'd landed when the liveried ruffian had pulled him from the carriage.

"I demand to know who you are and where that carriage is taking my wife and daughter." Lord Wentworth's face hovered inches from one of the four black-and-gold-clad men.

"They're likely bound for Black Tower, my father's house in Regent Park," Jemmy said, dusting himself off and hurrying to Wentworth's side.

"Your father's house?" A snarl on his lips, his lordship peered at the men.

"Yes, I recognized the livery as soon as they appeared. You"—Jemmy snapped his fingers and pointed at the nearest man—"did my father order this abduction?"

"Sorry, my lord." The young man stood straight, fear in his eyes. "He ordered us to bring you to the house as quickly as possible. To get the ladies away first so you'd follow."

"That certainly sounds like Father."

"That's Blackham, all right," Wentworth echoed. "He has gone too far this time, Brack."

"I agree, my lord." Numb with an outrage he'd never before experienced, Jemmy's whole body quivered. How dare his father abduct his bride? If this terrifying ordeal harmed her or the baby, his father would pay in the most horrific way possible. He would make an end to this for once and for all. "You!" He pointed at the servant again. "Father would know we'd need horses to go to Black Tower. Did you bring them with you?"

"No, my lord, but there is a carriage." He indicated a conveyance off to the side of the road he'd not noticed in his rage.

"Very good. Lord Wentworth, we will follow them in this conveyance, and I promise you," he said, clenching his fists until his nails dug into his palms, "it will end now." They climbed into the carriage as the liveried men mounted their horses.

They jerked forward, and Jemmy began to seriously contemplate the possibility of patricide.

"Do not panic, Elizabeth." Putting on her tone of righteous indignation, Mama was ready to do battle with whomever had orchestrated this outrage, be it the devil himself. "Whoever is behind this kidnapping has not taken into consideration who they are abducting. We will make them pay for this outrage to the fullest extent of the law."

"I suspect it is Lord Blackham again, Mama." Elizabeth sighed. She would have some sharp words to say to the marquess when next they met. "Who else would want to kidnap us?" She forced her words out calmly, despite the fact she was seething inside. How dare this tyrant abduct her—and her mother—and try to keep her from marrying Jemmy. Her mother might have a golden nugget or two to tell Lord Blackham, but she wouldn't get the chance until Elizabeth had finished with him. If there was anything left.

The carriage wound back into London, quickly reaching a very fashionable area.

"This is Regent Park, my dear," Mama peered out the window. "Perhaps your suspicion is correct. Blackham has a house on one of the terraces, as I remember. Part of his enticement for me to marry him was his listing of all his properties." She sniffed. "Thought he could sway me from your father with the promise of material possessions. True love will trump that any time."

"I certainly hope so, Mama." Craning her neck, Elizabeth gazed back and forth at the tall, stately houses, built in the classical style that seemed to be preferred on the street they were now passing down.

"Remain steadfast, Elizabeth. No matter what Blackham may offer as an inducement to abandon Lord Brack, do not be tempted." Mama nodded even as she looked back and forth at the splendid marble columns and stoops gracing all of the residences they were passing.

"I will hardly give Jemmy over with his child on the way, Mama. It will take more than a marble floor and a Regent Park address to make me give him up." Elizabeth hung onto the strap grimly as the carriage turned a corner onto York Terrace. "Do you think Jemmy and Papa are following behind us?"

"Most likely." Mama peered out the window, trying to see behind the carriage. "I cannot get a thing from this window, though. Oh."

The carriage bumped to a stop.

"We seem to be here." Thank goodness, it had taken no longer to arrive. All the excitement was extremely wearing on her these days.

The town house they had swept up to was imposing, if a trifle austere. Four smooth white marble columns framed the façade, a small portico carved with Greek statures. The house itself seemed to exude cold, and Elizabeth shivered at the thought of confronting Lord Blackham once more.

"If this is Blackham's doing, he's going to rue the day he interfered with my daughter's life," Mama huffed as she emerged from the carriage, assisted by another liveried servant.

"Yes, I suspect he will do a deal of ruing before the day is finished." She glanced back the way they had come, hoping to spy another carriage or horses with Jemmy atop them. No such luck. Well, she'd give the marquess an earful for causing them all this bother.

The door to the mansion opened, revealing a tall, dignified butler who did not speak but motioned for them to enter.

"Cat got your tongue, my man?" Mama threw at him, never pausing as she strode inside.

With a doleful smile, the butler led them down a corridor, up a short flight of stairs, to a dark, forbidding door. The whole household was dim. Elizabeth couldn't remember seeing more than two or three lamps or candles in the whole place at Blackham. Such dark-natured places always frightened her; however, anger sent fear flying out the window. She pushed the door open before the butler could make a move.

The chamber itself was as dark and gloomy as the corridor. A sullen fire burned in the grate, giving off indifferent heat. The wizened figure seated at the desk looked exactly the same as the one she'd met ten days before. A single difference in the man jarred Elizabeth, sending an icy trickle down her spine.

Lord Blackham was smiling.

She straightened her shoulders, drawing imaginary battle armor around her.

"Blackham, I demand to know what you have done with my husband." Pushing past her, Mama sailed forward on a cloud of indignation. She didn't stop until her feet almost touched the desk, and she towered over the marquess, staring at him like an avenging fury.

Crossing his arms over his chest, Lord Blackham sat

back, his disconcerting smile widening. "You have aged gracefully, Lady Wentworth. I will give you that. You were a beauty as a girl and are beautiful still. I had hoped time would ravage you a bit more severely, but I confess I find now I am happy you have retained your looks." He stared at Mama like a moonstruck boy.

"Little good flattery will do you, Blackham. After the hell you have dragged my daughter through, and now Wentworth and myself as well, you had better pray for divine grace and my sense of Christian charity to save you rather than weak flattery. Where is Wentworth?"

"He will be along shortly, never fear. I wanted a word with you, Amelia, before he arrives." His lordship rose, his eyes still fixed on her mother. "Shall I ring for tea?"

"You can go to the devil for all I care, Blackham. I demand that you release me and my daughter this minute." Mama's eyes blazed, and Elizabeth feared she would resort to violence against the marquess.

"Come, Mama." Elizabeth clutched her mother's arm. "We will wait for Papa and Jemmy in the foyer. We need not speak more with his lordship."

"Not so fast, Mrs. Easton." Blackham peered at her as he came from behind his desk. "I have something to say to your mother. To you as well." He headed for the sideboard and a glittering decanter of spirits.

"Then, for God's sake, speak your piece, my lord, and let us be done." Elizabeth's nerves crackled, and she clutched her reticule in a death grip. This madness had to end.

"Does she know that her troubles with her marriage to my son can be laid at your doorstep, Amelia?" He hefted the decanter and poured several inches into the glass. "Does she know she would have been a marquess's daughter had you done your duty and married me?"

"Yes, my lord, I am afraid I do know that." Elizabeth drew herself up to her full height and stared the man down.

"I know, and I understand completely how my mother must have felt. If she was in love with someone else, she had a duty to follow her heart and marry the man she loved."

"Pah." Lord Blackham's mouth twisted in disgust. "Romantic twaddle. Damn Lord Byron and all his ilk. They've ruined every woman with the ability to read." He glared at Elizabeth. "Do you realize you will make my son miserable for the rest of his life if you marry him? It is not too late. If you will release him, he can still marry the daughter of a duke."

"One that he does not love." Defiance welled up in Elizabeth's chest, and she glared at the marquess. "I rather see it that I am rescuing your son from a life of misery, to be fettered to a woman he would never love."

"Just as you never loved his mother." Mama thrust in that barb.

The marquess paled, then his brows lowered almost to his nose. "You have no right to speak of her."

"I have every right. Louisa was my dearest friend. You married her to drive a wedge in our friendship, to keep her from ever seeing me again. And I never did, once she married you." Mama's chest heaved, and tears threatened. "But she wrote to me. Did you know that? You couldn't keep her from doing that much."

"I did forbid her to correspond with you. I didn't want your sentimental claptrap to ruin our perfectly amicable agreement." Blackham shrugged. "I found out eventually that she had written to you. Found your letters in her correspondence after her death, although I still have no idea how she accomplished it." His smile flickered again. "She was a spirited woman. I enjoyed that about her. Fortunately, she valued the title marchioness far more than you ever did." A long pull at his drink, and the glass stood empty.

"You married her to spite me. Because I wouldn't have you." Mama's voice had risen to a shrill pitch, anger underscored with hurt. "So you struck at me by taking her away." Her lips trembled. "She was so sweet, so good. You didn't deserve her."

"Come, Mama." Elizabeth slid her arm around her mother's shoulders, trying to steer her away.

"She was sweet, and perhaps the best woman I have ever known." Lord Blackham's words fell like a stone into a well.

The plaintive tone, so foreign to the marquess's normal voice, made Elizabeth jerk her head around. "And you did not marry again, did you my lord, after her death?"

"There was no need, Elizabeth. He'd gotten the two things he wanted most, children and to hurt me for my refusal." Mama's tears began in earnest. "He didn't need another wife."

"With five young children and a marquessate to manage, he needed all the help he could get, I imagine." Something lurked in the back of Lord Blackham's eyes, something she'd not seen before. "You didn't want to replace her, did you my lord?" If she poked at him enough, perhaps they'd arrive at the truth. "You fell in love with her, didn't you?"

Waving a hand, Lord Blackham suddenly turned away, hiding his face. "We had had sufficient children. I did not feel that I need marry again." He turned back, his hand crashing down on the table. "Louisa and I had a perfectly fine marriage without all the trappings of love. Had you married me, Amelia, you would have understood how that could be an asset."

"Because it would be inconvenient to grieve a wife that you loved, I suppose?" Men could be such cowards about love. Elizabeth shook her head. "So sad to deny your love for your wife because you might lose her. I suspect you and Mama would have had a much less successful marriage together."

"Neither would Elizabeth nor your son be here today."

Papa strode into the office, followed closely by Jemmy, who rushed to her side.

"Wentworth, thank goodness." Throwing herself into Papa's arms, Mama burst into tears. He enfolded her in his arms and glared at Lord Blackham over her bonnet.

Elizabeth flung herself into Jemmy's arms, praying the nightmare of the day would soon be over.

"Are you all right, my love?" He kissed her cheek and held her tightly against him. "What has he done to you?"

Lowering her voice, she whispered in his ear, "Only talked to Mama about her refusal of him long ago. This whole scheme seems to hinge on his revenge for a very trivial slight. Has he always been this vindictive?"

Jemmy chuckled, sotto voce. "You do not know the half of it, my dear." He rubbed his face and glanced at his father; he and Papa were squaring off like two roosters in a hen coop. "I think we must tell him about the child. It may be the only thing that will change his mind."

"Blackham, this is outrageous." Papa had drawn himself up and puffed out his chest. "How dare you abduct my wife and daughter? How dare you interfere with the children's plans to marry? If you won't allow them to wed in London, then, by God, we'll see them all the way to Gretna Green, if we have to fight off your men at every tollgate."

"We have friends, Father. Perhaps not as influential as yours, but people who will stand beside us and help us do what is right." Jemmy drew Elizabeth toward the dark desk. "No matter what you do, we will find a way to marry."

"After a quarter of a century, can you not let this go?" Papa implored him.

Lord Blackham glared at all of them, face like a stone gargoyle.

"My lord," Elizabeth spoke up quickly before the marquess could begin. "Your son and I will marry. Not only because we love each other, but because we must." Squeezing

Jemmy's hand, she raised her chin and continued. "I am carrying his child. Perhaps his heir. Your heir. Is that precious commodity something you would destroy by preventing our marriage?"

Lord Blackham's face twisted with the shock of disbelief, eyes opened wide, then instantly narrowed. "You lie."

Jemmy surged toward his father, mayhem in his eyes.

Grabbing his arm, Elizabeth hauled him back. "Wait." She turned to Blackham. "It could be a lie, though it is not."

"You would have told me when you came to Blackham Castle."

"Your son wanted to. I pressed for his silence so you could not use my condition against me," she said carefully, staring full into his eyes. "As, I am told, you have in fact already done."

"Lady Locke is from home this winter, Blackham." Mama looked up long enough to throw the words at him. "This pair will be long wed before she reads your slanderous words."

A glint in his eye, the marquess opened a drawer in the desk and fished around. "I withheld this after Brack escaped the castle." He tossed a letter onto the desk, the direction clearly for Lady Locke's home in London. "Once he left, the duke withdrew his daughter's acceptance. If Brack felt so strongly about you, young woman, I'd likely get no cooperation from him, letter or no. And I wanted no stigma attached to an heir on the off chance there would be one sometime." He stared at Elizabeth with the unblinking gaze of a snake ready to strike. "Do you vow that you are carrying Brack's child? My grandchild."

"I do, my lord. Almost three months now. He, or she, will be born sometime in July." Elizabeth gave Jemmy's hand a squeeze as her heart dared to hope for the first time that all would be right. "Are you willing to let the past go? If my mother wronged you in any way, let that old feud be laid to rest. Let this new life, a new generation, bring our families together. You and my mother will share grandchildren, just as you might have in other circumstances. Let that legacy of hate turn to one filled with love, for the child's sake."

"For all our sakes," Jemmy added, then sucked in a breath. "May we have your blessing, Father?"

The marquess's face had undergone a transformation as soon as Elizabeth spoke of the child to come. The brooding eyes, the lowered brows had relaxed into an almost pleasant countenance. "I will give my consent to the marriage on one condition," he pronounced, sitting back in his chair.

"Name it," she and Jemmy shouted together and laughed.

"The condition is that you will name this child after me if it is my heir. If it is not, then whenever the heir is produced, he will carry my name."

"That's all?" Incredulous at this simple request, Elizabeth looked from Jemmy to her parents, all of whom seemed equally stunned.

"Yes. Your mother would never let me name any of the children after me." Lord Blackham's mouth pursed as if peeved. "I always wanted my heir named after me, but that was the one thing she ever refused me."

"But the heir will bear your title, my lord. Is that not enough?" Not that she was protesting; however, if the marquess's wife had denied this to him, Elizabeth could only imagine what that name might be.

"No. His full name will be my name." Blackham stared them down.

"Is it truly that dreadful?" What was the worst name she could think of? Marmaduke? That was rather hideous. Octavius? But he wasn't an eighth son.

"It is distinguished, madam. I don't know why the marchioness didn't see it that way," he snorted.

Giving up, Elizabeth shrugged and asked Jemmy, "So what is it?"

"Deuce if I know," Jemmy returned her shrug. "I always thought I was named for Father. This is news to me."

"Mama?" Her parents were fidgeting, not a good sign.

"Well, I believe his first name is Dionysus." Mama wrung her hands. "I have heard that name accepted in *ton* circles. Once."

"Hah." Blackham scoffed, his eyes filled with glee. "I told you that, Amelia, but I wanted to surprise you at our wedding. I will assure you, Dionysus is not my first name. And you must agree to the name to get my blessing." He looked expectantly at the pair of them.

"Oh, dear." Dionysus. That was dreadful. And it wasn't even the correct one. Elizabeth's stomach began to roil. She would love the baby, no matter what they named it.

"Yes, Father."

"Yes, my lord." Elizabeth looked at Jemmy and sent a prayer heavenward that the name would not be too outrageous. "We will agree to name him whatever you like as long as we can be married."

"Very well, then you have my consent and blessing." The older man cackled, and Elizabeth feared he would jump up and cut a caper on the carpet.

"Thank you, my lord." Now for Worth House and some much-needed rest.

"Father," Jemmy paused as he turned to go. "Why this whole abduction scheme if you knew there could be no marriage between me and the duke's daughter? Why risk harming Elizabeth and her mother by bringing them here?"

His father shrugged, the ghost of his smile returning. "I had not done with my revenge yet. I had waited more than twenty years to make her feel guilty about what she had done to me. I wanted to see her, make her squirm for a change." Lord Blackham chuckled, a dreadful sound. "Also, I had a few more tricks in my deck, inducements that might have worked, had Mrs. Easton not already been breeding. I told you widows with children had an advantage, didn't I, Brack?"

Anger in his eye, Jemmy started to turn back to his father.

Elizabeth took his arm firmly and compelled him out the door.

"Good day, Blackham." Papa whisked Mama after them. They followed Elizabeth and Jemmy to the front of the house, until Mama halted in the foyer, and whirled to stare straight at Papa. "Wentworth! Do you know what this means?"

Dazed, Papa shook his head.

"I shall have to organize two weddings at the same time!"

Epilogue

Elizabeth stretched and settled down with a sigh next to Jemmy in her bed at Worth House. The wedding had gone off without a hitch, quite a contrast to their turbulent betrothal. Even the weather had cooperated, and the sun had shone brightly as they had left St. George's, laughing in relief that they were finally, truly man and wife.

The wedding breakfast had lasted forever, it seemed, with both sides of the family wishing them happy. Charlotte and her other widow friends had attended, including Georgie, under dispensation from the marquess. Elizabeth hoped once she and Jemmy settled on a residence, they'd be able to convince his father to let her come to them, at least until her marriage was finalized or they could persuade him to break the betrothal with Travers. One hurdle at a time.

Basking in the afterglow of their first intimacy as a legally wedded couple, Elizabeth sighed in contentment. Truly, she could wish for nothing more save . . .

"When do you think we shall find out what we are to name this child?" She slipped her hand over her belly, reveling in the tiny flutterings she had just begun to feel yesterday.

"Hmmm?" Jemmy sleepily tuned over toward her, running a finger down the curve of her breast, bringing her nipple to quick attention again.

"I still don't know what we must name our child, Jemmy. I can't help but dread it. And knowing your father, he's liable not to tell us until we are standing with the godparents at the christening font."

Jemmy chuckled and slid close enough to grab her nipple in his lips, his tongue flicking the tip.

"And I thought you were asleep," she purred and pressed him closer, waves of desire beginning to rise once more down below. Her second marriage would apparently be as lively as her first.

"On our wedding night? Perish the thought." He kissed her breasts, and his shaft bumped against the seam of her legs.

"You will have to keep me completely occupied for the next six months so I will not think about what your father might be named. Do you think it very bad?" She had to have asked him that a thousand times in the past three weeks.

"Well, it is not what you would call a common name, no." He rolled them so he lay atop her. As his prodding member made its demands known, she opened for him, eager as he to join together again.

"What do you mean 'not common'? Of course, we know it's not common. Your mother wouldn't name you this dreaded name."

"It's truly not that bad, Elizabeth." He groaned as he seated himself deep within her. "Oh, love, you are glorious."

Heat kindled at her core as he began the long, slow strokes that drove her wild. "Hmmm. That feels so nice, Jemmy." But he was distracting her. What had he just said? "What do you mean it's 'not that bad'?" What's not that bad? His name? Do you know what it is?" She jolted up in bed, flinging Jemmy off her in her excitement.

"Good Lord, Elizabeth. You can't just do that to a man

mid-ride." He threw himself on his back on the mattress beside her.

"I'm sorry, my love, but you found out your father's name? How?" Elizabeth sat up in the bed, the disheveled sheets pooling around her hips.

"When Aunt Augusta wished me happy at the wedding breakfast, I took the opportunity to ask her if she knew Father's Christian name. And she did." He grinned up at her, wickedness in his eyes.

"Oh, my goodness. What is it? Is it truly awful?" Elizabeth held her breath.

"Well, it is certainly a Christian name." Jemmy reached out and cupped her breasts.

"Ahhh." His touch always drove her wild. She wanted him to sink himself into her again, but she was even more determined to know that name. "What is it?"

His laugh echoed in the chamber as he slowly rose up and pushed her back onto the mattress. "Now, where were we?"

Groaning with too many kinds of frustration, Elizabeth threw her arms around his neck and her legs around his hips. "Here."

He slid home once again and, with several quick thrusts, brought her to perfect completion again.

She shuddered around him and sank into the mattress, completely sated this time. She might not wake up until evening tomorrow.

Jemmy lay panting and smiling beside her. "Onesiphorus."

"I beg your pardon?"

"Onesiphorus. That is Father's first name. An early Christian elder, at least that's what Aunt Augusta told me. She always considered herself lucky to merely be named after her father's mother." Jemmy raised up on his elbow. "So now we know, are we going to renege on the promise? We're married, there's nothing Father can do to us if we name him something else."

Stunned, but recovering, Elizabeth slowly shook her head. "He seems so set and proud on having this child bear his name. I somehow can't quite take that away from him." She took Jemmy's face in her hands. "As long as we are together, I won't mind a jot if we name our son Marmaduke, or Jehoshaphat, or Onesiphorus." She snuggled into her husband's arms. After all, what was in a name?

Their future finally looked bright as a shooting star. Pray God it continued so.

Connect with